'She whispered h[...]and into the wind. For there is, after all, no light to this darkness . . . not even in the morning, no, not even at the end of the longest, blackest of nights.'

Spirit of the Sea
'Escapist reading *par excellence*, with appropriate dashes of du Maurier romantic suspense and dollops of smuggling, witchcraft and the supernatural for good measure . . .' *Million*

The Light to My Darkness
'A novel of the highest quality . . . the writing is starkly realistic without resorting to cliche . . . A dark and brooding tale that will hold you enthralled' *Sunday Independent*

'She tingles one's spine. She makes you think about people. She's marvellously literate and the similes really bring writing to life' *Jilly Cooper*

Georgina Fleming, who also writes under the name of Gillian White, is a journalist. She lives with her husband and four children in a farmhouse in Devon.

THE LIGHT TO MY DARKNESS

Georgina Fleming

ORION
LONDON

This Orion edition published in 1993

Copyright © 1991 by Georgina Fleming

First published in Great Britain in 1991 by Random
Publishing Group, 20 Vauxhall Bridge Road, London
SW1V 2SA

Published by Orion, an imprint of Orion Books Ltd,
Orion House, 5 Upper St Martin's Lane, London
WC2H 9EA

ISBN 1 85797 118 3

Typeset by Deltatype Ltd, Ellesmere Port, Cheshire
Printed and bound in Great Britain by Clays, Ltd,
St Ives plc

For Jamie

1

There are twelve hours left. Twelve hours of night. They are coming to kill me in the morning.

To kill me!

I daren't scream. I daren't cry. I am trying to hang on to something – sanity? And something else, something that seems more illusive than that – hope.

Confession?

Is that what you want, Brother Niall? Is that why you're here with all that sadness in your dark brown eyes? You look like a man who has spent too many nights listening to the ravings of the damned, holding the hands of the frightened dreamers whose stories are destined for tomorrow's winds.

You gave me your name and you looked at me simply – to see if I was fit for your God? Hah! Are you intending to reunite us? Well, let me tell you that I was born without a soul and therefore your God and I have never been united, that He is a stranger to me and I to Him and that I have never believed. There has only been one God in my life. My man is my God to me, brother monk, and he is more heathen than I!

You'll wish you hadn't come, monk, with your rough brown cowl and your belt of knots and your ragged, filthy sandals. The hatch above you snapped shut like a trap and you whispered, 'We are in the hands of God, my child, we are in the hands of God.'

Well might you take your place over there with your head bent and your hands together in prayer. I warn you, you'll not last the night! I'll shock you with my ravings, with my madness, I'll drain that weary resignation out of your eyes. For mine is not a comfortable tale of innocence wronged or advantages taken, nor is it a story of love and a heart that was broken. No, far from it, this is to do with something other, darker, stranger. Something a long way away from love. Mine is a tale of *obsession*. There – do you understand that? Do you know what I'm talking about . . . so that it made no difference if I was near him, if he spoke or what he said, if he glanced in my direction. I had my own images and I had my own meanings.

I know all about gods. I made one up. Mine was a powerful god, lord of the moor and the wild places in it, the gorge and the downs and the valleys he rode. The hunt, the lonely span of it all, the laughing wild-power of his life. Wicked, they called him, king of that terrible clan of godless men, and worse, much worse.

And we were death to each other. Some people are death to each other, aren't they, Brother Niall?

My obsession turned me into the creature you see, into the creature I am.

What do you see? Why won't you speak? Why do you look at me strangely that way? Don't pity me monk, for I would not have had it otherwise. I might have lived on the edge of a precipice but at least I lived! Did you? Have you ever known passion? I wonder. Have you ever longed to be rid of your brown, to be painted crimson, have you known desire?

Oh, I am frightened of this place, this dark pit with the sullen river out there. No longer my river, the river I loved – I think it smells of blood. I am frightened of the morning. Of pain, of the light, and of the way I might behave when they come for me. Of the things I might say when they come for me and of how they will handle me.

And I do not mean to insult you, monk. It is terror that drives me to do it.

When they first brought me here I held my breath against the rancid smell of it all and yet how easy it is to adjust, for now I don't notice it. Yes, that's right, have a good look around you, they don't provide many comforts in the dungeons of Lydford Gaol. No light. No warmth. No tenderness here. Having no lantern, it looks as if we must share the moonlight that peeps through the crack, its beam weakly shining. Does blue make you sad? And for warmth, for protection against these weeping stones, what shall we use . . . our memories? A fire would be a comfort, wouldn't it? We could watch the flames and poke the little grate, we could pretend it was warming us. Look, even the floor is too damp to sit down on, the straw is mildewed and rotten, and the ladder that stretches up to the hatch is merely a series of wooden planks tied together with hemp.

He will not let me die, monk. He cannot let me die! Rowle, after hearing of my intentions, will not abandon me. You will see, when dawn breaks he will come for me. And it will not be as it was before, for at last I will see real love in his eyes; after what I have risked for him he is bound to love me!

Hope. Yes, I will tell you exactly how it will be. I know because I have imagined it so many times. Listen – no, not like that, open your eyes, put a sparkle in them and listen – they will take me out of this dismal place, my eyes will be sore from the cruel light of morning. I will see the people small and far away, their mouths open, gaping. And just when I taste despair, just when I believe that all is lost, at that last minute Rowle will come and slice the gibbet rope, sweeping me into his arms. Magnificent, as always.

'Where were you, Rowle?' I'll say.

'Not so far away.'

Picture it, monk, as I do. The sky will rush past us. The slope down from Lydford is steep and dangerous. I will see that it has snowed in the night and the trees we pass under will drop it from their branches.

I will clasp the waist of my god, my king, my head against his back, rocking. I will want to scream out my joy, sing a lullaby, cry and laugh at the same time. I will want to shout, 'I love you I love you I love you,' and I won't just mean Rowle, oh no, but life and love, the whole world . . . even you, little monk.

I will smell him. The leather on his back. The rainy smell of his hair. My cheek will stick to his back, the snow and the tears will hold it there. When he moves it will hurt and I will enjoy that pain because I will feel it and know I am near him.

And oh monk, I will feel the stallion's muscles rippling and straining. His neck will lunge forward and his veins will start out near to bursting when he shrieks like a night owl calling. I will feel Rowle tense and tighten, faced by the gorge . . . *no bridge* . . . it will be just as they said. They will have set their tiny trap and I will smile at their smallness while the stallion makes a white whirlwind in the snow.

Rowle's whip will fly as he lashes the stallion's flanks without mercy. Life or death, it will lie in the leap he is so afraid to take. There will be no going back. I shall hear the chase behind us and turn to see, a quick turn made through tears that have run backwards from my eyes with the speed. Awful sounds behind us, sounds of men and horses in pursuit. But I will smile, for I know that they cannot catch us. I know that no one can touch us or hurt us or tame us or imprison us or teach us right or wrong. Close to Rowle, I will no longer know fear.

I will cry out to warn him, *'The bridge is down!'*

'I know that the bridge is down.' And our words will echo as though they come from the deepest of dreams. Rowle will turn and we will laugh together, in love as we have never been before!

We won't have time! And we cannot go back, straight into the trap. But the stallion once again refuses! And again we rush the ravine and again he will try to rear. He will nearly take us backwards, caught underneath him and flat in the snow. His body will shudder. He will tremble as the power in his body ripples through his fear.

Rowle will spur him on and strike out, shouting, 'Get on, go now!' And my eyes will be wet from the crying.

A deep weal cuts the stallion's sides. Still now, he spits pink spume from the cruel bit in his mouth, sniffs the air and stamps, deciding if he will be man or animal, foolish or cunning. His body will quiver and his ears prick forward: he will go with Rowle.

I will go with Rowle. I will cling, my lips to the leather. With all my heart and all my consciousness and all my will, I shall cling. Again we will slither towards the edge of the terrible chasm. The drop below us is dark and black and I know that the waterfall waits. Freedom – it won't be long now. At last the stallion leaps . . . at last, frenzied, we are one . . . animal, human, sky and water.

One mighty leap and then air, green air churning, green sky spinning, green water hurtling, bursting, screaming. Loving.

Just as I dream it. Just as I secretly know it will be. Oh yes, tomorrow Rowle will come. Tomorrow we will start the rest of our lives together and at dear last I can put all my terrible mistakes behind me. But for now there is only the night – and silence – and all the fears and uncertainties that darkness brings.

*What if he does not come? What if there is an accident . . . or no
one tells him where I am? What if he is captured by the constables as
he comes to find me?*

The world is dark and I am cold and I remember when we
made love by the waterfall. That was like this, like waiting,
helpless, between two worlds with sheer cliffs before and
behind to shield us. But the sun went in, turned the light from
green to dark, and I shivered when Rowle said, 'Go home'.

Without my secret hope I would be standing here now facing
oblivion. Well, I can picture that, I am a clever dreamer: I would
want to face it aware, like I loved Rowle – eyes open, aware.
Down by the water we loved, by the dark pools that were his –
black water thundering on rock – and the light, white water
which slid like wine from the lip of the fall, that was mine. In
love, in death, it must be the same.

So, how to get back to the girl that I was? I feel worlds away,
like an old, old woman, prying. I touch my rags and they could
be the scraps of me, all that is left inside. Can I get under the
skin and into the heart of that wild young creature that was
once me, when she seems to be missing now, missing as though
she had never existed.

The girl that I used to be was invisible to herself, as I am
now. Ignorant, she did not know she had no one but me, and I,
now that I am threatened by death, no one but her. That silly,
dreaming scrap of a maid with the streak of white hair in the
black that Lizzie called the taint-mark, the stigma of my birth.

Confession? But why – when I've told you how Rowle will
come . . . I am tired. Somehow we have to pass the night. And
there's nobody here but ourselves, alone in this very still place.

And I am so frightened. I go down the cavern of memory,
my lantern high, searching for something real, something I can
take with me tomorrow to give me courage while I wait . . .
this might be my very last chance so I mustn't make mistakes. I
want to talk – I want to tell you . . . obsession is like that. Call it
confession if you like, I don't really care what you call it. I
clutch at the memories that tease me, beckon and go again,
leaving only shadows behind.

Each year has a different colour and quality, lighter as they
go back, lighter and touched with a glittering magic, darker
and more shadowy as I reach the now time. I have to move

Rowle in order to see past him. He clings, he brushes my face, my arms, my eyes, my hair. He brushes with all his soft loving, holding me back from other things that mattered. They did matter to me then, those things, before the passion came. It was only of late that Rowle became my world. I hold the lantern higher and I see my grandfather Amos, my father, Amos, my mother's father, Amos . . .

But Amos is dead.

So that's where I'll start my confession. Pay attention, Brother Niall – but then you have nothing else to do, for there's no other sound but my voice in here, in this place gripped by such sombre winter.

Seven years ago. I was still a child, three weeks away from loving Rowle when the men came from Lydford to fetch us. I was three weeks away when I heard the howl of the ban-dog and saw the puffs of dust from the hooves of strange horses approaching Amicombe Farm. I was out at the newtakes putting in turnips, for life must go on even though there might be no tomorrow.

'Life has to beat to a rhythm. The crops must go in an' the cow must be milked. Just because Amos be dead that doan mean ter say the world has stopped turnin' or that the tasks need not be done,' said Maggie, nagging.

I was digging away in the hard earth angrily for I had quarrelled with Maggie that day. Oh, may your God help me, monk, for the last words I spoke to her were bad ones. All red-faced and furious I'd muttered and turned the mutter into a shout and the shout into the ugliest face I could pull. And I could pull ugly faces because I'd practised in the river.

'Doan tell me that! I'm not goin' ter hear you! I knows I'm hopeless an' mazed. Whatever I do 'tis not quick enough nor good enough, an' I carn make you like me but do you think I care? Well, I doan . . .'

My words were all ugly inside me. They hurt me coming out. They were raw in my throat and somewhere deeper down, even, than that. I remember the look in Maggie's brown eyes – but she didn't answer me then, or go for me.

Oh, I know we were all frightened, not just me. It was the whole terrible atmosphere while we waited for the men to come back. For we knew they would come back, as surely as night follows day. Fear jumped all over the house like ticks in straw, making us itch and scratch and slap, making us do mad dances with our eyes. And my three aunts, they lost their expressions and sat and waited, with Maggie saying, 'We has committed two measly crimes. We ought to have buried Amos in a right an' proper manner, an' we should not have gone at the men wi' the long-gun. An' fer that these roogs come after uz. For this we sits an' waits ter be taken. See how low we has come down. You'd swear 'twas impossible.'

I went out because somebody had to. But then I was never quite one of them, having shocked them all with my coming and killed my mother in the process of being born.

They had not buried Amos for the simple reason – it seemed simple then – that my three aunts were afraid to go out. Dartmoor can do that to you. We called it the Forest. Our land was a gaunt land where the wind swept over the raw-boned frame of the earth, giant breakers in the distance threatening to roar towards the lapping land-waves that were ours. Good and bad, same as people, and nothing simple about it –because bats came by night but so did the stars, yellowhammers by day but also came the hawks with their hovering shadows. Good and bad, black and white and I loved it. It was life, sweet with campions, honeysuckle, celandine and violet, and foxgloves grew between the blackthorn. And always, there in the distance beside us or behind us was the mast of our ship – the cone of Brent Tor with the dark church on top, a pennant against the sky.

I was born on a Monday morning in March with winter still on the high moor and only a granite line to show land from sky.

The cattle were close to home then. The mutton was hanging and the cider kegs were still half-full. They called me Bethany out of the Bible and Ruthy my mother said she hadn't a clue what was happening because I was the last thing she expected when she said to Amos, 'I's off upstairs to my bed 'cos I's got the gripes again.'

Amos my grandfather put his hand right up inside my mother because I was backwards coming and would have been stuck. He turned me like a lamb.

They told me what happened. 'Poor doer,' said Amos when he saw me. But Ruthy didn't get to argue because she was dead from too much bleeding.

15

My mother was the prettiest and the silliest. And I would have loved to have known her.

They lowered her down through the coffin hole in the bedroom floor because the windows were too small to take her and it wouldn't have been decent, anyway, to lower her out that way. And they put me in the basket with the sad lambs in the downstairs place which we called the room . . . the beasts were to the right and we were to the left. It was warmer that way. And safer.

And I think it was at my mother's funeral when Maggie, Lizzie and Birdie, my mother's sisters, were last out. Amos went three times a year with the sledge to Tavistock market – for there were no wheels on our farm, no road, only a sledge path, how it had always been. And I suspect it was the speed of the church responses that upset them for they never went again. They didn't like the new service: they called it a 'bliddy Christmas game'.

And then there was the strain of getting themselves there and back. Even on the yonder common out by the newtake meadows I can remember them getting bewildered, unsteady to be away from our own piece of land, their eyes all suspicious with the unfamiliar landscape; only when they were back on home land with the tor behind them did they stand steady again, did their faces take on that benign, wide open expression that I knew.

So on the day the men came they were stuck in, and while they waited for 'they varmints' to come back Birdie sang sad songs. Lizzie's black eyes stared, but she did not get up and brew her yarbs as she once would have done, to stave off ill luck. Fear seemed to have taken the magic from her. And then, as I left the house, out of my fear I shouted: 'I hates you, Maggie Horsham! I've allus hated you. An' now I knows that I really, really hates you!' I screamed at the aunt whom I loved best as I ran away to the fields.

God forgive me.

I looked back at the house out of hot angry eyes. The mist had dropped from it and it suddenly seemed so alone. Thatched and granite, mottled with lichen, our house was scooped from under such a great basin of sky. It hung from a slope of black granite on a pendulum of smoke, struggling outwards with its upping-block toe, pushing outwards with kegs and pails, washpans and pitchers, great cloam vessels and saplings for folds. It tiptoed out with its turf-rick and peat-stack, into the gorse and the blackthorn, but tight and safe with its arms round itself, tight as the shutters when winter came.

And winter was early to the Forest and late leaving us.

The front door sheltered under a granite bough. In winter you stepped up to it, in summer, with the dung out, you stepped down. I could find it with my eyes closed and just a hazel stick for balance. Many times I practised coming home like that because when I was little I had a terror of going blind. Then the ban-dog used to rush at me and knock me over and I'd flail at him with my stick and be disgusted that he could be so insensitive to a poor, blind girl coming home. I would limp, too, and hop on one leg like a cripple. I used to wonder if they would bother with me more if I was blind or maimed in some way . . . and almost want to be.

But the day the men came, that sad, angry feeling I felt could only have been the presentment of death. I dug and I hoed and I planted. And then I heard the ban-dog howl and saw the distant puffs of dust. And I ran and I ran and I ran. And I might even have been screaming so fast did I run, so hard did my feet pound the turf and so loud was the tearing of air round my ears.

But, Brother Niall, you with your prayers and your stained eyes, I did not run fast enough. And throughout the whole of the rest of my life I have had to live with that.

2

When I reached the farm it was quiet as night. Then I found the ban-dog, a bolt from a cross-bow in his chest and a piece of leather britches like a flag in his mouth. And Amos' gun, last fired by Maggie, lay broken by the trough in the court.

And I knew that this was the thing of which we had not been speaking. This was the thing we had been dreading.

I had no way of knowing what they were going to do. I didn't know the ways of the world then, and if I had known what was going to happen – does this sound too cowardly? – well, I wouldn't have followed. Night after night after night after that I wished I hadn't gone, hadn't seen it, because if I let my mind on it I thought that I would go mad. And for days my mind, all contrary, would not move to anything else. My eyes wouldn't see anything else. My mouth could speak of nothing else and then only in whispers.

They brought them here, to Lydford, and this cell could have been the very place where they waited, all of seven years ago. I followed a safe distance behind, sick in my heart for I knew how they would be feeling . . . each of them . . . three sets of different horrors. And my own hopelessness gave me a red-hot horror of my own that made the back of my neck burn with the sick heat of sunstroke. But what could I do? How could I help them? There were twenty men for three old women – but one of them was Lizzie Horsham, so I suppose they thought that if they sent a sufficiently large number she could not set her evil eye upon one more vexatiously than upon another.

They put the three of them in a cart and a bullock dragged them to Lydford. The marks of the wheels in the earth as it followed the lychway into the town and over the bridge made me think of the thin, wiggly burn-marks Amos made on the land when he scorched it. The town was empty of people when the cart pulled in, for it was around mid-morning and everyone was to their work. Just a few straggling fowls and children and

18

one or two women came to their cottage doors and looked out as if it was nothing but an ordinary day. Just a look, a shrug, and back to their houses again.

I hid in the churchyard behind the graves from where I could see all that happened. Even then I saw that this cursed place, this Gaol, was designed for and devoted to pain. There was no other reason for its existence. It rose up out of the grass and seemed to stop before it could reach its height, as if the sky had ordered it back . . . to retreat . . . not sully it further. It was squat and square and ugly with cracks for windows, sly and barred, but nobody would have wanted to see in and those inside could not see out.

They took them in here and I slept – not because I was tired, Brother Niall, please don't think it was that. I slept because I was scared, deep-down scared, and my brain seemed to crave that sort of oblivion. But while I slept I was aware. I woke when a wagon rolled down the street, when a shepherd took a short cut through the churchyard and out again along the road. I woke when an old brown woman came puffing by, sat on a grave and lit up her pipe, blowing smoke rings into the last clouds of mosquitoes. I was asleep and yet I knew what was going on around me. I woke the moment they brought them out and I knew that someone had hurt them.

I stood up too suddenly and hurt my ankle . . . I even remember that!

'. . . all waives, strays, echeats and presentments of assault or bloodshed, plains, writs of right according to the custom of Lydford . . .' I didn't know what the gaoler with the bored voice was calling. An ugly man with a head like a sheep's, long and moaning, he read from a scroll. And his small, withered ears stuck close to the side of his face.

At least I had a trial this afternoon, if you can call it that. But for Maggie, Lizzie and Birdie there was no trial, no chance for them to speak. The Justice wasn't due for another twelve-months. It was all decided by the keeper, and then it was that I saw Mallin. Our friend Mallin, standing apart with his packhorse loaded and a woman looking as if she was chained to his side. She wasn't – but she might as well have been.

The sin of hatred . . . Oh yes, Brother Niall, I'll confess to that. And what's more, I carry it still. Mallin, our friend, trader, with the face of Christ, longsuffering with anguish in

19

his eyebrows. Maggie made gloves for Mallin. Mallin would come to our house with soft leather pelts hung from his mule, but under his saddle were charms, amulets and the bitter scented vials that Lizzie secretly bought. Mallin was the only man she would let come near – the only man she needed.

Do you know, Brother Niall, that when I was small I believed Mallin to be my father, for he was the only man who came by. Later I found out the truth, but even then I didn't know it to be wrong. For I didn't know good and I didn't know evil . . . our lives were not divided like that. It was not so simple for us as it is for you.

Mallin would tell us stories when the weather was bad, while Lizzie spun, rocking backwards and forwards with her green eyes sharp on the others, feeding the wool to the spindle like harsh music played between finger and thumb. Birdie whittled, annoying Amos, fashioning a pipe to play on the down. Maggie sewed, and I sat in a corner pretending to dip candles, perched on a stool and looking out, my back to them but listening. I didn't want to get Amos' eyes on me. All the hatred in the room, and our fear of him, closed in on us on days like these. We were all sly-eyed and watching, while the peats glowed crimson and the room grew warm with the beasts sheltered next door. And the ban-dog bayed outside to get in.

But when Mallin came we forgot our fear for a while, forgot to stare at his shaking hands with their wormy, tortured veins. He would get out his silver-ringed purse of velvety leather and count out the coins on the trestle table for us all to look at. After an hour or so by our fire he would go, taking the wonderful gloves that Maggie had made and his stories with him. The Queen might well speak Greek, might speak to universities in Latin, might address any amount of foreign ambassadors in their own tongues, but I believed she was not as clever as Mallin. A war of religion went on in France, Mallin feared a Spanish invasion, and the Scots Queen's husband was a fool and a decadent. And I swore to myself, oh I swore that I would never love a scoundrel. All this Mallin told us until we could see it happen in the flames.

So why was Mallin in Lydford, standing so still and not helping, but watching intently like that? I had trusted him, but there was nothing to trust in his face that day and his smile was strange and thin.

I have to tell this: I have to tell it as I saw it. They clamped them, my mother's sisters, away from their home and afraid, they clamped them in the pillory. Screwed them there by their necks and wrists. It was cruelly done, more cruelly than any criminal could ever merit, yes, even for murder. It was done to them by men they didn't know, men who must have had wives and children at home who would run to them when they reached their doors with arms open . . . men with beards and bad teeth and hairs on their arms. I felt I could reach out and touch them, so near was I. Yet so distant. Never before so distant from any other human beings.

Birdie's feet did not reach the platform. I saw her struggle, then stop too suddenly, her eyes very startled and wide. From where she died she would have been able to see the black ridge. She choked to death very quickly, as if she didn't mind, and the men took no notice. I wanted to push my aunt's hair back, go over to her and straighten it, for Birdie had always cared so much about her frazzled, woolly hair and she would not have liked it sticky and matted together like that. Through my clenched fists I saw.

Time must have passed but I wasn't aware of it. I scraped out a little memorial and rammed a stone in the earth, torturing and dragging it this way and that in order to get it in. 'So that I'll never forget,' I sobbed, as the edge of the stone cut my hand. It was a very small stone, mocked beside all that smart granite. It would hardly stand up. I wonder what happened to it. I wonder, Brother Niall, if it's still there now . . .

Tomorrow, if something should go wrong . . . I'm sure Rowle will come but . . . afterwards, for me . . . do you think you could go and find it?

They were wary of Lizzie, avoiding her eyes, but they clamped her in that monstrous wooden frame just the same. She didn't spit. She didn't curse. But when the people came later in the day they threw such stuff at her that she lowered her head and moved her eyes off them. And then came the man with the sheep's head and a hammer and nails, and he nailed her ears to the board so that she couldn't move. She screwed up her face and clenched her teeth and then she went away.

They threw what they had at poor Lizzie. They killed her as she hung there and I saw the moment when her clenched fists opened. They appeared to be calling for more, defying the crowd, shouting: 'Come on then, please yourselves! Now you carn hurt me.' As if she had cast her last spell. With fate in her eyes and resignation in her hands she died. Through my streaming eyes I saw.

My heart broke then. I would have sworn it was not possible for it ever to break again but it kept doing so, there where I crouched in the churchyard. And I had to bend over to hold it together, for it was like a knife going into a meal-sack, and all the grain spilling out.

Mallin still watched from a distance. It was no longer afternoon but some time of day I have never known before or since. The first grey shadows of night cobwebbed the castle wall and torches were lit up high in their iron brackets. People came from nowhere, chanting, brute-faced creatures. Birdie and Lizzie were dead, for the pillory is designed for the frames of men, not women . . . women and children often die . . . but the knowing of that was no help to me then. Maggie was hanging on, living. They called my poor Maggie 'the Crockern whore', and Birdie, they said, as they lifted her poor, black face, was out of her mind. They poked their foreheads with their fingers and with their bad teeth showing they laughed at her. 'The unholy daughters, all three o' 'e,' they screamed with their high-pitched, silly voices while they kept on throwing their filth and their sharp stones, rocks, pebbles, sticks, even a bucket with flour in it. But there was no longer a need.

'Unholy . . . 'er filthy mother, 'er were t'Abbot's whore, the Devil's daughter.'

She was the only one of the Devil's daughters still alive when they took her out and to the pond, where they tied her to the ducking-stool and made her suffer their vengeance for all three sisters. The water was skinned with dark black like a pot of yarbs Lizzie might brew. Again and again Maggie went under, and the foam that rushed from her skirts – I closed my eyes and saw white sea birds with wide wings beating.

'Again! Again!' called the people as the heaving men bent the wooden pole and Maggie surfaced once more. And again it happened. And again. Until there was no space between . . . just black water and black sky . . . and the tracks of red across the surface where the torches scarred the sight of it on to my eyes.

And I saw that Maggie – whose skin smelt of chicken mash

and apple skins – was too tired to resist, to fight for her life as she might have done. They had taken everything out of her, and she knew that the farm was gone and her sisters were gone and she had nothing to live for now. I willed her to think of me, and I wondered, afterwards, if she'd known I was there, so strong was my willing of Maggie to live. You would have thought it stronger than words between her and me. But it didn't work. Through my trembling fingers I saw.

I do not know how much my aunts suffered. How can you tell that for anyone else? I only know what seeing them suffer and reliving that suffering did to me over the years. I turned away and walked over the bridge back to the Forest, not caring at all if they saw me or what would happen to me. I wanted to die so these feelings would not be in me. I thought they would kill me.

Ah, where were the priests that day, Brother Niall? Where were the holy men – afraid of corruption, afraid of the clutching fingers of the dark old religion? Or were they, too, in Mallin's pocket or too busy saying their prayers, as is the way of the righteous?

3

I worried all the time, but they can't have known about me or they would have come looking.

It would have been a simple matter to find me: I could not move from Amicombe. I stayed, hung around like a small, abandoned ghost and I watched Mallin move in with his girl-woman beside him and his silly long-eared mule laden with bundles and packages. He looked wrong on Amos' cob. I wished we had killed it when Amos died as Maggie had once, in a fit of uncharacteristic sentimentality, suggested we should. Mallin was too dainty for that horse with his long thin hands and his anguished air. He looked like a clown. That old white horse needed somebody down to earth, of the earth and with the earth like Amos was. Still, it didn't protest. It remained obedient to its new master, but I thought I detected a sly look about it as if, one day, when Mallin was off-guard, it might throw him and then, with all its great weight, trample on him and squash him. Mercilessly.

Mallin didn't have much of his own to move. All our things were there – all our animals, and I considered the cow a traitor to give Mallin milk, the hens to give him eggs and the stream, yes even the stream I hated, for it gave him our clear, sweet water.

Only the little rowan pony remained faithful. The wild creature that I had tamed stayed proudly staring from the hill. She would come to no one but me. She would go back to her wildness now, and forget. And I very badly wanted that so I left her.

We should have been able to guess it was Mallin who told. Well, there was nobody else for only he came by.

I watched Amicombe. Did I have a past? Did this place have a past? Was there anything of it left, or had it all been taken away? I forced myself to remember. The changes that happened inside my body as I grew up were natural and caused

24

me no ill-effects but the change that was happening outside I did not consider natural at all. Amos was gradually growing old only we didn't notice.

And then one morning he didn't get up. We came downstairs, and for the first time in my life there he was, lying on the settle with his long-gun in his arms, his head on his saddle and a sack pulled over him. Nobody knew what to say or do, for his eyes were open and glittering wildly as ever.

Amos and I – we passed each other with blankened eyes. His beard waggled grimly and even seemed to turn away if I was near and his mouth, always grim, went grimmer. Stern and immovable like the house he had built with his own bare hands, when Amos chose not to see me then certainly I did not see him.

Amos always fed first. We stood back as he ate with his fingers from his trencher and mopped up his eggs, six or seven at a time, with a thick step of ryebread. And the yoke ran down his beard in sticky rivulets. His face came out from under his hood as he fed, otherwise he stayed in it. We tiptoed round him, we women, almost lifting our skirts to get by without touching or annoying Amos.

He was out first thing in the mornings and back last thing at nights. He poached the deer with nets. He smelled of harness and horse. He also smelled, like Rowle, of the moor, but his smell was tickled with damp homespun and years of unwashing.

Father and Grandfer both, with his violent swings of mood Amos could be laconic and cold one moment and laughing all glitter-eyed the next – but his eyes rolled wild like a stallion's and you could never be easy with that laughter. Normally he was moody and morose, and now I am sure he verged on the edge of madness. His perfectly erect, small wiry frame carried a weight of silver-white hair and his beard seemed to hang from his heavy underlip, pulled like that through the ages of his life. He could drag a red deer home on his own. In the dark. Without a lantern.

So the morning when he wasn't up we got on with our chores, Maggie most naturally taking over his. I knew that as soon as they were together outside the house they would discuss the whole extraordinary situation so I stuck to them carefully all morning, listening hard.

"Tis not the ale,' said Lizzie, seriously. She scratched her chin, which was one of her ways of thinking. There are three kinds of witches – black ones, white ones and grey ones, and I suppose that Lizzie was grey. She had the habit of fixing her eyes in malevolent stares that meant nothing. She was skilled with the yarbs and screamed at any stranger who came near . . . 'Do 'e try my bit of charm, do 'e? Do 'e dare come nearer?' She spat, and her spit bubbled and sizzled wherever she put it, as if it had landed on the hearth. So nobody came to the house. Nobody dared, except Mallin. She kept the Gubbins away. Lizzie was the eldest and offhand with me, feeling, I suppose, that by my coming I had killed Ruthy.

Lizzie saw everything about her as a monstrous antagonist: everything that went wrong was a trap and she a fool to fall into it. That's why she screamed at everything wherever she went, but she didn't scream on the morning that Amos didn't get up. She scratched her chin, and that was the texture of the great black settle that lurked by the spiral stone stairs – polished, hard and knotted.

The settle where Amos lay dying.

"E's that stubborn, 'e woan take a potion,' she said.

"Tis not the ale,' agreed Maggie. 'No, 'tis something other than that.'

'Someone will have to go to the drifts on along.' And all this conducted in fierce little whispers with one eye on the door in case Amos came out and caught them doing nothing.

There was silence as they contemplated that, standing in a circle with bent heads as if already round his open grave, looking down into it but seeing nothing old there, or decayed, just some new, terrible other thing like going to the drifts, and suddenly a hundred other horrors that seemed quite out of the question. For they never went out. They never went off our land.

Pierced with anguished remorse I muttered, 'Doan let 'e die.' And saw that Birdie was praying, also. Birdie's 'Lord help me' was merely an echo from happier times. I think she would have liked to keep the religion but Amos wouldn't have it. Savagely shy, with eyes defensively sharp like flints of slate, Birdie could pull off a hareskin in one. She reminded me of fairy creatures and deep woodland thickets. Birdie's hair had the watery sheen of the cold, slate floor, as black as mine but

26

without the taint-mark. She was the singer with the eerie, wintry sound which came on a moan before it rose and affected the sway of the candles, making Lizzie cackle, 'Fer the love o' God, Birdie, pull yousself together. You sound like a vixen on heat!'

They whispered, the other two, that Birdie had once been in love and that she had made a fool of herself over someone who hadn't loved her back. They said she had a baby buried up on the ridge, and I'd looked at Birdie, and I'd seen how her thoughts and her dreams dropped off her fingers, and I'd always felt that some time ago her soul had flown out of the window, like a sparrow.

'Doan let 'e die!' And it wasn't that I wanted Amos to live – I hated him just the same, with the kind of habitual hatred that is never red-hot. It was just that I was suddenly struck by the enormity of the change that would take place in our lives without him there.

But my mother's sisters were powerful women, weren't they? They had not let me die and I was not half as important as Amos. Birdie had her religion, surely she could pray for him, and God, after the dreadful things that had happened to her in her life, would listen and act for her. I had heard that God could be merciful and Birdie had only once been a sinner.

Lizzie had her spells and the skills to bring anyone, man or beast, back to life if she wanted to. She'd practised enough – she was experienced enough. And Maggie, broad and fat as a November pig, pink as a ham coming fresh from the chimney, well, Maggie could nurse him to health with all her sensible loving.

Days went by but Amos just didn't stir. He was too ill to spit but you could see that he wanted to. It was at meal-times we missed him most and yet felt his presence most strongly. With the freedom of the table we could pick out the plump, best bits. And yet with him there, with his tortured breathing behind us, feeding like this felt like stealing. And the glimmer in his eye told us he thought so, too.

I dared to turn round and stare at him then. His eye caught mine and for the first time in his life he held it. Chilling, that's what it was. And I suddenly knew there was no help coming from anywhere. Not Birdie's God nor Lizzie's Devil. I knew that he knew that, too. I don't know what made me get up then and go to fetch Birdie's crucifix. But I did, and I walked towards Amos with a beating heart and put the metal cross on top of his blanket, on the thin, wiry flanks of him, trying not to notice how his claw hands clutched the sack edges, or how his beard had the life his face had not.

I was thinking of Granny, and of the fact that she couldn't possibly have loved him. And I knew, I saw in his eyes, that he was thinking of her, too.

And then Amos died.

We should have taken Amos properly into Lydford, shouldn't we, monk? We should have organised the proper church burial so strictly decreed by the law. But my aunts had this inward turning that I've already tried to explain, so we buried him under the cows in the shippen, taking turns with the digging and cursing the shifting beasts who watched with the juice of cud, like blame, foaming in their mouths.

We dug a steamy hole and laid him in it, Maggie with her mouth set grim and Birdie praying, 'I have gone from the hearin' o' God an' 'tis all dark around me.'

'This is something we has ter do,' said Maggie. 'So now let's be gettin' on wi' it an' savin' our breaths fer later.'

They'd closed his eyes or else I couldn't have helped them to carry him. This wasn't Amos. This was a thing, a creature. I couldn't stop yawning and shivering for I felt that I – that we – had failed him somehow. I was ashamed of my feelings, for tears for Amos were unthinkable. It was surprising how light he was, he who had always felt so heavy.

And then we blithely carried on with our lives, pretending that no one would miss him, that we could survive without the journeys to market, the paying of tithes, the turns at the drifts. It was not as simple as that, Brother Niall. There is nothing simple in madness. And madness . . . it was all around us and it was inside us and after Amos died it seemed to be what drove us. We moved in awkward silence, sharing the knowledge of our crime, our otherness. And we kept his chair at the table, his gun on the settle, in silent agreement that he was still there and we were all waiting for him to come back. And that's what we would tell anyone who came.

Why? Is that what your eyes are asking me? Well, I don't know why. That's how it was then. But it wasn't any longer how it had always been. The core had gone from our lives.

And then came Mallin with his questions. 'Where's Amos?' he asked, as he came with his hides to our fire. As he came with his stories, his warmth and his magic, as he came to our fire. How were we to know that Mallin had his name down for Amicombe Farm? Or that he'd found a young wife, contrary to his natural inclinations, more as a beast than a breeder, and wanted to settle down? We were not to know then that he'd had his eye on Amos, was counting the years as he put his money so cunningly down on our table. We were not to know there were steps that Amos could have taken to prevent this from happening. He could have put his cross on a paper at Exeter, but I suppose that he, like the rest of us, considered the death of himself impossible.

Then came the men with their sly-eyed enquiries. They brought a power with them which was quite new to us. Lizzie dealt with it in her own way – she spat and she swore but she didn't keep the sheriff away. Nor the men who came afterwards. 'Come for a good squint now t'maister's gone, has 'e then? Dare 'e, dare 'e come nearer?' And they did dare. And they came right inside before Maggie backed them out again with the muzzle of Amos' long-gun. And fired it. And missed.

And that, it seemed, was a crime every bit as bad as not burying Amos.

They went away, and after their horses kicked the dust I let loose the ban-dog and he did the rest, tearing off after them and going for the horses' feet so they kept up the speed until they were well out of sight.

Brother Niall, let me tell you that it settled nothing, just the fact that our fellow Borough men did not consider us suitable neighbours, nor the Duchy us suitable tenants. The law had been broken and Master Mallin had laid his claim. Justice must be done.

We could no longer work for the watching. It exhausted us all and our eyes grew sore with it. We could no longer move to the newtakes because we had to guard the house. We could not be caught outside it, helpless. And we moved the ban-dog in with us and he howled like hell to get out.

We sat and we stared as the nights drew in, our hearts beating together, saying little with our voices but much with our guarded eyes.

'They'll come back,' was Lizzie's dire prediction. 'Have no doubts about that, they will.'

Birdie was combing her hair, picking the nits from the thick of it and feeding them one by one to the fire. 'We'll be ready for 'e,' she said. 'We have done nothing wrong. But mebbe we shouldn't have put 'e there. 'E were human, after all.' And because of the peculiar look in Birdie's eye and the vehemence behind her words, I thought of the baby buried and I wasn't quite sure who she spoke of.

Maggie just looked at me. And said nothing.

It was me they sent to fetch and take the cattle. To milk, to carry water, to feed the pigs, to collect the eggs, to shut up the geese, to put in the turnips, to carry the dung-pot out to the land, to dig and store the potatoes.

So it was me who saw the cloud of dust coming up over the wastes when the man came back with the constables. And it was me who was too far away to warn them.

I watched the Farm, wandering about in my memories. Why hadn't Mallin told them about me? Maybe he'd forgotten, or maybe he thought me too insignificant to worry about, merely a child and a peculiar, silent child, at that. Maybe he thought he had done enough to the family of Amos Horsham. Whatever the reason, they didn't come looking as I expected them to. Mallin could not have known I was there, watching, next to Birdie's baby, from the black ridge. I slept by day and I moved by night. I felt secret and magic like the wisht hounds and I howled like the wisht hounds out loud into the darkness and Mallin must have heard and wondered. Yes, Brother Niall, don't look like that . . . I raised my head and I howled at the moon and I shook and wrapped myself in my arms as the pain came out.

For the first time Dartmoor became a desolate place, a place of shadows.

Where was God, Brother? Where was God?

I fed from Mallin's hen-house and the shadow the moon gave me as I crept, that shadow I carried like terror beside me. My constant companion. I pushed my hands through the rough wooden flap I had stood and watched Amos make, and I pulled down the basin of mash. I was not hungry. I didn't feel hunger but I knew I must eat. Mash and scraps from the house.

I sat, crosslegged on the floor of the court as I had when a baby, and ate them, my black eyes darting about and my ears listening hard. For I hated Mallin and feared what he would do to me if he caught me. Why was I there courting danger, then? Is that what you want to know?

Well, I was there because I was ashamed, full of shame that my aunts had died and not me. Wanting to be with them, yes, even in that way. Wanting to make up to them with my own death, wanting to make myself into a sacrifice. Half-hoping for, half-fearing capture. Playing with my fear.

I was mad. Mad with grief. And I wanted it back . . . my childhood . . . that hauntingly beautiful, harrowing world that had once been mine. But it did not come back, no matter how I willed it.

One night I heard Mallin's woman crying. I was sorry for her and I marvelled that there was still room in me for that. She was no older than I was. I wasn't happy being myself, but I preferred my life to hers.

Why didn't I move on, away from the place that held such sadness? I think I kept going back for the smell. The Farm smelled of home and of Maggie and Lizzie and Birdie. I went round the court by night, touching familiar things, trying to absorb them like food into my body so I could hold them there, so Mallin wouldn't get them. I wanted to burn it, to sneak to the house, take a faggot from the fire, bring it out to the mowstead and start the blaze. But somehow I could not destroy Amicombe, even with Mallin in it, Mallin and his poor whore. I couldn't wipe it away like that. Fire wouldn't take it away. It was in me. It was me. To burn it would be to burn myself.

And I must have managed to love just a little part of myself then, for I did not burn Amicombe.

No, Brother Niall, I watched it.

4

Did I always have a passion for self-destruction, this morbid desire for martyrdom? I came to Lydford yesterday full of good intentions, but didn't I secretly know what was bound to happen? Didn't I always long to be a sacrifice?

I ask myself questions. I try to listen to the answers. But everything has vanished and gone into darkness.

I am a listener now, and listen very hard for the sounds I want to hear. Voices, birdsong, the rustle of owl's wings, Lizzie, dark and witchy, scratching me with her voice. 'I told you so, I told you so.' Maggie's commonsense voice backing out from the potato store but with no commonsense in the words: 'Did anyone find that comb I bought from Mallin, the one with the studs in?' There was never any comb. And Birdie's voice, ethereal, mystical, in a softly savage singing.

Were we, and Amos too, all mad? How can I make comparisons? You . . . you silent, frail old man with the sad brown eyes, we are not in the hands of God, monk, we are in a trap, snared by our own emotions. You will not answer my questions, either.

Sounds – the sounds of a Dartmoor summer. Sheep bleating, the whinny of the tethered pony, the thrashing of Amos' wicked hook, the squelching bog and the buzzing of bog-bugs, the milching cow pissing on brown grass – me pissing on brown grass, smelling sour, fermented as the hay, pungent as the foaming ale.

'He's the best man with horse in the whole of England!'

NO! NO! Go away, Rowle! Go away and stop coming between me and the memories I want. I wanted him suddenly: there was that one, fatal moment when my mood was fixed for me, my fate fixed as Lizzie predicted all fates were.

There was I, an angry wild creature, dark with a glare of white in my eyes, a breathless, excited snarl baring my teeth – *picture it, Brother, picture it*. I can't blame Rowle. He didn't cause it. He merely noticed me, took a fancy to me, used me and discarded me, and I loathed him until the fatal moment when I must have decided to turn all that raw energy into loving.

Loathing was far easier, Brother, but then you wouldn't know about that. To start with, when I changed and began to love him, I had to deal with his aloofness and apparent indifference, amusement even. It was just no good me flouncing off, tossing my head and kicking stones – if he saw me he laughed, and we were over-polite when we met. I remember his hard, sardonic humour, his arrogance and the way he said eventually, 'Go home'.

And the brazen doxy who sat beside him feeding him with her fingers, her bitch's eyes telling me, 'Bethany my dear, go home, he's mine,' while a sour smile teased her lips. That was Lucy – that was how I wanted to see Lucy.

My pathetic desire to be near him. The looks that I sent him, timorous, hurt, fluttering . . . he must have seen . . . he must have. All that rushing out when I heard horses coming, the barking dogs, the bouncing lanterns, the raucous laughter, the curses, and me with the rain on my lashes and at last, at last, his lips, incredibly soft on mine and the raw-leather smell of him. Me there, frenzied with stupid, misplaced delight. That kiss, that kiss was the kiss of death.

For after that kiss, vivid colours burned on the moor for me. As for him, well, he didn't even bother to lie!

Laugh, Brother, laugh! But tell me, please, if you can, what was all that laughing and crying about?

What sort of person was she, that girl out there, half-living like that? Often in dreams I return there, to that safer place before the passion came. Before they left me, Maggie, Lizzie and Birdie, half-child, half-woman, half-mad with grief. And I often ask what gave me the need to love Rowle. I have spent whole nights searching for the answer, rising at dawn to walk and remember and try to work it all out. And then I looked up at the night sky and wondered . . . because all round the rocks there were always the skies, daunting, brooding, temptingly-wonderful skies. Did they make me, the skies and the yearnings inside me?

Was it the skies that gave me the need to love Rowle?

I don't know how long I would have stayed there at Amicombe, for time meant nothing to me, but the cold began to come through. It was the only thing that could penetrate the hard crust around me, and I knew it was there because it became almost impossible to sleep.

I tried, as moonlight edged the moor with silver. Hard by a black velvet lake I found a cleft in the rocks, its mouth filled with rushes and I slept on a bed of brake-fern. But sleep and waking, for me, seemed to have joined together. I drew bracken up around me and my head, my knees, they were all tucked in, so that when the men came I thought I was having a dream. I had many lurid dreams at that time. They came, like dream-monsters, out of the dark. I thought they were constables: they had me in their arms before I awoke properly or they would never have kept me. I would have outrun them.

I was over the neck of the horse before I realised that these were not constables. They were ruffians, without the neatness of the men from the town nor the quiet conversation that passed between them. These were silent men, in a hurry, alert and on the watch. For what? And why did they want me?

I heard Lizzie's voice then, just as crackly and strong, as discordant with foreboding as it used to be: ''Ware lest the wolves, the wisht hounds, the Gubbins get 'e!' And I knew whose horse I rode on! I knew who these men were! I can't have been as indifferent to consequences as I like to suppose because I screamed and they hit me without any thought. Hard. Not the warning that Amos might give . . . but a real blow.

The smell, the bouncing, the noise, the sweat . . . a terrible turmoil of thundering hooves which my arms dangled over made me limp like a doll, helpless. I stayed where I had been put, and I heard my own breath squeezed out of me each time I thudded down on to the saddle.

The Gubbins, the Gubbins, the Gubbins . . . the childhood threat that had sent me scuttling to bed . . . the padding ones, the night ones, the unseen ones, *the other ones* . . . more 'other' than we had ever been. The darker people.

I knew I had seen them just once before. The day when I spotted the wild men I had the ban-dog with me and mistook the black, fuzzy shapes down by the water for furze bushes. His ears pricked first and his hackles rose and I dragged him down behind a ridge and lay there, never noticing how the gorse thorns tore me until afterwards. The ban-dog noticed.

His body was all a quivering growl but he could not bite for the thong round his muzzle.

We were high on Amicombe Hill and they were in the ravine, down between the boulders in the river, six of them. I might be confused about the outside world but I knew who these men were. Even so, in spite of all the warnings and all the terrible stories I'd heard I had to fight to stop one ridiculous part of me from standing up and waving, calling to them down below me just to see what would happen. And then chasing away, with the Gubbins flying after me and my breath pounding in my throat and the grass whizzing under me. I didn't do that. I sank down beside the ban-dog. We had the full brunt of the wind, and the ban-dog and I were shivering with fear, cold and excitement, as we watched them.

They were fishing. Most successfully, for one of them had a staff on his back and more than five or six fish hung on the end: I could see their tails glistening as the man negotiated the boulders. I saw knives flashing, too, glinting steel from their belts, as they moved along the valley.

Cannibals. Murderers. Rustlers. Scavengers. Drunkards. Some were branded with a V for vagabond on their chests, I'd heard. These were the men I looked down on that day.

I couldn't make out their features from that height but they were dressed as Amos dressed against the cold, in leather jerkins and long boots tied with sacking and one had a sheepskin cloak loose around him. All but the man with the staff carried sacks on their backs. They moved at a leisurely pace, not nervous or watching for danger. They looked dark, and bearded, but all men look dark from far away. And their shadows slipped after them as they moved off through the ravine, growing larger behind them as I watched. One threw a stone in the water and the echo from that came up to me. I thought that was the nearest I would ever get to the outlaw band.

It was said that no one dare touch them, that constables and sheriff alike would rather turn a blind eye than earn the vengeance of the Gubbins and their terrible clan. They were leaderless then, or if there was one he had no name. If he had I would have known it: Mallin would have told us.

It was only later that one came along and called himself king. The ban-dog growled. I saw his teeth, yellow fangs bared

35

with a slithery tongue rearing up between them. I pulled on his chain to shush him. And then a shadow so long, so menacing it put out the sun, settled on me, and I could not breathe. I turned round so slowly a night and a day seemed to pass by for the time it took me.

It was a goat!

Only a goat! And the goat that stared down on me that day gave me such a withering, scornful look, shook so crossly at me with its pointed black beard, that I laughed out loud with relief. The echo took the sound down and startled, I followed the sound with my eyes. But there was no sign of anyone then. The Gubbins had gone.

I took a blackbird home that day. Quick with fear I caught it.

And these were those men!

And these were those horses . . .

The images of that nightmare ride open and close. They are shrouded one moment, clear the next. We were away and moving fast. No point in a struggle now, and why should I struggle for life? I could fall and kill myself and I knew that the rider who held me so painfully under his gloved hand would not have stopped for me. You know these things. You know them and they are more powerful than any other message given. The rider who captured me had less concern than he would have had with a stag he had killed or a sheep he had taken.

Every now and then their shouts broke the silence, sounding muffled and far away. Sometimes I imagined it was Amos speaking, then Lizzie, then Maggie, then Birdie. Perhaps my conclusions were wrong, perhaps I was dead. Perhaps I had died of the cold in my sleep and the Devil and his riders had come for me. I stared at the hard, black boots that gripped the sweaty flanks of the horse and felt dizzy. I closed my eyes tightly.

Hanging upside down, engulfed by the sounds of the violent motion, I went into another world, only half-conscious I'm certain. Under the real feelings of the hard, stabbing pain, of the great discomfort I was in, there was a queer unnatural twilight, and the moor was water green and everything we passed just shadows. How else could I see the world from the state I was in? I was half-starved, maddened with anguish, frozen nearly to death and dazed by lack of sleep. I must have looked like a spirit from the mire – filthy, ragged and half-alive.

That journey must have lasted, at worst, twenty minutes, but for me it seemed like a dark and endless night.

They wanted more women, I heard. Well, they must have been short of women to stop for me, mustn't they, monk? It was hard to imagine how they realised I was one.

I, who until one week later, hardly realised the fact myself.

5

It's funny, monk, but at times like these, when I draw near to Rowle, or even at a time like now when I come close to death, I experience a feeling of unreality as if I am suddenly dreaming. As I draw closer I look down at my arms, my legs, my hands and they look like someone else's, some body I have been given as a costume to perform in.

And then I get to feeling foolishly brave. It is, I suppose, a kind of mute arrogance, a method of rising above the rest. A trick that I use, of withdrawing from reality and allowing imagination to take its place. And are my dreams of rescue just another part of my game? No, no, I cannot think about that. Rowle will come. I am quite certain he will come.

My judgement is impaired, or I have no means of judgement left, for I cannot tell you which was worse – the confusion and terror I felt when I arrived in the Combe seven years ago, or the terrible events that happened in Lydford yesterday.

I didn't meet Rowle until one week later, if 'meet' is the word to use because it was hardly a meeting of hearts and minds. It was a meeting of flesh. We didn't talk, not on that day. He took me then and he didn't know me, nor I him.

And I loathed him. Detested him even, quite fiercely. Yes, Brother Niall, isn't that often the way? Surely that was a warning, some primal knowledge asserting itself. Animal instinct. If only I had clung to that state of loathing.

Oh yes, once the very idea of him touching me was loathsome! But then came the change, sudden and severe, one night when I saw him dismounting, shouting, 'Take him, John, I shan't want him again tonight,' as he passed his horse to his groom. Then I longed to throw myself into his arms, longed with a sense of suffocation, humiliated by it, too, and feeling that I had betrayed myself, my pride. After what he had done to me. Subtle, sickening excitement. Oh, how pitifully and how long I have nursed my wounded vanity.

Surely another sin for your little book?

Women, for Rowle, were a necessity. No wonder he preferred his other ones, who were less obsessed than I. Fun and laughter they gave him, adoration and a measure of safety, but not me, oh no. He saw that my love was dangerous: he knew that from the start. Passion isn't pleasant. There was little delight for me, either, in loving Rowle. I didn't want to love him, no, not at all. Our love was a struggle that grew into a war, with vanquisher and conquered and he was the tyrant and his voice was the voice of the tyrant, angry and quick.

He was heathen, Brother, heathen!

Ah, but we had our times together, our secret times when no one else was there. Times when I stopped, I managed to stop for a sweet while my ravings, my angry recriminations. Nights of blazing moonlight when everyone else slept and we lay in shady recesses, consumed with fiery longing while the dawn broke over Lynx Tor.

We loved, clawing for frenzied release from the blissful, agonised tension.

But Rowle must go back. He draws me towards him steadily, even now, with all that has happened between us. Look at me . . . look at me shaking. I can't wait to speak of him, be with him, see him, touch him . . .

There was only one entrance to the valley, and at this a watchman stood, hairy and huge in his weatherproof garments, clumsy like a performing bear with a lantern in his hand. He dipped it as we passed and it looked like a little moon going down. He and my captors exchanged a greeting that I could not understand.

Hell itself, Brother – I could be forgiven for seeing the Combe in that way. I think you might have crossed yourself and kneeling, raised questioning eyes to the sky.

How can I describe a place that started as a nightmare and then became my home? Surely in all the world there can be no other like it? Such a strange, hollow, unworldly place was the Combe where the Gubbins lived. Barren – a lair to live and wait in – a place of bats and jackdaws. A thin slit in the earth coming off the valley, a crack in the land hidden by two banks of swelling heathland. The black cut – for that is what it seemed from above, was fringed with gorse and clumps of hawthorn, dark green and becoming cooler, paler as you took the steep paths made by sure-footed horses and descended between the silent green walls to the valley floor below.

The Combe was hidden from sight, and by day the only signs of life were the blue threads of smoke that came from the women's fires. And such echoes – I had never heard echoes like these, and at the beginning I wondered what they were and thought that I must still be dreaming, the sort of dream where you call out with no voice and are answered by strange words beyond your understanding.

But when I arrived at the Combe I was sick and weak and broken-hearted. My teeth chattered from exhaustion and cold. And I was confused, bewildered by the people who took me from the men when they lumped me down off the horse. They clustered like burrs around me, clutching me, pinching me, feeling me as if they were blind beggars come upon a sleeping drunkard.

I did not move. Or speak. I was hardly breathing.

It was night when I came, and black. The night was always black there and without shades, and the days were yellowed and shadowed, only ever lit by the slanting rays of a peeping sun. Oh, yes, even the sun was in hiding there. When I arrived the sides of the Combe twinkled with lights that seemed to come out of the earth itself. And then, on my feet again and the right way up, my dizziness left me and I could make out what looked like more than fifty different dwellings with doors but no windows, fires but no chimneys, following the natural riddle of the rock that fell into caves and inclines around each jagged point.

Caves large enough and dry enough for people to live in.

What people?

People with livestock and families, obviously. Beside the caves were roughly built wooden pens where sleeping pigs grunted in fat dreams. Bare-footed children came from the caves and followed me with their eyes, fingers in their mouths while they stared. I stared back, in horror. For I saw one without an ear, one without a hand. Another had no hair. Was this, then, just another dream?

Some, preferring more open ground, had erected crude dwellings on the lips of the Combe where the shelves were wider, nearer the floor. And these were such simple, temporary-looking places that they resembled the telling houses shepherds use at the end of the season – no more than piles of specially placed boulders, packed with straw to keep out the rain.

People lived here?

'Hutt 'er ain, Mat, wull 'e, if'n 'er tries ter run.' I could scarcely understand what the man was saying. Their accents were broader than ours. They spoke in a mumble as if they were used to keeping their voices low – rarely using words but many signs and gestures. If I had understood I would have assured them that I was too weak to run anywhere and that hitting me would make no difference.

And all the women who gathered round me held shawls round their watching faces.

The horses were led off into the darkness by men who got up still wiping the grease off their hands. They came from a group who sat in the open air round a long trestle table that served the lot of them. They were shaggy, dirty men with rough beards. Three lanterns burned, one at each end and the third in the centre. The men were companionable in a way that showed they were used to each other, that they always sat round the table like this. They cared not a jot for the drizzle that silvered their shoulders, that sat like slithers of sleet in the creases of sheepskin blankets they wore, and their hands were protected against the cold by rough strips of hide.

Those that had turned to stare at our arrival soon turned away losing interest. I stood and watched as a woman passed round a cauldron of fierce-smelling stew. They dunked thick crusts into the communal bowl and took it straight to their mouths. Their teeth looked fierce and white in the false light. They wiped their mouths with the backs of their hands, their hands on the thick material they wore.

Savages!

By now I had done my trick and I was without fear. I wouldn't have cared if they killed me. All I could think of was Lizzie, Maggie and Birdie: their deaths and the manner of their dying haunted my waking and sleeping moments, and so did the last words I had spoken, 'I hates you Maggie Horsham, I really, really hates you'. My head roared with confusion and I would have given anything for a moment's forgetfulness, to give my tired brain a rest from it all.

All this – the dark valley and the people in it . . . does this make sense, Brother Niall – well, it seemed right, somehow. Perfectly ordinary and natural, just another layer of the madness that gripped me. I felt as if I had been here before and I was so tired of it all. I didn't question why they had brought me or what they meant to do with me. If I hadn't been there I would have been lying outside in the cold, shivering in the dark, praying for the oblivion that refused to come.

Yes, I was weak with the hopelessness of total despair when Rowle found me.

He thought I was a doxy, for that's what they told him when they took me to him, or a dell not yet broken. Just ripe for Rowle and there for the taking. He thought I didn't care, that I was as hard as the rest of them, and that's the impression I gave. I didn't bother to fight him, I was too busy fighting the monsters that threatened to take my brain away. He seemed far away then, more like a dream than reality . . . hah . . . that does nothing for his proud virility, does it, knowing that when he took me he felt unreal!

He could have been anyone, Brother, he could have been ANYONE!

Why do I lie when there's only you, monk, to hear me? Why do I continue to try and cheat myself?

Yes, a harlot, that's what he thought, banished from the town and doomed to make a living where and how I could. To go with men for any money just as long as it paid for a meal in my stomach and a bed for the night. I wasn't like the women he was used to. No wonder he was never easy with me.

I remember, I asked him once, and he said, 'I'd never have done what I did if I'd known your true feelings.'

Incredible! So I told him, 'That shouldn't have mattered! I was a human being! And if I had been a whore I still would have had my feelings! Nobody wants to be humiliated like that. It shouldn't matter to you who you think people are – why are you so heartless? Why do you treat women so?'

And later, when his actions drove me to madness, to jealous despair, he would not change his ways for my sake. He used to tell me, 'You're a woman. You can't possibly understand how it is between men. I need their respect. I have to earn it every day of my life, to fight for it if necessary.'

'But you don't need to prove your manhood, Rowle, not all the time, not in those ways!' And I didn't believe his crude argument. How could I believe it? No one was about to challenge Rowle, he was not a wild beast about to be tackled by younger stags coming up to fight him. No, I suspected he behaved as he did because he wanted to. His arguments did not hold water. And that knowledge drove me to sleepless nights, to kicking and writhing with red-hot anger, to jealousy so intense I could have killed over it.

'We wanted more women,' Rowle said. 'We were becoming too much of a company of men. Women wear down the rough edges. We were in danger of becoming too rough.'

Then it was my turn to laugh at him. Too rough! I couldn't conceive of there being such a state in Rowle's imagination. And I tried to force him to admit that the reason he wanted more women was because he was bored and dissatisfied with the women he had.

'I'd tell you if it was done for that.' And yes, Brother, Rowle would have told me. He never bothered, never took the trouble to lie. 'No, we had spoken of it in the council and decided on it, so when they passed you by they picked you up – couldn't believe their good fortune. You didn't struggle at all. You were asleep when they found you and you seemed to stay asleep. I'd tell them to leave you there now, if I'd known. I'd tell them to put you back.'

There was always a hard, sardonic truth underneath Rowle's humour. He rarely smiled, not at me, anyway, and when he spoke like that he tended to search your eyes. Not funny, really, was it, although frequently in order to ease the tension we tried to make it so.

I pulled and I pulled. I should have let go of my end of the rope before it snapped, should have sensed it would take no more tension.

6

'Take some broth while 'tis hot. 'Tis good an' full o' energy an'
you look as if you can do wi' energy . . . all life gone out o' 'e
like that, all limp 'n listless like.'

I listened to Mary, trying to decipher her words, but I did not
eat and I did not speak. I sat in the corner of Mary's cave with my
back to the rocky wall from where I could watch and listen and
not be disturbed. From outside, her home might look like a cave
but not from within. It felt like a safe place. For several days I sat
dumbly like that, eventually coming to understand that if I had
been brought to the Combe before Rowle was king then my
experience would have been quite different.

'We lived as savages in they days maid, wi' no order nor form
to uz lives.'

I tried to listen and concentrate, I tried to escape from the
thoughts that pounded in my head. Since Rowle's arrival five
years before, the Gubbins had started to live in families, no
longer in communal groups as they had done previously. Mary
was a kind woman with six children of her own and several
loose ones who came and went at whim. Orphans, some, with
memories that showed in the scars behind their eyes as well as
in their bent and crippled bodies.

Mary chatted all the while and she looked like a wizened
brown monkey with a wide, cheeky smile. Her silver hair stuck
close to her face like down on a sticky bud. Now and again she
would leave a bowl of broth on the floor and go by, not caring
whether I ate it or not but patting my head and whispering
gentle encouragement.

Mary had hung curtains across the vast open space so that
the whole cave was divided into three quite cavernous rooms.
And this cave was special because Ned, Mary's man, had
managed to hew a shaft in the rock above so that a fire could
burn indoors and the smoke find a way out – sometimes. So the
smell of smoke was pungent in there. It clung to clothing and
food and even the water tasted bitterly of it.

44

'But I 'asn't the heart ter tell 'e after all 'is hard work,' she explained to me happily, seeing me silently searching the water for charred, woody flecks before I drank.

And everything, apart from the smoke, was clean, neat and tidy. I watched and saw how Mary bustled round and enjoyed playing house. There were even shelves in the rock where she stored her earthenware pots. A whole flitch of bacon hung beside the chimney, well-smoked. Her own sow and piglets ran in a pen beside the door and a tethered goat, a vicious creature with horns, lived on the mossy roof above.

She spoke of her husband with resignation, 'Dead. An' 'e were a tinner – in them days we lived in caves worse than this.' And Mary looked proudly around her. ''E fell an' 'e broke 'is leg. We had no money fer doctors so of course the leg got worse an' worse till 'e couldn't walk, let alone work. We started ter beg. We were allus moved on.' She opened her bodice and showed me the branding scar. The terrible V dragged down between her breasts and I thought it looked mocking, like an in-growing necklace of pearls. 'Then 'e died,' she said simply, doing herself up. 'An' there was just me ter look after all o' they. No work ter be 'ad. I was told o' this group o' ruffians where I might, as a woman, be taken in. Oh yes, I was afeared o' comin' 'ere.'

Mary talked as she worked on round me. One of the children had made her a broom but the twigs were too loose and kept coming out so she left more mess behind her. 'But I had no choice when winter came so I brought 'em here, nigh on starvin', an' not one pair o' boots between uz.'

Mary smiled, as if there was something fond about those early memories. I wondered how she could find any humour there. ''Twere quite different then. 'E weren't here, 'twas just the rest o' they.' And she jerked her head to the door and pulled a rueful face as if to include all the men. 'A wild lot, an' not a brain to be found among 'em. But I put up wi' it all ter see the childer fed an' warm. An' fer once we could get uz heads down in the same place twice wi'out the fear o' allus being moved on, even wi' the little ones sick. That terrible, terrible road. Oh, sometimes 'twere never-endin', I'm tellin' 'e. 'Twere such a relief – such a blessed relief. An' then me an' Ned, well, we had these two,' and Mary patted the head of the smallest child who pretended to bite her. 'An' we go well together, you knows, fer 'tis not nice bein' lonely an' carryin' everythin' all on youm own like.'

I didn't answer her but I was listening, and encouraged by this Mary went on. 'Oh, I knows what they calls uz outside – the Gubbins – an' I knows 'xactly what that means. Lowest of the low, filth, dirt, the dregs, the leftovers. Well, they would now, wouldn't they, 'cos they is afeared o' uz. We sticks together in ways them out there would not understand.' And Mary cackled and showed a row of broken teeth underneath her sweet monkey smile. 'Well, we'm never likely to be moved off out o' here now, are we? I carn see the constables or the sheriff comin' in 'ere all bold ter move uz on. Not wi' 'e in charge. Not wi' Rowle.'

Whoever you listened to it was exactly the same. To the Gubbins Rowle was a god, or the stars or the moon, essential as an element, water or fire. I listened, I watched, but I never heard a bad word spoken against him. In fact Mary seemed even to bow her head a little whenever she heard his name, as some do, monk, when they hear the name of Jesus or pass a holy place. And I had time to wonder about this Rowle, about who he was and why they worshipped him as they did. About where he lived and why we never saw him, for he did not eat communally with the others. And he was not a fellow cave-dweller, nor did he live in one of the shacks.

Mary could divert me for minutes at a time, and thoughts of Rowle intrigued me by day but through the nights, I lay by myself while the monsters came to devour me.

Look at my right hand, Brother Niall. Do you see the white scar? Well, I used to sit with my back to the wall and bring it up, right to my eyes. I screwed them up and I stared at it and I licked it with my tongue while I tried to remember my name.

I needed to know who I was and I couldn't remember! I think it was this scar which saved me.

For me to be shut inside for more than an hour was hard, for I had always been outside. From a baby I was outside, whenever I got the chance, whenever the door was open. So I fingered the scar and I conjured back all the wetness on my bare feet, and the weight and the itchiness of the sopping rags I was wrapped in on the day I was bitten by the adder. I was always close to the ground as a baby, amidst the rushing draughts of legs, at the kicking level of sheep, at the fluffily tempting level of horses' plumed fetlocks, at the bend in the tale of the muzzled ban-dog, at the top of buckets and under my aunts' skirts.

And I had seen that wonderful adder among a secretive pile of leaves, with a decorative V on its head and a flicking tongue. I remembered it had been raining. The ground was wet. The sunshine lay with a sharp angle on the court which was full of peat-coloured puddles, a whole chain of them I could follow across the court and dabble in. When Amos came over the pack-bridge, grey and white, the colours of the fat old cob and the same set expression on their faces, the puddles seemed to tremble with the weight of the two of them.

I sat and I stared at my scar and I began to remember.

I crawled off after the adder's whipping little tail, thinking it was harmless like all the other creatures I picked up and played with at whim, marvelling, I suppose, at the unhairiness of it and the slithering quickness, unlike the slow-moving creatures I normally found. I was furious that it should escape my pudgy, clasping fingers – no wonder it bit me. But I'd seen it and I wasn't about to let up on it. Even in those days I was a fast mover and determined once I knew what I wanted.

My hand swelled up like a purple paw, and red whorls spread up my arm before anyone noticed. I was sick, 'sick as a dog, an' when there were nothin' more to come there was all that retchin' an' you not knowin' where you was or who we were. We thought we'd lost 'e,' said Maggie. 'Even Amos went about wi' a drawn look on 'is face. 'Tis the sense of failure in losin' a child, like losin' a lamb. 'Tis such a bliddy waste after all that feedin'.'

I was put on the trestle table before the fire. 'Kept rollin' off yer did, yer had ter be tied on in the end. You frightened uz,' said Maggie crossly, as if I had done it on purpose and I can't have been older than three or four. 'Yes, you did, you frightened uz. An' all the while the ban-dog, as if'n 'e knew, set up a horrible wailin'. Nothin' Amos could do to 'e would quiet 'e. 'Twas truly terrible, what wi' Amos cursin' an' Lizzie chantin' an' Birdie just goin' on wi' that mazed singin' o' 'ers. An' you, groanin' an' rollin' yer eyes through it all wi' even yer little face all puffy.'

Lizzie had given me henbane in nettle wine to put me to sleep before she cut me and pushed into the wound a brew of heads and wings of crickets, stewed with whole beetles in oil. ''Er pounded it up wi' that filthy old pestle o' 'ers an' rubbed it in, but first 'er sucked the poison out,' said Maggie.

But the bravest thing she did was to overcome her life-long horror of snakes, to go with a stick to the adder's tree trunk to seek out the culprit, catch it, skin it, reduce it to cinders on a stick on the fire, and powder the wound with the ashes. 'An' 'twas that, no doubt about it, 'twas that that saved 'e.' And Lizzie sat with me, went two whole nights without sleep to watch over me.

'An' nobody knows to this day from where 'er wondrous knowledge comes,' Maggie finished off with a firm smack of her mouth. ''Er were born wi' it. Just as you was wi' yer taint-mark.'

So then, Brother Niall, as I sat there in Mary's cave, I licked the scar that was part of me, and I pulled my black hair down around me, fingering the tress of silver white, for it was these memories which told me who Bethany Horsham was.

Oh, it was hard to be in the Combe. These were not the people I knew. This was not the home that was mine or the freedom I had come to accept as my birthright. I had lived free as air, but in a world of fantasy made up by myself, for there was no one else. We were never a family for speaking, or confiding – or sharing anything other than the work.

But that never mattered to me for I had the Forest and I had the dreams. I lived in my fantasy world, resenting anyone who made me come out of it. Sometimes in those lost days I'd turn Amos into a Gubbins, no better than the wild Irish they said, marauding and pillaging. And then he rose, tall behind the leaping shadow of his temper with a knife between his teeth. Some said they were cannibals so the meat that he tore I made human flesh. It suited Amos, my fantasy of him, pagan like the Gubbins, pagan to a man. My view of him sat well on his gusty shoulders.

Then Maggie would slap my head and I'd duck away and take off with a spear to go salmon fishing, to the spot that I knew under the packhorse bridge, for the blood month November was coming and we would be living again on salt meat: fresh fish was precious. Oh, I knew where the piskies danced by the rings that they made, and the caves where they lived. I always turned my pockets out when I went by the piskie garden or I knew I'd be piskie-led. And I let all my dreams come in when I was seven years old and out fishing or riding the jet-maned rowan pony – held her with a halter, no harness – wild I went. And to make myself sad on purpose I used to go to the grave of the child, the granite cross by the black ridge.

She was the only one I could talk to – her under the cross that hardly had arms. I sat in a special way, cross-legged, to talk and tell her about myself. Sometimes when I didn't feel too silly I used to kneel down and put my hands together and rest my head against her cross. On dark nights I challenged her to come out and face me. I didn't know how she had died but I liked the sadness she gave me.

'My name is Bethany Horsham,' I used to say over and over until the words sounded like nonsense and then I'd lay flat and shout them at the sky. 'My name is Bethany Horsham and I am good at catching fish. I am quick and sly, Maggie says. I am alive and I have a name. And I never want more than that. I have a dread of anything being different but I know that one day it will be. Can you hear me? Can you understand me? Were you frightened of something you couldn't see when you were alive?'

And more awful than that I would ask her, 'Did you die when you were little? Did dying hurt? Is it cold down there where you are?' Sometimes I went too far deliberately to upset her. So that I knew what that felt like.

I practised whistling there. I made up poems and songs. I pulled faces at the stone. 'These are my faces,' I told her. I never gave her a name. 'Which is the nicest? Which is the one you think I should wear? Do you think I am pretty? Or ugly? Do you think I am nice? Am I your friend?'

Yes, sometimes I crept out in the dark to keep her company, only returning when the way was clear to slide, unobserved, between the soft, warm bodies and the tumbling blankets of my mother's sisters, for my bed was a pallet. I slept among the limbs and snores of three scratching women, safe between great rocks in the twilight where Amos couldn't get me, safe while I heard him snoring downstairs on the settle with his saddle for a pillow and his long-gun, a lean-limbed lover in his arms.

Awake all day and all night, I was sometimes, but never tired, avoiding the bogs and the dangerous places, the caves where the wild men lived. Dartmoor nights, running barefoot in the combes: those nights, like sleep, refreshed me.

And then, in the Combe and no longer a child, I still wanted to ask those same questions. 'These are my faces. Which is the nicest? Which is the one you think I should wear? Do you think I am pretty? Or ugly? Do you think I am nice? Am I your friend?'

Please! Please, Mary, stop talking and tell me – *who am I*?

She must have considered me half-baked. I did not speak, but by now I trusted Mary enough to go with her.

''E built 'isself a house.' Mary took me by the arm and we went outside. I was struck by the freezing cold and the white Combe light which later I would get used to. Holding me tight with one arm she pointed with the other. 'See,' she said, screwing up her little eyes. 'See that stone house at the end of the Combe, just where you sees the valley comin' into it? Well, 'e built that soon after 'e arrived an' 'e lives there wi' 'is woman, Lucy Bishop. That's where they holds their meetings an' takes the council an' haves the monthly court. 'Tis grand in there, they say, but I've never bin. Never 'ad a need to.'

I frowned and Mary answered the question she saw in my eyes. 'We choose to live like we do. We could build houses, too, if'n we took ter doin' that. But we're wanderers, all o' uz, not used ter bein' in one place fer long an' it takes time to adjust. No, we'm happy as uz are. We'm different ter Rowle. Rowle needs ter live in a house. Now Rowle, 'e be a proper gentleman.'

We went back inside the cave together, trying to warm up after the cold. And I sat back later, sipping hot soup and wondering about Roger Rowle who was so well spoken of, who was such a wonderful leader, and yet who could choose to live in a house apart from the rest, happy for the others to live like beasts in burrows while he ruled from above and was contented to be called a 'gentleman'.

7

I blink, bewildered, when I think back to that time, for the memories come with such shocking intensity. I want to stay with the memories. *What will I do if he doesn't come?* I can't stay here. If I stay here I will be mad by morning. Madness for protection? Should I let myself? It would be so easy. That is something I will consider later, for there's lots of night to go yet.

Tell me, Brother Niall, if love brought me to the state I'm in now, if it's because I fell wildly in love with Rowle, then what is love? What is it I'm talking about? If I'm to die because of it I need to know.

Could it be nothing more than a sexual desire, the kind of desire that drove the animals at Amicombe? A ten, twenty-second frenzy satisfied with squawks and a fluttering of feathers? Can the depths of it be measured by its durability? If so, seven years of love as intense as mine and I must surely pass all tests.

Is that really all we had – seven years?

And do I regret it? Even now can I say that I would rather have lived without it? Certainly my life would have been calmer, happier, wouldn't it? But that would be like choosing to see the Forest in summer, denying the Dartmoor winter. And without those sensations together I would never have experienced the dizzying, fatal, agonising ecstasy of such intense suffering, such anguished delight. My love . . . my obsession for Rowle was to do with winter, the hard diamond of it glittering, embedded in my heart.

My young self – she doesn't want to stay with me. I feel her pulling away as she would from anything she didn't understand.

This is a plea, Brother Niall, a plea for clemency. Listen to me and write it down, or make it an intercession to put before your God. There are no other excuses – only this one.

It was unkind of them to bring that child to the Combe. It

51

was unfair to put her in that position. She was still too much of a child at heart. She should have been left running over the moor with the juice of elderberries dripping down her chin, the dark bunch of black she squeezed in her hand. She should have been left to grow up, still whispering to Birdie's baby's grave, plaiting corn dollies to hang from the rafters, believing in good luck. Still ducking from Maggie's great fist and casting her eyes down going past Amos. Still wary of Lizzie and screwing up her nose against the noxious smell of the yarbs. Forcing the rowan pony on, faster and faster, and wondering over the exhilaration and where it came from. For she was too young, too innocent for Rowle. Too young, with all the shame, all the heartrending mistakes to make and all the joy to come. She hadn't yet learnt to laugh at herself, and when the obsession came it didn't leave much room for laughter.

I was cleaner. I had a fresh, new woollen skirt and bodice made for me specially by Mary, who dismissed my smiles with, 'Oh midear, 'tis no bother. I likes ter sew an' make things when I'm blessed wi' a spare moment.'

She could not know that I had possessed nothing so fine as this before. I would have liked to have thanked her but I still could not speak. At Amicombe I wore cast-offs or sacks with holes in, and I hadn't ever thought about clothes before. Now the shift that I wore was soft and fresh-smelling and over the top was a skirt of gentle green and a bodice of red which drew up tight and snug around me. Mary gave me a cloak she had done with, and that matched the bodice. She had dyed it, she said, with a dye that would last, from a lichen she'd found growing on rocks at the bottom of the Combe.

So – warm, fresher and well-fed, after a week of Mary's careful gentle ministrations I was well on my way to mending. As far as the inside of my head was concerned, well, that would take much longer, for when I held up my hands, no matter how hard I tried to stop them, they still shook.

I wonder why Mary never told me what was going to happen. She must have known. Perhaps she assumed that I was worldly-wise enough to know, myself.

They had men aplenty. They were short of women, that's why I had been captured. Rowle used people, animals, situations. He used men, he used women, he used horses, each for their own purpose in his life. And when he had finished he discarded them, some of them the worse for wear.

When they took me to the house they said, "'E's asked ter see you. Quick now, 'tis best not ter keep 'e waitin'.'

I did not question his intentions. In all innocence I went with Ned, holding my cloak tight around me, interested, even, to meet the man who was held in such awe. I had no preconceptions . . . if anything I was disposed towards liking him. It appeared he could do no wrong. It seemed they could not survive without him. I think I must have been just a little bit nervous for I was hardly at home there yet, having been at the Combe for just one week, and that inside the cave all the time.

Picture it, Brother, for it is not hard, in fact it is quite distressingly simple: a studded door, not unlike our own at Amicombe, and a granite lintel, the same. I thought the house well built and in a good position, tucked in at the end of the Combe like that so Rowle had a view over everything if he opened the small mullioned windows. There were stables beside it, new and built of fresh wood, and I could hear voices from the back where the kitchens were, and my mouth watered as I smelled good cooking.

It felt strange to be in a house again. Sad feelings came to me as I remembered Amicombe. But inside it was not at all like our house. There was furniture and lots of bright, clean floors with rugs on them, and it was larger than the house where I grew up. There was pewter, sparkling, and real glasses, and chairs with arms that looked like thrones which I had never seen before. I stared. The panelled hall was spacious, and silk pictures hung each side on the walls. I stepped back, uncertain, made nervous by the sort of place I was so unused to.

And then I saw him, monk!

For the first time. And am I trying to say that I loathed him? Is it shame that makes me say that . . . makes me keep repeating myself over and over again like a poor liar? Shame, because of the feelings he gave me? Feelings I have never, ever admitted, until now. Because I am determined to tell the truth, monk, no matter how shameful, no matter how much you will not want to hear it. But now there is only you to tell. Rowle can't hear me: now it's too late.

53

Tell me, should I have known? By the feel of the room should I have known? I was fifteen . . . and innocent . . . wasn't I?

Ah, what is innocence?

The room was made warm by a large fire. Fine furniture winked along the low-beamed chamber, polished to a glow and burnished by flame. He was not alone but two companions stood by the table where a pewter jug glinted against dark oak. Beside the jug were three tankards. Rowle was just home. He took no notice at all when Ned knocked on the opened door, and I watched as he carried on, unclipping his spurs and handing his companions his whip. They gave him his tankard of ale and he sipped, licking his lips and turning round at the same time with his eyes half-closed as he savoured it . . . which . . . the ale or I?

What did he see? What can I say? All bone and eyes and hair, that's how Maggie described me. 'Bad eyes,' she said to me once, 'too bold, too black . . . you could be one of the piskie folk, you could be a tree elf with the way that you look, secret and mysterious. You are a child of the Forest, midear, no doubt o' that. Fer I've never seen anyone like you. An' yer taint-mark, it doan help yer.'

I saw his black eyes narrow as he nodded for them to leave. He ignored their secret smiles, but I saw them. He closed the door with his boot and I kept my eyes to the space on the floor and the jet black boots that came so surely towards me. I was not going to raise my eyes to any man who so clearly expected me to do so. He might be master to them, perhaps, but not to me. I had called no one master in my life and I didn't intend to start now. But I stole quick glances under my lashes while keeping my head demurely down. How rich were his clothes, so unlike those of the savages that he ruled. Rich and sweet-smelling, particularly compared to the cave-people I lived with. His boots squeaked as they moved towards me and I kept my eyes firmly on them.

Humiliation! I stung with it! For when, after long moments, I lifted my eyes to enquire, I saw that he might be inspecting a horse, running his hands over its withers, checking its age by its teeth, noting its haunches for breeding. And all this he did with his eyes alone. I held my breath as he caught my eyes and I shivered, unable to help it. He spoke. I could hardly understand the words and frowned at him to repeat them. But then I knew that he wasn't requiring an answer, his comment was made to himself and all it seemed to require was a laugh.

He sighed and appeared to relax then and I had a chance to look round. I stood very tall with my chin up, as arrogant as I could make myself, as arrogant as he. My eyes scanned the room as he watched me. Fire, oak furniture, some painted silk on the wall which I knew from my Mallin education to be of a Chinese garden. And rush candles burning in brackets giving those dark and light shadows. But one dark shadow, I saw, as I lowered my eyes once more, was round his feet and mine. Joining us in a pool of black. Together.

Something in the room, it must have been the high-stacked fire or the smoke, but something made it difficult to breathe. And I kept having to swallow. And Brother, I knew exactly why I had been brought here. I am no longer going to lie or pretend otherwise.

I should have turned and left, shouldn't I? I knew what was going to happen and I knew that he would have allowed it. He might have laughed . . . but he certainly would have allowed it.

Unsure and frightened I bristled when he caught my arm so arrogantly and led me towards the fire. I would have preferred to have been asked. Until then I was unaware that I had been backing away. And then I became defensive and glared at Rowle with ferocious eyes.

Oh monk, to fall in love at first sight is foolish. I had my own ideas of love and how it was going to be. I'd dreamed of being courted one day, given bunches of flowers and garlands of coloured ribbons. But oh, he was too handsome! Tall, slender, elegantly cool with a collarful of curling black hair. His eyes were so black they could have been seams cut from granite, and he was bigger than any man I had met, just by his sense of command. The half-smile he gave me showed very white teeth and he was pulling me to the seat beside him.

'How beautiful these moorland people can be.' Yes, those were his first words to me. I have never forgotten. 'Such hair, such skin, such eyes, just a wild, natural beauty.' I bridled. I flushed, determined now that I felt so vulnerable, to hang on to my pride. But I sensed menace in him as he bent to swish the blue cloak from his shoulders and loosened the lace at his throat.

There was silence except for the fire so I watched it, pretending to listen. We could have been conversing most seriously then, that fire and I. A tense silence, just me and Rowle and all the time in the world. My throat tightened, the silence extended and became just part of the time and the space we were in.

I wanted him, monk! He was a stranger and yet I wanted him! And how could I cope with the feelings I recognised, that desire which had so terrified and repelled me during the last few years of my life? A desire I had only seen in an old man's eyes. Amos' hands, Amos' smile, and only a bad man could smile like that. A desire I had fled from, a desire which had driven me out to spend night after night alone on the moor to seek safety, confessing to the child on the ridge, while my aunts at home suffered the violent repercussions of my cowardice.

I didn't like love with Amos. I hated making love with Amos.

'Look at me!'

So I did not hesitate. And by staring brazenly at him like that I thought I was hiding my shame. So I didn't resist, but kept on staring as I felt him undo the strings of my bodice, as I felt his hands on my arms and my belt coming undone, and he and his cold hands slipping the rough material down my arms. I crossed my arms in front of me, then, sensing the uselessness of that, put them by my sides while pressing my hands flat on the rich material. My hands, oh God, where to put them? I didn't know what to do with them for they shook too much and I shivered.

And he didn't smell like Amos. And he didn't feel like Amos.

But his voice, when it came, seduced me. 'Look at me,' he said again gently, while with his fingers he stroked me. And then, with no hesitation he took my breasts, released from the tightly-laced bodice, into his hands and he fondled them. As if they belonged to him. As if they were fruit he had been to the market to buy! As if he had haggled over them and now they were his and he had the right of ownership over them! 'Look at me until I tell you to stop.' And I saw with amazement that his eyes were trying to dominate mine.

So I laughed then, straight in his face. And I would have

cursed and got up to go, bridling with self-righteous resentment except that he held me, caught my wrists firmly and pulled me up. And when I stood for a moment, unbalanced, my untied clothes fell off me. They spread around in a pool at my feet and then I was with him, down on the rug, not knowing how I had got there, surrounded by my useless, crumpled clothing. How easily he had done that! Did he always strip women in this calculated way?

The rug was rough beneath me and the thick embroidery on it scratched like rough grass on my skin. I struggled with Rowle. I struggled to make sense of the situation. I struggled through my fear and my agitation, relishing them but refusing to admit that, just the same.

He was doing bad things to me and I said so.

Rowle bent over me where I lay, savouring my nakedness with penetrating eyes. He smiled and I saw his teeth. He smiled at my fear and his expression was cool, cool with fascination for his latest captive . . . and afterwards he called my behaviour deliberately coy and shy. He slid his hands under my breasts again. They were not large like Lucy's but small and apart and separated. He squeezed before bending to take one nipple into his mouth. He held it between his teeth while his hand calmly explored the rest of me and I felt his fingers soft on my sex before he slid his fingers through the heat to the burning inside. 'Is this bad?' he asked, raising his mouth and licking his lips. 'Is it bad to do this?' And I could not answer for I was wanting to arch towards him and so I arched away.

I murmured and moaned for I could not help it when he teased me with his fingers like that, when he caressed the inside of my thighs, spreading them with my own moistness, first with his fingers, following them with his eyes, and then, to my shame, with his lips and his tongue he traced the path of his fingers.

'The skin is so soft just here.'

Ah but his touch was soft, and his words were soft, and his glances were soft as he stroked me.

'Stop, please . . .' At last I had found the words to speak, and they were full of pleading.

'We'll stop when I tell you.'

Positioned by Rowle, I tried to close my legs but it was no

use, he held me. I stared at his face as he lay beside me, I stared at the smooth, dark skin of his face, the gleam of his teeth and the moody black of his sweeping lashes.

I could no longer deny my own desire for it stormed inside me and showed in the sweat that soaked me and in my trembling legs. I wanted to do whatever he asked me for I knew he was master of what we did . . . I knew he could take me to places . . . I wanted to bask in the pleasure. He took my hand and he held it down and he said, 'Let me watch you.'

'I can't do that . . . I can't touch . . .' and I moaned. Ashamed. As I did it.

Embarrassment and shame were soon forgotten, and then I was sighing, caressing myself in front of his cool dark gaze with awful abandon until I cried out for wanting him to help me. I was afraid of being unable to bear it. I was afraid of what he might not do.

He replaced my hand with his own. It was my body and yet he knew the hidden places far better than I. He knew what to do better than I. And all the time, detached, he watched, as if he played with a butterfly.

After he'd finished and I was quiet I stared in his face to shame him, flooded with misery because of my own wild abandonment. For I did not know this man and he was a stranger and what had I done? Where had these feelings come from? He showed no shame but his eyes were frozen like sheer black ice and I said, 'Let me go now. Let me go back.'

'Who are you running from?' he asked me gently. 'Me or yourself?'

I didn't know how to answer.

'You belong to me now,' he said. 'This is your home. You are one of us. Do you understand me?'

Oh, Brother Niall, he was strong and full of power and gave such a sensation of safety. And I wanted that to be true! I so wanted that! But I also wanted to be the only one for him. Was that wrong? Was that so impossible?

The flames danced soundlessly now. The flagstone floor, beyond the rugs, shone wetly black. The fire smelled sweetly of applewood and I heard ashes falling softly upon the hearth.

He pulled me towards him. I tightened, fearful again before relaxing for a second time into a kind of delirious, delicious hunger. *This is not Amos this is not Amos.* I might as well have been a slave and in chains for all the will-power I had of my own. He kissed me with gentleness, for reassurance, and his lips were moist with the wet, musky smell of myself.

With his hands round my waist he turned me over until I knelt before him, open to him, my breasts swaying gently and my stomach resting on a fur stool he moved there for the purpose. I no longer owned my own body. He was the master of me, body and soul, and his hands roamed expertly over my nakedness. First my hair, then my neck, my breasts, my belly, my thighs, even the backs of my knees and my toes, he thinned my lips and eyebrows with the tips of his fingers. He took every part of me that evening in the firelight and made them his. Everywhere he took with his fingers he claimed for himself. I closed my eyes and shuddered but he calmed me with his soft words. But all the time, I knew later, he was measuring me with his gaze, comparing me to all the others.

When I felt the force of him behind me nudging the slippery wetness I grasped the corners of the stool with both hands and almost screamed out in fear. But he edged in deeply and slowly, spreading me wide apart with his hands. Wracked by an ecstasy beyond my belief, time turned endless. We moved together in pure timelessness. I think I cried some time, because I must find that delirious absence from myself once again. My cries turned to a scream, my body writhed and contorted as we moved faster and faster towards the release that I craved.

My brain had let go of one nightmare. One madness was over — another, far more dangerous, was about to begin.

'No one has ever done what you did,' I told him, honestly and timidly. Because Amos had never given me anything like that.

'So . . . you want me to do it all over again?' I was afraid of that smile.

I have become more afraid of it since.

I wanted to cry then, monk, both terrified and sad, and half in love, yes, I know that now. But I hated him! Hated him for using me, and hated myself for allowing it . . . no, for wanting it! For the willingness in me and the need that made me humiliate myself like that!

I stayed very late. It was almost morning before I left.

Ah, monk, but as I left that house, much, much later, in the pale blue dawn of the Combe, I heard a woman singing a lullaby to a sobbing child from an upstairs window.

But I didn't go straight home to Mary's. I wandered down to the bottom of the Combe where a trickling stream made ponds between the boulders. I waited there until the small breeze calmed so I could see my reflection in the water. I knew that I must be different, and I wasn't sure that, now, I would be able to recognise myself.

I was a woman. And loved. No longer the child with quick flashing laughter and those darting black eyes. She had gone away for ever. Her day was done. And a different Bethany Horsham had come to replace her. I had found a new self. One that Rowle had called beautiful.

8

How could breakfast take so long?

'He called me beautiful,' I said to Mary.

Bustling about with a pan in one hand and a hot loaf leaping in the other, she threw me a smile and she chuckled, 'Oh, well, fancy that, so you do speak! Beautiful . . .' and she cocked her head on one side to consider as she banged down the loaf on the shelf by the fire. Her smile was broad when she finished, 'I suppose yer could be called beautiful in a black an' a gusty kind o' a way. Stormy,' she said, and obviously pleased with the word, considering it just right, she repeated it, blowing hard on her burned fingers.

And I dreamed on. You see, monk, I thought that because of our love-making I was going to be special! So when Rowle passed me later that morning, aloof on his horse, his companions around him, I was shocked to receive not even a nod of recognition, although I'm quite certain he saw me. I had spent what was left of the night dreaming. Not bad dreams – they were fading. Fantasy, I suppose: I was trying to escape, trying to deny reality again.

I am ashamed of this, Brother Niall, but I feel I have to recount it because it seems important. I might even blush when I tell it, so be gracious enough to ignore me. I had imagined being called to the house, summoned there immediately, taken to Rowle who would love me, care for me, make me his and one day, yes, one day marry me. So simple! So horribly naive! But so vivid were my imaginings that I was sure this was going to happen. When time passed and no message came I went and sat outside on the grass gazing down the Combe towards the granite dwelling with the court outside, the court which, at that time of day, was full of horses, men and action. I did not listen to Mary who chatted on as she scurried about getting the children dressed and preparing the breakfast.

The mist of the morning was cold. It sat wetly on my

shoulders and dampened my hair. Maybe there was a reason for the delay. Maybe he wasn't there, or maybe there were arrangements that had to be made. Eventually, too cold and anxious to sit there any longer, I returned to the fire, my head filled with questions that Mary was going to have to answer.

And did I feel some surprise that she had not immediately asked how I'd fared last night – what I thought about Rowle – why I was so late back and why my sleep had been so restless? Mary, who was always so shamelessly inquisitive? I had had to get up in the end to sit by the fire while the wind moaned outside, slapping against the ill-fitting door and shifting the sack-curtains. I sat and I thought, trying to clear my head. But Mary didn't ask. Mary only went about her morning tasks as if this day was going to be the same as any other.

I resented Ned with his slow-moving ways. A gentle giant of a man with red hair and a flaming beard, he was out of temper this morning because he had drunk too much ale last night. Get on . . . get on . . . I wanted to shout as he kept getting up and sitting down, his sturdy limbs creaking as he held his great head in his ham-like hands. Mary didn't scold, but was quieter than usual, pandering to his ill-humour. The children ignored their suffering father and ran about with chunks of hot bread in their mouths, going to the entrance of the cave now and then to call their friends, their voices clear as fluting bells as they tinkled from one cold side of the Combe to the other. This morning they were going fishing. There were shrill plans to be made.

I sat and impatiently considered these ordinary people. Ned was a poacher by trade, like his father and grandfather before him. Only now, here in the Combe, his art was recognised. And when I heard Mary complaining, 'I do worry 'bout 'e, out in broad daylight sometimes fer so long in such dangerous country wi' all they man-traps an' leg-breakers layin' 'bout,' I smiled to myself for I knew there were those who considered the countryside dangerous only because the Gubbins were about.

Even back at Amicombe, a place of little conversation, the Gubbins had often been discussed on dark nights. We believed it was Lizzie's spells kept them away, they and the ban-dog and Amos' gun. But we knew it was mainly Lizzie's spells because guns and dogs didn't stop the Gubbins from raiding or stealing from anyone else.

''Tis time something were done,' Amos once said darkly, on hearing accounts of their latest escapade. He tapped his pipe on the hearth and blew down the stem to clear it. 'John Cobbledick lost two sheep t'other day an' afore that John Taverner found 'is milch cow missin' . . . taken from 'is door cocky as you please. I reckons 'tis Lizzie's evil eye stops they roogs from takin' from uz.'

'What can be done wi' the likes o' they?' asked Maggie with her crossest look. 'They'm a law unto theyselves, roamin' 'bout at night in the combes, comin' from they lairs like beasts an' waylayin' honest folks on the roads. They carn be catched. They runs faster than fleetest horses. No one be safe from 'e. No one.' And she clucked and sighed so hard her breath came in gusts from her chest. We all enjoyed discussing the Gubbins.

'They have allus bin here an' I suppose they allus will be.' It was unusual to hear Amos accepting anything. And he did it with his usual spit. 'Hundreds o' they buggers. Catch one an' there'll allus be more o' 'un. Beyond the law they is an' they knows it. They'm laughin' behind their cave doors, laughin' at every one o' uz.' And Amos blew foul smoke rings into the air with a kind of mournful satisfaction.

I had spent many hours thinking about this. It was amazing that we never saw the Gubbins. They came and they went with a stealth that was wild, that was animal. Apart from that one, brief encounter, I had never seen the Gubbins in my life and yet they reigned with a rule of terror and were never far away from our thoughts on winter nights. I had imagined them as fairy men with the power to become invisible, or turn themselves into hares or red deer, or padding, sharp-eyed foxes. Amos even lowered his voice to speak of them as if he talked of the supernatural. Not afraid, I think, for Amos was never afraid, but alert, always alert and watching.

But if the Gubbins had magic, then so did Lizzie, and hers was a powerful magic. Look how she'd started the stream up again after it had run dry. Look how she'd healed the sores on Amos' legs. So why didn't she pit herself against the Gubbins? People might like us, I thought to myself, people might accept us and start coming to our house if Lizzie defeated the Gubbins.

So I'd asked her once. I'd gone out and found her in the

63

court with Birdie. Her long-toed bare feet suited her sharp-featured face with the same dusty muck on it. She stood with a halo of chaff round her head while the sun frazzled her woolly hair and her threshel was raised up for striking. And she brought it down like the curse that I wanted when she heard my question.

'Why doan 'e curse 'em then, Lizzie?'

'They never hurt me or mine.'

Birdie, working beside her with a sack tied over her black hair, giggled.

'But you could if'n you wanted to, Lizzie, couldn't 'e?' Nervously I crossed my legs. I plaited my hair with my fingers. It was the first time anyone had seriously suggested that Lizzie might be a witch.

I remember that Lizzie came up from the work and bent herself backwards, her hands on her waist to ease it. Birdie stopped laughing and decided to hum a tune instead.

'Aye, maid, aye, I could.'

'Then why not? You're afraid it wouldn't work, aren't you?'

'I'm afeared it might come back on uz.'

'Why would it do that then?' I had her attention and for that I was surprised enough. I was not going to let it go having got that far.

'A curse as powerful as that and you never knows.' Lizzie stared hard at me, astonished, I thought then, to see me standing my ground. But now I know that there was more in her expression than that – a sadness I had never seen in Lizzie's face before. A sadness and an acceptance . . . for Lizzie had the second sight and life was proving her right once again. The traps were there, open-jawed, waiting to snap shut around her. How could she have cursed the Gubbins, the wild, godless Gubbins clan, when to do that she would also be cursing me, whose destiny was so hopelessly entwined with theirs.

I thought about this as I watched Ned leave, all disgruntled with his nets on his back, ducking the mouth of the cave, and I shivered.

At last they were gone, not only Mary's children but a whole string of 'other ones' too. Weird ones. Strange ones. Some for whom drink was to blame, for others, disease, deprivation and life itself. For this was a place for those who would be accepted nowhere else and, strange and silent as I was, I wasn't particularly peculiar or odd compared to the rest of them.

Breakfast was a sociable meal in the Combe. All meals were. There was much laughter and conversation, gossip was exchanged and plans made for the day. Some of the inhabitants, with their humps and their limps, their twisted limbs and their poor blind eyes, needed comforting, and some could only be tolerated. But somehow they jogged along together until such time as tension grew to a screaming pitch; then there was a brawl or a drunken spat, somebody's pig would be let out of its pen, somebody's cave would be ransacked, and the heat would die down until the next time. If not, if the flames of emotion didn't burn out then the tricky situation would be taken before the council – Rowle's council – which he ruled like a god.

'When I left the house I heard a woman singing,' I told Mary thoughtfully. 'The sound, it seemed to come from upstairs.'

'Oh, aye, that would be Lucy.'

'Who is Lucy?'

Mary turned round and looked hard at me then. I returned her gaze as artfully as I could. Her voice went patient. 'Lucy an' Rowle came here together all five year ago. They live together as man an' wife. Lucy has three children by 'e – Judd an' Matt an' Daisy. An' I hears 'er be 'xpectin' another.'

Hot. Hot inside and burning. Trying to swallow with a throat too dry so that when Mary added, 'I told you that afore,' I knew she was right but that I hadn't been listening. I knew she had mentioned Lucy, but I hadn't heard about the children. And I hadn't correctly understood . . .

'Are they to be married, then?' The question sounded stupid.

'Tush, what nonsense. What's ter do wi' marriage, then? Why would Rowle have a wish ter be married, livin' as we lives?'

'Lucy might. Lucy might wish it,' I argued, with my own words hurting me down in my chest where they came from. She didn't answer me with words. She merely raised her eyebrows so I said, 'You like 'e, Mary, doan 'e?'

'I'm a woman. You're a woman. Now I asks you . . . what woman wouldn't like Rowle?'

Oh, God, was I then just one of all the others? I wanted to

bend in half with my pain. I felt humiliated even by my need to force this conversation at all, hotly humiliated because I was quizzing Mary like this and making so much of her honest answers.

'The men like 'e too.' I tried to turn the conversation, to make it sound more sensible.

'The men need 'e. They admire 'e. They would be no good without 'e.'

And then I could play no more games. I had to come out with it. 'Is 'e . . . is 'e faithful to Lucy? As if they were married?'

At this Mary threw back her head and laughed and I thought how ugly she looked, oh so ugly, in her abandoned condemnation of my silliness. 'Oh Lord love 'e, Bethy. What can yer be thinkin' of? After last night how can yer be askin' me that? You've brought some odd ideas in 'ere wi' 'e fer sure. Lord! Lord!' She saw my discomfort and composed her face too solidly so that it looked oddly wise and ancient, like a small, intelligent animal with a face that was human but not quite. 'Listen ter me, midear.' And she laid her wrinkled face on my shoulder, reminding me of Maggie. 'Rowle can do as 'e likes. That's all right by Lucy an' 'tis all right wi' the rest o' uz. If'n 'e fancies a maid 'e takes 'er. Course 'e do. 'E's a man – which is what you discovered last night, didn't 'e?'

Mary's face softened when she saw the hurt in my eyes. 'One night, maiden, an' you'll get over it. Was 'e the first 'un, is that what all this is about? My! An' at your age! My goodness Bethy, I has ter tell 'e ter forget about it. Hang yer daydreams ter dry an' bring them in again all neat an' folded. 'Cos I'm tellin' you now there's no point in you carryin' on a star-gazin'. 'E's not fer the likes o' you. 'E'll break yer heart as 'e 'as done so many others. Oh no, doan look at I like that. It has ter be said. 'Tis kinder ter tell 'e the truth. Rowle has 'is way wi' all the young dells that come ter the Combe . . . 'tis something that is understood an' accepted, like. 'Tis allus bin that way an' it allus will be while 'e stays the man 'e is.'

And Mary chuckled dirtily and I just couldn't bear it.

The fact was, Brother Niall, that I didn't believe her. Over and over our love-making I went. Later, alone, I touched my body in the places he had touched it, remembering so exactly that it felt as if he was there again, caressing, teasing, tantalising, flooding me with warmth until desire nearly choked me. Until I needed him there, hot there, inside me, and I repeated over and over again the words he had spoken over the different parts of me, comparing me to everything from the fragility of birds in the sky to soft, ripe fruit that needed peeling slowly . . . slowly.

I loathed him!

And it was later that morning that the truth of Mary's words hit home. Later, when I sat outside again, pathetically staring hard-eyed at the house, making myself believe she was wrong and that any moment now he would come for me.

Because how could Mary know these things? She wasn't in Rowle's confidence, was she? Mary was merely an ignorant peasant woman, holed up here with a drunken savage she liked to call her man. How could she possibly know Rowle's feelings towards the Lucy woman? Just because they had children . . . well, what did that mean? I was sure he wouldn't have done those things – those things he did with me, had he not loved me. And he wouldn't have done them with any of those others, either.

Because I was different from them. Yes, yes, oh God I really believed that! They had been baubles children play with, whereas I was a woman, a proper woman, for hadn't I shown him that? Hadn't he said just that, over and over?

And I hung my head in shame, monk, remembering my abandonment.

Because I had trusted him.

And that's when he came by. That's when he passed me with hardly a look. Certainly no word, no nod of recognition. And me there, sitting on the ground, looking up at him with what must have been worship in my eyes.

Oh yes, monk, I loathed him! I hated him!

9

Put me down for the sin of jealousy.

His women.

His children.

His horses.

His dogs.

Oh God, I was jealous of all of them. And I hated him hotly for that. I must have an outrageous sense of my own importance since I felt he was obligated to love me just because *I* loved *him*. An overblown sense of your own importance makes it harder to die.

Oh, it hurts, the memory of my dumb, humble, instant response to his power. I could have been a dog, couldn't I? I followed at his heels, obeyed his commands, waited for hours in corners with my eyes fixed on him.

Yes, yes, yes! I was even jealous of the children whom he allowed to swarm up his legs, whom he pulled up on to the back of his horse, laid them over its neck, dangerously, for they squealed and the stallion's eyes and ears went back.

And oh, Brother Niall, I longed to be gay and friendly with him like the children were. Out from this trance that struck me dumb and silly whenever he came near me.

But it was Christmas now and a time to celebrate: new to me for I had never known Christmas before and I had only once heard of it. It was spoken of on a snowy day when we stayed in at Amicombe, emotions screaming all the time as the wind got up under the shutters and hailstones phutted the fire and it was too wild to go out.

I sat by the window, staring out, I, who never saw the house as mine but always felt like a rather unexpected and long-staying visitor who had come without wiping her feet on the sack at the door.

My aunts used to try and best Amos – that was their most awesome game. And after that they would try to best each other. Sly-eyed and watching we sat, shifting only in our heads as the beasts moved next door, our faces flushed so that Maggie kept wiping the sweat from her eyes with the grubby corner of her apron.

Birdie was annoying Amos with her whittling and those old bells rang on in the distance. We could see, from the sides of our eyes, sneaky, we could see. And him trying to clean his long-gun, spitting on it, spitting on the fire, spitting on the floor, spitting with mounting anger and wiping his lips in a savage way with the back of his hand, pulling them so his teeth showed sharp when he looked up. There were many noises in the room but most irritating of all was Birdie's whittling.

And I'm certain she did it on purpose. She let her long hair fall on her lap, over her head and down. But under that I knew she was wearing her most mysterious, sweetest smile. The pipe she was making was tight to her chest, but every now and then the knife squeaked on the hard wood and then she would stop, wait, and start again, nothing of her face showing, just her hair.

'Must you, mistress? Must you keep that up?'

'An' why mustn't I?' All from beneath the hair.

Amos spat again. 'You'll drive us all ter madness wi' yer scrape, scrape, scrape.'

'Oh, an' is I the only one then?'

'An' what fer anyway? Just ter make those terrible bleatin' noises away on the down? I've heard you, yes, I've heard you, trillin' like a bliddy matin' frog.'

'Music, Faither, 'tis called music.' Birdie shook her head then, parted her hair and brought those flint eyes up at her father.

'Church music, aye. I should put you up fer hire maid, or I should take 'e ter fair fer a wife. An' Mallin says there's apprentices wanted an' yer useless ter I.'

'Do so then, Faither, do so. I wouldn't care. I could get seventeen shillin' a year fer workin' in one o' them kitchens. An' I doan only play church music – I makes up an' plays my own.'

Lizzie spun more fiercely, making the fluff shift on the floor. The peats glowed more brightly and the ban-dog bayed to get in. Maggie pricked the top of her finger and drew in her breath. I sat silent, for I could see how it was.

And then I knew we all hated Amos, really hated him I

mean, deep down hated, in spite of the fact that he seemed to hold us all fast in the palm of his hand. I knew because I could taste the hatred in the air, along with the smoke and the mutton and the damp sheep wool. Yes, I could taste it – and yet we needed him. We did not dare defy him. The thought of being cast adrift into the world outside, well, it wasn't a thought you could easily dwell on. It was a nightmare. We could freeze to death if we didn't first starve.

Amos looked at Birdie then with the look he used when he bent down, hauled at an ear, pulled the pig's head to one side and precisely and deeply cut its throat from ear to ear. And Birdie was nervous as that pig, hiding and pretending not to be but I knew she was.

And I wondered, Brother Niall, and knew why we let him.

Put me down for another sin. Only I don't know the name of that.

Amos hurtled forward and with one swipe knocked Birdie and Birdie's pipe to the ground. He pressed on her head with one of his rock-like hands, smooth with power as if he was a preacher blessing, a baptism of obedience to himself. She lay still, but the pipe rolled backwards and forwards, backwards and forwards, as if it were a live thing and playing its music already. Stony music. Music to accompany the wind-driven bells.

The world went silent. Lizzie spun and Maggie sewed and I dipped candles, trying not to laugh because I always laughed when I wanted to cry. And Amos went back to his gun until the next time. For there would always be a next time: you couldn't leave hatred like that alone.

Later, out of the quiet, Birdie walked up to Amos. She held out the pipe she had finished. 'Fer you, Faither,' she said. 'I made it fer you.'

'Fer why?' Amos scowled up at her.

'Doan you hear the bells? It be Christmas, Faither.' She held out the pipe and he took it. 'Happy Christmas, Faither,' she said.

Ah, the pealing of bells, and I remember that first Christmas so well – the raw-aired feel of it that went so well with my own emotions. And now, with everything so dulled inside me, and hopeless, I wonder that I was ever that girl who felt with such intensity, pursuing an objective she could never attain. Impossibility – perhaps that is the factor that fuels obsession.

I thought about Mallin as I pounded the dough for Mary, punishing it. One day, oh yes, one day I would have my revenge. Snake in the grass, greedy, grabbing man with all that slyness about him. Somehow, somewhere, no matter how long it took I would take my revenge. With his wormy hands he had killed my mother's sisters, had tortured them there on the pillory at Lydford in front of my eyes. Oh, other men had done the actual deed, bovine men with farmyard eyes but behind their terrible actions had slunk the reptile Mallin. He had stolen from me more than bread. I wanted justice according to the law. I wanted those crucified hands of his, I wanted them off!

But even anger couldn't cool the fever that already burnt for Rowle. I rarely saw him as Christmas drew near, and if I did, he ignored me.

'Everyone will be there,' said Mary, excitement shining her monkey face along with the steam from the bubbling pot.

'Taste the lambswool,' said Ned with a hiccup, in Mary's way with his big body taking up too much of the small cooking space. He reeked of the so-called lambswool brew he was boiling, mixing the hot ale, spices, sugar, roasted apples, eggs and thick cream. He reeked of it and he tasted it anxiously, demanded opinions from everyone else.

'Yer'll ruin it, man, if'n yer keep addin' ter it. Leave it now fer 'tis well enough as 'tis and likely ter be overstewed. An' we carn drink wi' no food in our bellies fer we eat corn-porridge only until the morrow. Get out of the house, man, an' help wi' the goose-ridin' down below.'

The women baked while the men set up the gibbet-shaped structure for the goose-riding that would take place this Christmas Eve afternoon. I went outside to watch. The structure looked like a gallows as it took up its rickety position down there at the bottom of the Combe. Most of the men were already drunk and Mary came to stand with me, wiping her hands and her sweating brow and moaning, ''Twould be better if they fasted on ale, the buggers, ter make room fer more on the morrow. Look at they, braggin' an' goadin' each other like that!'

There were six fat geese to be won that afternoon. The fact

that they would be shared was beside the point. 'Ter win a goose be a matter o' honour,' Mary explained, 'fer they all take pride in their horsemanship, an' large bets will be made.'

I looked at the geese, curiously limp as though they suspected their fate as they waited in the pen down by the stream with their long necks all thin and stringy with grease. They honked their protests loudly, padding round on their big pink feet.

"Tis not a nice way fer the geese ter die, still livin', wi' their heads pulled off.'

'They's only fowls,' clucked Mary. 'They has no brains, they feels nothin'. 'Tis the men I worry about, ridin' so drunk an' so dangerously between all they rocks an' boulders.'

And I pictured those wild, drunken riders, rough brawny men with urgent faces, as they rode half in and half out of the stream, clutching at the goose on the beam as they passed underneath it, meeting their opponents in clashing eagerness to tear the head off the living bird.

Ned came back for his lambswool and carted it out in pails. 'Doan just stand about. Help me . . . help me.' And I helped him pour the thick scarlet brew into the earthenware bowl at the centre of the table, a bowl that had been lovingly decorated with ribbons and bunches of evergreen by the children.

'Wake up, Bethy, wake up! My, you'm turnin' into a proper dreamer! Penny fer 'em.' But no money could pay for my shameful dreams. And so I went back to help Mary again.

Excitement reached fever pitch when the game began. Cheered by the women and children the men mounted and took their positions, half the group by Rowle's house, the other at the opposite end of the Combe. People perched on the slope chattering cheerfully, everyone with a perfect view. And I sat with Mary and her children, silent now, and unnoticed, watching for Rowle.

'Judd! Judd!' Mary's youngest saw the boy first and ran forward to meet him. No more than four or five years old, Judd was a boy with curling black hair and enormous eyes, a Rowle in perfect miniature. They started squealing and fighting like puppy dogs and were instantly joined by other children who bundled themselves on top. I turned round, tuned in so fiercely to the names I had learned, and that's when I first saw Lucy. That's when I first saw Lucy and Rowle together.

And it was a painful experience. While he stopped and talked to everyone he passed, natural and relaxed with his smile coming readily, Lucy watched the children . . . Judd, a younger boy and another just toddling who held her hand. But I watched the pair, and although Rowle seemed to give his attention to everyone he spoke to, there was an invisible cord which attached them together, yes, even in the middle of all these people and all the shouts and the cheers. Lucy moved on. He followed. Just a few steps in her direction maybe, but he certainly followed. And if he lost her for an instant with his eyes it was not long before he found her again.

Clearly the other women liked her. She found a place and sat down, propping the smallest child on her knee and was soon surrounded by chattering friends. She looked – beautiful. And as I patted my hair and straightened my skirt, nudging my face to a smile, I knew that beautiful was her word and not mine. Oh, I might be beautiful on top where everyone could see, but not beneath where it mattered, down where my injured feelings raged and tore. Her hair was tangled and long, springing in even coils round her face and shoulders. She wore a simple homespun the colour of pale grey sky and a light blue sash held a cloak of darker grey round her shoulders. She had grace, I had not. She had charm, I had not. She had a sweetness about her face, her eyes, even about the way she moved – a sweetness that I, with all my darkness, could never have. Envious, I watched her, feeling the jealousy stir within me, real as any baby growing inside, kicking and disturbing me, swelling grossly and growing, feeding greedily off my own flawed emotions. Even Mary moved to be near her and I felt jealous and betrayed although I had nothing to be betrayed about.

'Come on over here an' sit wi' us!'

I stared past Mary pretending not to hear before I looked away. Hurting. He must look at me now! He must! But Rowle did not. And even into this I read what I wanted to read – he was avoiding me! And why was he avoiding me, Brother? Well, that was obvious, he was avoiding me because he could not deal with the feelings I stirred in him!

The afternoon of Christmas Eve grew darker and snow threatened in a leaden grey sky. We blew on our fingers, stamped our feet. Fires were lit behind us and some spectators, growing bored with the action, moved towards them in order to get warm. Soon the meat would be put on the spits to cook slowly all night. There would be many mouthwatering dreams tonight and tomorrow the fasting would be over.

Rowle – I watched him. He stirred Ned's wassail drink before lifting the ladle to his lips. He drank, and I can't be sure but I think his eyes caught mine. He looked away and beckoned to Lucy who came and stood beside him while he tempted her to taste it in a gentler manner than Ned's . . . slowly he lifted the ladle to her lips. Their eyes met. Their eyes danced together. I saw how pregnant she was as their bodies came briefly together and touched. And he smiled at her then.

I turned my back to them. Nor did I watch as the men below tore off the heads of the geese. I was not interested in their games – I knew what was happening by the hysterical roar of the crowd. They oohed and they aahed as horses stumbled, and men tumbled, clashed and cantered through a rubble of splashing stones and furze.

I hardly heard, I hardly saw anything. Obsession . . . it creates a silent, lonely world, quite of your own making.

Oh yes, Brother, put me down for the sin of jealousy.

10

So – Lucy! The lovely, voluptuous Lucy, who was a girl when Rowle first knew her. Who was a woman when I arrived on the scene.

Lucy was the shadow, the shadow at Rowle's feet, and even when he was with me that shadow was always there. Making its claim in all the secret places we went. In our bed. In Rowle's eyes. Even in his laughter Lucy's shadow was just the other side of his smile.

And the worst of it was that I liked her.

And she was good to me, in her kindly, beautiful, gentle way, seeing me much as a petulant child, understanding my passion, being kind to it. Blaming Rowle!

Oh Lucy, what would have happened, and how would my life have differed if you hadn't taken work at Amberry during that particular, fateful time – when Rowle was looking for someone to love?

I spent the whole of the night awake and plotting. Furious . . . burning with angry resentment. I tossed and I turned in my bed because how could he dare to humiliate me like this?

There were many young lads in the Combe but so far I had taken no notice, even when they blew kisses and whispered as I went by. These children, I thought to myself as I lay there wide awake, making my plans, these children with britches and cheeky smiles would not serve my purpose. I must find a man, and not just any man. I must find a presentable, eminently handsome man with whom I could flirt outrageously and disgracefully in order to make Rowle jealous.

I had to make something happen . . . I couldn't bear for it to go on as it was! And what other option did I have?

The choice was an obvious one: it had to be Silas Peverell, the man whose horse had carried me here. Close to Rowle, of the same age, same build and with the same quick way of speaking, Silas was Rowle's right-hand man. And once I had

Rowle dangling like a fish on a hook, lusting after me and unable to get me off his mind, well then I would flutter my eyelashes, turn round and laugh, dropping him flat with everyone knowing the ass he had made of himself. For didn't I hate him! Didn't I detest him? Oh yes, certainly I did, and people were giving each other presents – candles, wooden dolls, spices, garlands of evergreen – and this was the present I intended to give to the king of the Gubbins this Christmas. Wrapped. With love.

With my mind made up, a plan in my head, I smiled more readily that morning and it must have seemed to Mary that I was actually happy that first Christmas day.

'The merry-makin' 'as cheered you up an' that's good ter see,' she said. 'You have an added colour ter yer face an' it suits yer.'

I helped her and the other women to lay the great table. I asked about Rowle in roundabout ways that always managed to get me my answers.

'Oh, well I remember when Rowle first came to the Combe,' reminisced Mary, arranging the peacock feathers in a riotous display around the tail of the bird. I feigned disinterest. I concentrated on the feathers and pretended to be only half-listening.

Mary's tongue came out and tickled her top lip as she concentrated. "E were lucky they didn't kill 'e, but that tattered, bewildered group o' ruffians who captured 'e were impressed by 'is courage, intrigued by 'is clothes an' interested in 'is intentions. I watched 'e,' said Mary, standing back to admire her work. 'I watched 'e as they fingered 'im wonderingly as if 'e were some weirdly patterned insect. There 'e were . . . such a dandy in blue an' silver, a silver boy on a regal horse an' a fairy queen ridin' behind 'im. Oh yes, pagan uz were, but we was superstitious folk, an' it seemed it might be bad luck ter kill 'e.'

And, remembering my own confusion, I wondered how Rowle had felt when finding himself in this strange world.

Whatever their reasons, the Gubbins had let him live, although Mary said it was touch and go. 'Oh yes, there was fighting an' there was arguments over it, but back then there was fighting an' arguments over everything – food, women, drink, horses . . . until 'e came along an' took control.'

I followed her back to the cave to collect the cheese, knowing that now she had started she would gossip on. 'Yer would 'ave 'ad a bad time 'ad yer come then,' she said to me sternly over her shoulder. 'We all o' uz did, uz women. 'E 'as ter put 'is claim on you. 'Tis the only way these men can understand that they carn take you theyselves. How many times do I have ter explain it? How long is yer goin' ter refuse ter see? 'Twas nothin' in it, maid, doan yer see that?'

'I will never get over the humiliation of it,' I said to her contemptuously. 'An' I will never forgive 'e.'

Mary ignored me completely. 'They threw 'im into the pig-pen, the one back there in the rocks. It reeked o' pig in there, an' the old boar, 'e were still in it. Huge 'e were wi' ten-inch tusks on 'e.' And Mary pulled a face, snouting up her nose and using her fingers for tusks, and she did look, briefly, a bit like a bristly boar with her eyes all small and furious. But then she frowned.

"Twere worse fer poor Lucy. 'Er 'ad a terrible time. Well, Rowle had killed three men in 'is efforts ter break free an' protect 'er. They 'ad ter wreak their revenge on one of 'em. Rowle were nigh dead in pig-pen so it had ter be Lucy. When they let 'im out an' 'e discovered 'er had been taken by any who wanted 'er, 'is anger were almost too terrible ter see. Enraged, 'e took one look at Lucy, flung off the arms of 'is captors an' attacked them wi' all the strength 'e could muster. But 'e were weak an' ill an' his flailings merely amused 'em. They pushed 'e ter the centre o' the bull-baitin' yard, chained 'e ter the post an' set a pair o' dogs on 'e.'

Mary looked pained as she remembered that time. She stopped what she was doing, stopped dead in her tracks and sighed so that all the bustle went out of her and she looked like a fallen pudding with a curl like a wisp of steam on her forehead. For once in her life she was still. 'They left Rowle well alone. They'd been impressed wi' 'is swordsmanship. They were eager ter keep 'im alive to learn fer theyselves. Rowle saw that, an' 'e saw that the only way ter save 'is life an' 'ers was ter outwit 'em. 'E worked out who was leader from one day ter th' next, which o' they could be outsmarted an' which could not. An' wild as they were 'e knew they was human beings. 'E treated 'em so. 'E treated 'em wi' respect. Gradually 'e fought fer 'is rights. 'E fought fer 'is horse, an' then 'e fought fer Lucy.'

'He didn't fight fer her first, then?' I enquired sweetly. 'The horse were more important than his woman!'

Mary gave me a hard, suspicious look before she went on. I followed her out to the table again, where she sank down for a short rest, half-hidden under the mountain of cheeses. 'They fed 'e good food. Gradually more an' more was accepted an' 'e became leader. 'E built the house at the end o' the Combe. There were no challengers, no stragglers. 'E sorted the weapons. Their swords were poor battered things wi' no edges. They used 'em fer all manner o' needs – from the slicin' o' branches ter the guttin' o' fish. They were quite beyond repair. So it took Rowle time ter find the sort of weapons that were needed, an' ter bring they ter any sort o' decent discipline. 'E planned 'is strategies carefully, sendin' out spies ter the inn an' sendin' coins fer bribes. Parties went out ter surround an' lift what they needed from travellers till at last there were an armoury worth polishin' and weapons fit ter fight wi'.'

'Do 'e blame isself fer what happened ter Lucy?' I asked, turning away and making my voice sound casual. I rubbed my arms hard for there was a frosty nip to the air that Christmas Day.

Mary shook her head at me. 'If'n that's what yer needs ter think, maid, then think it. Who am I ter say otherwise? But knowin' Rowle as I do, I doan think 'e'd be influenced by feelings like that. No, thanks to 'e we learned ter belong, Bethy. Everyone is here because they want ter be – we is a family now. We survive on trust.'

'Ah yes, a family, a family in hiding, every member o' which be wanted by the law! Every member o' which goes from this Combe in fear o' 'is life! A family without a past. A family without a future. What as' 'e given you, Mary? Safety? Respect? Security? Ah no, I doan think so. I think 'e is actin' out some fantasy o' 'is own. 'E is usin' you all, an' the longer you stay here wi' 'e, the more dependent on 'e you become.'

Mary rolled up her sleeves as she stooped through the door, ready to carry the pasties out of the oven. 'If'n the answers be so simple, Bethy, then why doan you come up wi' somethin' better? You carn go round callin' an' criticisin' everythin' 'e do as if you've got some score ter settle yer carn let rest. Does nothing satisfy you? You must learn ter take what there be an' make the best o' it like the rest o' uz.' She moved from the oven to the table and back, fierce and quick like her words. 'There be no simple way o' turnin' the past round an' makin' it good. We has been poor all our lives, hounded an' beaten, starved half ter death an' forced ter wander from parish ter parish lookin' fer work when there was none ter be 'ad. None o' uz knew the meanin' o' order or harmony afore 'e came. 'Tis as much as uz can do ter work together now an' that we does not allus do. People from nowhere, some o' uz. People without hope. Uz has lived on our wits an' our cunning fer years. Some o' the kids has been viciously punished – their ears an' arms cut off poor little mites, I ask you – fer takin' bread! Most o' uz be hidin' from the hangman. No, it aint ideal, but 'tis a bliddy sight better than what we 'ad before I'm tellin' 'e.'

And anger flashed in my eyes and I flamed under Mary's attack. I couldn't be honest with her and I couldn't be honest with myself. I only knew that my heart hurt with the untruths I was telling. I ought to have shaken her and told her, 'No, no, I doan mean anything I'm sayin'. 'Tis all ter do wi' how I'm feelin'. If only Rowle would turn an' smile at me I'd follow 'e all the way ter Hell an' back.'

But I had upset Mary. The cave fumed hot and steamy, half with the baking and half with her anger. It twisted out of the door like smoke. I didn't care what they said about Rowle: I hated him and intended to get my revenge. I had little knowledge of the arts and skills of flirtation, having never practised them before, but I trusted they would come naturally. I decided that I had detected a look of loneliness in Silas' eyes. I had noticed him glancing at me with a friendly gleam of interest and I could tell that he liked me. A dark-haired man with flashing black eyes and an earring that burned gold on his dark skin, I thought I had summed Silas up. I thought I knew about life. I decided I knew about men.

So there I was, seeing things as I wanted to see them, refusing to help Mary and sulking behind the sack curtain. But I went wrong with Silas . . . it's easy to go wrong with people . . . sometimes I wonder if, in the whole of my life, I ever got anyone right.

11

Silas Peverell, Lord of Misrule and evil with the antlers he wore on a band round his head, and his long brown coat of wolf fur. It flowed behind him darkly in raggedy imitation of the robe of a king. Tall, lean, dark and with insolent eyes he took his place at the table to bawdy roars of approval. He banged down his goblet for order.

All morning we had been exchanging glances and I was sure that I had him. His dark brown eyes bored into mine, his forehead furrowed to a questioning frown, brooding, interested, amused. With terror, I suddenly thought of Amos . . . '*Youm my precious, my own precious, isn't 'e?*' sour and stained like the leather cup he drank from.

The Gubbins knew how to enjoy themselves, how to make the most of a holiday. They tore at the feast on the table, wading in with their knives and their fingers. A great tusked boar, glazed black and obscenely naked, with an apple in its mouth and a garland of rosemary round its head, stared back at them out of hot little eyes. Peacocks plucked for the cooking, demure with their fantails colourfully spread round them, fell into succulent pieces and ended up as thin bones on the floor. The feathers were grabbed by the children. There were haunches of venison, the six poor geese that were used so badly yesterday, and of course as much wine or ale as anyone could want to drink.

Seeing me silent and pensive beside him, Ned cheerily urged me to drink. ''Tis the answer, maid. You'll see if you just try a few more sups o' my brew . . .'

Mary wasn't having it. 'Leave 'er alone, Ned yer vule. Drink woan help what's ailin' 'er.' And she nudged him away with a cluck of disapproval, saying to me, 'Take no notice of the stupid bugger. 'E doan know 'is own name when he's into 'is cups like this.'

Her painted face was almost shocking. Mary looked so unlike herself that even the children looked up and smiled and seemed nervous. Her work-worn hands were rough with rings, a scarlet boa slithered round her shoulders and she wore a ravishing dress with trailing sleeves made of red cloth of gold. Some of the women flapped elegant fans and wore tiaras of jewels in their hair – no rags, no sacking, no reeking of the cooking pot today. The men were more sensibly clad against the cold, but even they looked festive in their furs and leather jerkins; they had even greased down their hair and some wore ruffs round their necks. Stolen! Everything stolen! And Mary, who must have sensed my thoughts, leaned over and said, 'Every single item at this feast is somethin' ter be hanged fer.'

And I shivered and saw that every man present had a dagger in a sheath, and that the watchman on the hill remained at his lonely post.

Silas watched me calculatingly over the rim of his golden goblet. He fed himself with a knife, stretching over for meat, and each time he ate his teeth flashed whitely. 'The men to act as slaves to the women! No matter what they ask for. The men to serve the women and the women to be the masters!'

Rowle sat beside him with Lucy at his side – Lucy, in blue, wearing a silvery fur.

They drank and they laughed. Mary fell off her stool berating Ned with a drumstick and Ned, in order to make amends, crawled off under the table and came back with the parson's nose. The feasters clashed their goblets together as they obeyed his instructions, while Silas watched, drinking heavily at the end of the table. He observed his subjects, and his brown eyes darkened and grew broody.

'An apple to be passed from mouth to mouth and forfeits set by me for the fools who drop it!'

And it was done. The forfeits were so terrible that I trembled when the apple, battered and overripe, came my way. It became a matter of life and death to pass it on successfully . . . and I had Mary on one side, the worse for wear, and Ned, who didn't know the time of day, on the other. The tension in my face must have sobered them up momentarily, for they did not drop that apple and when we passed it I saw apprehension in their eyes. They cared! They cared about me, they wanted me to be happy and yet I had eyes for only one – I was too absorbed with Rowle to be interested in anyone else.

So I laughed too loudly and I drank too much wine, seeing

the chances of happiness going to waste around me, and I loathed myself for not being able to take advantage – I felt jealous of the flirting maids and the rowdy lads who chased them. I would have liked to be one of them, light-hearted, happy . . .

Then came the brandy snapping, overseen by Silas. A bowl of nuts was set aflame and the young girls forced to pick one out. Burnt fingers meant loss of virtue. There was squealing and squalling amidst all the laughter, for the pain of this was very real.

Nervous, I held back. I saw Silas' eyebrows raise as he watched the proceedings from high in his ornate chair. He sensed, in my sullenness, an opportunity for sport. 'Oh no, midear,' he boomed so that all at the table could hear him. 'It is quite unthinkable that any untaken maiden be left out. Today every little chicken must obey the rooster's orders.' And he stepped down from his chair, rolling up the material of his trailing, heavy sleeves, and dragged me, shrieking, towards the high white flames.

'Leave me!' I shouted, for this was no game to me and I hated it. I kicked at his shins and I spat and I cursed but he didn't appear to notice. Ned whispered something I couldn't hear but Mary pulled him down.

'No one disobeys the Lord of Misrule on this day, not even you, little one.' I wondered why I had picked him out and wished like hell that I hadn't. He thrust my fingers into the flames and his hand was like steel round my wrist. I grabbed for a nut, knowing it was the only way and burning the ends of my fingers. 'To play with fire means getting burned,' he whispered softly into my ear so nobody else could hear. But out loud he said, 'No virgin this!' and he lifted the sore, blistered ends of my fingers for all the world to see. There was uproar then, and banging on the table, but by then they banged drunkenly on the table over everything that happened. 'You maiden,' said Silas, in the hard voice of the Lord of Misrule, 'you are to serve me for the rest of the day and through the night if I ask it!'

His command was given only half in jest and everyone round the table knew it. But to refuse, even surly, foul-tempered me, to refuse him would have looked churlish. For it was Christmas Day and the bells rang on in the distance. I had to go back with him to his chair and I had to obey his commands. I knew it and Silas knew it. But this was not the way I had planned things. How had it gone so dreadfully wrong? I glanced towards Rowle with a pleading look but he was talking to Lucy and I doubt if he knew what was happening. I longed to call out, 'Please, please stop this!' but he would have thought it all part of the fun, for he had seen me flirting with Silas. I had tried my hardest to make it impossible for him to miss it.

Where had my earlier recklessness gone? Obediently I sat there on Silas' knee, timid and hating to be there. The games went on, and the drinking, the laughter; the children put on a pantomime, and the Gubbins lost interest in me, but Silas did not. 'You're trembling,' he said, with humour in his eyes. 'Am I so frightening? Stop trembling! I'm not going to hurt you . . . not in ways you don't want me to, anyway!'

'I am trembling because I am cold. Certainly not through fear of you!' And I was pleased that my voice sounded calm and icy.

'Come closer then,' said Silas, and he wrapped his fur cloak around me. I could not move as I sat there then because he had his arm tight round my waist and with determined fingers he touched me. His hand moved under my clothing. We were quite hidden from the rest of the world, or the parts of me that he touched were quite hidden. He made a pathway for himself, moving the clothes that were in the way and he was an expert at what he did. I squirmed on his knee and resisted.

'Don't! Don't do that! Leave me be! Let me go!' And with one hand I scratched his face but he grabbed for my wrist and twisted it. He brought his face close to mine and repeated his words in anger. 'I've told you, maiden, play with fire and this is what you get. Isn't this what you've been asking me for all day . . . with those bold black eyes and that charming pout? You can hardly refuse me now, my lovely.' And I begged him to free me with my eyes, but his were determined, unflickering and insolent.

I burned with shame as he took his hands to intimate places and stroked me with his long fingers. He smiled as he entered my body and thrust inside with no gentleness. He bit his lip and looked like a wolf, for his movements were slow and stealthy. I sat on his hand, I was helpless, I wriggled and twisted but could not call out for shame.

'Still cold?' asked Silas, his lips in my hair. 'Or warming up?' I kept my expression steady. 'It's warm and moist and inviting, just as I like it. Later I'll see. Later, sweetheart, you'll feel more than my fingers.' I gritted my teeth but he laughed, quietly, like a wolf, and I saw his tongue flick like a wolf, but his eyes held an unasked question.

I was afraid to cast even a glance in Rowle's direction although, from where I sat, I had a fine view of him. He was magnificent, decked in royal blue, padded and sparkling with jewels, larger and more handsome than any other man there, joking and flushed with enjoyment. I decided he knew what was happening to me but just didn't care. This was a more painful torment than Silas' roaming fingers, his cruel hard kisses and his hands, possessive of my breasts now as he teased the nipples between finger and thumb having brought them out from my bodice. I was forced to hide in his cloak, forced into nakedness for his eyes only. And I tried to bury my face in the shaggy, stinking fur of his cloak, wriggling to get away.

Silas suddenly released me, turned me towards him and took my face in his hands. And I saw, not drink in his eyes, but all seriousness there, and his voice was cold and hard. I pulled up my bodice, adjusted my skirt, all flustered under his curious expression. 'You have learned one lesson the hard way. You have flirted with me quite wantonly, telling me lies with your body and your eyes. I am not a man used to being fooled with. What did you think . . . that I'd enjoy such games . . . that I'd imagine your coy protests to be part of the fun? And are you blaming me now, for your own folly, for taking you at your word?'

I was silent, red-faced and anxious, not knowing what to say, for his accusations were true. I had seen him, summed him up and used him, assuming that he would be happy with that.

'Consider yourself fortunate that it was me that you chose for your childish games.' Silas nodded towards Rowle. 'Your scheming, sweetheart, has not worked, and nor is it likely to do so.'

I started to protest, for how could he think . . . 'You are very appealing,' said Silas, taking my chin in his hands. 'And certainly very beautiful. But you are still a child and you are dealing with adult matters.' He put a sweetmeat into my mouth and I sucked it, feeling a fool. And his voice was very

84

grave and his expression was extra thoughtful when he said, 'Pay heed to my warning, for it is given with well-meaning in spite of what has gone before. You play for the wrong prize, sweetheart . . . leave it. Leave it well alone. For all is often not what you see . . . not what you imagine. There are reasons for you to leave Rowle well alone, apart from the obvious ones which you clearly reject as unimportant.'

'Obvious ones?'

'Lucy . . . the children . . . the difficulties that could ensue . . .'

I spoke with unthinking aggression when I said, 'I am certainly not the first . . .'

'Nor the last, little one, nor the last. But one night of fun is quite a different matter.'

'Why should I listen to you? What do you know?'

'I think I know more than you. I have known Rowle for much longer. And what are your own reasons, I'm interested to know? What is your need for a man such as this? From where did you get your desire for pain? There are plenty of others, little Bethany, more suitable, nearer your own age. Just cast round your eyes . . .'

I blustered, scarlet with humiliation. 'You have read me quite wrong! I do not want Rowle. I have not the slightest interest in Rowle and what is more, I detest him!'

'Ah!' And the Lord of Misrule sat back and contemplated me under the lashes of his all too-knowing brown eyes. 'I think that I have not taught you your lesson yet. Well, there is still time – there is still the night to come.'

Silas only let me go when the game of football started, for he was taking part. He laughed when he pushed me away, whispering something in my ear that I did not catch, or that in my ignorance I did not understand. Free from him, free from the beery smell and the coarseness of him, I ran to Mary's cave and hid under my blanket. I feared he would come and get me. Who could I plead with? Who could I go to for help? Rowle would not listen. Ned was too drunk to hear and Mary was only a woman. I trembled. I shrank inside myself, wanting to hide, wanting, for the first time, to be gone from this place.

For I believed my ordeal was far from over. I believed that when this rough, violent game that took place all round the Combe – with no boundaries, no rules, just two equal teams both vicious and savage – I believed that when it was over Silas would come to find me. I disbelieved his good intentions for he was an untrustworthy man. Look how he'd played with me . . . look how he'd used me! There would be plenty of broken arms and legs by morning and the women would be busy with their splints. But when it was over I was certain that Silas would be back, for he was Lord of Misrule until midnight, and even after that Silas Peverell was a man who was used to being obeyed.

Yes, I lay down, Brother Niall, and I trembled and I hated Rowle. Unable to blame myself, unable to admit to what I had done, I had to blame him. I wanted to blame him.

Oh monk, *I wanted to hate him*!

If only I could have that time again and make something different of it. It's unfair! It's unfair that we never get a chance to go back!

12

Running. It seems to me now that I have always been running away, from circumstances and places to which fate and my own wilfulness have led me. But this time in Lydford Gaol I have nowhere to go . . . The walls are too thick, my gaolers too cunning and the wooden slab that covers the entrance at the top of those rickety steps is too heavy for me to move. They have rested a stone on top, Brother Niall, so that even you and I together would not be able to shift it. And when morning comes, when morning kisses the furthest Dartmoor hills with her wintry lips, then they will move it. And lift the slab. And I will see the sky . . .

And no one knows I am here save for the sheriff and the constables. And what if the Gubbins did know? Who would save me? Who cares enough to speak for me?

Now I feel self-pity, and that is a dreadful thing for it is wearying and leads to nowhere except more blackness and I have too much darkness around me already. I feel my tears come again, welling up from my chest with chokes and shudders, but I press them back because time is short and I do not want to waste what there is left of it in weeping.

Rowle will come. Of course Rowle will come. I might have made part of him up, but I understand him well enough to know that he will not abandon me here.

What, I keep asking myself, what could I have done to change things? Should I have stayed in Mary's cave, waiting, that Christmas, for Silas? If I had stayed and listened to him sensibly might that have changed things? Should I have acted more cautiously and made certain of my escape . . . fled from there and gone on walking from horizon to horizon until I was far, far away? But how could I have known about the waiting mists?

As it was my actions were born out of panic, and while the game of football was still going on, just as dusk came creeping round the edge of the Combe, I slipped out of the cave door and turned immediately upwards, clambering up the shingle between the furze towards the whiter light, with no other thought in my brain than to outwit the terrible Silas Peverell.

I wasn't used to drink and Ned's lambswool concoction had gone to my head. The further I went the dizzier and weaker I became until my legs would hardly carry me. But still I climbed on, forcing myself, reminding myself of my fear – for it was gone now, overtaken by practical matters like how to reach the next outcrop of rock and heave myself over.

I reached the top quite out of breath, and from here the sounds of men shouting, children wailing, women laughing – dramatically ceased. A frost had settled on the short grass which splintered, fragile as glass as I walked over it. The whiteness cast a sheen of fire on the air so I walked to my knees in frost-smoke. I saw an open gate on a hill and it seemed like a hanging hole leading to nothing but sky. I wanted to pass through but it was too far away. Could that have been a gateway to Heaven, Brother Niall: could I have found Heaven then? Had I the innocence? But as I stood there, uncertain of my direction, the rolling ridges and valleys were smoothed with sudden shadow as the moor became swathed in mist. With the mist came the silence – an eerie, lonely silence, and I longed for it to be broken by the cry of a bird, the bleat of a sheep, the comfortable munching of a pony. But no, there was nothing.

I shivered and drew my cloak closer round me. A child of the moor, I knew the nature of the mist, its amazing speed and how bewildering it was to the senses; how the familiar pitfalls of Dartmoor became suddenly so dangerous – hidden holes, outcrops of rock, swamps and mires – and worst of all, the endless tramping in circles that led to exhaustion and confusion. Until you were driven to hearing voices . . . into seeing the craggy shapes of witches and hounds, ghostly black through grey curtains.

I could see no further than one arm's length in front of me. Using this small gap in the fog I inched myself along until, with my outstretched hand I felt a boulder, followed the lichened curve with my fingers, found the crevice where it jutted from the ground and bent myself double to crawl underneath it. Just as I brought the last of my pieces of cloak in behind me, just as my breathing slowed and grew calm again, I heard the voices and saw two dim figures creep past like denser clouds of mist: I knew they were after me.

Two more. Then two more – they moved in pairs. They, too, knew the mists. They had hoarse, foggy voices and carried rush flares but all these gave out was a dirty, orange light that melted in the damp air. I bit my lip, clenched my chattering teeth. If I closed my eyes perhaps they wouldn't see me. Fear of Silas flooded back to me then as I crouched there: I am always afraid when I hide. Even in fun I get frightened and want to come out and show myself before anyone finds me. I crave for the end of the tension, monk, for the end of the game.

But this was no game.

'Hell, it be freezin' out here. Ol' Artful issel cud die o' this cold.'

'I carn feel it, 'tis windervul. I carn even feel me nose. I be quite numbed wi' ale.' And the searcher gave a saturated burp.

'I kipth on a-tellin' 'e, how be we cum ter find t'maid in this?'

'Yers right on that.'

And they, and their little tableau passed the rock. Water collected on my makeshift granite roof and dripped steadily on to my head. Thoughts of Mary's peat fire, of her rich, warm rabbit stews, of her chattering children and the dry pallet awaiting me, maddened me with want. And with them came the dread of my alternatives – emptiness, loneliness, nothing, leading back to the madness from which I had come.

When Rowle came by I stiffened. Was he with Silas? I had to wait to hear the man speak before I dared show myself. But then they found me – and it was a relief when the weak light beamed straight at my rock, took a turn over and under, and then I blinked as I was illuminated, doubled in half and shaking.

'Call them off,' Rowle drawled to his companion. 'Go back, Dicken. I'll bring her home.'

Home . . . and in that word were all the safe meanings I wanted. I was glad I had been found, glad the decision had been taken for me so that I didn't have to hide there wondering anxiously what to do. And better than that, I was alone with Rowle. Now was my chance to talk to him.

Dicken, Rowle's beefy companion, faltered as if considering I might be too much of a burden alone. He came out of the mist behind Rowle like a shaggy red bullock with a fat, wet nose, just short of the horns. He scratched his beard, looked at Rowle and then, deciding there could not be much of a contest between us, ambled off, shouting to his friends.

I crawled out of my cramped space aching with stiffness and damp. I straightened, my face twisting with pain, while Rowle held the torch up high in his hand and considered my plight with amusement. He leaned back against the face of the rock and laid his lantern down. 'Why?' he demanded, staring straight at me.

Oh, he was handsome, powerful and menacing. Disordered curls, damp from the mist, rested on his collar which was unbuttoned, and a cloak of thick fur hung casually round him. I could not look at his hands, my eyes stopped at the flurry of lace at his wrists. And yet with all this he carried an air of neatness and unruffled gentility, his dark eyes full of knowing and reproach.

And I? Small for my age which was barely fifteen, straight, except for my new breasts which were growing firm and round . . . thin-waisted, light-boned and airy. My skin was gypsy-brown from always living outside and my teeth were white for I kept them clean with a stick. My eyes were black as I'd ever seen anyone else's, except for Rowle's, and Maggie used to tell me they'd take over my face one day if they grew any bigger.

I looked away into the distance as if suddenly struck by a most magnificent view. But the mist swirled thickly round us and he caught my chin in his hand as he asked the question again. 'Why?'

'I was afraid.' I made my voice firm.

'Of what?'

'Of Silas.'

'Of Silas?' Rowle frowned first before he broke into laughter. And then he shook his head and said, 'There! And I thought how well you and he were both getting along!'

So! He *had* noticed the antics of the Lord of Misrule! He had noticed and done nothing! ''Tis not Silas that I want,' I said, making the most of the moment which, with the mists swirling around us, seemed weird and unnatural. And all the while I flirted, or thought that was what I was doing, looking up coyly through the corners of my eyes, trying on that little half-smile I'd practised down by the water. And was Rowle flirting back, or did he always look at women in that bold way? I thought of running again, bolting away suddenly and dashing off so that Rowle would come after me. But I was aching all over, and stiff, so I knew there would not be much of a chase. Besides, I had the nagging feeling that he might see through my scheming and not follow and then how foolish I would feel, creeping back into the Combe looking pathetic and childish with everyone knowing what had happened. There was no point in running anywhere in the middle of a Dartmoor mist, and everyone knew that.

'Oh?' Rowle frowned again and adjusted his back into a more comfortable position against the rock. 'And who is it then, that you want?'

'I'll not tell you who but 'tis not Silas Peverell!'

And then he said, 'I'm sorry.'

Quick as a flash I asked, 'For what?'

And he answered me straightly. 'That you feel the way that you do. I am not the right man. It would be foolish . . .'

I did not let him finish. I did not care to hear this – I did not want to be reminded of Silas' warnings. 'You are not sorry for what you did to me?'

'No,' he said slowly. I saw how a small frown brought his eyebrows together. 'Not for what I did to you, no.'

And I wanted to ask if what we had done had meant nothing. I wanted to ask if he had any feelings for me at all. But I had my pride so I shook my head, glared at him angrily and said, 'Well, you should be! What are you then? An animal who knows no better? I was against it. I had no alternative but to let you. It was the last thing I wanted and I hate you for it! I will always hate you! Take me back!'

'Certainly,' he said. And then, 'I wouldn't have taken you, Bethany, if I'd known you were so against it.'

And I flushed with delicious pride – because he remembered my name.

But oh, Brother Niall, those were just a few precious moments and I knew I had wasted them. Perhaps my wits were made sluggish by the mists, for my opportunity had gone.

And I spent the rest of Christmas night sipping a hot posset by Mary's fire, morose and shivering in spite of the rugs wrapped round me.

13

Spring gave way to summer, and along with summer came the storms. Grim masses of darker cloud did battle with the white ones until the whole sky seemed to boil above my head where I lay on a bare rock, watching. I went with the clouds, my arms stretched out like eagles' wings, so real I could feel the rush of them, and the lightning flashed and tore through the Combe, the thunder clapped the distant tors, and the rain soaked me through my clothing, beating me down on the rock until I felt part of it. I wanted to scream out loud, exulting in the roars and flashes that fitted so well with my emotions.

Something set inside me and I thought I felt my hatred harden. But I wasn't driven as I once had been – I was free to live again, and felt like a baby starting a new life. But I know better now, Brother Niall, for that is just one stage of obsession. It changes: that was merely the lull before the storm.

There in the Combe it was not possible to be lonely, bored or sullen, not for long because of the energy of the place. It could almost come from the earth itself, so primal was it and so governed by the seasons. Nobody was without purpose. Nobody was without value. Even the old men who sat telling tales of terrible times and faraway places while whittling their pipes and singing their songs were the holders of many, many secrets. And it showed in their wily brown faces. Even Rowle went to them, sometimes, for good advice.

The old women had their cures and recipes: Dancy had been born there, so had Maud and Bell, and they loved to talk of the past, could trace their ancestry back as well as any noble, to all of two hundred years ago, when two wicked women had come and set up home in a cave to safely bear their brats. A village had grown up around them, and that had grown nearly to the size of a town, so that now, in this narrow Combe, there were five hundred people all told – men, women and children. And those they called the lost ones, who seemed not to fit into any category . . . the children who lived in the shadows.

And if we were called savages now, what must have been the word for the Gubbins in those days? I wondered how any had survived such a troubled existence, for in those days the Combe was lawless. Gangs of bullies reigned supreme until they themselves were defeated by force, and unspeakable tortures were carried out on any who flouted the will of the leader.

To live here as a woman back in those days meant a hard and anxious life.

'Ask Bell,' said Mary, ''Er'll tell 'e. 'Er's a memory like a book, 'er forgets nothin'.'

And yet Bell had survived. She was old and bald and wattled like a turkey but she laughed more than anyone, gales of whiskery laughter that set her off coughing so she rocked backwards and forwards to calm herself while she pleaded for breath from the sky with her eyes, just so she could go on talking.

'The men didn't have it all their own ways then, oh no certainly not.' And she smacked her toothless gums together. ''Twas touch an' go for they. They wasn't organised, like now, an' never knew when the next raid was planned or from which direction the menace were comin'. The landowners from round about, they formed their raidin' parties an' they came fer uz an' carried uz off in the dark . . . men, women, children, it didn't matter to they. Ter work fer 'em. Ter fight fer 'em. 'Tweren't like now. In they days you was lucky ter raise one little 'un out o' a brood o' seven or eight – aye.' And her wizened old face screwed up in memory and her hard eyes twinkled merrily. And even if Bell died tomorrow I knew, and she knew, that she'd lived! That's what the fires in her eyes were about. And I wanted to live, too, and not just through the medium of a thunderstorm.

Sensing and wanting her wisdom, I tried to talk to Bell about Rowle but all she would say was, ''E's worth 'is weight in gold. You new ones doan know, yer doan realise what it could be like . . . that's why I sits 'ere an' keeps tellin' yous. You has ter believe it!'

And all the old women said the same. They all defended Rowle to the hilt, told their stories and sucked on their gums while the babies climbed up their skirts and I don't know which dribbled the worst.

'So you just listen ter what they tells 'e an' doan go round foul-mouthin' Rowle any longer,' Mary warned me.

'I doan foul-mouth 'e. I just doan trust 'e. An' I tells the truth as I sees it,' I said.

So Mary roared with laughter, saying. 'You've even started ter talk a bit like 'e. Haven't yer realised, Miss Airs an' Graces.'

Everyone had their place in the Combe, except for the lost ones. There were the beggars, some of them real rogues, and they went out in groups to fairs and markets, but always with an armed guard mingling somewhere amongst the crowd. Some went as deaf mutes, others as madmen and they were called the Bedlam beggars – they made us weep with laughter over their grotesque antics. Some went as hookers to steal from open windows, and then there were the priggers, or horse-thieves. The palliards painted revolting scars and deformities on themselves and were paid money by respectable folk to go away. Some didn't need to use paint: some were terribly scarred already, blind, or had limbs missing.

They all dressed carefully for their parts: their calico cloaks were dowdy and patched, their boots torn and in holes and they wrapped their legs with clouts to keep out the cold. I watched them go longingly and with admiration, for they were cunning and bold. They could dupe the most cynical citizen.

Some of the women went, too, posing as pedlars with baskets on their heads. They filled them with the cheapest trinkets they could find – laces, pins, needles and ribbons – and they would call at the big houses in the towns, persuading the stupid kitchen maids to exchange beef, bacon and cheese for their twopenny baubles. They always came back laden with more than they could comfortably carry.

No less skilled but with a little more class and authority was the defrocked parson, Sam Gaunt. I was always a little afraid of him for his eyes shone with fanatical zeal. A thin, stringy man with a ravaged face, he conducted unlawful marriages for money. He also presided over all the marriages in the Combe, although I wondered why anyone bothered with it at all, seeing it was just a sham, but they persisted, possibly for the sake of the dancing and feasting.

Tom Paten was the cardsharp who worked in taverns and inns, but he would take money from anyone, even his friends. ''E is not ter be trusted,' said Mary severely. Nor did she think much of Daniel Holland the gentleman pickpocket. Daniel was a nip . . . he cut purses from their owners with a knife. ''E liked ter practise on the women 'o the Combe by attachin' a bell ter their purses an' creepin' up after 'e all stealthy-like ter see if'n 'e could get the purse wi'out the bells ringin'. But 'e 'ad ter be stopped by the council. 'E were too familiar. 'E never stopped at the purses an' sometimes 'e went too far. You would hear a bell ring an' then a scream, often a slap. No, they had ter stop 'e from practisin' here.'

Fighting men went out to win money lawfully, and they were tough and scarred and I didn't envy them their skills. We watched them practising in the sawdust ring and they always drew blood. They came home black-eyed and exhausted, and so, very often, did little Jack Fitch who climbed church steeples for money and often fell off. The others told him not to drink, just to hold back a little before he went out, but Jack took no notice.

'One day the lad'll kill 'isself,' said Mary, 'you mark my words.' And she so reminded me then, of Lizzie.

The cony-men like Ned went out at all hours of day and night to the poaching, and bands of others trained for the purpose took sheep and chickens from neighbouring farms, choosing carefully so as not to annoy.

While the lost ones watched from the shadows.

It was Rowle and his band who put themselves most at risk, for they roamed the highways and robbed the inns, stealing large sums of money, jewels, clothing and sometimes horses. It was they who, if necessary, killed for their plunder, but their actions were always most skilfully planned. Spies went out first to study the lie of the land. And Rowle's gang were mostly the younger ones, from sixteen to twenty-five, expert riders and skilled swordsmen. It was considered a privilege to be chosen to ride out with Rowle: I knew that if I had been born a man I would be one of them, and I dreamed of being able to go with them.

The Gubbins went short of nothing. There was money enough left over to pay hefty bribes to coachmen and lackeys, tavern boys and innkeepers, and there were always constables who could be persuaded to turn a blind eye.

All these things I learned as summer came to the moor and I helped Mary with the washing and the cooking and the caring for the children. It was all I could do, and I used to wish I was clever at something else and wondered if one day they would teach me. For if I couldn't ride out with Rowle I would have liked to have gone with the women to bring back a basket of supplies. I did not intend to take a husband and settle down to have children which is clearly what was expected of me. I declined every offer from every swain, and not politely, either. If I saw Silas I put down what I was doing and walked quickly away in the opposite direction. Afraid of that man who knew too much about me, my heart used to leap even if I recognised him at a distance. I soon gained a reputation for being snooty and the others left me alone. I remained surly and suspicious, for after Mallin I would trust no one again. Not even Ned and Mary who were kindness itself to me.

I enjoyed my life. I had plenty of places to put my love – six sets of plump little arms and six mucky faces. Yes, I loved Mary's children. I was happy as I could be, in the circumstances. I was warm, comfortable and well-fed and if I thought a great deal about Amicombe, if I cried sometimes at night, well, that was how it would have to be. I would always carry that sadness with me. And it seemed that I was dealing, somehow, with my hatred of Rowle. I put it to the back of me. I would not let it destroy my life, especially now summer was here again and I felt Dartmoor call to me, as it always had, as it always would while I lived.

But obsession is so full of cunning. The Gubbins, the hookers, the priggers, the palliards – oh, Brother Niall, they had nothing on me. And the strange thing is that I was almost unaware, during all that time, that I was manipulating anything!

But when the message came from the house I knew that my scheming had paid off. Gradually and craftily, during that long dusty summer, I had come to know Lucy – not well – but well enough.

Her fourth child had been born in the spring and now she needed someone to help her. When I was told she had asked for me I hid my excitement and argued with Mary. 'Why? She doesn't even know me. Why wouldn't she ask one of her friends?'

'They has children o' their own ter cope wi'.'

'Well then, why not any of the other young girls that she knows?'

'If'n yer doan want ter do it say so, an' stop whinin' on about it, maid.'

'I do want to do it. I just want to know why she asked for me.'

Ned said, 'Yer bright an' yer strong, yer healthy-lookin' an' everyone knows yer good wi' Mary's.'

I knew that these were not entirely the reasons, for we had met, Lucy and I. We had met in the dark by the dying fire, had talked while we watched the small shadows. I had watched and I knew that she went there, too upset to accept the fact there were children who did not want love. If Lucy had not been there I would have come out to sit, to stare at the stars alone and to think about Rowle. But Lucy was there, her pale grey cloak around her. She looked like a statue she sat so still, she looked like a church Madonna. And it was strange to see her without a child hanging round her neck, another at her knee. I thought that she ought to have a bunch of flowers in her hands and I thought that they ought to be bluebells.

Nobody liked to speak of the lost ones for that was to speak about failure. There had been many attempts to tame them even, once, to drive them away, for these were people beyond Rowle's control and he used to say that they threatened the safety of all. I'd heard him: 'For we don't know what they're up to, and considering the everyday dangers we face, it is unnerving to have all this hidden, seething underworld right here in the Combe.'

While we sat round the fire Lucy said, 'We should be able to help them somehow. We shouldn't just leave them like this.'

And we sat and we watched together, and I stroked my tress of hair while the dying fire went white and sent flecks of silver into the air. We watched as the one they called Marnie crept nearer to the fire. 'Don't let her see we are waiting,' said Lucy, holding her breath.

As the child approached she reminded me of my own small self. She wore sacking with holes for the arms and round her waist was a thong of soft twine. What age . . . seven, eight, it was hard to tell, for her face when it came from the shadows was wise, more animal than human.

There were others behind her, crouching, waiting to see what she would bring them. The remains of a leg of mutton hung in tatters, burnt, from the spit. If Lucy or I leaned forward to hook it off and pass it, the child would run away. She wanted to take – not to be given. Anything worthwhile that she had ever had in her short life had been taken: given things were bad, cruel and dangerous and not to be trusted.

'They are pests,' said Lucy sadly. 'There are no two ways about it. What Rowle says about them is true. But if only we could get nearer . . .'

The lost ones looked pale and familiar as dream people do, a rough and ready rabble of horror with the veil of distance over their eyes and the timeless look of the unborn on their faces. They ran in a band yet alone, a clan within a clan but with no single voice. They took meat from the fires at night, corn from the bins and fowl from the pens. They watched from a distance but scorned all offerings put out for them. We knew that two were blind. Such a number of them were crippled that it was easier to assume they all were, yet without legs, hands or feet they got about agile as hares on their rough crutches, and they would not be helped.

Word must have got out in the gusty alleys and underworlds of the towns from which they came, usually singly, and it was often weeks before anyone knew that another child had arrived. Some had been found by members of the clan and brought home in kindness, but they had run from these families and joined the others.

They lived at the far, far end of the Combe where few of us went, for it was always dark there, but under the earth there were passageways which twisted and turned and went far back under the moor to come up in sandy hollows amid stunted copses. The lost ones knew their way across the moor and under it, people said without being able to see. They were like moles, like rabbits – like wolves.

Mary had told me, 'They 'as allus bin here, far back as anyone can remember. Whey they tried ter drive 'e out 'bout twenty year ago, the men went wi' sticks an' stones an' dogs, but when they got to the end o' the Combe, there were nothin' there. They'd all run away. Just empty passages! But some o' the men came back an' swore they could hear 'em breathin'. They said they felt the lost ones were lookin' at 'em from somewhere but be damned if they could see they buggers anywhere.'

And I had thought to myself – just like the piskies.

Lucy ran a school of sorts for the children who wanted to learn. I sat by her side and listened to her tell of it. It was a most disorganised affair, for someone was always shouting for her to look at their somersaults, and someone else was usually netting a butterfly or trailing a lizard. She took them round the Combe and taught them the names of the flowers, she explained the ways of the animals and brought in Dancy and Bell to tell stories and old Nat with his fiddle to teach them songs. She used a slate and charcoal to show them their letters and demonstrated how to make paint out of plants and lichens so they could make pictures. She made brushes from badger hair – fine, delicate brushes – but mostly she used these herself for the children preferred to paint with their fingers. And I knew how badly Lucy would like to attract just one or two of these lost children to her school in the mornings.

Oh yes, monk, we had spent long hours together, so it was not by accident that Lucy asked me to help with her children.

Mary was staring at me hard. 'I shall miss 'e,' she said rather stiffly.

I flushed with pride, for compliments did not come often from that quarter, but then she added, 'Aye, I shall miss yer moanin' an' yer moon eyes round the place.'

So I went round smugly for the next few weeks, secretly imagining that it was Rowle who had asked for me to be brought to the house so that I could be near him.

I took time to make up my mind. Like a lover would, I thought to myself. Coyly.

14

Because of the close life we led in the Combe there were bound to be differences. I had not been away from the place in six months, and by now I felt restless. The energy the place exhaled demanded that something be done with it. Some of the most vulnerable members were the women who hardly ever left the place, forever shut off from the sunsets. How must they have felt, those who lived within the confines of these steep walls from one year to the next, depending on news of life outside from the lucky ones who went, from time to time, to ply their strange trades?

And would I, one day, be one of them? Trapped with a man and a bunch of children?

There was nothing to prevent anyone from going out or from leaving, it was just considered wiser not to take chances and if you had children you were not likely to take those chances. But I watched and I saw how the small matters of everyday life engulfed them. I saw how important to them were the minutest details, like who was wearing new calico and who was cooking with new pots. I, too, was used to an insular life having never strayed far from Amicombe, but, knowing no different, I stayed satisfied with what I had. It was not so easy for them. And in my childhood I had had to get along with only four others, while they had to get along, somehow, with hundreds.

And some were bad-tempered and some were difficult, some were argumentative and some downright trouble-makers. When Biddie Canter's man Phineus started sleeping with that trollope Jessie Lang, the Combe buzzed with the gossip long before Biddie knew. And Mary said, 'There'll be trouble over this, you mark my words,' and I did not like the way she said it, as if she was telling me about some special meal she was preparing.

I was not used to gossip, nor the viciousness of women who spent so much time together. My aunts had been vicious in different ways – and, of course, we had only one main enemy at

Amicombe and that was Amos. Our hatred of him had held us together in a close bond and I suppose I have to be grateful to him for that.

The first thing that happened was that everyone took sides. The settled, more mature women sided most naturally with Biddie, who had three children to look after, and the younger, saucier types with Jessie, saying, 'We should be able ter lie wi' whoever we wishes. We are not cattle ter be owned an' nor is we tied ter a man by law.'

It was a warm summer evening and we sat outside in a circle on the ground, slapping at the midges as we talked. 'But it doan work like that,' said Mary comfortably, loving a gossip, as the four of us sat round cutting up turnips for the communal pot. 'Life carn work if some o' uz ignores the rules while others try their best ter keep 'em. It makes the rest o' uz look pathetic, that's what it do.'

'Who made the rules, then?' asked Dolly, who was my age but already the mother of a sleeping baby which she held on her knee – a baby I thought she seemed angry with. 'Men?'

'Nobody made the rules,' said Mary, enjoying her position as defender of the moral way. She dipped her scrawny hands in a bucket of water to get the pith off. 'They're rules fer the livin' an' they has allus just bin understood.'

'Not by me they haven't,' said Dolly petulantly. 'If'n my Robin wants ter sleep wi' another that's fine by me just so long as it gives me licence ter do the same.' Dolly was thin and spindly and looked like a little girl. Her thick, husky voice made you wonder where it had space to come from.

'It doan work like that,' said Sal, the shy pretty one. But she, too, was on the side of the wicked Jessie Lang. 'There's one law fer the men an' another fer the women . . .'

'Only 'cos we lets it be that way,' gusted Dolly, turning her baby over on her knee so that its tiny head drooped over the turnip pile and it started sneezing.

They had taken this scandal and made it theirs so it was little to do with Biddie Canter and Jessie Lang any longer. And I noticed that every little bit of blame was laid at Jessie's door so I said, ''Tis Phineus' fault in the first place, so why is you blamin' Jessie? You are all blamin' Jessie.'

''Cos women ought ter know better,' said Mary sternly to me, a little surprised, I think, that I had spoken out. Normally

I only watched and listened. 'Women doan have the urges that men do – women can say no, or they ought to be able to.' And Mary sighed and they laughed, rolling their eyes round a secret from which they considered me excluded.

But I knew what they said was untrue. I wanted Rowle with a ferocity I was sure was the same as a man's, physical as well as mental. And yet they seemed to be saying that I was unnatural.

'I wouldn't say no,' I said bravely, 'not if I was wi' the man I loved.'

Mary gave me a sharp glance of disapproval, knowing of whom I spoke. And even this most secret speaking of Rowle sent a glow through me, made me restless and angry.

Dolly said, ''Tis different at first. You'll find out, maid – wi' the same man it gets borin'. I'd prefer a selection . . . wouldn't you, Sal?' And she gave a salacious giggle which seemed odd coming out of someone who looked so young.

'So women do feel the same as men,' I said. 'So why do you agree to tie yourselves down?'

'Fer the sake o' the children,' said Mary. ''Tis essential ter have a man ter provide.'

'Not here 'tisn't,' objected Sal. ''Twould be easy, here, where everything comes fer free.'

We'd forgotten old Bell was there just rocking and sucking and listening, preoccupied, I thought, with the clouds. 'Nothin' comes fer free,' she cackled. ''Twere like that when I first came here. You wouldn't like ter go back ter that, I'm tellin' 'e.' Her face hardened and her skin was brown like a wrinkled old nut. She spat as she rocked and she leaned forward suddenly. 'That's what 'twere, an' every man, every woman fer 'erself. There were no choosin', not on the part o' the women. An' the men, they fought an' they died fer a night o' pleasure wi' the wrong man's woman.' Bell scratched her head – there was no hair on it, just old flakes of skin. 'You be glad o' the rules,' she said. 'They're there ter protect you . . . an' women like Jessie Lang should be drummed from the place. They is dangerous.'

Mary nodded round at us all as if she'd been the one to say that, grateful to have her opinion supported by one so staunch and wise. And I saw they were all prepared to accept Bell's words, so with my face flaming with the unfairness of it I turned to Bell and asked her, 'But what of Phineus? Shouldn't 'e be drummed from the place then, too?'

'Phineus Canter, 'e breaks the horses. 'E is a valuable man an' needed here. 'E is needed by poor Biddie an' 'e must be made ter accept 'e's responsibilities an' not act so flighty. An' they should find that wretched Jessie Lang a man o' 'er own afore 'er causes more trouble.'

But we could talk over the rights and wrongs as much as we liked, and we did, delighting in it, but talk – it doesn't settle anything.

We watched, we whispered, we gossiped, and poor Biddie Canter went past straightbacked and with her head held high as if nothing was happening that was out of the way. And that bad Jessie Lang wore a secret look of quiet satisfaction and stayed quietly in corners watching from under her eyelashes. And I came to thinking what a shame it was that people weren't allowed to love more than one person – and wondering whether Biddie and Jessie would be content to share Phineus. But then I thought about Rowle and knew that I would never be happy with that, so why would either of them? But it still seemed sad that there was no satisfactory answer. Just compromise. And that, over such powerful feelings, seemed a shame.

Just a few nights later we woke to the sound of screaming. Ned pulled on his cloak, picked up his knife and ran out of the door, alarmed. Mary gathered the children from their beds and I saw great fear in her eyes. 'What is it?' I whispered, all in a daze and badly frightened so that even my hair seemed to crawl with fear on my head.

'I doan know.' She made them wait by the door alert and ready for flight. 'We'll know when Ned comes back. 'E woan be long. 'Twill be all right.' And I could see, then, how she depended on him, how hopeless it would be for her in an emergency to cope alone with these little ones. Even I found comfort in the knowledge that Ned would return and would fight to the death for their protection. So I saw, yes, even I saw that because of the way we lived there had to be a man for a family and that he would only fight if he thought them his – such being the way of men.

Fear and unease filled the cave thicker than any smoke as we waited, breathless and trembling, for Ned to come back.

Our eyes, and I know that mine did too, glinted like fires in the darkness. Like beasts, we were, and sweating hard, for I had seen beasts trapped like this and now I knew how they felt. But Mary's fear was worse than mine because it wasn't for herself that she crouched and panted there, ready by the door. Her fear was for her children. And the set of her face was terrible.

Time went slowly, cruelly slow, and every sound, every splutter of the fire came like the crack of a gun to our ears. Our breathing was silent. We held our breathing tight so we could listen.

But when Ned came back we all relaxed, for there was laughter in his eyes and ease in his movements. He slumped like he did when all was well. My heart took an age to quieten its quick beating. He dismissed the children back to their beds with a wide sweep of his arm, and they, in sudden awe of their father, quietly obeyed.

"'Twere the Canter woman,' he told us, accepting a mug of hot ale from Mary who never normally fed him ale. ''Er has crept into Jessie's shack an' thrown a bowl o' scaldin' water over 'er. The poor maid be badly burned – 'er pretty face'll never look the same again. Vicious, 'twere, the way 'er did it. 'Er showed no mercy ter the maid. 'Er went an' tipped the lot.'

'Are there people wi' 'er?' Mary could relax now. She could afford to be generous, to be all concern.

But I wondered if, somehow, by our gossip and meanness, we had caused this disaster.

'Aye.' Ned sat down, enjoying his moment of importance. 'Aye, they've sent fer Peverell . . . 'E'll be able ter take away the pain if not the scars. Phineus, 'e were there, in bed wi' the maid. 'E narrowly avoided gettin' the lot over 'is backside an' 'e scuttled home like a startled rabbit quick as you likes wi' 'is tail 'tween 'is legs. But I doan envy 'e the next few months o' 'is life wi' that shrew!'

I couldn't help feeling for Jessie Lang – not Phineus, whom I considered a cheat and a coward and not Biddie Canter and the smug self-righteousness that had made her burn some other woman's face. I wondered about Lucy, about how Lucy would act if Rowle came to me . . . surely the sweet-faced, gentle Lucy with the wide blue eyes would be more understanding than that? Surely she wouldn't, for the sake of herself and her children, attack me, destroy me, so great being her fear?

And I said to Mary unkindly. 'So are you happy now? Do you consider that justice has been done?'

'I carn say what I would have done in the same situation,' she told me. 'An' you can hardly criticise others fer what they do. 'Twere a bit extreme o' Biddie I'll grant you that, but someone will take Jessie Lang, what wi' the shortage o' women, an' nobody's goin' ter be bothered wi' the state o' 'er face.'

No, nobody but Jessie herself. It could have been the only thing she had and now she would have to turn herself into a different person, use different weapons to fight her way through life, debilitated, always, by what had been done to her.

So you see, Brother Niall, how quickly fate can whip out a knife and scar you – Lizzie believed that – Lizzie was hobbled by fear. It turned her cunning and bent and sent her scurrying for unnatural signs and cut her right off from the world. Put there to hoodwink her, that's what life was to Lizzie and she saw each day as if it was one of her own noxious brews, but unlike her yarbs, quite out of her own control and always malevolent.

She didn't sit for hours like I did, hours and hours watching nothing more interesting than bugs scuttling about under a log. If Lizzie had done so, then she would have realised that life isn't like that: life is random, nothing says yes and nothing says no, and the earth can fall on you the day you least expect it.

I can criticise Lizzie, but I didn't remember the lessons I learned under that log, for why else was everything I did in such a hurry and why am I waiting, now, to die in the morning?

Brother, if only I had realised that those long summer days in the safety of the Combe were to be the most peaceful, if not the happiest of my life, but I would not have that. Peace and contentment were not what I wanted. I was not satisfied with them.

For I was still beautiful, wasn't I, and shouldn't I make the most of that while I still had it? And I was young and free, not trapped like the other women were. Freedom – the wild things had it, the sheep, the buzzards, the ponies, the wolves – they all ran wild and free. And I lay down that night, safe in the cave and delighted in the awareness of my own freedom, un-shackled by children or a husband I did not want. I delighted in the realisation of these things and the sense of power that they gave me. I had freedom to choose and freedom, surely, to follow my own desires.

Whatever the consequences might be.

15

Oh, please God, help me. Oh, please Rowle, why don't you come now? Why wait until morning? I don't think I can be brave any more.

Sometimes I can forget for as long as fifteen seconds where I am and what is happening. I time what might be left of my life by the moonbeam that throws a silver line across the floor. It slid along the wall to begin with, now it lies halfway across the floor. The moon must be full tonight. The moon is taking away my life, monk, while you just stand there, head bowed, watching meekly. What use are you to me?

Go! Leave me here on my own! I am perfectly happy to wait for my lover without you.

The moon is taking away my life and yet I have always felt a kinship with it. I won't get moonlight on my face. I won't let it stain me.

Sometimes I can convince myself that I am back in the Combe and that this dungeon and the tomorrow that looms over my head is nothing but a dream from which I will wake, sweating with fear, crying with relief. And I will go to Lucy and I will say, 'It was so real! It was so real! I truly believed they were coming to kill me and that Rowle might not rescue me, and I spent the whole time trying to think back over my life and work out how it had come to this. Oh Lucy, I'll never be able to forget this night.'

And Lucy would light her candle, pull on her wrap, and if Rowle was away she would move over in her bed and let me in beside her while she comforted me, saying, 'I know what those bad dreams are like. I have them, too. We all have them – Rowle more than most. There's times and times I have to wake him in the night and tell him it's all right. He's just like a child. We'll talk together for a little while until you are fully awake. Come closer and let me cuddle you, you're freezing cold.'

But I, unable to believe that Rowle could need that sort of comforting, would return to my own plight and tell her, 'It was cold in that dungeon. Cold like a tomb and wet and dripping. Even the stones stank of decay.' And I'd get close enough to feel her heart and I'd be so grateful for her comforting arms.

I, Bethany Horsham, who fully intended to break her heart.

I knew when Rowle was in the house – did Lucy? I didn't have to see him or hear him. When I picked up Judd or Matt or Daisy, when I cradled the tiny Bessie in my arms I felt I held part of Rowle, the hidden, delicate part.

Every day I went to visit Mary. I thought of her as the mother that I'd never had but I don't think she would have liked to have me as a daughter. She recognised the darkness in me. She was wary. She rarely failed to ask about Rowle and I'd say, 'I'm all right now. He's just a man and not a very respectable one at that. I don't hate him. I don't feel anything towards him.' But Mary would look at me sharply and sigh. Because Mary knew.

There were pretty curtains at Lucy's windows and flowers in her garden. There was a softness here that did not extend to the rest of the Combe which, from here, looked dark and forbidding. The evening sun stopped at Lucy's house, washed it and dipped, missing the Combe and bringing darkness early.

We were friends. I liked Lucy. She wore loose, flowing robes and shawls and hardly took any trouble with her appearance yet she wrapped herself in loveliness, simple, soft materials which she used as a kind of safety. She didn't need to try. We would go to the stores where Rowle kept chests of clothing available to anyone should they want them, and spend hours there, just like children, dressing up, shaking out the damp, screaming with laughter and marvelling over the fine workmanship and the richness of the materials. But they were not the practical clothes we needed for our own lives so we rarely kept anything save for an occasional brooch or a feather.

Within a week of my arrival at her house Lucy was saying, 'I don't know what I'd do without you. Were you brought up in a large family? You must be used to looking after children.'

'Animals. No children,' I told her.

'Oh? No brothers or sisters?'

And she sounded sorry for me but I told her how I'd enjoyed being alone. She was the only person I told about what had happened to my aunts at Lydford. She watched me tell it, she listened to me and afterwards she said nothing but just came to put her arms round me and rested her cheek on my hair – she didn't seem to mind at all about the taint-mark and when I told her that's what I called it she smiled and said, 'Tush, what nonsense.' And I realised that my story, though terrible, was nothing compared with the suffering endured by so many others before they came to this place. But it was none the less for that and Lucy was telling me so.

Sometimes, in a soft voice, re-living it with faraway eyes, Lucy told me her own story. She was animated when she talked about her travelling childhood and all the people and places she'd seen, less so when she explained how she had come to Amberry, how she had come to meet Rowle. She didn't talk at all about feelings, only events, but the feelings were in the story, showing in her face and in the pauses between her words. She started to tell what happened when she first came with Rowle to the Combe, but couldn't go on so she concluded, 'But I am more of a coward than you, Bethy.' She picked up the chortling Bessie and jigged her on her knee. 'I still can't talk about that time.' Her face went suddenly hard and she stared through the window. 'I can't even think about it. Perhaps it's best. I'm not as strong, not as brave as you.'

She had that way of speaking so immediately I felt brave and strong – new feelings for me and something else to think about. I wasn't sure that I liked this image of myself. Maybe Lucy was weak and cowardly, maybe Rowle knew that and that's why he wasn't attracted to me, knowing I could cope alone while his sweet Lucy could not. So I wished I had known that when I first arrived so I could have acted coy and frightened, and not the fierce, wild abandoned creature I had appeared. For deep inside, I told myself, I was soft and gentle, like Lucy, too. It was just that I found it harder to show that part of me.

No, Brother Niall, it is no use pretending. Lucy was self-contained. There was nothing that screamed inside her, longing for a wild ride through the night. Lucy was peaceful, like a woman drowned in bright daylight, and the atmosphere round her was peaceful, too, while the one around me boiled and bubbled like a brew of rank poison, although I swear I tried to make it otherwise. Oh, I tried.

Because Lucy was happy with her man and her children she

always thought that's what I wanted, too. To stop her from trying to match me off I shocked her by telling the truth. 'Do you know what I'd really like to do?'

We were sitting down by the stream at the bottom of the Combe, letting the children play in the water and cooling our feet. Draped over the stone like she was with her long hair sweeping loose behind her, I thought Lucy looked like a mermaid, wistful and with all the secrets mermaids have which they won't tell mortals like me. I was always wanting to shock her. I would have liked to make Lucy angry with me so that I could hate her, fairly and squarely, with reason.

'I would like to ride out with the men.'

I squeezed my knees to my chest and held my breath as my imagination took me. 'I would love to feel the thrill of the chase, the wait, the pounce, the kill . . . that mad ride home and all the exhilaration that can only come from fear.'

'You don't like being with me, helping with the children, living in the house with us?'

I shook my head impatiently. 'Yes, I like it. 'Tis nothin' ter do wi' that. I feels there is something lacking in my life an' only that can fill the space. I was allus free before.' I dropped my eyes, for what was the meaning of my freedom word? 'I had the whole moor. I had my rowan pony. I dreamed daydreams then, but if I go to the place where the daydreams are, the nightmares have room to come in.'

Judd had a dragonfly in a net. 'Don't touch it,' said Lucy. 'It'll sting.'

'But it's beautiful,' argued the sturdy, black-haired boy, waving his net towards us.

'Beautiful things are often the most dangerous,' she said. I looked at her sharply but she smiled back at me.

'Do you think 'e ever would let me?' I whined, while I helped Daisy with her castle of stones.

'If I were you I wouldn't ask,' said Lucy.

'But if I don't ask nothing will happen.'

'Make it happen yourself,' she said, getting up and seeming tired, for it was time for Bessie's feed. 'Just take a horse and go. If you dress correctly no one will ask who you are, not in the dark, not if you pick the right night. Not if you're careful. There's danger in it, Bethy.' She didn't believe I would do it.

'Danger? From Rowle?'

I couldn't see her face when she answered me. 'No, Bethany, Rowle will never be a danger to you. Not in that way.'

I didn't see much of him. During the day he was out, only eating breakfast with us and seldom returning in time for supper.

Sometimes he would join Lucy upstairs when we put the children to bed and then he was a funny, gentle father, telling his children stories and having play-fights on the floor with his sons, giving horse rides to Daisy. Very occasionally he would sit with us in the upstairs chamber, drinking mulled wine and discussing the people, their needs and their comforts . . . just like a king! It was at his insistence that Lucy set up a group for the women where they could meet regularly and air their grievances as the men did. But sadly this failed because nobody bothered to turn up: if anything was seriously wrong the women found it more convenient to nag their men. They met round the cooking pots as they always had, and their concerns were quite different concerns, and mostly they solved their problems themselves – or put up with them and just grumbled.

Rowle treated me not as a servant but as a family friend. I spoke little. My speaking was all done inside my own head. I was angry with him . . . I hated the way I waited all day for his arrival. I did not like the way I behaved in his company . . . sulky, self-aware . . . not able to laugh and make a fool of myself as I so often did with Lucy.

Maggie would have shaken me hard. She would have said, 'Fer goodness sake an' what's ter do wi' 'e, tummit-hed.'

Once Lucy asked, half-bemused, half-exasperated, 'Are you frightened of Rowle? It's just that you're always so different when he comes in. If I didn't know you better I'd think you disliked him. He won't bite, you know.'

So I quickly defended myself, relieved that my angry opinions had not reached Lucy's ears. 'I don't want to intrude,' I told her. 'It's you he wants to be with, not me.'

'Nonsense,' said Lucy. 'Rowle is very fond of you. He wouldn't have agreed to have you here living in the house if he felt otherwise.'

Ah! And I took this piece of information to bed and mulled

over it, wondering, again, if it had been his idea originally, or hers.

Oh, what an abysmal, pathetic fool! I feel nauseous when I think of my grotesque stupidity. Did I really believe for one moment that Lucy did not suspect? I thought I was a worldly, grown-up woman. I thought I knew all there was to know about life and the world! Lucy was only seven years older than me, but so much more experienced. She had travelled, seen life on the road, life in a big house, life as it used to be lived here in the Combe. She was wise for her years. What did she think – that this was some sort of childish passion that would leave if I was introduced to Rowle's world, into his household? Did she think that my hero image would die once I saw more of him as he really was? Did she think that? Is that why she agreed to keep me in her house? I know she sympathised and that she gave me every opportunity to discuss my feelings with her.

She knew me. She knew Rowle. She knew how dangerous it would be for two such people to love.

She didn't even blame me . . . that was almost the worst, the most insulting part of it all . . . she actually blamed Rowle!

16

Ah, but if Lucy had her mermaid secrets then I was soon to have the first of mine – and there would be many. I came upon my first secret by accident and nobody knew I found out. It should have made a difference to my feelings – I know that, Brother Niall – but it didn't.

The room downstairs was a place where Lucy and the children seldom went: it was the room where Rowle had made love to me that first, fatal time. Often, since coming to the house, I had crept in there, knowing it was not allowed but wanting to see if it held, in its sun-dusty rays, some of the sensations I so vividly remembered.

The room had an opulence about it that made me think of the pleasure dens Mallin told us of; by day, the sun shone in on the elaborate rugs and cushions while by night, as I knew, the firelight took over. In here the men met to discuss their plans for the day – one select band of men, the men Rowle rode with. But I, inquisitive and suspicious, wanted to know how they acted together, what they did and said: I wanted to know everything about Rowle, even the secret things, and so I found a place behind the wainscotting where a knot in the wood was missing, and when I knelt down in the boot cupboard I had a central view of the whole room as far as the casements.

On this particular night they were late home, and when they arrived there was more shouting and cursing than usual in the court, and loud exclamations from the waiting grooms. Lucy had let me go early. I had lied to her, saying I was tired and she, never questioning me, told me to go to bed and I could miss breakfast, too, if I would rather sleep. So I'd taken up my position, taking care to lock the door behind me but knowing I was quite safe because no one would come in here until morning.

I expected a short meeting, a few drinks, a summing up and some final goodnights. I was tired, (I had not been totally untruthful), and it was uncomfortable in there, crouched up on one knee and with a cold draught coming through the knot-hole that made my eye water. However, I was quite shamelessly determined to miss nothing, although later I wished I had given into my earlier instincts and gone straight to bed.

There was a scuffle at the door. It took time for anyone to actually pass into my line of vision, but as soon as they did I made out that they had taken a prisoner – an event I knew to be rare because of the consequent dangers of interference from outside authorities. And the prisoner was a fine one, a fat dandy of a man with a curling, beribboned wig and a bow on each pastel leather shoe: a gallant in black and silver, with his arms lashed behind his back and a gag making his fat cheeks bulge. Even so he managed to look appalled and disgusted, his little eyes buttoned out of the podge of his cheeks like the eyes of a startled hog. Seeing him there, trussed and indignant like that, I wanted, in spite of my perilous position, to laugh.

Rowle's horsemen were rough with him, ignoring his fidgetings. They pushed him down in Rowle's chair and tied him to it – his waist being hard to find they held him instead to the back of the chair by his neck, making it impossible for him to turn his head in either direction, and to the seat of the chair by his knees. He could raise himself only a little, quite hopelessly, and hardly an inch. And his small, piggy eyes were glaring, staring furiously about him. Closing his eyes was the only way he could avoid watching what was going to happen.

I moved my fascinated gaze from him and took in my breath sharply, for he was not the only prisoner they had taken that night, it would seem. There was a woman, also, but she was not tied. She walked stiffly, a handkerchief held under her nose as if to prevent her from fainting with the horror of it all or from some unknown, but indescribably gross contamination. Well-heeled, both of them, flounced with lace and dripping with gems, and I wondered why these hadn't been already stripped from them. But no, there were rings on their fingers and sparkling diamonds glittered from the woman's dainty ears. Her face was whitened so it looked like porcelain, and a beauty spot was daubed on one of her cheeks. She was a woman, but nothing like me or any woman I had ever seen in my life. As different from me as fire is to water.

She walked like somebody made from stone. She looked, if she bent, as though she might split.

Tonight had been special. The full party had ridden out, so some important encounter had clearly been planned and executed – but something unexpected must have happened, and now the whole band of men, twelve in all, filed into the room and took their places. It looked as if some sort of trial was about to begin, but the prisoner was gagged and had no way of speaking.

Rowle stood back, pulling at the lace of his cuffs, and left the stage to Silas. 'I cannot,' I just heard him whisper while moving back towards the shadows, away from the light. 'I cannot . . . I am too much involved with all this.' And he said the words as if he had earth on his tongue, or bitter herbs in his mouth. And his mouth was a firmly drawn line and he looked at the man in the chair with such loathing it was as if he would have preferred to draw his sword and put an end to this session immediately.

Silas said, 'This is not the way. This is no answer. Consider the consequences of what you do! For Lucy's sake . . . or if not for hers, for the sake of your children!'

But Jacob Gifford, a man with a face like an axe and a reputation as cutting and hard, was there and had scented the kill. He would not pull back. He turned towards the woman with a small smile on his thin lips, and she, unafraid, not knowing his reputation, looked back at him haughtily. He ignored this, but took his time contemplating her, as if deliberating on whether she was young enough, pretty enough or suitable for his own purposes. Tension stalked the room and I knew that look of Jacob's: he was about to torment her. I watched and I wished that I had chosen some other night. I did not want to see this and yet I had to . . . I had to know . . .

She stood very proud and still as he stripped her. He did it in such a way that she must have known she counted for absolutely nothing. His calm, even voice, when he gave his orders, pierced an absolute silence, apart from the squeaks that came from the little man tied to the chair. But her neck never bent, no not even when he was down to her most intimate undergarments. Quite gently, with a horrible care and concern, Jacob Gifford removed her clothes one by one, putting aside her wrap with gracious politeness. But when he reached her petticoats and her shift the man in the chair writhed and kicked his pudgy feet and strained to get up. Rowle stepped forward to push him down with the blunt end of his whip, and stared at him in such a hard, strange way that I wondered who this man was and what he could have done to make Rowle hate him so. And then Rowle nodded to Jacob, turned his back on the company as if finally agreeing to something he had not been sure of, and walked towards the window, towards Silas who stared at him steadily. There Rowle stood, looking out. But there was nothing to see because it was quite dark.

Now the stranger moved with a passive endurance I had to admire, as Jacob led her, naked but unbowed, her high blonde hair coiled about her neck, to the seat where Rowle had led me. She obeyed, her eyes – I caught a quick glimpse of them – glittering proudly like a queen's. What would they do and why were they treating her so? And suddenly I realised with shock that they all meant to share her! What would Lucy say if she knew that this was happening down here in her house while upstairs she tucked her children into bed? Did she know? Was it possible that she knew and yet ignored it?

The lady was no longer mistress of her breasts, her belly, her legs, her hands, or those long thighs that were bare and openly displayed for all the watchers to see. Foolishly, she attempted to struggle and I wanted to call, 'Let it be . . . let it be! You can take yourself off to some other place . . . 'tis quite easy!'

She ground her teeth in rage and fought when Jonna moved forward – Jonna, a mere stripling, with his trimly cut hair and his ruddy complexion . . . commenting brutally, handling her coarsely, joking and calling the others to join him. They came, they held her, and then she looked like a doll, just as limp, just as accessible with a body stuffed tight with feathers. And still I felt there was nothing of this woman that resembled me.

It was Jacob who sat at the end of the seat gripping her legs in a vice-like hold while the others took turns to rape her. They undid their britches right there in the room and they thrust their thighs between her legs and drove themselves into her helplessness, while Seth had her arms above her head so her heavy white breasts were stretched and the others handled them cruelly, with coarse, animal comments. And when they had stretched her neck back they made her take them into her mouth while some were using her the other way. Her long hair came loose, fell down over the seat and almost touched the floor. It reminded me then, of Lucy's hair. Couldn't Rowle see that?

Rowle could not see anything. He stood with Silas at the far end of the room, his back to the proceedings, shutting them out.

As time went on the men became quieter, their heavings, pantings and jibes lessened, but the plump prisoner in the chair grew more and more agitated. Finally, Rowle gave a signal for the men to release him. They did so, and he immediately stood up, a little fat man with a bright red face and a wig askew on his head, his whole body protesting.

He squeaked. He tried to speak. There was no time.

They held the woman tightly, while a party of three propelled the fat man towards her. They unbuttoned his britches, they stripped off his leggings.

'This is your husband,' said Rowle, 'and I believe this is your wedding night, so it is your duty to accommodate him.' And I have never heard his voice so grim.

She struggled again and sobbed in fear, but they would not let her up. And they moved and manipulated the man with the wig until he was over her and they made sure he entered her. Each time he tried to emerge from the enforced embrace they pushed at his buttocks and held her wider. Until, it seemed, he was with them in the game because his little face puffed up and he caught his breath and before long he had stopped protesting while all she could do was to cover her eyes with the hand they had loosed. And it took him time – longer than all the rest put together, and I think I heard Rowle say, 'Make the most of this, Charles, for this is the last time you will fuck anyone. Make it good, little man, make it last.'

I'm sure that the man called Charles did not hear him, but it was as if he had. He showed signs of slacking but the men, led by Jacob, were at him again, whispering lewd words and crude jokes as they forced him, grunting, into his wife. But the woman was nothing to me.

My eyes were sore with the staring. I could not tear them away.

Eventually, worn out, defeated, Charles sank on to the body of his wife and lay there moaning and crying.

Rowle laughed, an icy sound, but his face, bone-white, matched the woman's. And Silas said, 'Leave it there . . . leave it there . . . remember what you are doing!'

But Rowle turned away, refusing to listen, and shook Silas' hand from his arms as he gave the order, 'Take them away,' with no emotion whatsoever. And the woman was pushed out, naked, and the man, helpless and shuffling, went without his britches.

I turned away then, realising I did not know Roger Rowle at all – a man who could do such things . . . for although he had not taken part in these grisly events, his men had acted on his instructions – and with more than his blessing.

Later I found out what happened to the prisoners: in spite of Silas' violent protests, Rowle had them killed.

Was I shocked? Oh no, not after the stories old Bell had told me, and the world is a cruel place, but I was surprised – because wasn't Rowle opposed to this sort of cruelty? Hadn't he put a stop to it in the Combe, referring to it as 'descending to the level of the animals'.

But I knew that animals did not behave in that way. Rowle changed the whole world in order to suit his mood: this man they loved to idolise, this man they called king – he was, as they said, a law unto himself.

It wasn't until much later that I found out that Charles was his brother . . . that the riding party had chanced upon the Amberry coach coming home, and that Rowle had recognised Charles and his new young bride, the daughter of an earl.

My informant was Hugh the blacksmith who came to the kitchens the following day to deliver the mended boots. He looked around him carefully, making sure Lucy was not about before he confided to me uneasily, 'I have never seen Rowle in such a rage. It was truly terrible. What that man must have done to warrant such anger is anyone's guess. Rowle wanted them dead, and nothing that Silas did or said that night could dissuade him.'

So I wondered why Rowle hated Charles so, and why he had waited so long for revenge.

According to rumour . . . and rumour spread in the Combe like forest fire . . . that was not to be the end of the matter. For it was almost a year later that word went round that Rowle had gone secretly under cover of darkness, and had burned the great house to the ground and everyone in it, until Amberry, Rowle's former home, was just an E of ashes on the ground. Somewhere among them, it was whispered, were the ashes of his stepfather, Gideon and everyone else who happened to be in the house that night – brothers, sisters, cousins and visiting friends. To Rowle, so great was his need for revenge, guilt or innocence seemed irrelevant.

I listened to the rumour, which grumbled round the lower reaches of the Combe heavy and dark like incipient thunder. I listened and I frowned, for I knew what they said could not possibly be true.

For Rowle could not have gone out that particular night with his men to raze the house to the ground.

Rowle had been with me. And at no time that night had he left me.

He must have heard the rumours. So why didn't he deny them?

And why had Rowle never returned to his former grand world? Why had he and Lucy remained for so long in the Combe after their capture? There were very many things, then, that I did not understand.

But would it have made any difference to me, Brother Niall, if I had? I doubt it.

17

To everyone except Lucy, Rowle showed no visible signs of emotion. From everyone else he kept himself distant. I felt him inside my own head – all the time – but I could never reach out and touch him. Chilly and stark like a man carved from granite, he'd never allow it.

Nor was I going to ask him if I might ride out with them. He would certainly have refused me. Women were there for the pleasure of men, to bear their children and to keep their houses. And if they did those things smilingly and without scolding they reaped their just rewards –they were loved in return and provided for. And if, occasionally, a man needed to take his pleasure elsewhere, well why not? And why should Rowle hold different views from everyone else?

But I thought everyone should be free to follow their own desires.

And all the women I spoke to disagreed, except for one, my friend the wicked, scarred Jessie Lang. She felt as vehemently as I did over this, cheated and angry with all the smugness of it. I thought these traditions made people narrow and closed, and I wanted more than that from my life. Why should women be different from men? Were my unusual views to do with my peculiar upbringing? It was because Maggie, Lizzie and Birdie had held such low opinions of themselves that they had been destroyed. They could have run that farm easily without Amos! They should have enquired about the tenancy them-selves, should have rejected their lowly lot and fought for their rights – instead, by their docile complicity they had allowed the worst to happen to them. As all women did.

Yes, I was not only angry with myself, but I was angry with them for dying and leaving me.

I spent most of my spare time with poor Jessie, who had been 'given' to Caleb the blacksmith's son by decision of the council of men in order to keep her quiet – to keep the women quiet. Jealous, I thought them, and so did Jessie. No one else bothered to visit her. She had moved from her shack and now lived on the other side of the Combe which was a drearier, sadder place, where the alternative people chose to live. She had insisted on going there. Now she said to me, 'You're strange – different.'

'How?' And I thought she meant my hair, for it was the taint-mark she was staring at.

'You has no idea o' right or wrong. You are all messed up like that. 'Tis a little like talking to . . .' and she paused, stuck for a comparison, 'like talkin' ter the wind or the water – there, but wi' no idea which way ter run or ter blow.'

We sat side by side on a pallet in her cave with the door closed hard against the wicked weather. Jessie wore a filthy shift which hung off her drably. She was thin and pale and the woolly material of the garment came to her feet and almost drowned her. She was not the girl who had once gone secretly round the Combe with satisfied cunning in her cat-like movements. Her gestures, as we sat there talking, were listless and lacking all energy.

I didn't know what she meant. I was all concern because I thought I could understand her torment. Jessie's terrible wounds were healing on the outside thanks to Silas' ministrations, but as we talked I learned she would never accept her fate. For the first time I listened to ideas that echoed my own and I was excited by them.

'I'm leaving,' said Jessie rebelliously. 'I'm not stayin' here ter submit to that an' grow fat an' ugly bearin' e's brats.' And she pulled her dark hair forward to cover her face as if she thought I might be distressed by seeing her scars.

I tried to reassure her. She needed reassurance all the time. The scar on her cheek was terrible: it stood starkly against the winter pallor of her skin. 'When people know you they take no notice. It's only when they see you for the first time that they feel shock – and then it's only because the rest of you is still so beautiful. Don't hide your face from me.'

'How can you knows what it feels like? How can you, wi' a face like yours an' yer fancy way o' speakin'. How can you come here givin' me advice?'

But I didn't feel it was like that so I fell silent again, imagining that I knew what she must be suffering. She lived with Caleb in one of the lower caves and would not keep the door open to let in the light and fresh air, even when it was warm outside. And today it was cold and squally; the rain tore down the sides of the Combe leaving red peaty rivulets in its wake. Jessie hid from everyone but me. She sat on her pallet of blankets and moped, arranging her hair with nervous agitation and never cooking anything for Caleb to come home to.

'I marvel he puts up with you this way,' I told her. 'And I've heard he's a good man, kind, like his father. You could have done worse.'

'I couldn't have done any worse at all!' she shouted at me. And the terrible scar on her face reddened and seemed to pulse. 'Havin' a man thrust on me – chosen for me. A prisoner here in a cage! Livin' down here on the dark side o' the Combe wi' all the queer ones. How can you say I'm lucky? How can you honestly come here an' say such things to me?'

'Because I don't think you should leave,' I told her, worried. 'How would you survive in the outside world now . . .'

'Now what, Bethy? Now that my face looks like this? Well, I would be better off than I was afore. Then I had only myself to sell, till my face grew pocked an' old. Now I am really lucky – I can beg for ever, hold out a bowl instead of my body an' get paid fer it. Blessed by disfigurement. 'Tis much easier. There are gangs of beggars would be glad to have me now that Biddie Canter has arranged my face for me. I should be thankin' 'er most probably, 'stead o' hatin' 'er like I do.' And Jessie's smile stretched her face and made it go lopsided until it leaned into laughter and I thought I had never heard such a cold sound. She bent forward and clutched me. 'Come wi' me, Bethy! Doan you want ter see some o' the world? You carn want ter stay 'ere fer ever! Fer what reason do you stay?'

And I couldn't tell her at that stage because I wasn't even admitting it honestly to myself, but I felt I was letting her down by not going with her. I tried one more ploy. 'You'll break Caleb's heart if you go. He cares about you, Jessie.'

And she spat in an evil way that reminded me of Lizzie. I couldn't think why such a girl would go after Phineus Canter – a thick, boring, sullen sort of a man with a paunch on him the size of a pregnant heifer. Once I asked her, 'Did you love him?'

And Jessie shrank underneath all her hair and took her little body into a knot. 'Well,' she said defiantly. 'An' is that so funny?'

Rain dropped in yellow drips from the back of the cave

where it tapered and disappeared into a dark crack of rock. There was nothing soft in this place, or forgiving. It was spartan, stark, and Jessie had done nothing to make it otherwise. Perhaps she felt more at home in a place as grim and dismaying as she felt her own life to be. I shook my head, looked into her ash-grey eyes and forced a steady gaze. 'Not funny,' I told her quietly, 'but hard to understand.'

"'E told me 'e loved me!' She flung the words at me and I thought she would have liked to have slapped my face using them as wet fish, defying me to contradict her, even call her a liar, as he had. 'An' no one has ever said that to me before.'

So I looked away and wondered if it was this then, this craving to be loved that denied the freedom of women. Was this the fatal flaw that we all seemed to share . . . even the most self-assured and confident women of all, like poor Maggie, who had gone off into the snow to find it from those hard-bitten men up on Crockern Tor. I looked at Jessie, sulky and gaunt, but I remembered Maggie, yet the two were as different as night from day. I had followed my aunt once and found out where she went, because as I grew older and Maggie did her disappearing I always thought it was my fault. I used to end up being particularly nice to her and trying to help her when I could, to stop her going away again. This would work for a little while, and then I'd forget and go back to ignoring her as before. I used to get really worried when she went in winter: in summer I knew she would survive.

Maggie never gave a sign that she was going. She just took off and went. For me, though, each time she went it was worse. I became distracted, befuddled, wild with rage and resentment and sick with fright. Was it the ugly truth that she didn't care about me at all? Didn't care about any of us, in spite of her lovingly made beef puddings? Why hadn't she told me? Why did she have to leave like this? And why did she never say when she was coming back?

And then I realised that it was only at certain times of the year that she went . . . Once I understood this I felt a little better because it was no urge that took her, no sudden, inexplicable anger at me and at what she called my lazy, sluttish ways. There was some control over the madness, unless it was a particular time of year that called to her, some wink of the moon she had to answer.

She set off before nightfall on a window-rattling, fire-puffing day when no beast should have been out of its shelter. She went out the back store with her potato sack round her and her clogs all wrapped against the weather. At any other time I would have sat near the fire, waiting for her return, experiencing that tight, hurt pain of despair as the hours went by and still she did not come back.

But not that time. That time I gave her five minutes and then I fetched my cloak and followed her.

We went, blown by an icy wind behind us, to the ferns and mosses, crisp that day with ice, of Crockern Tor. What drove her? The cold was in my bones and I ached, I spun in clouds of sleet. And this, when we arrived, was a desolate place. But there was life here, it seemed – voices on the frost, the breath of mules, the clank of tools hung from rough saddles, forks with seven prongs, wicked looking mattocks – and I knew this to be the place where the tinners met.

At the top of the Tor was a fire and I smelled mutton roasting, so sweet it made my mouth water. They had set up taut shelters of skin against the wind, and lanterns hung from the willow frames of the shelters: sleet frail as dust-motes danced in their beams. What could the tinners be wanting with this big, ham-boned mountain of a woman who smelled of goose grease?

I waited and I watched. I saw the men as shadows in the firelight. They greeted her, knowing her, fond of her. This wasn't my Maggie any more. I felt I ought to leave – partly from fear of being found and partly from some other strong feeling, something to do with Maggie and freedom and solitude and the need to go one's own way. I knew that need: it was granted to me, and I should grant it to Maggie, too.

Three times a year Maggie made her lonely way to Crockern Tor where the tinners met, those men on their seats of stone round a massive stone table. I followed her only once.

They had business to do there, important business. And it appeared that Maggie had business there, also, for when she came home two days later there was a sparkle in her eye and money in her pockets. I heard it jangling. Her step was lighter, quicker, and she took to singing for a little while.

So was there no way out? And were men able to free themselves from this need? Were they made differently inside that they didn't crave love as we did? Make themselves prisoners as we did.

Then, shivering, and a little sick from the pungent odour of mouldy rushes in Jessie's cave, I told Jessie my secret. I told her of the night I watched and saw Rowle's men with Charles and his wife. Jessie was not surprised. She said, 'Men! They is all the same, especially wi' a score to settle. I heard what happened after your story – rumours spread. The woman was killed cleanly, 'er ordeal were nothin'. But I did hear that the man fared worse. Rowle made them cut out the lady's heart after, an' forced 'e ter eat it!'

Horror and pain – it was everywhere, but even with this, life was kinder in the Combe than the justice meted outside it. I said, 'I thought Rowle was different. He's always talking about considering others and never ill-using those weaker than yourself. And he has the nerve to call this place a sanctuary! I've heard him say it – talking to Lucy.'

''Tis to 'is advantage to do so,' said Jessie. ''E's worse than all the others put together only no one be sharp enough ter see it. Rowle this, Rowle that, 'tis time someone stood up to 'e. There isn't a man here who isn't afraid o' 'e. There isn't a woman here who 'e 'as not taken an' thrown away.'

I could hardly bear it. 'You too then, Jessie?'

'Of course me too. Why wouldn't 'e?' She touched her scar. ''E wouldn't want me now, though.'

And, ashamed, I knew that it was because of her scar that I could still remain friendly with Jessie.

I said, 'And yet Lucy doesn't appear to mind. She stays with him. She loves him.' And I wondered, once more, if Lucy would cease to love him if she knew about the terrible things he did.

'Ah, an' what is love?' Jessie huddled down further into her shawl and I thought I smelled the damp in it as she pulled it round her. But she knew what love was: she had the scars of it all over her face. And I loved to hear her call Rowle names – I shivered delightedly. I joined in viciously, yet knowing, somewhere deep, that I played games.

The early twilight deepened so that we could hardly see each other across the low, stone room. She groped for a candle, picked it up, but decided against lighting it, preferring the darkness as I did. The ceiling appeared to sink lower, the door to come nearer. We were close, Jessie and I, close in our love and our pain, but keeping our secrets.

We talked about how women ought to protect themselves from their feelings until Caleb came home and it was time for me to go back to the house. I walked back with my head down against the rain, my ankles deep in the mud. The weather suited my mood. We had searched, but had found no answers.

Lucy stood at a table that was heavy with meat, fruit and wine. A comforting fire burned behind her. 'Help yourself,' she said when I entered, 'and are you quite sure you are properly dry? You'll catch your death sitting for hours in that woeful place with Jessie.'

'She needs some comfort. She needs support. Lucy, she is so very alone.'

'You can't help her, even if she is your friend. You must stay out of this. It is strictly between Jessie and Caleb.'

I knew that Lucy disapproved of Jessie. When I told her that Jessie was about to leave the Combe she gave a startled laugh and I thought there was fear in it. Lucy's loyalty to Rowle, her obedience as a wife, her disapproval of anything slightly disruptive irritated me beyond endurance. Later that evening she moved to sit by her window, waiting for Rowle, sensuous in flowing black with her hair gathered into a loose knot at her neck, looking like silver against the black satin gown. Her wide lips smiled their sleepy smile. She only half-listened to me – with the other half of her she was watching – her eyes slid past me to the court outside.

'They're late back,' she murmured. And I wanted to be the one who was waiting for him, worrying.

'I'm going to help Jessie,' I told her, agitated, walking up and down the narrow chamber which smelled of sandalwood, Lucy's favourite perfume.

'Jessie is your friend. You'll miss her if she goes.'

'That is no reason for me to keep her here against her will.'

'Leaving the Combe is not the best answer for her . . . if she's allowed to settle down she'll become a wonderful wife and mother.'

I was furious. 'How do you know? How can anyone else decide these things for others?' I wanted to go on and say –

'Look at your life, compared to Jessie's. No wonder you can sit there with that sweet look on your face. You live in this house like a queen, with four children you love and a man you worship. Compare your life here to Jessie's, down in that damp place with a man she cannot abide and her face all mauled and twisted. You should be trying to help her – all the women should be trying to help her – not siding with the men to keep her, criticising her for her wicked ways, making her come to order.'

Out loud I said, 'She would be safer if she was given a horse, and she wants to wear boys' clothing. Some food and some money would get her a better start. Lucy, if you were prepared to help it would be so much easier for Jessie. And she'd also know she had friends here who approved of her, she'd know she could come back if ever she needed to.'

'It's not as easy as that,' said Lucy in her soft, vague way. And I know she was worrying if Rowle's hot food was spoiling in the kitchens.

So to get her attention I said, 'Jessie wanted me to go with her.'

'But you wouldn't.' She looked startled again, and I realised for the first time, with surprise, that Lucy was lonely, and that's what I was, too – lonely. And I had thought that impossible in the Combe with so many people about. 'I couldn't cope without you,' she said. She bowed her long white neck and her lips barely moved when she added, 'Life is cruel outside, Bethany.'

'It can be equally cruel in the Combe, Lucy.' I wanted to tell her about Rowle but I didn't.

We had eaten early. The children were in bed an hour ago. There was nothing to do but wait. I would have liked to convince Lucy to help my friend, for I needed the storeroom key. I would get it anyway when I went to look for my own outfit – I had not forgotten about riding, one night, with the men, and Lucy understood how I needed to do that. But I would rather have her cooperation openly. I wanted her to sympathise with Jessie. Sometimes I trembled with the urge to shake Lucy out of her easygoing complacency.

I went to the window seat where she sat and looked out over her head at the dark outline of the moor. There were lights down in the stables. The moor seemed to heave and sigh in motion, like I imagined the sea would do, heaving as if trapped against the sky and between the two great tors on either side of my view. With sudden panic I thought, my life is like that just now, I am writhing, seething, trapped between rocks, unable to change course, settled like this for all eternity. Life is short – I cannot bear to be trapped – perhaps I should go with Jessie. I shivered as the swirl of my dark emotions swept like a gale through the casements.

'I'm going down to the court,' I said to Lucy. 'I need some fresh air.'

'It is cold outside, and wet,' she told me, pulling her shawl around her.

'I am not afraid of the cold.' And when I said that I meant – I am not afraid of anything – unlike you! She gave me one of her strange, secret, mermaid smiles, and I took her picture with me, the picture that Rowle would see by the lantern light in the window as he rode home. A lovely woman, waiting, all softness and giving. Her eyes, looking out into the darkness, saw quite different things from mine. Safe things. Happy things. And it showed in the steadiness of their gaze.

I should have stayed in for the rest of that evening. I should have said goodnight and gone to my room and locked the door. But I didn't. I couldn't. I had to see him.

As I went outside I heard the distant sounds of horses' hooves on the path. Painfully I imagined the next few moments. Rowle would do what he so often did, he would dismount, hand over his horse, call goodnight to his men and stride straight up the stairs to take Lucy in his arms. His supper, the supper that Lucy so worried about, he would eat cold, later. Or he would leave it quite alone and make do with a cold platter of meat. And how did any of this concern me? I took the vision further – I always play with visions that hurt me. I saw her twining her arms round his neck, pressing the length of her body against him. I saw her head thrown back and those mild blue eyes burning. He would feel her breasts soft against him . . .

Like a mangy cur about to whelp an unwelcome litter, I found the shadows and stuck to them. Hiding myself. Hiding from Lucy who was watching from the window. Hiding my dark thoughts, trying to wipe them from my head. Ashamed, because didn't I hate him? Didn't he revolt me? Especially after the things I had seen in that room of secrets. Lucy, who didn't know, could love him – but how could I? Knowing the man he was.

The hollow sound of hooves turned into mellow clattering on cobbles. Rowle was sleek, polished blackness, just an image at first, becoming clearer as the men came out with their taperlights and their welcoming voices. Taking shape in front of me as I lurked there in the shadows.

Men, saddle-sore, weary, cursing; the sound of harness, the stamping of hooves, a whinney, a shadowy mass of people, suddenly, with the stark moor only an eye-lift behind them. He brought the wildness of all that home with him. He dismounted, and I heard him shout, 'Take him, John, I shan't want him again tonight,' as he passed his horse to his groom, *and then and then and then and then oh Brother Niall, oh you sad monk, I wanted to throw myself into his arms!*

That was the moment. I'll never forget it.

It was as simple as that – after all that simmering, all that pussyfooting around it – not knowing, not naming my feelings. I loved him then, as surely and certainly as if I had been struck by a lightning bolt. So this was what it was all about. I was in love.

Rowle went in. He didn't even see me.

From my dark place I glanced up at the window. Lucy was gone and I – I was trembling.

18

Jessie lived for her escape. I was frightened for her. I thought she was safer in the Combe and I said so, but I could not dissuade her. Half the trouble, I knew, was Phineus, who passed her by without even looking at her, his eyes hard and unloving, and he would not 'talk' to her which is what she craved.

'I's must ask 'e if 'twas all a lie,' she said sorrowfully to me one day as we watched Nat Hurley building a butter cooler down in the shadiest part of the water. I saw Jessie as pathetic and in need of help – but not myself – not then. The neediness of her angered me, embarrassed me. I believed that I would never be like her: I had Lucy's children with me and I always felt proud then, chosen specially to guard Rowle's most precious possessions. Because that's what they were, that's what everyone and everything was to him – he owned the lot of us.

I had stared long and hard at Phineus Canter, trying to understand, for Jessie's sake, what there was there to love. And I did wonder if her dramatic plan was deliberately intended to bring herself to his notice. Jessie still believed there was a choice for him to make between her and Biddie. If she was trying to force the issue I knew beyond doubt that she would not succeed. I looked at him – quite happy now to go back to his woman and his children when his work was done, somehow easily able to forget those secretly stolen nights of love while poor Jessie mourned as if over a death.

A great ox with his brawny arms and ropes and leathers – he was gentle with horses, had all the patience in the world, but for Jessie he had no time. I tried to tell her this but she would not listen to me.

The stones for the mound young Nat was building clacked wetly beside the water. His bright red hair burned like an auburn flame against the green beside him where rushes marked the deeper dampness. Apart from the sounds he made the moor was tight with its summer silence. I chewed grass and threw worried glances at Jessie. She was upset. Quick-eyed women had pursed their lips and shaken their heads as we walked down past their dwellings, Jessie and me. 'Hard-faced whores,' she whispered sulkily as we settled on the grass. 'You'd think I's were the only one who had ever been bedded by a taken man.'

'They do it out of their fear.'

'I doan care why. I hates the lot o' em. They're all glad about my face. It makes 'em feel safe.' Only to me did she show how she felt. The others would never know how they hurt her. Jessie sounded and looked just like a child, hardly older than Judd. More vulnerable even, for he was sturdy, a rangy child with wild good looks while she was thin as a bird and scarred. She would look better as a lad than a maid, would resemble a young boy even when she grew old. And I had the key to the clothes stores. Taking a horse would be difficult, but not impossible. And it was only fair, after what had been done to her here, that Jessie be given the best possible start in the cruel world that awaited her.

I wished that I could make Phineus love her.

If it wasn't for Jessie I would have been happy. I had moved, I thought, on to a higher plane of love which allowed me to worship from afar without the agonising, cramping pain that had been there before I admitted the truth. Now I was free to dream and fantasize, and it didn't seem to matter – then on that day – that my love was not returned. It was as it was, strong, pure and joyous, and I delighted in it. Thinking no further. Not needing to.

But, Brother Niall, as I've told you, that is just a stage of love. It changes.

Dartmoor in summer had all its usual loveliness, and yet it didn't touch me as it used to. It had become a dream place, and the people around me dream people. Rowle was all that was real – Rowle and I.

Lucy remarked on my daily visits to Jessie, and so did Mary, disparagingly. She said it seemed odd, but I thought it was odd how quickly people forgot and became self-righteous, turning out to be the hardest critics of those like themselves. When I asked Mary about Jessie she said she knew little about her except that "'er be a trouble-maker, 'er allus was right from the time 'er first arrived. Doan get involved wi' 'er, that's what I'm sayin'. You is too easily led.'

But I liked going to see Jessie, talking with her. Without a family of her own – she told me she couldn't remember anyone – before she came to the Combe she had wandered the road with a group of beggars doing everything and anything for money until their licences were taken away and five of the group were hanged for vagrancy. 'An' I thinks I was born on the road,' she told me, 'an' that's why I's finds it hard to stick to one place.'

But that wasn't the reason Jessie wanted to leave.

Jessie didn't have a high opinion of herself, either. 'I causes trouble wherever I goes,' she grumbled. She lifted her head to expose the scars as if she wanted me to see them. 'Sometimes I thinks I am a witch, Bethy.' And she drooped her hair again, afraid, I thought, of what I might answer.

But I knew all about witches, black, grey and otherwise and so I could say quite truthfully. 'You're nothing like a witch, Jessie. There's no badness in you.'

'No one's ever said that,' she objected in a cross voice, as if I disturbed her by saying it. 'People tell lies . . .'

'I'm not lying. Why would I lie?'

Jessie shook her head and we took to staring at Nat again, watching his efforts in the mesmerised, summery way of watching men at work when it's hot. And then she said, 'I was thinkin' o' weavin' a spell to make 'e love me.'

Exasperated, I turned to her and said, 'Leave him alone, Jessie! He's not worthy of you!'

And angrily she turned back and shouted so loudly that Nat looked up, Judd turned round and Daisy ran back to my knee, 'An' neither is that one any good for you!'

'That one?'

Jessie looked down and whispered, 'Yes, that one.'

'How did you know?'

'Doesn't everyone?'

'You're stupid, Jessie Lang,' I told her, 'stupid and nothing but a trouble-maker.'

'I leaves tomorrow,' she said as she got up and left me. 'So if you still wants to help me I needs some clothes an' I needs a horse.' She stumped off up the track, red-faced with temper.

'I'll help you,' I muttered as I gathered the children round me, as I watched Jessie flouncing up to her cave and heard her slamming the door. Tiredly I picked Bessie up off the grass. And did I imagine slights, snubs, stares and suspicious glances as I trundled the children back up the hill on the darker side, towards the lights of the house and supper? Had they all been directed at Jessie earlier on, or had some been meant for me? And how was it possible people could see into my head?

I was miserable. The sun, as was its habit in the Combe, had suddenly gone, there was no preparing for it. I shivered; the children sensed my sudden desolation and padded along beside me, looking up but not asking questions. As I passed Jessie's cave I paused and waited. She must have been watching for me, for the door opened slowly and she came out, a mess as usual, her hands on her hips and a scowl on her face. I had not been honest with her: I had been patronising, pretending, standing back as the others did, and critical when I had no cause to be.

Suddenly she laughed.

'What are you laughing at?' I was annoyed, went stiff and moved off again.

'You!' she shouted after me. 'You! You look so funny – so prissy and straight-laced and innocent! My, my! You wi' yer secrets, lustin' after a man same as I!' She hiccupped and went into a wild fit of laughter.

Aghast, I stood and watched her. What had betrayed me? Was I, now, a figure of amusement to everyone, or was it just Jessie who knew? I couldn't keep my face straight any longer. Suddenly the tragic absurdity of the whole business of life engulfed me and I laughed back, the children nervous round my skirts, tugging me back to sanity. But I couldn't help it. The more I heard Jessie rolling round there screaming and shouting with laughter the more I sank into hysteria too, until in the end we were hugging and kissing and crying with me telling her I didn't want her to go and she saying she'd known all the time and why hadn't I told her.

We parted as friends again, closer than ever before, and I shouldn't have helped her to leave the next day because Lucy was right, it was safer in the Combe, and I could have done with a friend as the next few months went by.

Oh monk, perhaps by talking it out with someone, I could

have cooled off a little, prevented some of what happened. It would have been far, far better if I had gone with her.

19

Except for the moon it is midnight dark. My feet are sore from pacing on this rough stone floor and yet I cannot be still. If I try I find it harder to breathe.

What if there is some terrible mistake and they hang me tomorrow? I am not ready to die – Brother Niall, can you hear me? I cannot die! I AM NOT READY. My scream comes as a whisper. I dare not scream, not here. And who can be ready for death who is not old or ill or in pain – and yet so many have died . . .

Jessie was not ready to die. Jessie was sixteen like me. Was I ever sixteen? It seems such a silly age when you say it over and over again, sixteen years old and yet I had started to sew my own grave clothes.

Did I make Jessie die?

I was twenty-three years old in March . . . now it is coming to the ninth of February . . . that might be the date of my death. Strange to know it – some might call it lucky. Death cannot creep up on me in the night leaving me with so much still undone.

When the constables come for me I will hear the beat of the gallows drum. And it will beat more slowly, I'm sure, than the beat of my own heart. I am in tune with it already; if I close my eyes I can hear it coming nearer and nearer until I flinch to the beat . . . and I will never see Roger Rowle again. Never. Never. Never. I will never see Roger Rowle again. Feel his eyes on me. Feel his arms. Feel his body. Feel his power.

Gone.

There were ponies tethered at the east end of the Combe, big-bellied tat-eared ponies of the deepest brown. Broken and yet not broken, like my rowan. They were set free in winter to roam over the moor, caught again in summer to be used as work-horses around the Combe and for the beggar bands to ride out on. The ponies gave birth in the spring and summer months; their foals enchanted the Gubbins children and after all the early fondling, were never quite wild again.

I didn't consider taking one of these to be stealing – these ponies belonged to no one. But to pick the sturdiest and most gentle-eyed, this was my problem. And having once taken my pick, Jessie must be ready to go and quickly, and ready to cling on, too, for she would have to avoid the main pathway and take a torturous route zig-zagging up the side of the hill.

I asked Lucy for the clothing cupboard key. She gave it readily, believing I was looking for something for myself. I hated the way she always believed in me – never looked for treachery. If ill-luck rebounded on her then it was her fault for her naive attitudes, I told myself firmly and guiltily.

I chose leather britches, a calico shirt, knee-boots and a thick sheepskin jerkin. To go over that, a woollen cloak with a serviceable drawstring that would hold tight against the strongest wind. There was a set for Jessie and a set for me. I was surprised to realise that we were the same size. Before I'd given thought to it I would have said that Jessie was much smaller than me. But no – we were both little, compact and wiry, more like lads than maids. I chose the thickest material for Jessie and took it along at midday. She was sitting on her pallet, moping. She rarely did anything else unless I forced her to accompany me outside.

She nodded when she saw me. ''Tis a good day for it – all the signs are right,' she said, trying on her witchy ways again. I snorted.

'It is nothing to do with signs,' I said, unfolding my bundle for her inspection, proud that I had chosen so sensibly. 'If you get out of here unchallenged then it will be by your own commonsense and skill, not to do with omens and portents.'

'Come with me, Bethy.' She tried not to make it sound as if she needed me to, but I knew how badly her heart was in the wanting. She untied her long, grey skirts and slid the britches over her narrow hips; the shirt-sleeves were too long so she rolled them up and the arms coming from the ends looked frail like sun-bleached bones.

'I can't come with you.' I started to cut off her hair, using Caleb's skinning knife. I stood above her and when her hair came off I felt as if I was weakening her, for her face – all the ugly mess of it, was exposed with nothing to pull across it.

'Because of Rowle?'

I sighed and stopped, staring ahead at nothing, a hank of hair in my hand and the knife resting by my side. Weary. Weak by my own admittance, in every way as debilitating as Jessie's scars. 'Yes, because of Rowle.'

Jessie wasn't going to criticise me. I knew that. How could she? 'Would you have come – if'n 'tweren't for 'e?'

'You know I would have. We're friends.' We both liked that word. We used it often when we talked together. Neither of us had ever had a friend before. 'Where are you going?'

'Into town. Where there will be others like myself. There are places in town that I knows. They is allus there, waiting, people like me. Before . . .' Jessie touched her face, 'before I used to see they an' run, disgusted, fearin' infection. Children are cruel. Now I am one of 'e,' And she smiled, almost prettily, and tried to pull her hair across her face only there wasn't any so she rubbed where it stuck up, messy, on her head, and her smile was turned into a grin – and yes – she did look better like that.

The deed was done. There was no turning back. If Caleb came home and caught her she would be beaten, dragged before the council and watched; too many times like these and Jessie would have no energy left. That was the amazing thing about both of us – we had such energy – we revelled in excitement. We were crazy maids, Jessie and me, screaming in the wind, crying in the rain together. And close, as I could never be to Lucy, who was owned so happily, so totally, by a man.

No, I didn't want Jessie to go. And she knew it. And that made us, suddenly, awkward together. I wanted to speak about it but I couldn't. We hadn't known each other long, no more than six months, just two seasons, and yet I was closer to Jessie than I had been to anyone else in my life. Hesitantly I put my hand on her shoulder. She shrugged it off. 'Doan. Doan do that. You make it harder that way.'

'Yes,' I said. 'I know.'

Then she smiled wryly. 'We woan meet again.'

'I can't think that way.'

'You must. An' then we can stay honest together to the end.' Her voice and her face were fierce. 'Doan you get yousself lost, Bethy, not like I did. You can still pull back.'

'No, Jessie. I can't.'

There was nothing else for us to do then but laugh, which is what we always did together when we were in difficulties with the speech. So we did laugh. But it was more of a crying, with tears just the same, and that feeling of weakness that comes after. Left with an emptiness that wouldn't be filled again this time because Jessie was going away.

'Don't worry, Jessie,' I told her. 'All will be well when the cuckoo comes.' Maggie used to tell me that, when as a child, I was down: 'Your cough'll go when the cuckoo comes, doan doubt it, doan doubt it.' And she was right – wonderful things used to come with the cuckoo, with the spring.

But Maggie was not the one who knew about love . . . that one was Birdie, strange, mad, wandering Birdie. It was Maggie who told me about Birdie and I was surprised to discover that all I had to do was to ask, 'Who was it?'

'Somebody who were no better than 'e ought ter have been,' said Maggie.

'That's no answer.'

'Back along they came,' said Maggie, 'an' Maither said we's should let 'e in. 'Twere snowin' an' blowin' an' we heard they comin', fer they shouted ter each other from way back on the ridge. The man in front were tryin' ter make out the wych way, the party at the back had the corpse, takin' 'e fer burial at Lydford. The snow, you knows, had obscured the track an' the wind were gettin' up strong an' they wouldn't have made it so they left the track an' came up here towards the house.'

'So they came in?' It was hard to believe that anyone other than Mallin had been to our house.

'All but the corpse an' 'e lay outside, properly shrouded an' crisp from the cold. They was men from Two Bridges so they had come a fair way in that weather.' Maggie smiled. 'I sees they now. I sees the water drip off 'e as they stands wi' theys backs ter the fire, stampin' the hots from their toes.'

'An' Birdie?'

Maggie looked hard at me. ''Twas love at first sight, Birdie said afterwards, all forlorn. 'Er said they locked eyes that young man an' 'er. 'Er came down in the night brazen as yer likes an' they went outside together, lay in the stable an' talked, 'er said. Talked, huh! That's talk fer 'e. An' that's what you gets fer yer hospitality, Amos said after. 'E said ter Maither, "I told you so," but Maither said, "well, we couldn't have known what would happen. We couldn't have let 'e perish in the cold. 'Twould not have been Christian." An' you knows how Amos hates the church.

'We never saw hide nor hair of 'e again, any o' theys. Went back ter Two Bridges they did an' Birdie grew an' as 'er belly grew so did 'er misery grow also. Maither wouldn't speak ter 'er an' Amos cursed 'er every time 'e passed. As fer the little maid, 'er only lived fer an hour an' we didn't show 'er ter Birdie, 'er wouldn't have stood the shock o' havin' that small corpse put in 'er arms. Amos wouldn't tell 'er where 'e put it so fer weeks 'er went searchin', 'er eyes ter the ground, an' uz wi' all the work ter be gettin' on wi', wanderin' around out there weak an' reedy like the music 'er plays until 'er found the piece of broken ground up on the black ridge an' then 'er wore 'erself out lumpin' a rock, rollin' an' gruntin' an' lumpin' it an' 'er were weak, then, from all the sadness, from the foot o' the ridge 'er rumbled that rock right up there.'

' "'Er's made a cross fer 'erself in more ways than one," Maither went round mutterin'. "The vule should have let 'n goo." '

And as I listened to Maggie that day and thought about Birdie with her struggle up the hill with all that dead weight, I felt a tight rope round my chest and knew that was how wanting to cry made you feel.

'I knew that,' I said to Maggie then. 'I knew about the grave. I knew there was a girl there. I goes there an' I's talks to 'er. I tells 'er what's goin' on.'

'Well, if'n you knews,' said Maggie to me, suddenly looking very annoyed, 'if'n you knews, then why has you wasted my time wi' the askin', yous tummit haid?'

Oh yes, I knew that loving and not being loved in return can turn you that way. I felt it was probably wise that Jessie had decided to act . . . to do something and not let it get her in the way it had got to poor Birdie. I helped Jessie pack a bundle with food and money. Knowing nothing of money, having never used it, I hadn't an idea of how much I had taken from the purse in Lucy's chamber. I just hoped it would be enough to buy Jessie a bed until she found safety. We walked together straight down to the stream, and followed it up the Combe, avoiding curious glances. Just a maid and a lad, we made our way to the tufted paddock where the ponies swished the flies with their tails and stamped their neat little feet.

'That one,' I told her, knowing. I walked towards the little mare I had been watching for days. The eye that answered my call was soft and willing and I was put in mind of the rowan. I had always had a good eye for horse-flesh – even Amos had given me that in one of his more expansive moods. Animals, all animals, even the wayward ban-dog would do anything for me. Lizzie used to eye this skill of mine with suspicion. It was not usual to be so akin with the animals. Once she saw me with the ban-dog's head on my knee and I ruffling his spikey snout – eye to eye we were – and she'd chanted one of the charms she used to protect her against malignant forces and said, 'Put 'e down, maid. Yous soul doan want to commune wi' such as 'es . . . wicked bugger that 'e be.'

And I knew, in the kind of way Lizzie knew, that this pony was right for Jessie. Cautiously looking around me, fear like a butterfly trapped in my throat, I pulled off the chain, flung on the dusty halter and called her. 'Go now. Quickly go.'

We didn't say goodbye. With a rattle of stones and a grunt from the mare they were off, heading up that steep incline into the shadows, with Jessie kicking the pony's flanks and urging her forward with her strong, thin arms.

I didn't watch. I sat on the grass and turned away, put my head in my hands but I did not cry. How could I cry, when Jessie was clambering nearer to freedom? I shouldn't feel sad – just for myself, for my loneliness. I had to fill myself with something and it is easy to find anger. Anger with Phineus, with Caleb, anger with Lucy and Mary and all the women. And, of course, anger with Rowle who could have prevented all of this had he been wiser. *Had he even been interested.*

Yes. Hate is so easy. It is love that is so hard to find.

20

I tend to forget about the in-between times. Looking back it seems as though everything happened at once. It didn't, of course, and it was more than a month after Jessie left that I first rode out with Rowle. A month of missing Jessie so intensely I became ill and depressed, so that Lucy was concerned for me and asked Silas for a cure. I argued with her vehemently, swearing that nothing was wrong, refusing to see Silas whatever she said. However, Lucy might look weak and feeble but she was stubborn, and when her mind was made up there was no changing it.

When Silas entered my room the following evening I was sitting on the edge of the bed and greeted him with an air of aloof composure, glad of Lucy's presence. I had not forgotten Christmas: I often thought of that awful episode as you do when you have embarrassed yourself and cannot shed the shame. Save for white ruffles at his neck and wrists Silas was dressed all in black, and a little dishevelled, in contrast with my neat, white room consisting of simply carved furniture. The bed where I sat was against the wall, small and narrow. Because my room was under the eaves the ceiling sloped and caught the first of the morning sunlight which flickered over it and woke me so that on some mornings I dreamed I was surrounded by water. In the evenings the glow of the small fire in the far wall played on the angle of the wall and ceilings, bathing the room with a rose-coloured light. Tonight the room smelled of burning leaves and reminded me of sad autumns.

'I don't want a physician,' I told Lucy sullenly, ignoring Silas after my first, cool nod. 'I'm just missing Jessie, that's all.'

'You're pining away to nothing,' she retorted. 'And Silas is a good physician with a proper medical degree. He worked at St Bartholomew's Hospital in London where he saw so much horror . . .'

I stopped bothering to listen. I didn't want to hear about Silas, hear Lucy's excuses for him.

'Trust him,' said Lucy to me, and I thought how naive and innocent she was not to know his true nature and my wariness increased.

Silas smiled briefly at Lucy before asking her to leave.

'Don't go, please,' I said. 'Don't leave me here with him.'

But Lucy was ashamed at my ingratitude. She clucked her tongue and admonished, 'You're a baby. You are quite safe with Silas. Be brave!'

When she'd gone, he turned round and smiled. I recognised that smile from the Lord of Misrule: his eyes seemed red like men's eyes go when they see a wench ready for the taking. I felt at a great disadvantage. Lucy could say what she liked about Silas but I knew his type. I sat on the bed looking wan and trying to revive my pride but Silas, who in front of Lucy had acted all charming and twinkle-eyed, wore his wolf face again as he sat down beside me on the edge of my bed. I sidled away, struggling under the beams to keep a straight-backed position. I crossed my arms in front of my chest. I felt trapped. There was nowhere to go.

'How long have you been feeling this way?' he enquired, and held out his hands to feel my neck. When I pulled back he smiled and reached further.

''Tis nothing, really, just a slight fever. It will go if I get more fresh air. If I eat more food.' And I wanted to call out for Lucy. I pulled my shift tight round me.

'More exercise, more food and more to think about,' said Silas soothingly. 'You're on your own too much and able to wallow in melancholy thoughts.' And he talked to me so gently, with such understanding, that soon I was forgetting who he was and telling him of poor Jessie and of how much I missed her. He began to look like a trustworthy man as he sat there, nodding and listening, so that suddenly his sympathy proved too much and my words turned to tears as, quite inarticulate, I tried to explain my solitary feelings of desolation. Self-pity changed my tears into wracking sobs, so loud that I thought Lucy would hear and come in to find what was happening.

Oh, I was tired. I missed Jessie so much that it hurt. And my obsession for Rowle was eating me up, wearying me – it would not go away. Food did not interest me, nor did entertainment or conversation. And now here was Silas, giving me such a safe feeling of understanding and confidence, and I didn't pull away when he took my hand into his and stroked it, letting his fingers run up and down my arm.

Lucy did not come in. She must have gone downstairs. Instead I felt Silas' arm move around my shoulders and he pulled me into the consoling warmth of his chest. I was happy with that . . . quite happy . . . and I sobbed on.

'That's right,' he comforted me. 'Weeping is as good a cure as anything else I could prescribe.' His free hand stroked my upper arm, then moved gently towards my neck to touch my hair before slowly retracing its path. I nodded, quite feeble now, stretching out for a handkerchief with one hand, plaiting the edge of my coverlet with the other. And all the time he spoke to me softly in words I did not really hear, until gradually my crying subsided and I became conscious of the light touch of the back of his hand on my breast as it travelled along my arm.

Ashamed, I felt my skin tighten as I became aware of his deliberate action; confused, I recognised the heat that came from my skin. But this time I was unafraid, happy to be there in the arms of the Lord of Misrule. I did not attempt to pull away.

Silas' mouth nuzzled my hair as I relaxed against him. His quiet words were punctuated with soft kisses as his hand stayed on my breast where his fingers, as surely as my own quick breathing, told him the effect his fondling was having on me.

Then we fell silent. And it was only when, long minutes later, that he lowered me carefully down to lie flat on the bed that I worried about what was happening and pulled the cover up over me. He saw the quick look of fear in my eyes, he gave his black-eyed smile, and I had to smile back when he said, 'If you are feeling better I think I should complete this medical examination.'

He twisted round on the bed to feel each side of my neck. He examined my ears, my throat and my eyes. He raised my arms above my head and left them there so they lay on the pillow above me.

'Stay like that,' he ordered and getting up, pulled the

coverlet down to the foot of the bed. He raised my shift until it was bunched up above my breasts and I heard his sharp intake of breath as he looked down at my nakedness. Our eyes met then, and I smiled. I, too, was enjoying this game.

He pretended to examine me. He started at my feet and ankles before moving slowly up my legs with a sure and experienced touch. He halted and pushed my legs slightly apart, before running his hands up the insides of my thighs, making them feel smooth and silky under his fingers. And then he moved on, and stopped at the hot, moist place between my legs. I tried to cover myself, tried to close my legs but Silas' hand stayed between them as he lifted his head with the sharp command, 'No, let me finish.'

He knew then that I was just as inflamed as he: there was nothing I could do to hide my desire. I made myself think of Christmas Day, when I had sat there, helpless on his knee while he played with me like a toy but this time, the memory came without shame. It served to heighten my passion, so that when Silas again moved his hand, I allowed my legs to fall apart. I know that I moaned as his fingers stroked me outside first, before slipping in. I twisted my head on the pillow. I tried to stop moving to the rhythmic motions of his fingers. I tried one last time to stop him: I could not. Silas knew the game was won when he ceased his movements and I whimpered.

'Do you still want me to stop?' he asked, and his wet hand moved up to my breast. 'I won't go on – not if that's what you really want.'

'No,' I moaned, and quite shamelessly I pulled him down to the bed beside me, guiding his hand back between my legs and pushing upwards to meet it.

Then I abandoned myself to Silas. I let myself move with delight. And as his fingers moved faster and faster his mouth came down to take my breast. I fell back, exhausted, warm tears on my face . . . tears of pleasure and weakness.

'Lovely,' said Silas, withdrawing his hand. 'Lovely. There is nothing wrong with you, nothing that a good bit of fucking won't cure. You need to be loved by someone who cares and thinks highly of you. Why are you letting yourself pine away . . . waiting for a man who can only cause you pain and distress? What has happened to you that you need to punish yourself in this way? What makes you ashamed of your own desires, what gives you such fear of your feelings? You cannot love a god, Bethany . . . you cannot forever see your body as a sacrifice.'

And I was immediately frightened of Silas. I was afraid of my feelings towards him, and of the things that he said. I saw him preparing to take down his britches and I saw that look in his eye again. I saw the bulge of his sex where it pushed against the tight material. My fear of Silas mounted and I realised just what a fool I had been.

Silas was wicked. The feelings he gave me were wicked. I belonged to Rowle who had taken me and who owned me and I had no choice in that . . . no decisions to make. I would never be anyone else's but Rowle's.

Before Silas could put out his hand to stop me, 'Lucy!' I screamed at the top of my voice, wretched and ashamed of myself now. 'Lucy, please come now – Silas has finished!'

And Lucy hurried in, all concern. I pulled the covers up over my nakedness.

'Well?' she asked Silas.

'She'll be fine,' said Silas, that wretched man. His voice was thick, his eyes were stern, and I noticed how casually he wiped his wet hand. 'Just a little more white meat, some more red wine. And I think a few more visits from me are the answer.'

'I'm so glad,' said Lucy. 'I was getting quite worried.'

'She misses her friend.'

'It was Bethany's fault that she went.'

'She will get over it eventually,' Silas told Lucy, keeping his back to me. And then he added, 'What this maid needs is a man of her own and children,' and he winked at me when he said that, his dark eyes direct and dangerous. I saw that bad twinkle in his eye again, but Lucy was at the door and missed it.

Lucy saw Silas out and came back into the room. She sat on the edge of my bed looking placid and beautiful, while beside her I felt like an alley cat, sly, scratchy and on the prowl. My body was like an alley cat's, too, for while Silas had touched me I had thought only of Rowle . . . hadn't I? I was thin, restless and held so tight as if readying myself to pounce, reckless, wanton. I could not have responded to Silas at all – it must have been Rowle I imagined inside me, Rowle's eyes on me.

Lucy lit a fire in my upstairs chamber. She often sat with me and I used to ask her, whenever I could, about Rowle. Now I spoke of Silas. 'That man is a bully, a drunkard and a womaniser and I don't like him near me. I don't want to see him again.'

'You can't play with a man like Silas and expect to get away with it completely.' I was surprised to hear that Lucy knew. She knew about Christmas but not of today.

'He's an animal.'

'He is a good man and wise. He's seen life – too much of life – you must make allowances.'

'And do you make allowances for everyone then, Lucy, no matter what they do?'

'I try to.'

'So did you make allowances for Jessie?' I knew she was angry with me for helping Jessie to escape. She was the only one who knew my part in it. My friend's going had caused a great deal of trouble: Caleb wanted her back, Biddie Canter took up arms again, turned on Phineus and brought the matter up in the women's council. 'How can any of uz be safe,' she asked with a baby on her back and another under her arm. 'How can uz live uz lives when there's whores like that about. Let 'er go. 'Tis best 'er's gone an' any other behavin' so wantonly like 'er should be drummed from the Combe also.'

Sadly, Jessie's going had started the whole seething nest up, stinging again. And I raged at them, marvelling at their lack of understanding, or at the pretence of it. Apart from feeling the sharp edge of Biddie's tongue, Phineus had got away with it lightly.

Now Lucy told me patiently, 'It's up to the women to set an example. Men will be men, but we must not pander to their lusts. Trust – that's all we have to base our lives on, and if we can't trust each other then we have no safe place to start from.'

I couldn't look at her. But I argued, 'Just one mistake and . . .'

'No, not one mistake, Bethany. Jessie has done this several times since she came to the Combe.'

'She's only my age. She can't have . . .'

'Age has nothing to do with it. Jessie started young.'

'Jessie had no alternative! Jessie's life outside the Combe was all to do with existence, she had to use everything she had merely to survive.'

I couldn't argue peacefully like Lucy did. She stayed calm while I was hot and flustered. She won the argument by staying placid and reasonable while I became more and more excited and silly.

'I know that. I understand that. And Jessie was given time to adjust, but she didn't, or couldn't. And there comes a time when we cannot be accepting any longer and someone has to take action. Biddie Canter was driven to do what she did. It was cruel; it was unnecessary. And after that, Rowle took action by giving Jessie to Caleb. That, we hoped, would settle the matter. But Jessie has taken things into her own hands again – with your help, Bethany. And let's hope the situation will settle down again now and eventually be forgotten.'

'I will never forget her.'

I looked at the stars outside my window and I thought about Jessie. I wondered if she was lonely, too.

Round the house I went quiet and dejected, deliberately making the most of my pallor to catch the attention of Rowle. I wasn't a wild, stubborn creature any more. Look at me! Look! I am helpless and vulnerable, worthy of your love and protection, just like Lucy! Look!

I even made my voice more like Lucy's – soft. And I took care with my appearance, brushing my hair a hundred times every morning and wearing the colours I knew suited me best . . . pearly creams and simple whites. These colours, I believed, disguised the black and made me look innocent. Wide-eyed and appealing.

I used my illness, my love for poor Jessie, to catch him, Brother Niall. I had no shame, no other ambition. He was my all, my every waking thought, and he teetered on the edge of every fevered dream.

Rowle's attitude to my new gentle ways was hard to interpret. We rarely spoke if left in a room together. Immediately, then, the air in that room grew tense, the silence in it hissed, my heart pumped and I know that my face went a violent red. I was most careful to avoid his eyes in that situation.

But I watched him. All the time I watched him. And when he tried to meet my stares I turned away. But I made sure he knew that I watched him. And I knew he must have known.

If we had to talk we were most polite, in a way we had not been before. In company he joked with me, more than was necessary. Everything he said was a joke, with a laugh, an uncomfortable laugh at the end of it. But every single incident, every remark, every time he brushed past me or caught my glance, every one of these things I took as a glittering gift, wrapped it up in my heart and took away with me. Out of the mildest, most meaningless insignificances came the most extraordinary fantasies. It was almost as if he might not have been there, for I was making everything up. It didn't matter that we hardly ever spoke; Rowle's messages to me didn't need words.

Awful? Shameful? Wicked? And in this way my obsession grew and grew until it was fiercer and hotter than any of these fires burning out there in the Combe.

When they brought Jessie back Caleb cried. I didn't cry: I felt nothing.

'She was killed,' Lucy told me, 'for the money she carried – she had fifty pounds in her purse. It was the money that killed her.'

Lucy knew it was I who had handed Jessie that stolen purse, not knowing what money was, anything of its value or what men did to get it. I had never owned money in my life. It was through my ignorance that Jessie had been cudgelled and left to die, broken and alone, in a bleak alley down by the river among the filth and rats of some unknown town.

They brought her back and gave her a burial. I didn't go to watch them put her in the earth, but Lucy did. All the women went – all those women who had called her names and scorned her. Some of them sobbed when they came away – with guilt, I supposed.

And Lucy looked at me so pained and sad, with such a question in her eyes but I looked away, monk, for I didn't know what I was most guilty of. I didn't know right and I didn't know wrong.

But I know what love does.

21

We recover from most things, I suppose, since our own life is always so much more important than anyone else's. We recover and come nearer to the waterfall. Can you see it, Brother Niall? Can you hear it? It starts as a tiny moorland stream, gurgling happily between primrose banks, hurrying, swirling as it comes nearer, gathering speed and energy, sighing as if it knows where its destiny lies. It comes to the gorge and the thundering shadows. Jetting foam, swirling round all obstacles in its path, it suddenly reaches the precipice. And in the light of morning, in the dark of night, it fits to the black rock and slides down over into the dappled space between the birchwoods. Letting go. Flying. Dying. And the sun bursts bright upon it, lighting up the moss and liverwort beside the slide. And the moon casts magic lights on the water and makes the rocks sparkle as if they are not of this world.

And what is the point in living after that? How can the stream bear to go on? Larger now, that it has met with more water, contented now, no longer a silly, splashing child. But ponderous, slow, sensible and careful, its energy gone deeper. And its agony. Wiser perhaps, as it turns to a river and calms, except in the flood. But if I was that stream I would want to go back and back, back to the waterfall again, not contented to leave it behind, further and further and further behind.

After that . . . after that place and that experience I would not be interested in meeting the sea, in meeting death, no matter how many might be waiting for me there. No matter how calm that might make me.

Oh, take me back to the waterfall.

I lived my life breathlessly, as though always on the brink of some discovery. I didn't like being careful – I have never liked that. There was no moment when Dartmoor did not call to me. There is no moment on Dartmoor when the light is not changing. One minute gloomy and mysterious, the next, as the shadow moves over the ragged peaks of granite the whole earth blazes, the summits bathed in glorious light. And the sun chases the shadows over the hills and you want to run with them, over the rocks and bogs and pastures until darkness comes and leaves you with the sense of the hills. And you feel as small as that wreath of mist under the moon. That pale mist, the colour of eternity. But the day has been scorched on your soul.

I wanted to ride on Dartmoor as I used to do. Always I knew when they were going, living in the house it was impossible not to know. For a start Lucy became very nervous. And there were always many more people about. The place throbbed with energy and a kind of expectant nervousness that wasn't usually there. So I knew the night. I was ready.

Lucy was with me in this, quite against her nature. And yet she encouraged me, knowing, I think, how much I needed the excitement. Hoping, I know now, that this would divert me, fulfil me, take away my need for Rowle. Maybe she thought it was all I required to calm me down. I was always with her. She cannot have failed to feel the turmoil inside me, the constant agitation.

I loved the horses and the stables so I was often round them. Hugh Northcote was the blacksmith. Some years ago an upset brazier caused by a bad-tempered horse had severely burned his legs, and although Silas had done all that he could to save it, finally, agonisingly, the leg had been sawn off. It was, I suppose, a tribute to Silas' skill that the blacksmith lived. Hugh stumped around on his wooden leg, a cheerful man, grateful for life, but sometimes, after a hard working day, the limb that was gone pained him so terribly he was forced to rest. And because Hugh Northcote was the man most likely not to ride, I had taken every opportunity to get to know Juno, his mare. A little wilful, with an easy stride and quick to respond to the slightest touch, she was a nice mare. A beautiful grey with dainty feet, full of easy power like a racehorse.

It was dark, with a storm brewing in the distance. There was controlled turmoil as the men mounted and met in the court, instructions already given and understood so there was no need for more talk. I kept to the edge, my back to the rest, adjusting my stirrups and pulling tight the girth so that no one glimpsed my face. I saw the light at Lucy's window and dreaded that she would betray me and suddenly call out. I glanced at Rowle but he was deep in conversation with Silas and Dicken. I felt very anxious, expecting to hear my name shouted at any moment to be followed by howls of laughter and impatient instructions to get back to the house. I held my breath, communicating only with Juno. 'Don't fail me,' I urged in my head. 'Keep calm. Stand still. Stay back.' She seemed to hear. She was not upset with her lighter rider.

We set off. We passed the watchman on the hill and he dipped his lantern and wished us luck. I kept my head well down, stayed in line, held the steady pace, the only one not knowing where we were headed. And if I had known it wouldn't have helped me for I didn't recognise this part of the moor, more westerly than ours.

All was quiet save for the squeaking of hooves and the breathing of the animals. The rain came and attacked us with hard, slanting arrows. Jacob Gifford cursed softly ahead of me, but we kept our heads down and rode on. Heavy clouds cruised overhead, and it felt as if we were moving like that – stealthily, unhurriedly yet determinedly.

We came near to the road and I recognised the high place called Gibbet Hill. We followed the route of the road north and then, at a wild and desolate spot where there seemed to be nothing to hide behind, we crossed it and immediately sank out of sight into the low curves of the land, tiny undulations in the ground, just high enough to accommodate horse and rider. We spread out. We kept our horses still. And we waited. There was communication between us, there in the silence, but it was unspoken.

There was great danger. I had been so eager to come, so bewildered by the smaller intrigues of it, so afraid that I wouldn't even get on a horse let alone beyond the court gate that this fact hadn't occurred to me. It did then! Every one of us was putting our life at risk. We could be shot – we could be caught. There might be an armed guard on the coach for which we waited. It kept us still – the danger. It kept us hidden and silent. It was with us as much as the darkness, as powerful and as intense. But most of all it kept us together as a band. As one. And I had never felt so close to Rowle before.

To hear the coach wheels, to see in the darkness a faint glimmer of light coming along the Tavistock road, was a relief. Any action would be a relief, for the tension was terrible. Yet nobody made a sound. There was no communication between us. I wondered if they had even seen the approaching light and wanted to tell them, just in case. I fought the urge and kept silent. I felt that my life, that every life here, depended on my silence.

The coach rolled towards us like a great fat baby expecting nothing but love. It even had cheeks and a little snub nose and it fell about and staggered in the potholes but came on, its lights wavering crazily in the darkness. It grew larger and larger. More purposeful, somehow, and older and more confident. No baby now, but lean and adult and threatening. It was on us. It was passing. And only then I saw that Rowle and Silas had moved out with a light and were before it with guns in their hands. Rowle was mounted but Silas was down and had the door open, the coachman climbing down and the horses stopped all in a second – no, less than one second of time. And we were moving in from behind, like shadows. Juno went when the others went, bringing me out from my hiding place and turning me into an outlaw.

Did the people in the coach even know we were there?

There was no fight. From where I was I didn't even hear any words. No request for money was made. I thought I heard, once, a sob, from inside where the brightest lights were, but I could have been mistaken. And then I realised that it was raining hard and this was what made it all seem like a charade, a mime with mummers behind masks and me watching in my own pool of sound. Wet and bedraggled.

It was done. Silas handed three large leather pouches to Rowle. He had handles on his saddle to take them. I did hear those pouches slap the sides of his horse. But we never moved. We stayed like shadows behind the coach, like the threats that are always there in everyday life, unseen, but waiting for the unwary. Breathing there behind you. Of course the coachmen and passengers knew we were there. They didn't need to look round to see us.

No order was given but then we were off and away – afraid of a trap. Galloping headlong into the night, alone now, each one of us, and having to get home somehow. It was to do with speed and courage, for we rode into total blackness. I had never ridden as wildly, as madly as this before. All my skills were put to the test, my knowledge of the moor, my feel for a horse, my instinctive reactions and my courage.

But how to find the Combe? We were taking a different way home . . . they were gone into the rain, into the holes of the night while I plunged through my own like a wild rabbit, crying.

It was no good like this. I couldn't see or hear. Juno and I could ride on forever like this and get nowhere but exhausted. I pulled up the mare and stood for a moment, listening and sniffing. I walked her – I let her have her head. She broke, on her own, into a canter. She was going somewhere and I knew it would be towards oats and bed. She would be able to hear the others, to sense them when I could not.

It was the watchman's light that told me we had made it, and I have never seen a more welcome sight. My heart hammered, my breath came in bursts, I had imagined everything that could possibly happen to me had happened. I had been caught and tried, found guilty and hanged. I had jumped a ditch and broken my neck. I had led the constables to the others and betrayed them all. So that when I saw that lantern, stopped, listened and knew there was no one behind me I almost sobbed with relief, but remembered not to answer his greeting – just gave a manly nod and a shrug as I took Juno down the slope and into the court where the others were already there and dismounting.

I watched. Rowle unstrapped the pouches and made straight for the house. 'Take him, John . . .'

Silas followed, and Dicken, and Will. What should I do then? They believed I was Hugh. But then I saw that two others left together and made their way back to the Combe, so it was all right to go off. There was no formal meeting, no counting of heads, no discussions. It was done, as they did it on so many nights – without comment, without afterthought.

I left Juno at her stable door, trailing the reins round the bolt, then made to go from the court but doubled back afterwards and slipped in through the door unobserved. I went to my room, my heart still pounding, my legs all trembling, and I sat on my bed and put my head in my hands, trying to calm myself.

I wanted to talk about it! I wanted to shout and dance and sing and glory in the frenzy of the exhilaration. I did not want to let it go, to slide out of me in sleep to be lost in the everyday dreariness of ordinary life. But there was nothing I could do but ditheringly remove my clothes –they were soaked with rain on the outside, with sweat on the inside. There was no one I could talk to, no one to tell, except Lucy, and she would be closeted with Rowle until morning.

So I had to let it go. There was nowhere to put it. And it felt just like love, Brother Niall – all that inside me with no way to come out. My powerlessness made the feelings explosive, and built them up into monsters inside me. They wouldn't go away. They could be pushed back, denied, but they would never go away.

It took me hours to sleep. I tossed and turned, came in and out of the wildest dreams which were peopled by Jessie and Maggie and Lizzie and Birdie. And then I was crying – but no, it was just the rain on my face. And Rowle. Oh yes, and Rowle.

For I had watched him carefully that night. And he had been magnificent. All the forces, all the power of the night, everything seemed to have come from him. And as I lay in my bed and worshipped, I wanted . . . I wanted . . . I passionately wanted to love.

22

I craved that excitement. I couldn't wait to go again – but I had to be careful.

'You look better,' said Lucy, 'as if some life has come back to you again. Danger suits you, Bethany, better than any of Silas' remedies. The very thought of it destroys me – but it suits you.'

'I'm going to do it again,' I said as I dressed Bessie and tried not to think about Silas and his remedies. 'And you won't say anything? You promise you won't tell Rowle?'

Lucy shook her head. 'Not if it means so much to you.'

I tried to nod naturally, not letting her see how much the danger I craved, and Rowle, went together, were one and the same. I couldn't do enough for Lucy these days. I was riddled with guilt because I felt that by aiding me in my schemes to ride with the men, I was asking her for Rowle, as well. And she was giving him, hopelessly fooled by the fox that was me, that licked its lips and watched her with such glittering eyes.

'Anyone else and I'd think you had found a lover,' she said, watching me back. 'You haven't been meeting somebody secretly, I suppose? You would tell me, wouldn't you. It would be so wonderful for me to know you were happy. Is it Silas? How I would love it to be Silas. I know how fond he is of you.'

I flinched at the sound of Silas' name and Bessie cried out. I must have pinched her, or held her wrongly. 'Oh my poor, poor Bessie,' I cried, making a great play of it while inside I ached in every limb. 'I'm sorry my pet, I'm so sorry.' And I held the pretty baby up and kissed her, pulled funny faces until I made her laugh, and Lucy also. 'How about a walk? Or shall we play in the sand? Or shall we watch Judd with his new falcon – see how far he can make him fly today?'

But I saw from Lucy's eyes that the question had not been forgotten, that I would be forced to answer. So I made a click with my tongue like Mary would and said, quite angrily, 'You know I would tell you, Lucy, but you also know that I am not interested in men. Some of us have better things to think about! Don't we little Bessie? Don't we?'

And Rowle's child gurgled happily on my knee.

*

The days must have slipped into weeks, the weeks into months, because time did go by – somehow. A slow and painful trickle of time with so many little barbs in it to torture me.

Don't think I was never happy, monk – I was – oh, I was! Even the miseries of loving Rowle made me happy. Does that make sense? No, not to a sensible person like you. Lucy wouldn't have understood. I don't suppose many people would understand. Looking back now it seems it was all plots and plans, and the more I plotted and enveigled myself to the right place at the right time the more trapped I seemed to become by my own cunning – trapped in my head with the loving of him. I had to be near him. I had to see him. Without that I felt bereft. Nonexistent.

I tried to talk to Mary but she wouldn't have it. She told me I was being pathetic and boring, dotty and silly and I knew she would never understand. I was doing nothing but harm to myself, she said. I should get on and lead my own life, keep busy, and then these feelings would go away. She wasn't a friend as Jessie had been a friend, and I thought to myself how lucky she was that she had never experienced life in the grip of such powerful obsession. I wondered how she'd react if it happened to her. And oh, I missed Jessie.

'Yos doan want to end up a woman like that!'

'A woman like what?'

She was going to say Jessie but she saw the look on my face and stopped herself. Instead she said, 'A woman who carn be trusted. A woman who carn find a man o' 'er own an' has to use somebody else's.'

'Nobody's getting hurt by it,' I said to her sullenly. She maddened me in the way she could not be moved. Her ideas were so resolute, dealing only in black and white.

'No – nobody's getting hurt *yet*. Only you! Going around pretending to Lucy – to Lucy – who has been nothin' but kindness itself to you . . .'

'I never asked her.'

'Bah! Get away from me. 'Tis like talking to a five year old child. 'Tis all a game wi' you, anyway. You'd run a mile if 'e

156

even looked at you seriously.'

'I love him,' I said, hoping to affect her by my direct simplicity, but I did not know what I meant by love and I did not know what I wanted from him.

'Love!' she sneered, too close to the truth for comfort. 'Doan make me laugh. You're not grown up yet. You knows nothing o' the meaning of the word! Just listen to yourself maid, just listen! You sound ridiculous!' For a moment I remembered how I watched him, sitting there, in the evenings by the fire, playing my secret and perilous games – yes, like Mary said, just like a child. I argued against myself, my own behaviour as well as Mary's ignorance.

With fury in my heart and what I hoped was cold dignity in my voice I said, 'Yes and one day he'll love me!'

Mary eyed me steadily. 'You're such a silly fool. When will you come to yous senses?'

'You forget. We have been close, Rowle and me.'

Mary laughed and maddened me further. 'Well, of course, if you're goin' ter count that!'

'And why wouldn't I?'

''Cos it means nothin' – that's why!' And Mary brought her face right close up to mine and I wanted to push it away, far away with both hands and close up her mouth and the things she was saying with my fingers. But she knew what I was thinking because, 'You're bad, bad, bad,' she said, turning back to her basket, the strands of which she bent and twisted with angry manipulations. 'Bad,' she said again, as if to plait the accusation into the shape of the willow.

And Rowle? Well, he knew of course by then. There was no way of him not knowing, with me going around with my eyes full of hungry, brooding intensity. He met those glances with amusement before looking away, and indifference – remote, when he wasn't being actively hostile. Sometimes a rush of commonsense would hit me, or a creep of primitive terror, and I would tell myself to stop, and convince myself that I could. But what would I have left, if I did as Mary bid and got rid of the feelings? I would be left with that sad, drab destiny – to marry and settle down. I couldn't have borne it!

'Heartbreak – torment – forever hankerin' after something you carn never have. Oh maid, that way lies disaster, carn you see that?' But I wouldn't listen to Mary, and she wouldn't listen to me, either. Still, there was one good thing about Mary, I could say anything to her and she would never be offended.

But something was going to happen. I knew, in the same sort of way that Lizzie would have known, that if I did nothing more, something would happen. And sometimes I even prayed, although I didn't believe and didn't even know who I prayed to: 'No, no. Please don't let it.' As if I, too, could see far into the future.

I took my spear down to the wide pool at the far end of the Combe to catch salmon. It was late afternoon, still hot, but autumn. Taking off my clogs I laid them carefully on one of the sleepy boulders, and safely away from prying eyes hitched up my skirt around my hips and rolled up my sleeves as I waded into the water. My hair was everywhere – it smelled of bracken and heather and lay around my shoulders like a luxurious shawl, a perfect black but for the taint-mark. Now I lifted it from my neck to let the cool air in. Everything was so still, so calm, and when I felt the sharp cold water biting round my ankles I remembered the summers of my childhood and wandered in the silver ripples, dazzled by the images of it.

I lifted the water in both hands, peering into it, trying to read sensations like the words of a book. I took it up over my head and let it pour down on me. Again and again, until I was like a child playing, soaking wet, the water streaming off me and clinging the material to my body so that I was slippery like the fishes and twisting, free. If only it was easy like that, if only I could just swim away. From everything.

Memory can play tricks. Was this a trick? Through the rainbows in my eyelashes I saw him then. Blurred, becoming distinct as I blinked away the brilliance and panicked, for I could have been naked there, so clinging were my clothes and my legs and thighs quite bare. But after the first shock I lifted my head and stared at him in the way he stared at me, letting my hands, the hand that had shot to my mouth, go loose to my sides, my ankles quite numb now with the freezing water that swirled around them. I am not ashamed, my stare was saying. This is me, who I am. You might not like this person, but I cannot change her.

For long, steady minutes his eyes never left me. We were

both quite still. Like animals who do not know each other, passing in a field. Way, way above him a hawk hovered, alone in the sky. All nature was in him, savage, merciless, beautiful, delightful and frightening. And there was secrecy in his being there. The knowledge of that was what caught my breath and made it impossible to swallow.

Rowle was half-smiling, but this time there was no mockery in his smile. Alone then – and Rowle was seldom alone. Too far away to speak, for if anything was said now it would have to be said softly. He was standing in a hollow in the upper slope among the brambles and gorse, the sun setting so fast now you could see it moving, see it tinging the lips of the Combe with purple before it moved fast away.

Then his smile disappeared, he turned and abruptly strode away.

My moment of exultation was as quick and as perfect as that sunset. Lights would quickly appear in the hovels but just then . . . that moment . . . that early dusk, the sun lit the lips of the Combe with purple, then crimson, and the day seemed to hush, awed by the premonition of night.

And just the lonely note of a nightjar broke into the stillness of the moor.

23

Twice more I rode with Rowle, and twice came home to safety. And only Lucy knew. Each time she said to me. 'You're tempting fate. Someone is going to find out.'

'How can they? Nobody looks at anyone else. Our minds are on what we're setting out to do. As soon as I see Hugh's wooden leg hanging on the front of the stable door instead of the harness, I change them round before anyone else can notice. Hugh is too engrossed with his pain, tucked up in bed with a bottle of rum, to explain to the others. No, I feel quite confident. I'm no more likely to be discovered the third time than I was the first time.'

This time the weather was cold and it was much darker as we stamped our feet and blew on our fingers, waiting for the horses with our backs rounded, cramped by the cold. We were impatient to leave so that we could get warm. As I was never present at the meetings held beforehand, I never knew our destination, and this meant I had to stay closely behind the next rider. Still, by now at least I could find my own way home. Tonight we skirted Amicombe, riding hard and fast across the moor to reach the Exeter road. I saw the lights of home burning there in the distance and felt an ache inside, hard and screwed up like a fist, knowing they were Mallin's lights. And I thought, as I rode, my teeth clenched and my eyes watering cold across my face, how wonderful it would be to pay a visit there to Mallin . . . I could take the sort of vengeance on him and his family that Rowle had wreaked on his own.

We stopped. Behind us Belstone Tor dominated the skyline. We were early, with time to kill. This had not happened before, and I froze as the men dismounted, tethered their horses and looked in my direction. I pulled my hood well down and appeared to slump on Juno as if I was dozing and happy to be left alone. They passed round a brandy gourd and I shook my head when they held it towards me. Two played five-stones and two kept watch, while Rowle took a stick and drew some map in the dirt and began discussing tactics with Silas. I became increasingly uneasy, wondering how long I could keep up my disguise, but they seemed uninterested, quite happy to ignore such an unsociable one of their number. I wondered how they could all stay so calm, given the nature of their exercise, but calm they were, exchanging jokes just as they would have at the table at home. The watchers were not relaxed, however. Not for a moment, I saw, did they cease to stare and listen out in the darkness.

We waited. It grew colder and somehow more silent. The cold seemed to creak my bones.

'Somebody comes.'

Ah! It was hardly whispered, yet heard and instantly acted upon. Three men took the horses and moved them to the clump of blackthorn while the others spread out and knelt down, their knives and swords at the ready. And me? I jumped off Juno, led her to the bushes and crouched down at her side, my face hidden in the warmth of her flanks, calmed by the rhythmic beat of her heart.

'Horses and pillions, using the bridle path.'

These were not the ones we waited for: it was not yet time. I felt instantly sorry for the travellers, for I knew there was no more uncomfortable way to travel than by pillion, and the bridle paths at this time of the year were a mess, full of puksey-holes and treacherous ruts so that the pillion rider would be bumped half to death. These travellers were already unfortunate enough, without coming across a group of savage highwaymen. Unknowing, they came nearer, until they were on us . . .

'Who are you? What do you want with us?' The man's voice was full of fear and surprise. A woman screamed, a metal sound in the cold. And then, 'We have nothing for you, we are poor men ourselves, travelling to Exeter for the fair to sell our pots.' His voice was gruff, his horses scruffy and ill-kept. A raggle-taggle bunch of wanderers they were, and his companions looked beaten and weary. The pots were the only respectable items present, being well-made and solid.

'The coach will soon be here,' Silas reminded Rowle, and his voice was sinister-quiet.

Dicken spoke with urgency, his movements sly as shadows. 'Put them round the back of the bushes, quick. We'll deal with them there.'

'Let us go peacefully on our way. We have seen nothing. We want no trouble.'

'That we cannot do . . .'

'Hush, Silas.' And Rowle stepped forward to look at the travelling party. Two horses were both dragging pillions on which rode two elderly, disreputable-looking women behind their gypsy men. And tied behind the lead horse was a mule almost obscured by pots of all shapes and sizes. Certainly what they said was true – they were poor and posed no threat. And yet they had seen us . . . they would be near enough to hear and to act when the robbery took place. And men would do anything for money. They would have to die. I knew they would have to die. They knew it. It was in their faces.

But Rowle said, 'Dooley?'

And the crone in the back pillion sat up – a horrible hag of some great age hard to pinpoint for the squash of her face and the hump she carried on her body.

'Dooley?'

The woman tried to hide her face. She gave no answer, and Silas was saying urgently, 'The coach comes . . . Look – far off there I can see it! Get them round into the bushes now.'

Dicken and Jacob moved forward, swords ready for action, and Garth pulled the horses.

'Let them go.'

'Rowle, we can't! We dare not take the risk.'

'I said let them go. And take your places.'

The spokesman for the travelling group could hardly believe his luck. A brutish-looking man with a broken nose and cauliflower ears, not a handsome thing about him, he walked his horse on, looking over his shoulder with his bloodshot eyes, expecting a trick. But there was none. For incredibly the Gubbins stood back and watched as the party moved out of sight, dragging their wares and their women behind them . . . bump, bump on the uneven ground.

Silas tried once more. 'Rowle, let me . . . there is still time . . .'

'Leave them – poor beggars.'

Astonished, Silas said, 'You knew that woman?'

'I knew her once, a very long time ago.'

'What is she to you? You must owe her some great debt.'

162

'We owe each other, but I don't know what. I only know we owe each other something.'

Silas shook his head. And Rowle looked up and seemed to shrug at the sky.

The robbery went smoothly as always, and we rode home. Who was the ugly old woman with such a strange look in her eyes? I could tell she meant much to Rowle. She'd looked at him, then looked away, and hidden her face, but I had seen her eyes. Did they hold doubt? Fear? Some hidden yearning for something that once, a very long time ago, had passed her by? It was impossible to tell. I dismissed her from my mind, for the evening was soon forgotten, reduced because of a tiny incident right at the end of it.

Back at the Combe, all was activity, bustle, with dogs barking, the sound of hooves on cobbles, voices, lanterns bouncing – without the aid of arms behind them, it seemed – steam from horses' backs and rain sheeting down, dropping off the roofs in fat splashes that in the dark looked solid as hailstones. I had left Juno and was creeping through the shadows to get to the door of the house so that I could go and change, get dry, get warm. I was not there yet. Not safe yet. I had the last, most dangerous yards to go. With my hood pulled well down over my head, scuttling, I bumped into the arm that was held out before me, blocking my path. I jumped, immediately lowering my head again and grunting some greeting but it was no good. The arm didn't move. Nor did the man who owned it.

So I stood there, watching the pool of water grow as the rain took me and my cloak for a target and used them to drip off. I daren't look up, so I kept looking down. And I would stay that way as long as necessary . . .

'Bethany, what are you looking for?' His voice was quiet – it came with the rain but soaked me through my clothing.

I swallowed, not able to answer, not knowing what the question meant. I still hoped he might let me pass.

'That's three times now you have ridden with us. Don't you think three is enough?'

Another question I couldn't answer. 'Lucy told you!'

Rowle shrugged. 'No, Lucy didn't tell me. Lucy didn't need to tell any of us.'

I felt so foolish, so full of humiliation. I had thought I had got away with it, had even congratulated myself on the cleverness of my cunning, on my disguise. 'Have you known all the time?'

He didn't bother to reply, just stood there still, blocking my way, and suddenly I felt angry and tried to push past but his arm did not give. So I lifted my head, my hood fell back and I glared at him, daring him to contradict me. 'I was as good as any of them.'

He raised his eyebrows. 'Yes, yes, certainly you were.'

'Then how did you know?'

'Don't be silly, Bethany. How could I not have known?'

All those conversations I had wildly imagined, all those wonderful things to say and here we were, alone at last, exchanging nothings. Guilty suddenly, I looked up at Lucy's window but the light was not on. She must have gone to bed, given up waiting. Ah – this could be taken away and added to my fantasy.

'What now then?' I asked him. 'I suppose you're going to stop me going again?'

'Yes. I'm going to stop you going again.'

'Why?'

'You know the answer to that.'

'Because it's too dangerous for a woman?'

'That's one of the reasons, yes.'

'And what do you care that my life might be in danger?'

Then he laughed. And I thought of kicking his shins, taking him by surprise so that I could pass by and take some dignity with me while there was still time. But I glanced at his face and changed my mind.

And then I knew – I knew what was going to happen. I'd imagined it often enough. He said nothing to answer my stupid question but, not touching me, not touching me at all, he bent his head down to mine and I felt his lips incredibly soft on my lips and I smelled the raw-leather smell of him. His hair was silver wet, the rain looked frosty on it. There was rain on my lashes, and tears. At last! At last! Me there, frenzied with stupid, misplaced delight. Hardly able to stand, my legs were trembling so. It lasted a long, long time, long enough for me to close my eyes, open them, close and open them again, and once more to glance towards Lucy's window.

That kiss. The kiss of death, Brother. It turned my world around.

24

I can hardly believe this is me – here – waiting in Lydford Gaol. I have to find another place to be, for I cannot bear this one. But I wanted to be a sacrifice, didn't I? I went like one, blazing all in white with my good intentions. I behaved like one. I asked to be one, didn't I?

'Serves you right then,' Maggie would say, her eyes blazing dark and furious. 'You brought it all on youssself.'

Jessie speaking, quiet and sad, 'Pull back while you still can.' Her dark hair swinging softly either side of her face.

And Rowle said, 'You want to ride with me? Come with me, then.' Was this a challenge? Was he testing me, his black eyes piercing like knives? Did he think I might not take him up on it? He handed me back my world of dreams, intensified. Of course I worshipped him.

I loved the man he saw himself to be – oh, I loved him through his own eyes and he loved me through mine, while Lucy saw us both as we really were. Lucy was the first to recognise the danger of two such child-like people loving.

All those voices. I push my hands to my ears to block them out, nursing my head. What's the point of going back over it all? It's not going to help me when they come for me tomorrow. Knowing isn't going to make the pain go away, knowing isn't going to dilute the horror.

And if Rowle doesn't reach me in time?

I WANT TO KNOW THIS – I WANT TO KNOW HOW MUCH IT IS GOING TO HURT. And how long it is going to take. *Please, please somebody tell me.*

The voices come together and seem to make a song.

NO! No lullabies. I'll have to bang my head against the wall if that song comes again. I can't allow it now – not in this place. I can think of Maggie, Lizzie and Birdie and bear it. I can think of Jessie. And I can think of Rowle. Isn't that enough for you, God, or whoever You are? Isn't that enough? Penance is it now? Are you making me pay? Isn't the threat of death enough? There is one whom I cannot think of and never will. Ever! Not even tomorrow. Not even on the point of death. GO AWAY, LITTLE ROWAN, GO AWAY. This is no place for a child and I am no mother.

I waited for his words with a kind of breathless suspense. My world depended on them.

Two long months went by, an eternity of yearning looks and awful anticipation. And then he said, 'You want to ride with me? Come with me, then.'

Did Rowle say that? Or am I making it up? For from that moment on we were make-believe people in the make-believe world of our own creation that we both so desperately wanted. Confusion – I don't know, he said something like that, but the point is that I went with him, didn't hesitate or pause to think – I went.

And Lucy knew. Of course she knew. Although I went round pretending she didn't.

It had been a March of menacing cold. Rowle and the men had spent long days hunting, had come home surly and tired. They chased stag and wild boar through the forest. Rowle came home once all covered with blood and Silas said he had killed a wolf with his bare hands. 'We hardly see you,' said Lucy, tending the ugly gashes and wounds. 'We rarely see you, sometimes, it seems, for days on end.'

And when spring finally unlocked the frozen earth, there were weeks and weeks of rain. There were sullen, brooding skies, and we all huddled indoors, restlessly, listening to the water rushing over the land. I helped Lucy beat out the rugs, flinging them out of the window, sprinkling them with sweet herbs, and ridding the house of its winter smell of damp. But now the whole earth smiled again. The hawthorns blossomed. The dew started sparkling on the dawns, taking the place of the hoar frosts.

'Open the shutters,' ordered Lucy. 'Let it flood in.' And from that time on, just as it had done at Amicombe, the oak door of the house stood open.

Early spring. The spring that Mary stopped looking into my eyes. The spring that I said to Lucy, 'I wish I had breasts like yours, legs like yours, a face like yours.' Smooth, silken and maternally tender.

I pressed my hands hard on my tummy and drew it in, looked sideways at Lucy as I brought them to my own small breasts. We dressed together by the fire each morning, and we dressed the children. Judd was playing with his top – over- excited he spun it too hard and it leapt off the floor and stung Daisy's mouth. She flew at him, a whirling small bundle of fury. But Judd tickled her until all the angry tears turned into laughter. Lucy, who never liked their rough play, who always showed concern and drew back from it, Lucy smiled, too, especially when Matt, sensing his mother's unease, went to her and put his arms round her neck. He twined his hands in her long, golden hair.

As soon as she could, Lucy liked to deck the house with spring greenery. She looked a picture like that, shadowed by green, standing naked before the fire with a bare-legged boy in her arms. I looked at Lucy, she looked at me, and I knew that Rowle's hands had touched her and soon I, too, would know the feel of them again. His answering eyes those days promised me that. Who would he prefer? How did he love her? In what way did he love her? Was I going to be good enough for him? Was I seductive? Was I cleverer?

No, I was not. I was a fool.

Everything was bursting, new. I had no mind now, no mind of my own. I ate ravenously, drank the new May wine, slept profoundly, and became saturated in every sensation about me. I drowned in it all. Another cycle of life was beginning when I went with Rowle to the waterfall.

Sodden, damp, dripping, fleshy, all of it. And me, clumsy with all the freshness, moistly languid with it, reeking of it. I think I even smelt damp, like the earth, I was so close to it. Wild flowers – long grass – water lapping – me.

And Rowle.

How can I tell you? Yes, he did everything well. What they said of him was true, and he was one of the best horsemen in England so it felt good to be riding behind him, faster and faster, tasting all that air, the delicious tang in it. He said he knew a place and that I would like it there. And oh yes, I certainly did.

'Keep your wits about you, hang on for dear life. He goes like the Devil once he is given his head.' And I did hang on. I was definitely not going to let go now. And then Rowle shouted, 'It won't be long!'

Bands of sunlight lit the greeny-air as we walked down to the water, hand in hand to the water deep down in the gorge. Thick undergrowth wet my legs and my skirt slapped as I went, following slavishly. One of the obsessed, like you might call one of the drunks, or one of the sleepwalkers, or one of the opium addicts, people who cannot help themselves – well, I went like one of the obsessed. It might have been distressing, even, to an observer, to see one quite so pitiful. But I went ecstatically. Poised somewhere between bliss and agony, tilted alarmingly now and again towards each extreme by merely a look or a tone of voice.

Down and down we went towards the silvery ribbon of water which showed as we neared it between all the green. And the steep cliffs were higher than we could stretch to see: it was Rowle's world – a magic world of emerald fronds, padded as if a million trailing sheep's tails hung from the rocks obscuring almost all the sky, damp with the moisture of silver. I laughed when a bird taking flight skittered out over the water.

An omen?

I let go his hand and ran to sit on the wide, smooth rock at the foot of the fall – posing, of course, for Rowle. Knowing I would look pretty there. Choosing the backcloth for myself and assuming a relaxed kind of posture which might deny the screaming tensions inside me. Was he taken in? I felt him come close and stand behind me. I felt him touch my hair and then he said, 'A stream of white water. My own white lady.'

Yours, Rowle? And were you mine, then?

It was warm for spring. The sun steamed off the rock. This time I undressed for him and he watched me with his eyes narrowed against the rays of dim green light, against the heady scents of the place. What did I look like, shivering there on the brink, staring across the distance of sex? I watched his eyes. I saw them glitter, in love with love and with my slim nakedness, and delicious. I was young and alive and beautiful. Not so curvy, not so graceful as Lucy, but beautiful. Oh yes, I knew I was beautiful. None of the nature around me, none of it, could compare with mine just then. I let my hands run over my body, in love with it as he was, and my hands were cold like the water caressing the smooth, bewitching shapes of the rocks it had moulded.

And as he stared I became more and more confident . . . no

longer shyly modest, even coy. I enjoyed standing there in front of him, I relished my nakedness, concealing nothing from his eyes. Wasn't this, after all, what I had been longing to do? We were both, Rowle and me, discovering beauty. Wherever he watched me his eyes made me beautiful.

I drew in my ribs, rose on my toes and lifted my hair – for Rowle. The admiration in his eyes made me flow like that, dancing erotically like that as if I'd done it a hundred times under the silks of a sultan's tent, and liquid soft as honey. I lifted my breasts, exulting in the softness of them, raised my arms above my head and swept my hair upwards.

'Yes,' he said to me. 'Yes, you are beautiful. More beautiful than any woman I have ever seen.' And still he stood, staring at me. Wanting more.

I was utterly, completely alive. When his hands replaced mine I could hardly tell. They moved down my body leaving welts of fire behind them. And when he was naked I knew it by the crisp feel between my fingers of the curly black hairs on his chest. I slid my hands round him and felt the subtle movement of muscles on his back. His breath was warm on my lips and fragrant, of rain. He drew me close. He swept my hair in his hands and put his lips where it had been. And wherever his lips went he made that into a secretive place.

His eyes were dark and large, full of strange tenderness. His body was lean and glistening bronze, tuned like a cheetah's, a very fine animal flexed for the race. I could still see, still hear the waterfall. And I knew he was guiding me, all the yearning in me, down one narrow path that could only end in falling . . . down and away into nothing, helpless and fluid as the water. Mindless as the water. All sensation.

I wanted to go with him.

He whispered, as he stroked me, as he guided me down, 'Are you afraid?'

'Why would I be?'

'You should be – a little – it's better.'

'It's happened before.'

'No, not like this.'

'I love you, Rowle.'

He smiled and I saw the sheen across the whiteness of his teeth, the texture of his skin as it moved on his face, the way his eyes changed, became brooding.

'Passion, maybe, but not love, little Bethany. A long way away from love.'

What was he saying? And suddenly I was afraid and tried to push away from him. He would destroy me, tear my body and break me. I couldn't let him do that, I had to stop him. But I was spread on the rock beside him and the sky was green and coming down, beating on the stone and driving me on to what seemed like unbearable sensations, sensations I could not control. Like earth in a storm I was swamped by a raging of natural forces, and on he went, touching me, stroking me, but where would this end? I feared annihilation. I would be lost, surely, and never find myself again. I clung to him. I tore at his back with my nails.

I felt and knew real terror then, but it was full of such sweet taste. He lowered himself upon me. The rock was cold and hard to my back as I lay wide open and under him. Rowle's mouth was on my mouth, setting me on fire. One of his hands was on my breast, the other he glided down, under me, tracing the roundness, feeling his way, and then his hand was under and round my waist, improving his hold on me, pulling me to him. And I was brushed by the man I needed so badly, threatening me, making me gasp with sensations. I was seething, rushing with pure desire, widespread and waiting. His back flexed under my nails. He lifted himself, went down deep into the depths of my body, and when I screamed out he bit my mouth.

If only he would let me catch my breath. If only he would have some pity. I received him as if I were receiving a god. I worshipped him with the moans of a lover because, Brother Niall, he was my God to me.

And then I was lost in a pleasure so exquisite, so shattering, that I lost sense of time and reality.

Later, a million years later, I lay still and had to swim back to the green sky to find reality again. Surprised, I opened my eyes to find him still there, lying on his side and smiling. All the dangers were gone. There was just gentle luxury left all around me.

'I was frightened,' I said, lifting a heavy arm, still trembling, playing with his damp curls. 'For a moment I was frightened.'

'This is a very safe place,' he said. 'It's a good place for love.'

And I, who wasn't meaning the place, said, 'It's our place now.'

He didn't deny it and so I thought he agreed with me. I saw him as a warrior with stern, black brows and hands that were capable of anything. Well, look how they had transported me! I drew one of his hands towards me now, opened it and stroked it. I touched his clothing, too, admiring the velvet of his britches, the soft lambswool of his leggings. I thought he felt as I did. Something nagged at me, telling me that he didn't, but I wouldn't let that in, not here in this perfect place. It was not possible that passion like ours could be sullied, could be wanting. My vanity was enormous. I had made this happen, therefore I could make anything happen just by willing it.

I buttoned my bodice. Rowle watched me dressing with knowing in his eyes. 'Not for long,' he said. 'I won't have you hide your loveliness away from me for long.'

I helped him with his boots and we laughed when he stumbled and fell. I tried to haul him up but he brought me down with him.

Of course it was perfect. It had to be perfect. It was my dream, my fantasy all come true. But things are never quite as you think they are, are they? Even then, even then I think I can remember shivering in that queer green twilight, before we left the gorge and went back to the Combe.

And the horseman sat still in the distance. Darkly silhouetted against a moorland sky. From this far away I could tell it was Silas, and I knew that he must have recognised Rowle and I.

25

I lived for those times.

All that spring and summer we went to the gorge together, sometimes at night when the others were asleep. Then we left the horses behind and walked there together, talking softly into the darkness, I holding his safe, warm hand and walking beside his shadow.

It was incredible – the gorge – in moonlight, making love in the moonlight. Sometimes, on hot nights, we lay in the shallow water below the fall and I felt we were the only ones on earth.

Rowle said he didn't bother with everyday things. He chose to lead his life this way, he told me, without ties, possessions, commitments . . . even emotions.

'I need such energy to live my life that small insignificances would weaken it. I've rid my life of inconsequentials: I have to tell you that.'

So what of Lucy? What of his house and his children? What of the clan which always meant so much to him . . . I didn't ask him questions. I was quite happy to believe him and listen. But I, I used my life in search of happiness.

'Happiness,' Rowle said dourly, 'there is no such thing.'

And yet many times in those days I saw him enchanted, laughing with his head back and his eyes sparkling, on fire like a child's. There were times . . . Who else knew? Everyone knew. But we crept out, pretending, just the same.

We talked. He told me me of Amberry, of Charles and Gideon and Catherine – of Dooley, his childhood, his school and how he had first met Lucy. I loved to listen, proud that he had chosen me to tell. I believed he told me some things he had never told Lucy, and like a fool I smiled to myself in the darkness.

And I told him of Amicombe, but it was just like telling a story, a way of joining with him like our love-making was and every bit as important. You had to trust to talk the way we did. Sometimes I knew what he was going to say before he said it.

And he was like Jessie in some ways – never blaming, never critical, and so sad sometimes. Yes, he denied there was such a state as happiness, but I watched him laughing there in the moonlight as we chased each other in the water, covered with silver, and I believed that he was happy then. With me. Only with me.

We talked of most things – things I had never thought it possible to speak about. But of love he would not speak, nor of the other women he had had in his life. These were his taboo subjects. I tried to trick him but he would not be tricked.

'I don't know why you are afraid to tell me,' I said to him as we lay in the spray of the fall. 'It must mean you don't trust me. All this,' and I spread my arms over my head, 'we have all this. We share all this and yet you don't trust me.'

And yet all the time I whispered my lies about Amicombe. I told him that I was a special child, the daughter of a Lord. 'He loved my mother, Ruthy,' I said. 'He loved her and promised to come for her and take her away one day. But he was killed in the wars and never came back, and Ruthy died from the heartbreak.'

I lied, but I did not know that I was lying. The truth, meanwhile, flitted away like a moth to a shadow – easy and silky with fluttering wings. It was so much better to tell it that way, so far from the stark reality. A whole world away from the rather drab truth of my birth.

'My mother was so beautiful, so graceful and so alluring that the Lord promised he would marry her,' I said to Rowle, believing it all myself. 'And when he knew I was expected he sent round silks and satins and a cradle crusted with seed pearls. He said he'd come back and fetch us, my mother and I, when he returned, all glorious, from the wars.

'He never returned, and my mother died with me in her arms, her tears for the noble life that eluded me falling warm and soft on my face. They were so much in love. But I was always considered to be a most special child, and treated with respect by the rest of my family. They didn't make me work like they did. They did their best for me, fashioned me toys and dolls, told me stories, played games with me. I was never alone, oh no, they always saw to that. They chose me a special pony – Amos, my grandfather, trained it. He wanted to make quite sure that the horse I rode would be perfectly safe, that we would never be in danger, me and that rowan pony. He taught her the most dainty ways,' I told Rowle. 'Amos was skilful like that. And she always had the most perfect manners.'

We lay naked together as we talked, and if we felt cold we moved closer into each other's arms. While I was telling him tales of my childhood he began to explain about his. And I should have listened harder then . . . should have heeded Silas' warnings, should have used all my commonsense. It was all there, laid out before me . . . the reasons why he would never leave Lucy, the reasons why he found it so hard to love. But to understand Rowle was to go into a very different world from the one I was used to, so different that it was always hard for me to picture, although I made him tell it again and again in a desperate effort to understand.

Amberry was not five miles from my home. I could have known Rowle much earlier – we could have had more than our seven years.

I would not have been allowed past the gates.

Amberry, Sir Anthony Rowle's house, was built in the shape of an E to flatter Elizabeth. It was erected on land purloined from the monastery that his father had bought from the King. Anthony's father knocked the old monastery down and then he died. His Catholic enemies went about saying it was an omen, a punishment. Then there was a time of laying low during Mary Tudor's short reign, and Anthony Rowle, having gathered the materials together and kept them in store, started on his house the day Elizabeth was crowned.

When building work was under way, he left the house in the safe hands of the master masons and carpenters and sailed away to Africa, to fetch slaves to the Spanish colonies in the West Indies. He sailed away, leaving his young wife, Catherine, pregnant, with the house going up grandly around her. He sailed away with royal backing, to make his fortune. And drowned.

When Rowle was born there was just one wing constructed and furnished – the middle section of the E and the long windy gallery which, eventually, would connect to the others.

I don't know how Lady Catherine took the news of her husband's premature demise, neither does Rowle. Was she heartbroken, she with her tiny son growing inside her? Were they in love, this couple who seemed to me to have been given so much, or had it been, as so many were, a marriage of convenience? A giddy, pretty woman, Catherine was given to spending long hours before her mirror applying ground alabaster to her high, smooth forehead and glazing her cheeks with the whites of eggs. But there must have been more to her than that – nobody is as empty as Rowle made her out to be. She liked hunting and riding and playing bowls, she liked acting and eating and dancing. She liked, it appeared, to live gaily, to entertain and to flirt. She never spoke of her husband's death to Rowle, who had little to do with his mother.

'She smelled of marjoram and nutmeg,' seemed to be his strongest memory of her. 'And her hair was bleached almost white. She wore long blue feathers in it and when she walked she seemed to move without the aid of such basic essentials as feet.'

But she was extremely rich, sufficiently wealthy to have the Queen call on two occasions to take part in the good hunting nearby . . . and that cost money – four hundred pounds for four days, it was rumoured. She could provide the Queen with gardens to walk in – terraces and lawns and a miniature maze, sundials, fountains and a bowling green –and a dignified entrance beside which rampant heraldic beasts kept guard. For the Queen she made available a special suite – a wooden panelled bedchamber with a withdrawing chamber next door where her servant slept on a truckle bed, and beside which was conveniently situated one of the five close-stools which the house boasted, covered with velvet over a pewter pan.

In Catherine's world they ate off silver plate downstairs in the great hall. But that world did not extend to the nursery, where Rowle ate with his fingers.

So wealthy and so well-connected was Catherine Rowle that she provided too much in way of temptation for Anthony's feckless and unworthy brother, Gideon. It was thought right and proper that the young widow should remarry, that the lands and estates should be kept in the family. Even so, eyebrows were raised over the prudence of such a match. After all, there were other brothers, and Gideon had a long reputation, outrageous for such a young man, as a gambler and whoremonger – these were just some of the traits one could speak of. But Catherine, it seemed, had little choice in the matter. She married Sir Gideon Rowle, her husband's brother, just one year after Rowle was born.

So this was the world Rowle should have inherited . . . had not Gideon Rowle's new wife borne him a son of his own. The rooms Rowle lived in had mouldings in gold picked out on the ceiling. The walls were warmed with tapestries. Rowle's world was richly beautiful.

But now Rowle had a stepbrother just two years younger.

Rowle's world was lonely.

Rowle's world was dangerous.

Rowle's world became one, long nightmare of brutality. He never, in the whole of his childhood, knew love.

'My first memories are all of that chimney,' he said to me. 'There was an enormously wide chimney in the nursery and whenever I was left I was sat on a chair by Dooley and told to watch it. "And if you move," she'd say from the door, "they'll come down that chimney, all those monsters you dream about in your sleep at night, they'll come down that chimney to get you. They're just waiting for you to move!" So I sat for hours, straight-backed, eyes staring at the dark hole. I can never remember a fire being lit in it. And I sat and I waited like that until Dooley came back.'

I thought of him sitting there cold and frightened. 'Couldn't you have told anyone? Were there no servants who cared, and couldn't you have told your mother?'

When I asked Rowle that it was at the beginning, when I didn't fully appreciate what was going on. No wonder he smiled at me.

'They went in fear of Gideon,' he answered. 'So did she. They wouldn't have dared to speak to me and I knew that. But at that stage I didn't know why. I didn't even realise there was anything wrong. You accept,' Rowle told me, looking resigned. 'You accept what you have when you are a child. I didn't realise anything was strange until I grew older and noticed the different treatment Charles received at the hands of everyone in that house. When I asked them they said that was because Charles was a good, sweet boy while I was surly and rude. 'Who could love you?" said Dooley to me, with that look of disgust that was never far from her face. "Look at you! Look at Charles! That's right, next time you see him you take a good

177

look and you'll see for yourself. You're clever enough! Oh yes, too clever." And I looked and I thought I knew what they meant.

'I was told I was bad from the beginning. You believe what they tell you, and you become what they tell you you are. I was rude and surly, sly and cruel. My thought were bad thoughts. I could feel the hatred inside me, it grew as I grew, like that scar on your pretty hand, Bethy. I had no other examples to follow. How else could I possibly have been?'

'You find it hard to trust anyone, Rowle. Is that why it's difficult for you to speak to me about Lucy?'

'There are some things you can never trust anyone with. You have to keep them inside yourself. They are too tender, too vulnerable to be put into words. You devalue them if you speak of them.'

'When you speak to me of Lucy you devalue her?'

He put a wet arm round my shoulder. I stiffened. 'Stop it, Bethany. You know that's not what I mean.'

'But Rowle, what are we going to do?'

He stared at me strangely. The moonlight made beads in his eyes. 'What do you mean, do? Haven't we got enough?'

'How can we make it so that we are together always? I can't live in your house forever pretending I am your children's nurse!'

He was silent. I watched his hand make patterns in the water, swirling patterns with holes inside and I knew there was a hole in what we were talking about. A hole that I might fall into. A hole that was full of dark places.

'Isn't this enough? Must you have more?'

'Yes, yes, yes, More! Is that wrong? To want more of you . . . more and more and more. How can I help wanting more?'

'All of me? Is that what you want? All of me?' He was staring at me in a way that made me feel uneasy. His face was dark, his curls wet and tight to his head. His mouth was a firm line and he did not move. He was marbled in moonlight, marble-still, like a statue.

'Yes, I want all of you.'

'You can never own anyone else. I find it sad, strange that you want to.'

'I love you.' I thought that might explain it. But he turned on me then and gripped my wrist so savagely that it hurt and I tried to shake away.

'Love!' he sneered, and his laugh was cruel. An owl screeched having snatched its prey and a cool night wind whispered through the gorge.

His voice cut sharp. 'You! A child of the moor. Brought up to be wild and yet you speak with all the smallness of a worm who has always lived blind and in silence. That you can say these things, Beth, it amazes me! Is this need to possess and destroy inside all women? You squeeze and you squeeze until you drain all energy, all passion out!' And it suddenly seemed as if he wasn't speaking to me any more, that he had forgotten I was there.

I spoke quietly, frightened of his anger. 'And yet you took me against my will. Possession – it is a trait of men, not women.'

'You think you can possess a woman by taking her body?'

'No, but Rowle I think that's what you believe. What men believe.'

'You haven't begun to understand what I believe.' His voice was full of quiet contempt.

'Tell me then, Rowle!' I almost screamed. 'Tell me what you believe!' I turned on him like a wild cat then, wanting to scratch and claw for something he would not give me. I couldn't let it go.

But the magic was gone from the night, and the jealousy that had formed inside me so many months ago began to grow. The seed of it was inside me, poisonous and vicious. Because I did want him – all of him. And I couldn't bear to share him.

Jealousy, it feels like insanity and you can't see past it. Once it was there I could not get it out. Oh, if only there were a way of uprooting it before it gets a hold and claws and clings like ivy, clutches the heart and twists and burns. If only I could have gone to Dancy with it as I would with an unwanted baby – and Lizzie could have done it, I'm sure, killed it with the yarbs. I could have wrapped it in leaves, packed it up and burnt it, mourned for it, maybe, such a little scrap of nothing – it and its yelling right to be born.

Nothing has a right to be born. I had seen monsters come into the world at Amicombe, monsters just like jealousy, and Amos had dealt with them while we averted our eyes. These were things we never spoke of, like two-headed calves and lambs with five legs and no tails.

And we walked in silence up the gorge, following the river to a deeper black until our silence was filled by a dark, wet roaring. Water thundered in shadows. Sight and sound and feeling – all our soft splashings – churned and turned into a fearful, threatening roar. I felt safe here only because I was with Rowle.

That's when he first said, 'The time is wrong for us.'

I hardly heard him, but I answered, shouting above the roar on a moan of terror, 'But when will the time be right, Rowle? When will there be a time?'

And he turned and kissed my tears. Which wasn't any sort of an answer, Brother Niall. Was it?

26

And so we met, secretly, and time passed by, measured for me by our meetings. The only time I lived without doubt was when Rowle was making love to me. I was blinded by those timeless moments. The gaps between them seemed like years, the times we were together passed fleeting as seconds – gone before I knew it. So I looked back a great deal, on our last meeting, on the last words he had spoken, trying, all the time, to make them into something more, trying to give them my own meaning and to take his right away.

I encouraged Rowle to tell me about himself. If I knew him I could understand him: if I understood him I thought that I could make him mine. But I did not like the stories I heard. Rowle was my hero . . . my god . . . and it made me uncomfortable to picture him as a vulnerable, frightened child.

Despite the deliberately harsh treatment, Rowle survived. And it was only survival, it wasn't a life.

Other children were born, but they seemed unimportant – it was only Charles who grew up to be the thorn in Rowle's side. It was because of Charles that he was treated so badly. Gideon wanted his son to inherit, and Catherine Rowle didn't appear to care either way.

When Rowle spoke of his childhood his eyes, always black, went blacker, and his forehead furrowed darkly. I never knew how to respond. But then I think he didn't want a response, just needed to tell it to someone who wouldn't show shock, or sympathy, or any of the weaker emotions that Rowle considered so enfeebling.

And over all the horror of it loomed the monstrous figure of Dooley his nurse. 'I can't imagine where they could have got such a creature from. I've never met anyone remotely like her, before or since. She had a hump, but no, that had nothing to do with it. Dooley was a mixture of a man and a woman . . . huge and dark and hairy and she always dressed in black. She was my gaoler, never my nurse. I can hardly explain to anyone else how dark Dooley was to me. And how terrified of her I was. She made up my whole world . . . I was rarely without her. Sometimes, if it was cold, she made me sleep at the end of her bed so she could warm her feet on my back. I had to lie there naked so that she could place her feet on me. They felt like two blocks of freezing iron, and I lay there shivering and shaking, never daring to move, until I guessed she was asleep.'

I tried to picture how it must have been in that draughty room high up on the top floor of Amberry. Dooley in her high, brown bed draped in heavily embroidered coverlets, Rowle in the little truckle by the side. It was an ornate room, apparently, with nothing lacking in it other than warmth or love. The other children shared a separate nursery, grew up together. Their childhood, as far as I could make out, seemed to be normal.

'When orders came from downstairs I was starved, sometimes for a week, but never longer. My stepfather had friends in important circles, and it would not have been seemly or prudent for my death to result from such obvious causes. At those times without food I used to hallucinate: I could fly higher than any bird, move to great depths in the sea. I was ten-limbed, five-eyed,' Rowle laughed. How could he laugh over something like that? 'No, I'm not mad. You wouldn't believe what the lack of food can do to you up here,' and he tapped my head.

It was hard to picture the Rowle that I knew being so small, so totally helpless. He told me, 'Sometimes, for days on end, I was not allowed out of bed. At the age of four or five, the hours pass slowly when you've nothing to do, nothing to watch. Dooley would sit in the nursing chair knitting, sewing, humming, grumbling. Rocking. And I tried to sleep, for there was more going on in my head than there was outside it. Always more in my head. It was a far better place to be.

'On other days, according to Dooley's moods, I was allowed to get up but not allowed to speak, not even to myself. And if I did, if I forgot and exclaimed, or cursed, or laughed, Dooley would get out the whip with the ivory handle that she kept on the door. It was a whip she had found in the stables, one used by the master of hounds. She could have killed me with it, I know that now, but she didn't. She must have applied it

182

gently, although it certainly didn't feel like that. Dooley was careful as she carried out this weekly ritual which had to be endured whatever the sin committed. Now, of course, I realise how much she must have enjoyed it. I can see the traps she set for me, so there was really no way I could have avoided her punishment.

'The whip lost all meaning for me in the end. I ceased to fear it, ceased to fear pain. Through pain I knew I was still alive. Pain and fear were my strongest emotions – I grew up with them shadowing me, as you, Bethy, grew up with the tor casting shadows on your mornings. I learned how to turn myself off so that nothing could touch me. I created a world of my own far more real than the one I lived in. It was the only way, so that when the whip came down it had no more impact on my naked back than a wisp of straw. Dooley knew this, and it drove her to terrible rages. I was tied to the bed for hours on end, spreadeagled like a stoat nailed to a tree trunk. She wanted to see me cry, for only then would she stop. She increased the number of strokes, but nothing she did could work – and then, of course, she handed me over to Gideon. First she threatened me with him, and that was enough. Then, when that no longer worked, she called him up to the room that they called the back nursery. Gideon. She well knew I was still afraid of him.

'I couldn't dismiss Gideon so easily. He was both in my dreams and out of them. He was everywhere, and I hated him. Whereas I could never quite bring myself to hate Dooley.'

'I would have hated her,' I told him simply, without thinking. 'I would hate any woman who could treat a child like that. How could you not hate her, Rowle, after everything she did? And why did you let her go free on the night she passed by with her brute-faced travelling companions? Why, when you had the chance for revenge!'

Rowle turned on me as if I had suddenly got up and slapped his face. 'How could I hate my only companion? She was the one who gave me my food, the one who was there in the night. Yes, I was afraid of her, but she was there, big and dark and strong. Big in my life. I was dependent on her for my life.' And then he was full of shame, and I wished I had not spoken and I knew that he wished he had not defended her. He thought I could not understand his dilemma, for how can you love a monster, how can you rise to defend your most pitiless persecutor and expect anyone else to comprehend?

But I could sympathise. You see, I knew. I never spoke about Amos because my reasons were the same as Rowle's. I knew I should hate him for all he had done to me, and I did, oh I did. But hatred is suspect because it is so empty and underneath all that frustrated anger there lurked something far more powerful . . . too difficult for me to define. It was something to do with a flawed kind of love, a love I was abjectly and humiliatingly ashamed of. I couldn't bear anyone else to criticise Amos. I felt defensive of his cruelty in a way I could never quite understand and I hated myself for my feelings, knowing them abnormal. I answered Rowle quickly. 'She wanted to take your life away.'

Rowle turned away from me when he said, 'Ah, but I didn't know that then. I think, if I had known that, I would have turned over and died.'

'And she would have won,' I said to him.

Rowle smiled. 'Things are never that simple. Dooley was my life to me, but remember, I was hers to her, also. She saw no one else, went nowhere else. I was all she had.'

And I knew for certain then – and only I knew this, only I could truly understand – that in spite of all Dooley had done, beating him, starving him, humiliating and warping him, he still loved her with a fierce, childish sort of love that had never been able to grow up. It was something he would never admit.

And neither could I. Until now.

In winter we met at a shepherd's hut – oh yes, he knew all the places. Dressed in fur he took me there, where icicles hung off the thatch that wrinkled over the window. We lit a peat fire and lay down beside it. So large was that fireplace and so small the room that it took up almost all one wall. In summer we went to the gorge.

Between times I spent all the hours I could alone in my room, that small spartan place at the top of the house with just a bed and a box. And a window that I could look out of and watch the skies . . . those fatal skies.

What did I want? *What did I want?*

I wanted Rowle to leave Lucy and build a house for me at the other end of the Combe. That would do to begin with. And I wanted to belong to him – I wanted it acknowledged that I was his, and to bear his children. Eventually I wanted him to leave the Combe and start a new and normal life. He had the money and the wherewithal. He was educated. He could change his name, marry me, and we could build a house of our own away from all this, away from the danger, deceit and the ties on his time. So what did I imagine? A house with land – a house like Amberry, perhaps – where we could entertain and live life properly instead of hiding, savages living in a crack in the ground.

Was that so extraordinary? Was the wanting so impossible?

When I put these ideas to him, oh carefully of course, at first he laughed but as I repeated them, wouldn't let go, he became angry and that's how our fighting began. To begin with, the fights were playful, adding zest to our already frenzied excitements. So I used to rile him deliberately, tease and tantalise so he would make me stop. And there was only one way he could ever do that.

When Rowle realised that I was serious beneath the jests he became wary. He never lied to me, Brother Niall, he never bothered to lie. 'You have to understand this, Bethy,' he said, kindly at first. 'I will never leave Lucy. And even if I wanted to, I could not leave the Combe. There is no place for me in the world outside . . . circumstances have made it impossible for me to go back.'

'Why will you never leave Lucy? Situations change. Feelings change.'

Oh, what a fool I was . . . I could not imagine Rowle as needy, as needing a mother, confessor, friend, ever-forgiving, ever-understanding, as Lucy was to him. He made it clear he was not willing to discuss his reasons with me, and that, more than anything, drove me to fury. How could I argue if he would not speak? Worse – if he smiled like that, looking down at me as if I was one of his children, unworthy of a serious answer. Unworthy! And yet he took my body gladly when he needed it, let me listen to his reminiscences and his musings. Even, sometimes, to his hopes and his dreams.

Our meetings, which had been so wonderful, became tearful, full of my angry recriminations. 'How long can we go on like this, meeting secretly all the time, only when it is convenient for you. I have feelings, too, Rowle! I have needs, and they aren't being met like this!'

'Did I, at any time, give you reason to think there would be more than this? Isn't this enough?'

'No, it is not enough. It was to begin with – it isn't now! I love you, Rowle! I need to be with you all the time. And I can't bear to share you!'

'You are not sharing me now. I am with you, body and soul. I am totally yours.'

'Tonight, yes, tonight. But what of tomorrow night, and the night after that? You'll be with Lucy – or even someone else. How can I know? How can I know that I am not the only one?' I raged and I stormed. I lifted my fists to hit him and he held me by the wrists and glared down into my eyes.

'You know because I tell you so.'

I wept, frustrated by my powerlessness to move him. 'How can I believe you?'

But then he pushed me away from him and turned his back, kicked the fire with his boot as if he wished it was me he could knock into shape so easily. And the fire flared as I felt like flaring. But then he stamped on the embers and they quickly turned into ash.

Oh monk, it's hard for me to keep the thread, to remember all that I said and all that he said. One minute it's clear, the next it's gone and I know that's because I don't want to remember, because I'm ashamed of it. I behaved so badly. I can see myself – I know I cried a great deal, I can see my skinny shoulders shaking. I can see myself kneeling, my arms round myself as I sank into misery so deep I could hardly bear it. And I can hear my own voice saying, 'Why won't you? Why won't you? You care less about me than you do about her, that's why. In fact you don't care about me at all.'

And his voice comes, laden, into my memory. 'I wouldn't be here if I didn't care. You know I don't bother to pretend.'

'But what do you feel? What is it you feel for me?'

And Rowle didn't answer, save to put his arms about me, hold me and say in such a deep, sad voice, 'I care as much as I care about anyone else in my world. I don't think I can love, Bethy, do you understand that? I think I am empty inside and only able to give by the hour, by the day. I'm trying to tell you, trying to explain, Bethy. Things make it hard for people . . .'

'You don't care for Lucy by the hour or the day! You care

about her all the time . . .' On and on I went. The sound of my own shrill voice makes me want to scream, now, more than the thought of tomorrow. That voice from the past, full of such desperate urgency, killing the very thing that it loved most of all.

And so I came to believe that I had to act to make something happen. I had to test him, bring the whole seething pot to the boil. And there was only one way to do that and that was to tell Lucy. I convinced myself it was right she be told. She was part of it – she was the reason I couldn't be with Rowle.

And oh, Brother Niall, I even convinced myself that she was so good, so kind, so sweet and so noble, she loved him so much that she might let him go.

27

It was hard for me to find the right time, to decide my best opportunity.

It was hard for me also to deceive Lucy, for she believed all I told her and never questioned Rowle. Rowle was her man and yet Rowle demanded total freedom and she appeared happy to give it. On the nights we spent together, I would go to bed early, saying I was tired and did not want to be disturbed. Then, heart beating fast, tiptoeing full of fear, I would creep back down through the house and out the back door to meet him, so frightened of being discovered, and yet half-wanting to be. The house was all creaks on those nights, all creaks and fluttering candles. The draughts became my enemies, little gusts of my own fear, and certain stairs caused my breath to catch in my throat.

By day it was no easier. I was often tired, falling asleep in the afternoons and having to invent excuses for that. There were no squeaking doors, no unexpected puffs of wind in the daytime, but there were eyes to answer, expressions and tones of voice. And every time I spoke of Rowle, or listened to Lucy speak of him, I feared that one of these gestures would give me away. Sometimes I thought I caught her giving me curious glances, but when I stared back with a careful expression I imagined that I was mistaken.

Silas was a different matter. He knew – and we knew that he knew. I had told Rowle nothing of the night he had come to treat me . . . the thought of Rowle finding out about that doubled me up with fear. But Rowle knew something of that Christmas night . . . not all . . . but something. I had not spoken of it but he had surely seen, everyone there on that night had seen.

Rowle and Silas were close. Silas had a room at the back and he ate with the men. Out and busy most of the time, he rarely returned to the house save to sleep or to talk with Rowle, and they spent many hours in that special room, talking and making their plans.

Lucy saw good where there was no good. She'd been uncharacteristically hard in her attitude towards Jessie. With Silas, Lucy was most deferential. Sometimes I watched them together and his genteel politeness towards her made me smile. They were great friends, and she was always defending him to me. 'He likes to pretend he's a rascal, that's all, and you seem determined to believe it Bethy for reasons I don't understand. He's good at heart and Rowle couldn't be without him. He's a strong man to fall back on. Totally reliable. Always there.'

How could she say that about a man such as Silas? You only had to look at him . . . only had to catch his eye to see the quick cunning there. Of course I avoided him. If I saw him alone in a room then I would not enter. If I realised that we would be left alone then I'd get up, make my excuses and flee. And all the time I felt his bold eyes following me. Sometimes, on those rare occasions when we all sat together, others would be talking but Silas would be standing, one leg on the hearth and his insolent stare wandering over me. Insolent eyes. Knowing eyes. Eyes that had been under my clothing before.

With Silas Peverell I had gone too far. I trembled and knew it.

There were times when we had folks to dinner. Sometimes, after a council meeting, it was just a few men from the Combe, but on other occasions there would be outsiders, fine men mostly with flaunting airs. On these days Lucy and I dressed up and the children were sent to bed early. Rowle and Silas discarded their rough outdoor clothes and dressed grandly . . . maids were brought in for the serving and old Mother Gant, who had a light touch, came to cook.

I remember the night we entertained John Furze. He was an important local dignitary, warden of the stannaries Rowle told us, so all must be perfect tonight. Most of our visitors had dubious reasons for coming to the Combe and they arrived stealthily by night, led by Rowle's men. Some were brought in blindfold, and others went away with money round their waists.

I remember the night John Furze came because he was so genial and gregarious. Rowle was stiff, Lucy was quiet and for the first time, Silas flirted with me outrageously and openly, deliberately taunting Rowle. John Furze, unwitting and a bit of a buffoon, encouraged him in this, but we all knew that John

Furze was here for the most secretive and important reasons. Later he, Rowle and Silas would go off to talk, would sit together in that room with brandies in their hands. But at this moment you wouldn't imagine John Furze could be cautious over anything, because his laughter was so loud and hoarse and his appetite was so huge.

John Furze was a big, theatrical-looking man with a large white wig on his head that resembled a cream pudding. He smelled like a brewery when he called me 'Midear', and brought his red face forward, gnawing a chop and staring at me out of bloodshot eyes. 'I don't think I have ever seen such an angel at the table, if the lady of the house will excuse, from politeness to my host, my not referring to her.'

I blushed, unhappy to be the centre of attention.

I felt alarm when Silas joined in, determined to cause trouble. 'She's not the angel you might suppose, sir. Look harder, look into this "angel's" eyes.'

'Ho! Ho! Ho!' Yes, John Furze, not a great wit, did laugh like that.

Silas had started drinking early and I mistrusted the hooded shape of his eyes. If our visitor had not been there I would have quickly made my excuses and left. As it was, that action would have been most impolite. I was keen to behave and use my new manners and so I was forced to sit, smiling and calm, while Silas lounged back twiddling his glass in an agitated fashion, his long legs spread under the table, his dark eyes sombre and his chin out – resolved, it would seem, to annoy Rowle.

John Furze tucked into a leg of mutton, and grease floated down his whiskered chin. 'I must say,' he started, staring round, 'what a life, eh? What a life you do lead with your pick of the gels . . . women like this, and waited on hand and foot.' And little Joan, a maid at best so dejected, so lost she was beaten by humility, scuttled from the room with a wild, fearful look in her eye. And then he turned to Rowle and said, 'You rogue! No wonder you were reticent to return . . .'

'You know full well that I could not return . . . duped as I was into thinking . . .'

'It is only the Amberry fire that stands between you and your birthright now! You're a fool, Rowle, and you know it. Your outlaw activities can be played down, with help from your friends. And the provocation that goaded you into the killing of Charles is now well understood. Your uncles have cleared you of that . . . with a little monetary influence and the friendly ear of the Queen. All this we have discussed, at length, before. But to go and destroy that house . . . your mother . . . Gideon . . .'

'I would rather not speak of that further,' said Rowle, and I saw Lucy's lips come together, hard, as she looked away into a stony distance. Why did Rowle not argue the point? I stared at him hard, for I knew he could not have started that fire! His freedom was at stake . . . his whole future . . . the possibility of returning to the world and taking up his life again!

Astounded, I realised that even Lucy did not know . . . even she believed he had burned the house down and from the looks she was sending him then it was something she would never forgive. So why? Why? Who had burned the house, and who was Rowle protecting? Maybe he did not know . . . but even in my confusion, I realised that just could not be.

Rowle smiled. He did not defend himself. He did not protest.

John Furze was his friend. The man was waiting for an answer. None came. He went on, 'Well, until 'tis otherwise proven, the suspicions will remain and you will stay a wanted man and an outcast.' Then John Furze went back to his joking, and banged his fist hard on the table. ''Tis monstrous,' he bellowed, and there were serious words under the humour, ''tis monstrous that you should live here like this, drinking wine as though it was water and taking what you want from the countryside, while the rest of us are forced to live within the confines of the law, pay taxes, lock our doors against you and lie with our own dry wives at night!'

Did Silas know who caused the fire? Silas, red-faced and well away by now, seemed determined to cause trouble. 'I think we might be able to find you some sport afterwards, sir, if you are that way inclined. I wonder now, what about Bethany? You seem impressed by her, sir, and I must say she has many fine points.' And now he leaned forward and tilted my chin with his finger as if to display just some of my more obvious charms to his guest, as if, when he'd finished with my face he might start travelling further down my body.

'Silas! Really! Remember you are at dinner! Please behave in front of company. We do not have visitors often, sir,' a flustered Lucy appealed to John Furze. 'And I'm afraid my friend is forgetting himself.'

But it was Rowle Lucy stared at that night. Rowle who sat back, dark and glaring at the head of the table, regarding Silas out of coolly perceptive eyes as if he saw for the first time that there might have, once, been something between us. And Lucy was not a fool.

'I must apologise,' said Silas, over-emphatic as he leaned across me to address John Furze. 'I have such little opportunity, these days, of meeting with those of daintier sensibilities.'

'Don't count me in among them, young man!' John Furze nodded brusquely towards Lucy. 'Don't stand on ceremony, please, just because I am here.'

'We were not,' said Rowle.

'And how long have you been with the outlaws, young lady?' John Furze's sleeve was now completely covered in grease. I moved my arm away, but there was no menace in the man. It was easy to see that he meant no harm, he was only used to being easy and enjoying himself among men. And I suppose he assumed that because we were women among such a company of rogues then we must be of the lower class he was used to . . . there for the amusement of himself and his companions. Lucy, by her manners and the way she carried herself with such quiet airs, was trying to persuade him otherwise but John Furze would not have it.

'I have been here a year and a half now, sir,' I said, turning my head from Silas and attempting to sound as demure as Lucy did. 'This is my second summer.'

John Furze slapped the table, greatly amused by my coyness. He looked at Rowle and then at Silas, sensing, perhaps, that there was some ownership game going on from which he might, as a guest, be excluded. But heady with wine he pressed on.

And I know that I did look special that night. I had made myself pretty on purpose, having said to Rowle last time we were out, 'Next Friday night when the company comes I will make you decide! You look at Lucy and look at me and decide who is the more becoming!'

So I had deliberately left my bodice low, pulling it tight so my breasts bulged over, nearly displaying the nipples. I had chosen a deep blue gown of silk and it shone and rustled like water, catching the light whenever I moved. Lucy and I had flapped it around in the court to get the damp out. It came from a chest of many others, but the blue in this gown emphasised the black in my eyes and I thought my hair quite stunning against it. Lucy had curled it for me so that some of it fell in ringlets around my face. I had rouged my cheeks and painted my lips just lightly with stuff from Lucy's paint pallet, so I suppose that to John Furze I did look available . . . He would not let the subject of me go and neither would Silas, and every time Lucy tried to raise the standard of conversation Silas would take it to me again and John Furze was a willing accomplice.

'She was orphaned,' said Lucy, seriously. 'She used to live at Amicombe.'

John Furze burped and thought about that. 'A bad business,' he said. 'I do remember something of it.' He turned to me, chin lowered as he bowed his way out of his belch, and he said, with as much charm as he could muster, 'If I had been warden there at the time, midear, you can be sure that such an event would never have happened.'

Rowle grew more and more silent, more tense at the end of the table. This was a touch of what I had intended but there was far too much danger in it now. I tried to ease the atmosphere with conversation of my own but I was not as loud nor as drunk as John Furze and Silas' voice, when he made it drawl slowly like that, always dominated conversations.

'However, I do not think, if you wanted a maiden, good sir, that this lass would suit you. Her charms do not lie in her virtuousness.'

'Oh, Silas!' said Lucy crossly. 'You are being insulting! Do be quiet and let us move on to the puddings.'

'How do you know that?' John Furze was all fascination. My pulse quickened with shame. I didn't know how far Silas would go. I was afraid he would blurt out too much and that Rowle would discover about the night I had been so foolish with the man who had come to my room as my physician.

Silas' words were slow and careful. 'It is what I surmise, sir, from my expert knowledge of such matters. Let us call it a well-informed guess.'

'My goodness gracious! And can you always tell such things?'

Silas gave his guest a deep bow. 'Yes,' he said. 'Yes, I think you could probably say I was rarely wrong on matters of such importance.'

I sipped more wine but it tasted bitter that night. I sent Rowle a few nervous glances. I wanted to kick Silas hard but feared that such an aggressive act might spur him on.

Finally my ordeal was over for Rowle stood up, pushed back his chair and announced, 'We have more important business to deal with than this, I think, gentlemen – if you, Silas, have not totally lost command of your wits.'

Silas was surly as he followed Rowle and I could see John Furze was reluctant to go because his fascination with me was complete. He had stripped me a hundred times over with his eyes, quite cocksure, not bothering to conceal his thoughts.

However, he was a well-meaning man, and before he left the room he stepped back, took my hand forcibly into his own soft fat one and whispered all whiskery into my ear, 'If you ever need help, midear, if you are ever in need of a friend, there's few with so much influence as I in this fair part of the country. I, John Furze, am at your disposal. Remember that, my child.'

He tried to click his heels in a gallant gesture to complete his little farewell, but failed and tripped instead and had to hold out his hand to steady himself on a chair.

I heard his jovial, 'Ho! Ho! Ho!' booming from the room next door. Even, later, when I was to my bed I heard it. So I knew that Silas and Rowle would be pleased . . . just another to pay off and take so easily into their pockets. For as Rowle used to tell us often, every man has his price.

Lucy and I sat on in silence for a while and she was rarely silent with me. She seemed very tired, later, when we helped poor Joan and the other maids to clear up.

'Go to bed Lucy,' I said. 'Leave this to us. We will do it.'

But Lucy replied, 'I wouldn't sleep, Bethy. It is not exhaustion that makes me tired tonight.'

'Then what?' I asked her. 'Are you ill?'

She gave just a small, sad smile over her shoulder as she carried the wine to the kitchens.

Once in bed and alone, I forgot about Lucy, my thoughts

returning to what Rowle had told me that day and the discussion they had held with John Furze. Why didn't Rowle deny any part in the fire? Why, by his silence, was he destroying his birthright, ruining his chances of ever returning to claim the inheritance that was naturally his?

And why had he killed his stepbrother?

Certainly he had good reason to hate Charles, for while Gideon Rowle ruled over Amberry with a rod of iron there was one person only who escaped his cruel discipline, and that was his own son, Charles.

No wonder Rowle hated Charles . . . but enough to kill him? Charles was special. He was taken early from the nursery so that he wouldn't become 'lily-livered and pampered'; he accompanied his father everywhere whenever he was home, even on visits to the nursery at the top of the house where the bad child lived with Dooley.

Mercifully for Rowle, Gideon spent most of his time in London, although, in some ways this was worse because when he was home he tended to concentrate on 'home affairs' more intensely than he might have done had he stayed.

Rowle was almost the first to know when Gideon returned. Sometimes, when he came to the back nursery he still had travel dust on him, his eyes rimmed with dirt from the road and streaks of horse-sweat on his britches. Dooley used to lose no time in scuttling down to make her complaints.

Gideon would open the door and Rowle would cower. 'He dressed like a dandy, like the gentleman that he was. He wore black velvet trimmed with silver and he was as dark as I was, having the same colouring of my own dead father. I could easily have been taken for Gideon's son, for I resembled him more than Charles did. I remember him most clearly in black and silver, with his black eyes and hair, and silver buttons down his padded doublet. Charles dressed in Gideon's image, even down to the lace that dripped from his wrists, the ruffs, wide and starched, round his neck. The cloaks he wore were always black with scarlet linings. Yes, Charles was Gideon in miniature, not just outside, but inside as well.'

Gideon came to the back nursery for sport, in much the same way as he rode with the hunt, coursed the hare or went hawking.

'Once he came in after a kill, and I'll never forget that time:

he was covered in blood. But it wasn't the blood that stands out in my memory, it was that insanely vindictive look in his eyes, as if some lust remained unquenched.'

When Rowle told me these things I shivered. I had thought Amos cruel and unfeeling but Gideon was a lion to his lamb.

'I was punished for anything,' Rowle recalled. 'Actions that were acceptable one week were crimes the next. It was all to do with Dooley's mood and Gideon's whim at the time. If I had sat with my hands crossed and not moved they would have found something to punish me for. And I understood that. Oddly, this knowledge left me free to behave as I wished. I could be as rude, as disagreeable as ever I liked, because my behaviour, in fact, made no difference to the severity of the punishment or the frequency of it. Gideon used a horsewhip. He liked it best when I ran so that he could put Charles to chase me. He opened the door and used the long, narrow corridor outside my nursery for the sport, for which, to add to the sense of fun, he often used a hunting horn. As one end of the corridor was a dead end, it didn't entail Charles in much effort to catch me and bring me back. Out on open ground he wouldn't have succeeded, for Charles was flabby and unfit, a fat, lazy boy who inherited his father's indolence.'

And I thought to myself as Rowle spoke to me that he could either have developed into a fearful, timid man, afraid of his own shadow – or the man he had become, hard, cynical and unafraid of anything or anyone. And I also thought that after a childhood like that he was lucky he hadn't turned into a dolt, a brainless stutterer with vacant eyes . . . for there were others in the clan who had been turned, by emotional torture, to that.

Sometimes, when he loved me, I thought that Rowle had gone back to that terrible place, because he was rough, as though trying to exorcise some ghost of the past, impassive to my pleas but full of remorse afterwards. I didn't care how he used me: I was even glad to be his whipping boy if it meant I had the whole of the night with Rowle. And I thought I understood him . . . him and his needs. I thought the fact that he used me as he wished meant that he loved me.

He never cried. And I thought that this was his way of crying.

It was Catherine, Rowle's mother, whom I found much harder

to understand: that gay, flighty creature who tried to stay like a little girl to keep her husband's love, tried to be all that Gideon desired her to be, even if it meant turning her heart to stone.

I could tolerate her indifference – for most noble ladies had little to do with their children once they were born, handing them over to others to rear and hoping for the best, hoping for some sort of survival rate after their terrible labours. And I could understand that she, too, was afraid of Gideon and didn't want to cross him. He was a terrifying, brutal man, with eyes in the back of his head. He missed nothing that went on. But there were times when Gideon was away from the house, so why did she never visit that back nursery? Why did she never try to soften the dreadful Dooley? Catherine, with Gideon gone, had power. She was in full charge of the house, the servants and the children. But she never, in any way, tried to make Rowle's lot easier, to find out what his life was, if he was well, if he was happy. Catherine Rowle stayed right away, quite remote from her firstborn son. This, at a pinch, I could tolerate.

What I could not forgive was her collusion in the cruelty, so complete that it looked as if she condoned it. Supported it. She knew, you see, oh yes, she knew. *She knew that Gideon wanted her first son dead.*

28

I was biding my time, crouched like a wolf in the granite smooth distance and howling into the darkness. I was still awaiting an opportunity to talk to Lucy when Judd went missing . . . And is this a clue to my whole manic state of mind, Brother Niall – because I have honestly to say that it was not the safety of the child I worried about, it was the relationship between me and Rowle, whether the truth would all come out, and whether he would still love me after suffering such a shock. And he was shocked. Rowle was devastated.

As it was, we were lucky not to be caught red-handed. I find this shameful to speak of now but we were together in the stables when we heard Lucy calling from the house. Her voice came nearer, straight towards us as she hurried out across the court. Rowle quickly adjusted his britches and I pulled down my skirts, dusted the straw from my back and tried to arrange my dishevelled hair.

Rowle went out to meet her and I backed against the wooden partition, head ducked against the cobwebby beam, half-crazed with fear and humiliation. I caught sight of my hands – they looked like claws. 'Don't let her come in . . .' I prayed. 'Please, dear God, don't let her come any nearer. Let Rowle be able to steer her away, let him be able to compose himself so she does not suspect that I'm here.'

And yet didn't I want Lucy to know? Wasn't I planning on telling her? Why then, would it be so unacceptable to have her find out like this? Dear God, did I imagine there was a kinder way?

I heard her voice. 'Is Judd with you?' and I imagined her strained face peering over his shoulder . . . over the stable door and piercing the gloom beyond. I shrank back into the shadows, shuddered as cobwebs clung to my hair and a wood louse made its way slowly along my arm. My teeth chattered. 'Don't let her come in. Don't let her find out like this.'

And strangely, in that short moment which can only have

lasted a few seconds, I hated Rowle. I hated him for turning me into a treacherous friend, a secret lover, someone who did not, immediately, care about the whereabouts of little Judd. Oh, I know it takes two, and I was equally guilty, perhaps more so. But still I remember that moment of hatred and, Brother Niall, it was like a sudden release! Immediately I saw, so transparently clearly, that he was just a man, and that because of him I was jeopardising my friendship with Lucy which seemed, just then, something eminently precious and sweet. I think it was something to do with the fear in her voice – rusty and sharp, cutting me like the jagged edge of a piece of tin.

'He is not with me. Where have you looked?'

And they had such an ordinary conversation then – husband and wife although they were not – exploring together the places where Judd went, the likelihood of his being with Saul or Peter or Davy. And I knew that Rowle would have his arm round her shoulder in that protective way he had when Lucy became alarmed. And I felt wretched, as if it was in some way my fault that the child was missing, and furious with Judd for being so foolish. I was angry with him – yes, angry with a six year old boy – for disturbing our love-making in this way.

'How long has he been gone?'

'I don't even know that. I assumed he was with Bethy and I've been trying to find her. You don't know where she's gone either?'

'No.' Oh, the lie slipped so convincingly off his tongue. I should have considered that: I should have registered the fact, then, that Rowle was a clever liar.

After that Rowle called the men out and the Combe was searched from end to end. Everyone was involved. I came out of my den, pretending that I had been searching, joining the throng of anxious seekers with the same note of nervous certainty in my voice. 'He can't have gone far. We'll soon find him.'

And Lucy, spying me, pounced. 'Oh, I'm so glad you're here! I am out of my mind. Nobody's seen him, Bethy. Nobody's seen him since sundown.'

'Take her in,' said Rowle to me, with nothing like love in his voice, he who just a moment ago had been caressing me with his soft loving, had been whispering over my charms, my sweetness, my skills as a lover.

Even my words of consolation sounded malicious in my own ears. And I saw Lucy with pity, a ghostly-wan creature with no warmth in her. That's how I saw Lucy's sorrow as I said, 'Come inside, into the warm. You can do nothing out here but distress yourself further. The men are searching the Combe and the nearby valleys. They will find him, Lucy, you know they will.' And I badly wanted her to smile so that I could feel better.

Did she feel it – did she feel as strongly as I did as we sat there together, as I tried to comfort her – that all that sweet intimacy we once had was nothing but cheating and lies? Was Lucy as aware of that as I was? The room grew darker . . . I was even afraid to light the tapers in case she thought that my mind was not entirely on my grief . . . in case she suspected me because of my cool concern for practical matters. Gradually the room and everything in it dissolved in its own shadows, so I let go her arm, took a rush to the fire and brought some light to the horror of it all.

Her face looked tortured. 'What can have happened?' She wrung her hands. 'He is such a sensible, practical child – well, I don't have to tell you that, Bethy, you know him better than I do. He would not get lost, forget about the time, linger with friends without letting me know. He was never a child like that, Bethy. Sometimes I felt concern over his sense of responsibility. I thought him too young to carry such loads . . .'

'He is like his father. He is concerned for others.'

And if Lucy looked at me quizzically I wouldn't have noticed because I was searching for reproachment in her eyes. I saw none. I realised, by then, that when speaking of Rowle Lucy and I were describing two entirely separate people. I saw the hero, the champion and the king. She saw the child who needed protecting, who needed forgiving. Would she forgive him for loving me?

Tom Masters came in nervously. 'I've to ask 'e what 'e was wearin', ma'am.'

'Why?' exclaimed Lucy, close to hysteria. 'Have they found him?' She rushed towards the horse thief and almost wrenched the lantern out of his hand.

And that was the first time I'd considered the possibility that Judd might be dead. I reeled as a list of dire possibilities flooded through my mind. He could have been captured by prowling constables and taken to Lydford for trial. He was six years old just, quite old enough. He could be caught in a man-trap, his small leg shredded and torn completely in half. He could have fallen into a mire – he could, even now, be struggling for life, his head the only part of him above the stinking mass that sucked at his body and pulled him down into the sinking, clammy depths of the swamp. He could have been taken by wolves. And I – all I could think of was Rowle and whether he might not still love me. Rowle in mourning – Rowle in guilt . . .

Nervously Tom rushed his words to make things sound right. 'Lord bless 'e no, ma'am. 'Tis nothin' like that. 'Tis just that the maister wondered if'n the lad might have got cold an' taken shelter under some bush ter keep 'isself warm. That was the reason that I was askin'.'

'What was Judd wearing, Bethy?' And Lucy's eyes were startled and wide. 'I can't remember . . .' Tears welled from her eyes and spilled down on to her pale cheeks. 'My God, my God, he is my son and I cannot remember!' she accused herself.

I could remember. I could remember patting his straight little back and telling him, 'Run off now and play.' I had heard Rowle arriving back early and was desperate to be alone with him, not waste an instant of extra time. 'Go off and play, find Davy.' So I said to the man with the ropes at his belt. 'He was wearing his thick brown jerkin and his hard woollen britches. He wore his winter boots and I know he had his hood in his pocket.'

The man backed out of the lighted room, nodding as men do when they think they are burdened with too much to remember, crinkling up his leery red face.

'I didn't know,' wailed Lucy. 'I could not even tell them what he wore!'

'You have far too much on your mind to pay attention to details like that.' And it sounded as if I had not.

Silas came next, with a vial in his hand and his cloak swinging out behind him. I thought he deliberately ignored me, that his straight back was a message to me for he went directly to Lucy and knelt by her side. 'I want you to drink this . . . all of it. I want to see it quite taken down. Every drop, it is bitter but worth it. And then I want Bethany to put you to bed. By morning all will be well, and you will have had the sleep you so badly need.' His words were gentle but persuasive.

Everyone, it seemed, could help her but me. Everyone else's intentions were good.

I helped her upstairs. I undressed her. 'What would I do without you?' she said as I pulled up the covers of Rowle's bed, as I tucked the thick coverlet Rowle slept under closely around her. Did I blush at the enormity of my betrayal? I don't know – I only know that I ought to have done. And I kissed her then, and sat quietly beside her stroking her forehead until her eyes closed and I knew that nothing would wake her from Silas' most potent medicine.

I looked down on her. Lucy was pure. I wanted to be pure but I was like a jealous black dog.

Of course I threw myself into the thick of the search. It was guilt that drove me and, oh yes, guilt is a drastic master. Instinct took over . . . and I was close to the animals, belly low, shaggy and slinking as I started my search, quite alone, not wanting to join the organised groups who were scouring the moor, overseen by Rowle who gave directions from the court. I did not go to him, knowing he would want to avoid me now as I wanted to avoid him. Was our love then just an empty thing, only thriving when life went easily . . . backing away and cowering like something in the dark when anything real took over? Shouldn't we have wanted to comfort each other in this agonising hour? As friends, surely, if nothing else.

But Rowle and I were never friends, monk. Friends are true to each other. Friends don't hurt each other.

All the children were under instructions never to leave the Combe, and knowing Judd as I did, I doubted he would, with darkness threatening, disobey this most necessary of rules. Had he lingered too long at play, had he stayed after darkness fell, every one of the Combe families would have sent him back home. Even a passerby on his way back from his work, even the swarthiest blaggard who did not know him well, everyone would recognise Judd and would send him on his way.

Instinct took me, nothing else. I found myself at the dark east end where the lost ones lived, in a silent world away from the lights and the fires. Away from the watchmen's lights. The track grew sandier as I went, calling softly, 'Judd, it's Bethany.

Judd, where are you?' And my voice sounded little and silly, and when I disturbed a watchful owl, when its wings beat suddenly, moving the night, I leapt for fear, and the violent rush of it felt like my own guilty heart.

And then came fear. We imagined we knew these children. We had talked about them so often, talked in safety, surrounded by warmth and people. Even during our lonely vigils together by the fire, Lucy and I had been together within calling distance of help. But these were wild children, who lived by nobody's rules. And if they had Judd, if they were keeping him against his will then why did they keep him – and what would they do with him? They were children but they were cunning and sly. They could use Judd in order to set demands. They could hold him for years and even the Gubbins would not be able to find him. And little Judd . . . thoughts of the child's cheeky smile, his attempts at daring, of his unswerving yet secretive need for his father's approval, came abruptly to me. I imagined his little brown body scrambling out of the river, looking drowned as a bear cub, shouting at the top of his voice, 'Bethy, Bethy, fetch Rowle, let him see I can dive! He said I couldn't . . . well look, I'll do it again! I'll show you! I can! I can!'

A child like this . . . a baby . . . taken by the lost ones?

A sob caught in my throat as I felt for the child that I honestly loved as my own – or thought I did until this night. Visions of Judd, so protected, so needy, *so unlike Rowle*, persisted in the front of my mind. I tried to put them out . . . they would not go away.

So protected. So needy. *So unlike his father.*

Monk, you must think me stupid or deaf or both – for hadn't I heard a thing he had told me earlier? Hadn't I listened, or was it that he was my hero and I did not want to hear?

It was at a Christmas banquet when Rowle was nine years old that he tried to speak. He was brought down because two of his father's friends were guests at Amberry for the week's celebration and had enquired about him, clearly refusing to be put off by nonchalant comments as to his welfare, as was generally the way. Perhaps they thought it strange that the second son was so much in evidence, while of Anthony's child there was no sign.

So he was to be dressed up and brought down, for their benefit. 'I was given a suit of clothes, measured by the seamstress who came to the house from the village and told me she hadn't even heard, before that day, of my existence. The woman had been in the house on many occasions and made clothes for all the family, except for Mother, who travelled to London once a year to acquire a new, fashionable wardrobe. Dooley watched, striking out at my fidgeting, lifting my arm so the string could be put underneath to measure, pushing my chin up, turning my head this way and that between her large, hard hands.

' "I didn't know there was an older boy," said the woman innocently, with pins in her mouth. "Fancy me not knowing that, and I've sewn for the other children all their lives! Where does he come now, in the order of things?"

'Dooley was most annoyed at her familiarity. "Why should you know?" she asked the woman rudely, turning me round on the chair so that I wobbled and nearly fell off it. "'Tis not everything can be learnt from servants' tittle tattle, from village gossip. The master and mistress of this house don't have to explain themselves or their goings-on to the likes of you!"

' "I was merely stating my surprise. Merely trying to make conversation," said the woman meekly, astonished by the ferocious reaction.

'But I in my naïvity, was more astonished. This was something new to me. Why did no one talk about me? This woman knew about all the others, everyone knew about all the others, but nobody knew about me. I could see that the woman considered this strange, and so, all of a sudden, did I.

'Dooley poked me hard. She could see I was thinking, mulling things over in my mind. It was something she was never easy with so I liked to do it often. So, the other children of the house had their clothes made for them by this woman who was far more expert at it, far gentler, than Dooley . . . but why them and never me? Until now, Dooley had made all my clothes, rough-cut garments taken from discarded curtains or blankets, or even cut down from her own old skirts. They had a hole for my head, two for my arms and two for my legs. And always, winter and summer alike, I went bare-footed. If my feet were cold I wrapped them in blankets. I must have looked like a real rag-bag to the long-fingered woman with the freezing cold hands who came with her needles and pins, her soft bag of cloths which she held up before me.

'So it was with this new knowledge, that I was not treated as the others were, that I went down to the banquet.

'No wonder I went downstairs with my head bent. I had other burdens to carry – instructions on how to behave and what to say – given to me by Dooley, and the threats of what would happen if I disobeyed were scorched on my brain. There were threats of Gideon and Charles, even threats that I would break my mother's heart. That was a new idea, one I had never considered before: could I break her heart, then, this remote Ice Queen with whom I had not spent more than ten minutes of my life? Did I have the power, then, to do that? The possibility of it was huge inside me . . . a new power . . . the only power I had ever tasted.'

When Rowle said this to me I turned my head away, not wanting him to see the thoughts that were showing through my eyes. For I was interested to learn that his first taste of real power should have been given to him by a woman.

'I found it incredible,' he whispered. 'The sumptuous grandness of it all, the tables laden with mutton, rabbits, partridge, geese – marvellously decorated puddings, all the silver shining, the chandeliers a mass of flame, musicians playing, hooped-skirts swinging . . . oh, for me, it was unreal, a dream. The sensations came rushing at me and I remember crinkling up my eyes and shielding them with my hand, not so much against the brightness but against the wonder of it all.

'Fat Charles came to meet me at the bottom of the stairs – I suppose he had been ordered to do so. My mother sat at one end of the table, which must have been forty feet long, and Gideon at the other. Who the friends of my father's were, I never discovered.

' "Walk with your back straight like this at all times!" Dooley had instructed me. "Remember who you are!' Who I was? This, too, was a new concept, impossible for me to deal with, for who was I? What did she mean?'

'I saw my mother and stopped in my tracks; no one was aware of my entry. The doublet I was unused to wearing felt tight, and the britches slowed me down. I was all in a silver blue, even the buckles on my shoes were silver. I pulled at the ruff at my neck and the layers in it. I could not move with it on, could not turn quick enough to see all I wanted. I suppose I should have gone with Charles to stand beside the great fireplace where the other children, dressed in laced finery, were waiting to watch the entertainments, the jugglers, the singers. And there was to be a bear baited, later, right here in the hall.

'I was unsure how to react when a servant who passed by carrying a silver dish high in the air bowed to me. I stared at my mother: she was astonishingly beautiful. The magnificence of all that great hall, the finely dressed people in it, the decorations – none of these things could rival the way she dominated that room.

'She stopped in her conversation – oh, I remember – with her hand halfway to her cheek and all the jewels glittering on it, halfway through some gesture, with a sparkle in her eyes, she stopped and she saw me. Her high eyebrows arched a little but other than that her expression remained the same – aloof, haughty, but with some secret amusement in her face.'

Rowle stopped. I thought he had gone to sleep, for it was late and we had been talking for hours. I shifted in his arms and saw that his eyes were still open, open and staring away into the darkness, and I knew that he was seeing back into that time, that he was no longer king of the renegade band but a small boy again about to go somewhere where there were monsters too big for him to handle.

It was the first time I had ever seen anything akin to fear on Rowle's face.

'Don't say any more', I said to him, touching his lips with my finger. And then I whispered, 'I know what happened.'

The fear left him. He sat up straighter, pushed me from his arms and picked up his ale. He gave a brief smile, one of those that never touched his eyes. It appeared he hadn't heard me because he went on, 'I left Charles behind and I ran over. A mile long, that short journey seemed to me across the marble floor, and all the time my eyes never left her. But as I approached I watched her closing up, like a fan. Her eyes lost their shine and became dull, blank. Her body first relaxed, then grew tall in her high-backed chair. She lifted her chin and her eyelids came down so low that I saw the lashes shadowing her pale cheeks. I think I stopped once, but undaunted, set off again. I should have turned back then . . . there was still time! Somehow I was aware that Gideon had stood up, that all faces were turned towards him, leaving me to reach my mother unobserved. But then the faces turned once more, and all eyes were on us as I rushed up to her and tried to bury my head in her skirts.'

Rowle tensed for a long moment during which he held his breath. I waited . . . not knowing . . . expecting one of his angry silences. Then he laughed. Really laughed, flung back his head and roared and I had to shush him because the others might hear. In a voice as relaxed and casual as if he were discussing the next day's weather he told me, 'She pushed me away as she might have done her spaniel. Well, of course she did. What else could she have done? She loosed my fingers from her skirts and from the other end of the table came the command, "Sir – to your room this instant!"'

'Then the silence was fluttered by conversation and I realised how deep, how total that silence had been. Faces turned away and only eyes were left – you know that feeling, Beth? They weren't watching any longer but they were still aware and wondering . . .

'I remembered what Dooley had said about standing straight and it was with a straight back and little clicks from my shoes – jewelled shoes, I must have looked smart – that I went back across that massive hall and started to climb up the stairs. I wanted to cry, not because of what had happened, but because of my wasted clothes. All that trouble, all that work to make me look proud, to make me look like "who I was". I was going back upstairs and Dooley would make me take them off. I might never get to wear them again. My mind concentrated on that . . . built that into the tragedy. The other, I suppose, was too terrible to dwell on.

'I wanted to look back, very badly, to see what expression she was wearing now but I didn't. I did glance at Gideon as I passed him, and he was watching me carefully with a different look in his eyes. Was it fear? I couldn't be sure. I was not old enough to read men's eyes – or women's, for that matter. But I knew that Gideon's eyes bored into my back as I disappeared, as the lilt of conversation grew distant along with the smells of the food, of the perfume, the tapers, the candles, the applewood burning on the fire and the pithy smell of broken branches as they wept in their bundles of decoration over the fireplace and over the doors. They grew distant then, and like a dream.'

Rowle turned to look at me, suddenly aware that he had a listener, that I was still there. 'Funny,' he said slowly, 'but I had the feeling I had disobeyed Dooley. I had the feeling that I might have broken my mother's heart. And I was glad.'

I was cold, freezing cold and chilled to the bone.

How could they have missed him? They were sitting in a sandy hollow between thornbushes, Judd and the scarecrow girl they called Marnie. The night sky moved purple over them, and as the moon slipped between the clouds it turned them into silhouettes: they could have been just two more of the stunted, twisted trees there. But when the light came again they were simply two children together, pewtered by moonbeams, hardly speaking but totally involved with the small bird on the ground.

It was a nightjar. It flapped there weakly in the dust but Marnie had it firmly. Its beady eye shone out like the brightest diamond in this pale moonlight. I stood, protected by the ring of thorns, and watched for a while. Marnie grasped the bird between her filthy feet. She held it between her toes, while with her black fingers and torn nails she manipulated the birch stick, wrapping it to the shape of the white-spotted wing with a length of straw which she drew from her mouth. Judd leaned over watching, mesmerised.

And all my joy in finding Judd – I have to say this, I have to admit it, monk, for it is the awful truth and I can no longer lie – all my relief and joy was to do with the fact that all would be well . . . that Rowle would be bound to love me more for being the one to recover his son! Mary, who kept me at a distance these days, might even forgive me! Lucy might be kinder on me on the day she at last found out about us. Oh, I suppose some of the relief was for the safety of the child. I am not all bad. Surely, even then, at that most fevered time of my life, surely there was some concern for somebody else other than myself and my relationship with Rowle!

But how to approach them? I was so unsure of Marnie.

Maybe she would take him yet, seeing how valuable an asset he would be to her and the children she led. Maybe she would see me and pounce, wielding a knife at his throat. For other reasons than this I was reluctant to disturb them. There was something so wonderful, so magical in their being together silently like this, joined in concern for the damaged creature that lay between them.

But I must have moved too suddenly, breathed too sharply, for Marnie looked up then and there were three eyes on me, the one-eyed stare of the nightjar and the equally wild, wide eyes of the girl. All alarm, I thought that at best she would flee, leave the bird to its fate and slink off into the shadows. I stayed dead still. She spoke to Judd but I did not hear what she said. And like a child in a dream my little Judd stood up, cast one last look at the bird and came silently towards me.

Only when we were out of sight, hand in hand, did he speak, and even then it appeared he had not realised he had done anything wrong. When I told him of the concern, of the search parties out all over the moor, of Lucy's anguish, he took little notice as if these things mattered nothing compared to the fate of that nightjar.

'We had to find just the right stick,' he said, with such seriousness on his small face. His words tumbled from his lips as words do when you speak of a dream, so as not to forget it. 'It had to be just the right thickness and length. And then I had to go and search for the right quality of straw . . . the mouldy stuff they use for the bedding was not good enough. It had to be perfect. Marnie said that, to meet perfection everything you used had to be perfect. And I was all worried because it was getting dark and I might not choose right. But I did . . . and she fed it live moths, Bethy, she held them by their fluttering wings, and she purred to the bird and it might have been answering her back for she seemed to understand.'

'You must have heard the men – you must have seen the lanterns, Judd! Surely you knew we were searching . . .'

'Marnie dragged me down a hole: it was a chimney with steps going into the earth and wide, sandy places where we could stop. We had to climb out to set the bird free.'

How could I scold him? I loved him. I led him home ecstatically, conveniently forgetting it was I who had sent him off in the first place when he had been entrusted into my keeping.

And when Rowle saw us coming – because of course I led the child straight to the court where I knew that Rowle was waiting for news – his face showed such pure joy, such intense relief and delight at seeing his son safe and well, that I did not stay to receive my acclaim. No, I slunk off to the quiet of my room, there to lick my wounds and wonder which of my musings was correct – would this awful experience draw us closer, or would the temporary, terrifying loss of his son unite him with Lucy?

You see, Brother Niall – I was so steeped in my own foolish fantasy that I could not believe, could not understand the one massive fact that eluded me. I could not believe that there was nothing to unite – *because they had never been truly apart*.

29

Time goes so slowly. If I crouch by the wall I can see the moon and it hasn't moved since I last stared at it. It hangs in the sky, telling my time like a majestic clock, the queen of the night-sky hunting with her pack of ghost-clouds, howling. Birdie was moved by the moon, they said. They liked to watch her carefully when the moon was full.

The mad are moved by the moon, it makes them restless – and women like me, who watch it through their bars. There are very many bars, not all ugly iron ones like these, but bars that imprison you inside yourself and stop you loving as you yearn to love. Bars that take the wildness from you and make you afraid of it.

The moon-clock has hardly moved in the sky. Time goes slowly when you're waiting to die.

When you're a child days pass slowly as months, months as years. A year is an enormity, too big to be contemplated. A year – and it would be quite possible that you would be dead, so old would you be at the end of its passing.

So childhood always lasts for a very long time and what happens in it is important. As my days were full, so Rowle's were empty, because he was a prisoner in that room at Amberry and rarely went outdoors. They did nothing with him. They left him there while life went on downstairs as if he did not exist. Charles was sent to school. He stood it for a year before he returned a good deal thinner and with a hacking cough that kept him in bed and pampered for as long as he could get away with it. It was only by guile and deceit that he survived the experience at all, that, and the vast amounts of money from home that he used to smooth his short passage. He refused, outright, to go back. I think he wasn't very bright, and being so fat and spoilt I suspect he must have been bullied terribly. So he was put to learning the managing of the estates with the bailiff, Tremain, but his experiences away from home had made him crueller, trickier than he was before.

They had failed in their attempts to subjugate Rowle by the use of cruelty and humiliation, and their methods had failed to kill him, for he was not frail and sickly as so many children are, as so many of his brothers and sisters were. Three of them died during his childhood. He didn't know them, other than their names and their faces. He didn't even know what they died of or how the bereavements were received by the family. He was just told the facts by Dooley in her ominous and threatening style; it was more of a, 'There – if they can die, so can you – but they have gone to Heaven whereas you are destined for a much more frightening place.'

During the year that Charles was away at school, and when Gideon was absent, Catherine took to summoning Rowle to her bedchamber just before she rose. 'Why she did this I don't know,' Rowle told me. 'She was risking a great deal. There was a good chance that her behaviour would be reported to Gideon on his return, and the whim –for that's how I see it now – the whim to have me about didn't last for long. It was probably something to do with the way I behaved when I was with her, petulant, wary. But it did result in the purchase of better clothes. She couldn't stand to see me looking, as she put it, "like a street urchin at a barrow of fish".

'The curtains of her bed would be pulled back when I arrived, pushed impatiently inside the room by a furious Dooley. My mother's clothes would be warming by the fire, lacy petticoats and chemises, silks and satins, and most times when I arrived her maid would have begun the long job of dressing her hair. Catherine liked to lie back on the pillow and have it brushed and brushed so that it formed a lovely halo around her.

'Everything seemed to be waiting for her – as I waited – breathlessly. Her tiny jewelled slippers would be laid in a line so she could choose which ones to wear on that day. "Stand there, Roger. No, back a bit so that I can see you properly. Don't fidget, for goodness sake stand still. You worry me, you make me nervous with your scratchings and your scowlings. You're jumpy as a flea, even your eyes seem to leap about the room. *Stand still child*!"

'My mother lisped in fluttery sentences, gasping between

them and during them and she chided me to be still but her own hands never were. She plucked and she pulled at her sleeves, her bodice, her bedclothes. They moved around her like a lover's hands, frustrated, as if she was trying to get at herself but could find no easy way in.

'I didn't know what I was there for but she used to stare a great deal at my eyes which she said were "so like your father's. Angry eyes, just like your father's. Slant them that way for me, now this, now the other. Raise your head a little, no, Roger, not like that! Perhaps, after all, you will grow up to be like Anthony. Stubborn, like him." And then she would fall back on her pillow and close her own eyes, finished with mine, and I wouldn't know whether to leave or not.

'It was always the same. When she got out of bed she would stretch, hold her hair, loose still, high above her head so that she looked like the statue in the entrance hall, and turn and smile at me before she removed her night-smock. She was like an actress coming on to the stage, gathering herself up for the performance of her life – another day. Her maid would be standing by waiting, holding her underclothes warm and ready. I was anxious to leave, anxious not to see this part because it always disturbed me. Naked, Catherine would turn towards me, smile in a certain languid way, bring down her chin and regard me under her eyelashes. Her body was smooth and girlish: there were no signs of childbirth, no ravages, no scars. And Bethy, I wanted . . .' Rowle stopped and stroked his chin, looked amused.

'What did you want?' I asked him coldly, knowing the answer.

'No wonder I couldn't stand still. It was a game she was playing, because I'm certain she knew how I felt. And I'm sure that she also knew how angry Dooley would be for the rest of the day – how she would punish me later for this visit, which was unfair because it was through no schemings of mine that I was invited, unless dreaming of it could be called scheming. But what my mother didn't know was that I was glad of Dooley's punishments, welcoming them, knowing I deserved all I got when I reached the safety of the back nursery again. Dooley knew. Dooley knew everything. Dooley had it right. Because I wanted to touch my mother. I wanted to run my hands over all that smooth skin. My palms even itched with the wanting to do that. I wanted to take her back to the bed. I imagined how warm it would be, how smelling of her it would be, how very unsafe it would be – and I relished un-safety. And it would be something I could hold, something very hard and powerful, as a weapon, a secret weapon against Gideon. But she never invited me there. Instead, accepting her day-smock she said to her servant, "It's his eyes, Annie. Don't you think he has the eyes of his father?"

'And Annie would nod and look nervous, but not half as nervous as I was feeling.

'I would stand there, not yet dismissed and yet totally ignored, while they made up her face and turned it into marble, brought up her hair so that it didn't look real any more and she lost all that had made me want to touch her, turned herself into Gideon's creature. And I knew she was punishing me. I wondered if she punished me because of Anthony, because of something that Anthony had done to her for which she could never forgive him – like dying and leaving her to the mercies of Gideon. I would have liked to have said to her, "I'm not Anthony. I wouldn't die . . . remember! I am the one who didn't die! I am still here and wanting to love you, only you won't let me." '

Rowle smiled and said unpleasantly, 'How innocent are children. Because then she would turn and say disdainfully, "What, still here? What are you doing still here" And then I'd go and have to wait until the next time. But the experience was addictive – every time it happened I began to look forward to it more, so that when Dooley said to me, "Your mother wants you again this morning," I could hardly bear the feelings those words aroused in me. And it wasn't just seeing my mother I ached for, it was also the punishments that would be dealt out afterwards. Life is so unsimple, Bethy, until I turn to you – and then it becomes impossible.'

Oh, Rowle! To hear him speak like that tortured me and I wondered if it was done deliberately, contrived as Catherine's torments had undoubtedly been. And I felt a hot flush of hatred towards this woman and jealousy, too, even though I knew she was dead – as if the mother of this man had been his first love, afraid in case it was always to be his only love, his fiercest love, to be conquered before he properly loved anyone else. And where did this, then, leave me? Where did it leave Lucy?

Oh, Brother Niall, I was even jealous of the piece of sky that Rowle moved under. I was jealous of the earth, seeing its subtle roundness as feminine and watching how easily Rowle conquered it just by moving over it. And I wished I could be cold and forbidding as Catherine was because I felt that then he might love me more. And I'd try, for a while, to be aloof and cruel in the way that she had been, to hold back from him and not let him touch me. But Rowle would see through me and laugh and say, 'It doesn't suit you, wanton. You were never anybody's lady! Come here!'

But I did undress in the way she did, and look at him under my eyelashes, seductively. And then, sometimes, I would see something like pain in his face and be glad. Because I wanted to give him pain. I thought it proof of his love: if I could be big enough in his life to cause him pain then he must love me.

I didn't see then, or was too pathetically infatuated to realise, that it was I, not Rowle, who associated pain so directly with love.

30

I was a prisoner long before I arrived at Lydford – for loving Rowle turned me into one. Once it had happened I was never free of him, but was surrounded and crushed by my own twisted emotions which shackled me, were so tight that I couldn't move.

But if someone had opened the dungeon door and stood back saying, 'Here you are – here is the way out, take it,' would I have done so? Would I have walked away with a light heart and never looked back? Or would I have stumbled about searching, unable to sleep, eat, speak, move, function at all without the loving of my sweet and terrible gaoler. Needing him for vitality, for reality.

Don't I sound sad, monk? Pathetic, feebly wasting my life like that. And I wonder, are there other women like me? I hope not. But if there are, and if you ever meet them, tell them about me, Brother Niall.

He used to tell me. He knew what it was like to be a prisoner. But the young man they kept upstairs in that house could not be ignored. He was no longer a child. He'd never, really, been a child.

And when Gideon gave him that horse for his tenth birthday I think it was a last, desperate attempt to do away with the heir he so despised. The stallion should not have been ridden by a man, let alone a boy – and a riding accident would be quite acceptable. Rowle was given the horse and then invited to the hunt, not one week after. Gideon gave him the horse and Catherine gave him a ring, which she said had belonged to his father. She stopped inviting him to visit her bedchamber. 'She paid me off,' said Rowle, contemplating the black opal he always wore on his ring finger, 'as she'd have paid off an unsatisfactory servant. Well, all I could do was admire her from a great distance, and that wasn't enough. No wonder Gideon was desperate, because I don't think he could touch her either, not where she felt anything. And he, a proud man and very vulnerable when it came to his sexual prowess, knew it.'

Rowle told me, 'I'll never understand why Dooley took my side then. Perhaps she knew her time was over and it was a way of fighting back against Gideon whom she considered, in some weird way, to have let her down. Perhaps it was that she did, after all, feel something for me, felt able to forgive me for growing up. Perhaps this was a battle she wanted me, for some perverse reason of her own, to win. I just don't know. But she did encourage me to ride that horse as much as I could in the week before the dreaded hunt, allowing me the freedom to do so, shouting at me to persevere when I came home bruised and in tears of anger, making me dress in my hunting clothes the next day, and the next, forcing me back to the stables, forcing me to conquer my fear. Because I *was* afraid of The Turk – named by Gideon, and chosen and broken by him with me in mind.

'We connived together in combat, me and Dooley, because I had to ride in secret while Gideon was away. I was up and out at dawn and back, crossing the cobbled courtyard, before breakfast. The other end of the day, I was riding in semi-darkness after the other horses had been stabled and fed. The grooms grumbled but took The Turk, the steam rising off him, and tended him while I fell, bruised and exhausted, into bed, and into sleep that was just a continuation of the day's terrible ride.

'He was fifteen hands high and almost magnificent. Easy with power, a dark chestnut, he was flawed by the temper that rippled him like a streak of evil, that showed in his stamping feet, the foam at his mouth and the wide wild whites of his eyes. I could have refused to accept him and backed down from Gideon's challenge. I could have refused the invitation to the hunt. I could have saved myself in many, easier ways, but I didn't, and Dooley, I think, approved of that. I think she must have taken some pride from the knowledge that, whatever else I was, she had "made a man of me". And that to die in a hunting accident on such a beast would not have given me, in her eyes, a sporting chance. Gideon, thought Dooley, was cheating! His scheme was much too obvious!

*

Listening to Rowle I could see how it had all started – this needing to beat things, to conquer them, to overcome – it was all a way of life to him. As for myself, as a woman I couldn't understand it, and Dooley's attitude, the way she encouraged him in his foolish recklessness, made me think of her more as a man than a woman. For I see backing down as a way of winning, without much dignity perhaps, but then what good is dignity and who ever needed dignity? Certainly, I think ruefully, I didn't. And pride – pride is as bad. Perhaps if you lose it early you're not plagued by it for the rest of your life.

Rowle should not have accepted that dangerous horse. By doing so he was condoning Gideon's wicked game. He should have aloofly declined such a horrible gift. He had no interest in hunting – not then.

And I had the nasty feeling that he had possibly accepted the challenge, not because of Gideon, but because of Catherine. He always showed off in front of women. And maybe he thought that by beating Gideon at his own game he would make his giddy mother . . . what . . . love him? Admire him? Rue the day that she rejected him?

That's the conclusion I came to, and it made me very angry.

'The moor, on that day, was bright and dry and good for galloping. I had supervised The Turk's feed, made sure Gideon did not slip him extra oats. There was a little too much of a wind, and wind excited the chestnut: there was a wild gleam in his eye as we set off. But I took great satisfaction in Gideon's stare of surprise as The Turk stood obediently to be mounted. We had conquered that, after hours of painful practice, that horse and I.

'I was also careful not to move too near Gideon, who had the nasty habit of leaning across and flicking other horses' flanks with his whip, for fun. All the riders were wary of Gideon, but no one dared confront him openly. The Turk would not stand to be shocked like that. I felt his muscles rippling underneath me as we led off close behind the master, flexing, testing himself and his rider as he always did.'

Rowle leaned forward and whispered to me, 'I can never remember being so frightened in the whole of my life. His ears went back when he heard the hunting horn, the greyhounds and spaniels round his feet unnerved him. A bird chirruped in a narrow lane and he pranced so unexpectedly he nearly unseated me and the two riders behind us. And all the time I was aware that Gideon would do something. This was his plan. This was his chance, possibly his last.'

I turned away from Rowle, pretending not to listen. He was bragging, pleased with himself and happy to see me so impressed, but I was thinking that he had no need to have been there, putting himself in danger like that.

'Once we were out in open countryside it was a different matter. Quickly the fear left me and I realised it was fear of the fear that had been daunting me, not the fear itself, which I exhilarated in. So did my horse. Under fast-scudding clouds the hunters galloped, tossed their heads, flung up their heels as we moved across Dartmoor, and for the first time I felt that The Turk and I were pulling together, excited by the same sensations, moving in the wind – one being. And I forgot about Gideon, forgot about everything except for the chase and the wild sensation of freedom all about me. I was too fast, Gideon could not catch me. The Turk and I, together we had power. I remember, Bethy, I laughed out loudly, the sound fell in streamers behind me, and I laughed because it was Gideon who had given me this: inadvertently he had given me the best moment of my life and he, who had taught me fear and all its subtleties, had shown me how to conquer it. I was breathless, quite breathless with the discovery of it.'

'How,' I asked Rowle then, 'how do you conquer fear?'

'By gripping it and taking it and mastering it. By challenging it full in the face. By remembering that it's the fear of the fear that is debilitating.'

You see, I was always like that. I didn't allow him to tell me a story without directing it towards myself, towards our desperate 'relationship'. On and on and on I went, predictable, oh so transparently predictable. 'How simple,' I said, as cuttingly as I could. 'What simple philosophies you use in your life. I wish I could steer my own life to your simple patterns.' Rowle referred to the big events in his life, never the little ones. It was the little ones that defeated me, but as he always told me, he never bothered with those. Never minded what people thought about him, how they reacted to him, whether they liked him or disliked him. Never cared enough, I suppose, about them, as long as they obeyed him or gave in to him.

That, to him, was all that seemed to matter. And his charisma was such that he made it work for him, painlessly, most of the time.

I had forgotten that I used to be like that, that I, too, was fearless before I met him. I had to think very hard to remember how I used to gallop over the moor, drinking in the wild excitement those feelings gave me, the same feelings he talked about with such wonder. He had discovered them but they had always been mine. I was afraid of nothing, then. When had I changed? Was it because of the horrors I had witnessed at Lydford? Was it because of what Rowle did to me – and has that been between us ever since? Or was it because I fell in love with him?

Could it be that loving him had turned me into the feeble creature I perceived myself to be, and that all my fears were directed towards Rowle and whether or not he loved me?

Whether or not, and when he was going to stop loving me? And, if that happened, could I bear it?

Rowle ignored my selfish mutterings and went on. I could see, by his expression, that this was important to him, that he wanted to tell it to me. *And that's what mattered to me then . . . those words only . . . to me, to me.*

'And it was on that same day that I learned to love the land itself. The texture, the shape and the deep, rich colours of the moors, the woods, the streams. It made me feel ecstatic but, at the same time, humble, seeing how small I was, I, who had always considered myself the centre of the universe up there in my room with poor Dooley. Life wasn't at all like that . . . there was all this, waiting for me, my time would come . . . and it would be here long after I had gone. There! Another discovery given to me by Gideon. He thought he would kill me that day, but instead of that he gave me life.

'And as if to clinch it, when we brought down the prey he jumped off his horse and was first to the stag, shouting at the dogs to leave it be. With his hunting knife he cut its throat, slit its belly open, called me from my horse and, with great delight, thrust my hands and feet deep inside the hot, wet body and daubed me all over with blood. He hadn't achieved the ultimate, but he could wash me in the victim's blood and imagine, maybe, that it was I, slippery with the crimson mess, who was lying there, broken, at his feet.

'So it must have been with great surprise that he heard me laugh, laugh long and loudly as I never remembered having laughed before, great shouts of joy that echoed back to us from the surrounding moorland like song. It was my moment, Bethy. I was the vanquisher, I was the powerful one and vibrant and he, but a little man doing little things – and failing even in those. He knew it and I knew it as we faced each other then, panting, wind-blown, grimy with dust and mud and blood as if we had fought each other almost to the death and now it was over.

'I saw Gideon gulp as he took a deep breath. I saw him shake his head. I saw bewilderment on his dark, haunted face. And when he wiped his hands together on his way back to his horse and stooped a little, it wasn't blood he wiped from his skin but his power over me. Oh, he kept me – I was still a dependant, still made to live upstairs with insufficient food and Dooley for company, but I would never be vulnerable as I had been before.

'I didn't go back with the rest, I wanted to be alone. I rode The Turk the long way home, loving him, trusting him, understanding his wildness now and his need to be free. Of course he would resent me, his master, for his captivity, for his taming. And now I could respect him for that. The sounds of that shifting, creaking saddle, his hooves so sure on the earthy paths, the way his nostrils quivered, opened to every stimulant, his senses missing nothing . . . I know that I could have ridden that way for ever, letting all those new wonders flood through me, getting used to the new person that I had become.'

I listened to Rowle but I thought of the beautiful Catherine, regal as a queen, up at her window and watching her son, her champion, riding home. Had he looked up at her window, doffed his hat, bowed and smiled, that day when he came home covered in blood, no longer a child? Had he? I couldn't ask him that. He wouldn't have answered me – he would have been disgusted by the meanness of the question.

And I did understand what Rowle was saying to me. I did. I knew how important his freedom was to him. He would never submit to taming again, not by man, woman, animal, elements, not by anything.

Oh yes, I did understand it but I couldn't accept it. How could he think that I wanted to reduce him . . . I thought that loving me might make him larger. Wonderful, isn't it, how I could believe that, knowing how fragile loving him had made me!

Rowle was the wise one. He always was, while I stayed the wide-eyed, adoring fool.

31

It is easier to stick to the facts when I think about Rowle's life, because all I knew of that was related to me, while when I think about my own I become unsure whether a thing really happened, or whether it was a figment of imagination.

I have to keep saying to myself, 'I think,' when I muse on my own experiences, but with Rowle's I can safely say, 'I know.' Everything about him is firm, unflinching and hard. His image is a flint in my mind, whereas my own is wishy-washy, fluttery as a candle-flame.

To see Rowle, to meet him, it would be quite impossible to guess at the pitiful bleakness of his early life. As far as I know he never spoke of it to anyone, but I knew that Lucy knew. He was swift and certain and determined about everything he did, intolerant, certainly, but quite fearless, never shy or unsure as I was. Never dragged backwards by what had happened to him. but he had one weakness that stands out for me, and that was that he could never bear to be laughed at. I tried it once, and at first he smiled – I can see him now, standing before the fire, his hands behind his back, his cloak tied from the epaulettes at his shoulders, his jaw down in his collar and his black eyes unswervingly on my face. Not by a flicker of an eyelid did he betray what must have been going on in his head.

I went on, undaunted, teasing him, testing him, trying to see how far I could go.

He moved so quickly. He grabbed my arm and twisted me round and said, in a voice so filled with ice that it made me freeze, 'No, Bethy, damn you, don't ever do that.'

So he had his soft underbelly, just the same as everyone else. I found that one, and I used it occasionally, carefully, in situations when I needed to win.

From the day of the hunt Dooley's power over Rowle diminished. Until that time he had always believed his life

223

would be stagnant, that he would always be a prisoner, dependent on others for his very existence.

'The change was so subtle,' said Rowle, 'it was hardly noticeable, but it was certainly there. She began to feed me proper food and to serve it decently with a knife and a spoon. Until then I had been left to eat with my fingers, had grown up learning to use the bread as an implement. She began to allow me to leave the nursery at night, pretending she didn't know where I went, which was to fetch books from Gideon's library – *The Treasure of Knowledge*; *The Whetstone of Wit*; *A Hundred Good Points of Husbandry*, and all sorts of joke and riddle books from which I taught myself to read. Dooley marvelled when I showed her what the words meant, how a page could tell you things you never knew about places you had never seen, about monsters and serpents, mountains and oceans, how neatly the pen could speak. She had never picked up the reading. But most fascinating of all to me were the Italian novels, translated into English, that Gideon kept in a separate case; I found the key in the top drawer of his desk in the library. Of course I never read Dooley these – strange, erotic tales that spoke to me of feelings I already recognised.

'And the next time Dooley went for her whip I fought her for it. I lost, as I knew I would lose, and she was all the more ferocious for that. And as I fought her, as I raged and tore at her clothes, thumped at her chest, grabbed at her hair, I suddenly realised, with awe, that Dooley was a woman, as my mother was. Incredible, but so. And that I was a man and would one day be stronger. So I knew, and she knew, that one day I would win.

'Fat Charles was nicer to me, too, and gradually my position in all this turmoil began to slip into place – my position, and their attitudes to it. When I first learned I was the future master of Amberry I was astonished, not just with the enormity of the realisation, but because it was then that I understood why I had been treated so differently. It was the bailiff Tremain who told me, inadvertently I'm sure, because the servants were strictly under orders to say nothing, but Tremain had been a friend of my father, had known him as a boy, so perhaps the way he leaked the news to me was a deliberate attempt to warn me. And I remained on my guard from that moment on.

'Tremain was a huge, jovial man with a voice like a bellowing bull and the most extraordinary eyes. They crossed, but they seemed to locate you first and then cross, so that you felt you had moved out of focus and the watery blue was trying to place you again. Tremain was married and lived on the estate which was largely and profitably populated by his myriad offspring, all who grew, those from the right side of the blanket and those from the wrong, to look exactly like him. You could tell who they were – even the tiny toddlers – from their lumbering gait, their bellowing voices and their give-away eyes. All, it seemed, had inherited that same trait, so his wife must have known and accepted the distressing situation or, more than likely, felt unable to do much about it.

'On this particular day Charles had invited me to do the estate rounds with him. Gideon was away but he liked to hear that Charles was showing an interest – he liked his son to accompany Tremain at least once a week. As far as I could see, Charles hated the whole business. He was not a natural rider and on a day such as this, windy and cold with sleet in the air, he was happier staying by the fire feeding himself sweetmeats.

'Charles, Tremain and I were riding round the Beacon Hill when we came upon the vagrant woman. She was just round the bend in the track and we came upon her so suddenly we nearly trampled her. As it was, she darted back just in time, but one of her babies was still on the road, its fingers in its mouth, squatting there looking like a bundle of shawl, crying. There were four others, only the eldest higher than a man's knee. Two she carried under her arms and the other hung on to her skirts and looked up at us – we had pulled up in a great lather of confusion – out of big, wide eyes.

'She dropped the two and rushed forward for the baby. Tremain looked down at the motley collection of travellers, tipped back his hat and bellowed as gently as he was able, "Doan yous knows youm trespassin'? This is Amberry land, there be no footpaths through here."

' "'Tis the quickest route to Tavistock," the flustered woman answered quickly, pulling her shawl back over her head as if, for decency, she had to have it there, exactly right. "An I's has to get there by nightfall in order to get a bed an' supper for these." '

' "Be on yous way then," said Tremain, relaxed and letting

225

his reins loose again. And he would have gone. He kicked his horse, looked over his shoulder and inclined his head for us to leave them be. He wanted to finish his rounds before dark, but Charles hung back.

' "Not so fast!" he called out after Tremain. "These people are trespassing. Are you going to leave them to carry on, to set a bad example to others? Hell's teeth, man, before you know it all the waifs and strays in the district will be roaming over our land, taking what they want to supplement their appetites and pockets along the way. Sir Gideon will not be pleased about your attitude, Tremain, when I tell him of it on his return. By God he will not."

'Tremain had reined in his giant white cob and now it was pulling on the bit, clinking the harness, impatient to be off. The horse's breath and ours made white wreaths in the air. Sleet landed on Tremain's hat and melted there and I thought it must be enormously hot on that spot because I could see the man struggling for composure. He tried to speak in a quiet voice, to keep to the same measured politeness he had adopted all afternoon, even in reply to Charles' most futile questions, but he was not by nature a patient man. "They'm be beggars, Master Charles, a beggarwoman wi' five brats to cope wi'. I's doubts if 'er'll find the time, or the energy to snare any rabbits on 'er way, or bring down a snipe, or take yer sheep."

' "I don't care what you doubt or what you do not doubt, Tremain. The fact is that the law is being broken and you are turning a blind eye. That would not be Sir Gideon's way. I have ridden with him many times and he is most particular, as you know, about who travels this main path."

' "What do yous suggest, Master Charles, that I's do?" Tremain's voice was laden with sarcasm as he looked down from his sturdy steed upon his smaller, fatter travelling companion.

' "See her off here and now," said Charles in that reedy, high voice that he always reverted to when in temper, or challenged. "See her off and make sure in the seeing that she will not repeat the misdemeanour." He drew his winter cloak around him, his face looking fatter than ever as it set into one of his pouts. "We lead by example, Tremain, remember that. By example, man."

'Even I knew that Charles was betting on a loser. Tremain

was strong in the knowledge that Gideon Rowle would never dismiss him . . . the whole success of the quickly accumulating estate depended on Tremain's skilful management, and there was not only him but his whole troupe of relatives as well. They worked on the farm, in the stables, up at the house, in the mill and on the river. While it is true that servants could be hired for two a penny, Tremain's were a trusted and willing lot, dependable people and not easily replaceable. No, Gideon, who was not a fool whatever else he might be, would never dismiss his bailiff.

'But Charles seemed to be driven by some strange illusion of authority and carried on regardless. It was embarrassing – Tremain was laughing at him. The woman, sensing her chance, had moved along, laden with children and baggage. Charles saw his quarry disappearing in front of his eyes and became furious. "It's a point of principle," he blustered. I don't think Tremain heard him, or if he did he didn't bother to answer. Charles took his horse-whip, turned his horse, and trotted a few threatening steps towards the scurrying beggar. He brought the whip down in the damp peat-black soil not an inch from her trailing skirts so that she jumped, turned and went very pale. Her hand at her mouth was trembling. The whimpering children fell silent. Before he could bring it up again for a second crack that whip was out of his hand and on the ground. Charles' small eyes shrivelled angrily as he looked at Tremain who had used his cattle-whip to knock the weapon from his hand.

' "I'll not forget this," said Charles in a querulous voice, staring first at Tremain and then at the whip below him on the ground. It was a good whip, a new one, and he didn't want to abandon it, but nor did he want to lose face.

' "That'll not worry me," said Tremain, the polite veneer gone from his voice so that he sounded natural, his voice fitting his face for the first time that day. "That'll never worry me, lad. 'Tis wi' relief that I's know yous'll never be my bliddy maister!"

' "That's enough, Tremain!" Charles decided to dismount.

'But Tremain was in full flow now: his blood was up and he refused to be silenced. "No laddy," he guffawed as he turned his horse to lead away. "Yous'll never get yous bliddy hands on these reins. Not while there's a boy like the one behind yous coming on! Not while Anthony Rowle's son lives yous woan."

'And I travelled behind, mulling this over and lost in the wonder of it. Would I, then, one day inherit Amberry? And would it be mine? Yes, I came to understand a very great deal that day, by accident, although no one ever referred to it again and when I asked Dooley she just snorted.

'So that, little Bethany, was my brother Charles.'

I smiled and looked away, because I still couldn't understand why Rowle had had to murder him – and nor did I dare to ask him why.

32

The winter that followed was the worst in memory. Sam Gaunt, the defrocked preacher, dressed for death all in black. He stooped about mournfully, his long, broken pipe clutched between gravestone teeth – while Silas strutted savagely beside him. He could never really bear to accept death. 'He has seen too much of it in his life,' Lucy said, 'and if it were any other man it would have turned him. Even the old and the weak, he fights too hard to keep them alive. He upsets them,' she said accusingly, 'for they are accepting and willing to go but Silas pulls and struggles. Silas will not let them be.'

'God's blood!' shouted Silas, flinging his hat on the wall in a gesture of angry defiance. 'Anne Hartley, Martin Rudd, Shamus Dogherty – how many more?'

Silas could not say whether anyone actually died from the cold, but it seemed to bring out all the dormant weaknesses in folks who had been doing quite modestly well when they could bask in the summer warmth or while the comforting autumn lights played upon them. The Combe lay rigid, frozen stiff in an icy grip like the old men's faces, such mists . . . ice mists . . . they floated cloud-like and blocked out all sight and sound. So thick were the mists you could not see from one narrow side of the Combe to the other. You could not even see the house next door. Every breath taken in haste felt sharp as a knife in your chest.

Even the children seemed to be coloured by the cold, and their little faces under their hoods were grey and haggard. 'Even when I'm in bed at night my teeth are chattering,' said Matt. And then, quite suddenly, he started to cry.

'It's affecting everyone,' sighed Lucy, 'this winter melancholy. When will it end?'

There was no softness about it. Drifts of snow shone like glass matting, making all movement treacherous. The children had long ago abandoned the snow, its novelty soon gone. When first it came they had used it delightedly, sliding down the steep Combe sides, chasing and racing on complicated, firmly structured sledges made out of wattles and sacking. Their voices pierced like blades in the cold. They had constructed weird and magical statues, and such was the extent of the freezing grip that these watchers – for that is how they seemed, sitting staring into nowhere like that – 'they look still and condemning as ancient ancestors,' said Rowle – these watchers remained in all their fine detail; not one glossy eye slipped out of place, not one shiny button slithered to the ground – so fierce was the clutch of the cold.

I regarded the weather wearily. It was my enemy, for the difficulties it created made it harder for Rowle and me to meet, threw us into dangerous assignments where it was more likely we be caught. We still made for the shepherd's hut sometimes. No one could follow our footprints, for we made no indents in the crisp snow, despite the heat that was in us, that flooded through us . . .

Sometimes, Rowle asked me of Silas and I answered warily. I was becoming more and more afraid of Silas as the cold kept us in and the deaths mounted up and he scowled more often and cursed more wickedly and stared at me more insolently as each day went by.

'Silas is nothing to me,' I assured Rowle with a deadpan face. 'I wish he would leave the house and build a home of his own. I wish he would find a woman and start a family. He is a man with no scruples, Rowle. And he frightens me. I wish he was far away.'

'There is only one woman that Silas wants,' said Rowle, poking the hut fire angrily and glowering through the dusty bars of heat. 'And that's you.'

I was placing stones round the hearth, tidying it up as the jackdaws had got in through the chimney in our absence and caused a mess. Rowle moved away from the fire, held me by my shoulders and stared directly into my face. He was so big, so black, so wicked at that moment. 'I would kill him, Bethany, if I thought . . .'

'You have no need to kill Silas, Rowle,' I said, squeezing the cold stone tight in my hand. 'You know I am interested in no man but you.'

But I shivered in my fear because I knew how Rowle feared the loss of those that he loved . . . or, more correctly, Brother Niall, those that he considered his own.

While the stars twinkled, frozen above us and we cuddled together for warmth against the world outside, he told me of his first encounter with love.

'I learned that lesson a long time ago,' he said in his smooth, soft voice, 'just before I left Amberry for The Mountford School. I was going for my last ride when Gideon informed me casually that he was giving The Turk to Charles, and that in future I would not need a horse of my own, I could use the pool.

'I argued with him that The Turk was his present to me. I told him the horse was not his any longer to dispose of as he wished. I reminded him how wild The Turk was when I had him, and that it was I who had trained him into gentleness, persevered with him over the months, made it possible for others to handle him without danger. I didn't want Charles to have him. The Turk belonged to me!'

I told Rowle, 'Gideon knew how much that horse meant to you. He wanted to wear you down, that's what he was doing.'

Rowle said, 'Yes, I loved The Turk as I had never loved any other living thing in my life. I tried to keep my calm. I was trying to unclench the fists at my side and to keep my voice from trembling.

'Gideon was angry with my audacity. He smacked his whip against his boots and scowled as he strutted about, waiting impatiently for his own mount. We stood and argued in the courtyard, Gideon just about a head taller. I remember thinking, quite clearly, it won't be long – it won't be long before I can lick the bastard. The clouds gathered like my temper that day, and Charles chuckled paunchily and told me, with a sneer, that he would treat The Turk with every consideration, just as if he was one of his own. And I had seen how Charles treated his mounts, and it was nothing so simple as cruel, but more disagreeable, petty-minded and bad-tempered. I knew that I would return from The Mountford at Christmas and The Turk's head would be down, his eyes blank, and everything that made him bold would have been ground out of him.

'I went for Charles then,' said Rowle. 'I turned and prodded him with my whip, letting it sink deep into his stomach until his face went red and his mouth turned into an O as if bloated by cherries – like this. And I gave a series of stabs to the handle, wanting to push it right in and silence his squeaks forever. That that flabby apology for a boy could be the possessor of such an animal as The Turk was quite intolerable. I would rather that Gideon had claimed him for himself.

'Gideon called me off, I ignored him. I threatened what I would do to Charles if I had my way. And then Gideon's whip flashed over my back so fiercely, so unexpectedly, that it cut the material and I had to let loose my fat prey, just as I had backed him conveniently against the wall and he was about to beg for mercy. I fell back, clutching at the pain. Gideon smiled, and when he smiled his mouth drew back from his teeth and his eyes went cold as flint. I knew that he would never change his mind, that The Turk belonged to Charles now and there was nothing I could do about it.'

I watched Rowle carefully as he spoke, but saw nothing of fear or failure in his face – no – just a desire to win, to outdo his opponents. And he would – I had no doubt that he would find a way to prevent them from having The Turk.

'I called to the chestnut under my breath. He came to nuzzle my hand but I bore no titbits for him that afternoon. He smelled warm, of life and of love. I tugged on his mane and mounted. I leaned down over his neck and I whispered into his ear. We left that stable like a bolt from a bow: The Turk reared up in the court and took a five-foot wall. For a moment I thought he would throw me, but we jumped the wall and went. It was all I could do to hang on.'

I remembered something of that feeling, riding wild with my little rowan, when we never knew where we were going or what was going to happen to us. I had often let her have her head – just for the sheer fear of it.

'It was our last ride together,' stated Rowle. 'I let him take me. He could go until he was exhausted and he seemed to sense this. I galloped my hatred out. The pounding in my head became just the gentle rhythm of The Turk until both our frustrations were out of us and we had both had enough of them. He pulled up by a river and we stood, just he and I, at a place of his choosing, alone for some moments, listening to the silence, breathing it in. We needed it. We were waiting, just as the approaching storm was waiting to break. Then I dismounted and let him drink. I caught the water in my hands and cooled my forehead, smoothing all that was left of the hatred out. I wanted to be clear, clear as the water and as pure when I did what I had to do. The first hard drops of rain came then, making puddles in the water like stones being dropped, and sweeping from bank to bank with the whorls that they made. I took my knife from my belt. I hung on to his head, there as he stood, trembling, his hocks in the water, his tail lashing, his ears pricked to the thunder as he used to prick them to the hounds.'

Rowle's face was resolute. His lips came tightly together and I thought that he wouldn't go on. I squeezed his hand. I wriggled closer.

'I plunged my knife deep into his neck, and with all my strength I brought it down. I tore. He trembled. I struck again and again, at love and the wheaty smell of it, the warm breathing of it, the sweat and the pain of it. He staggered and went to his knees. I sank with him, clinging to his lifelessness, no strength left. His eyes were blank. They never accused me: they never had time. His life went into the river, Bethy, and the water boiled with it, a furious maelstrom in the storm. The river rose, thrashed at its contents, crying, crimson with blood. The lightning came and printed his name in jagged letters on to the sky, recording them forever there in silver. For even on a summer day, after that, I could screw up my eyes and see his name.'

Rowle turned to me. I expected to see pain in his face, to see it softened by that memory, awed even, by an experience so powerful that he had forgotten not one detail of it. After all these years, not one detail, so that I, the listener, sensed the sombre atmosphere of that dark place, the storm, the horror, the dying horse and all the power leaving such a beautiful thing.

'You weaken yourself when you love,' said Rowle quietly. 'It is essential to keep free.'

There was nothing on his face. Nothing at all.

Back in the Combe, my fingers quite numb with the cold, we drifted towards the action pretending we had not been together.

'Fifty on t'brown bird . . .'

'Take ten, Matt! No, make it twenty.'

'Yer a vule . . . carn yer see that one 'as no stamina, 'e'll not last the course.'

There was a roaring and a bawling as men haggled for prices. Steam came off the crowd, a rush of misty excitement, hot as a boiling kettle it rose into the air as we approached the cockfight, where a patch in the gloom had been lit up with watery lanterns. Children had pushed to the front of the small ring and now they looked fearful as though they would be crushed with all the frenzy of it, but they held their ground. Men and women, fatly bundled up against the weather in every garment they could lay their hands on, thrust themselves forward to see. Some had sticks and staves and were poking their neighbours, jostling fiercely for position, and others, less frantic, were sitting round small fires they had lit high on the steep slope above. These were the sensible ones – for they would have a far better view.

And there stood Ned, Mary's man, huger than ever in his swathing of deer-skins and sacking, a giant with his vast red beard that matched the colour of his face, swollen with pride for his champion bird. He held it high in the air between both hands like a winning prize-fighter, calling out for all the people to see and approve. His opponent this evening was Daniel Biggins, a thin listless man. Normally morose, today his long face was animated and he was eager to pit his bird, his precious bird, against Ned's. He had spent long hours on his own, secretly in training, for his fighting birds were the love of his life. Arguments rippled from the front of the crowd to the back, occasionally breaking out in friendly play-fights round the edge where the younger men, released from their winter stupor for a few precious hours, punched and fooled around like boys again.

Coins were thrown down into the ring and the backers were well tuned to catch them.

The fighting cocks were almost featherless. Their combs and wattles had been chopped off for the purpose, their wings had been shaped into sharp points and their beaks fashioned to be cruelly sharp. They looked aggressively thin and ugly. Ned stooped to place his bird on the ground, to allow it to strut and familiarise itself with the sawdusty ring. Then it was Daniel Biggins' turn, and he was not amused when the audience threw out their insults. His face was wicked and white, and I thought how much he resembled his bird.

At the same time exactly, the two vicious fighters were released to their fates and such a roar rose from the crowd that I had to clap my hands to my ears. The birds rose, squawking, into the air. They struck at each other with their sharpened spurs. Time went by but none of the excitement lessened. I climbed up the slope, heading for Mary, having, for decency's sake, to keep apart from Rowle in public. He had pushed forward and now stood watching, just as excited as the rest, from a place in the centre of the crowd.

"E has such faith in this bird,' said Mary, watching the scene below with gritted teeth as I drew my skirts round me and sat down beside her. She had on her knee a small wooden coffer which I knew was normally full of coins. She had it open before her – it was empty. 'Yes,' she said, not moving her eyes from the ring but sensing my concern. ''E has staked everythin' we 'as on it.'

Mary screamed as wildly as the rest of them, beating a blackthorn stick on the ground so that in the end it could take no more and snapped in half. I wished it would end. I bit my lip and watched the proceedings. It was hard, with the blood, to tell whose bird belonged to whom. I knew nothing of the subtleties of the game but Ned's bird seemed the stronger, and I called out with the rest. There was something infectious about the fray, about the mood of the crowd so that for a while we could all forget we were cold. We could forget about everything except for the wild, flapping mess of beaks and wings below us in the dust, and the crimson pool that was spreading.

There was such a sudden silence. Such an inrush of breath. You could even hear the thin cry of a child. Daniel Biggins' bird tried to strut and crow, but its beak was half off and one wing trailed along the ground behind it drawing a bloody circle, while Ned's bird slumped in the corner, where it had trailed its body, heavy with death, accompanied by the jibes and jeers of its frenzied supporters.

'That be that, then . . . I told 'e . . .'

'The best bird won . . . 'e had a clean pair o' heels. I can allus tell . . .'

'Neither o' they'll live ter fight agin.'

The winner was declared and money was pocketed. Mary's coffer stayed limply open, staring back at her vacant eyes with all its wooden emptiness. "'E 'ad such hopes,' she moaned. 'An' now 'e'll have to start all over.' It was not so much the loss of the money she bemoaned, but the loss of poor Ned's pride.

And then Ned's bird, sly and only feigning death, rose in the air like a cunning ghost from the grave with its wings outstretched and its spurs at the ready, and fell upon the declared champion with such evil desperation that its opponent, startled and half-crazed with pain, fell down with its legs in the air and died instantly.

There was a deeper silence. Awe. Bewilderment. And then the ugly anger of unfairness rose in a growl on the air.

'Ned's bird be the rightful winner! The result were announced afore the fight were properly ended!'

'No one can doubt who the real winner be!'

'We'm must 'ave our money back! 'Tis unfair play! 'Tis cheatin'!'

All the supporters of Ned's bird called out in pained self-righteousness. The crowd began to argue amongst themselves. The shadows of the lanterns played yellow and menacing on the shifting mob. Their faces, some of them well-known to me, looked drawn and sharp . . . all flinty-eyed. Strangers. Savages?

'Oh Lord,' said Mary to me, 'let's go home, there'll be trouble.' And many of the women felt the same for they picked out their children skilfully as short-legged birds pecking about for grubs, squawking about among all the feet, shouting and drawing their children to them . . . children in danger of being trampled now under the blind fury of heavy-booted, hard-done-by men.

I was all concern for Rowle for he was down there in the thick of it.

I was all concern for the outcome, for old enemies, sensing the chance, were singling each other out and it seemed as if this episode would serve as excuse for the sorting of longlasting disagreements. It had to be stopped – and stopped right away.

And then I saw that, a little way above me, a group of Rowle's men had appeared, as from nowhere, surrounded by others, council men. Silas was there at the front, and soon Rowle came. The scuffles ceased, uneasily, one by one. The cold came again to the Combe, and a mist rose up into the sky, uncannily chilling.

'Ned's bird is the winner,' said Rowle, not loudly, but softly, conversationally, but with great power behind his words. 'The outcome was concluded too soon and it is to those who backed Ned's bird that the winnings should go.'

Mutterings. Growlings. I averted my eyes for a moment. I was horrified and sickened by the menace in the air. The tension he spoke into was like a monster seething with an animal life all of its own.

Silas and Rowle stood together side by side, dominating the group below them and flanked by armed men.

'And those of you who have lost by this have learned an important lesson,' and Rowle smiled sharply. 'Never trust your enemy until he is well and truly dead, and proved to be dead. If you're not sure then you should find out. You are nothing but fools to do otherwise. You deserve to lose your money – think it lucky you have not lost your lives.' He glanced casually round, but I could see how he deliberately caught the eye of every man in that crowd. Some he held longer than others before he moved on.

It was quite impossible to think of this man as ever having been vulnerable and lost. That he could talk this way . . . insult them even . . . and that they would accept his criticism, even in their angry mood, was a measure of Rowle's control over the Combe and all life in it. The wrongfully-taken money was given back with a surly reticence – and certainly I heard threats made under the breaths of angry men – but they did give the money back. And nobody stood up and protested.

I had seen how swiftly and surely Silas had moved to Rowle's side, and it was only because I sat where I did that I saw the brassy gleam of the gun that Silas held behind his back. And I knew then, that had there been serious trouble, Silas, without hesitation, would have taken the trouble-maker and dealt with him firmly, fatally. Silas – who hated death – and yet he would mete it out coldly, unblinkingly, and without a second's hesitation if forced by the need to do so.

Ned was triumphant. I knew he would have to be put to bed, near out of his head tonight. Mary would forgive him and his children would call him champion for a little while. Daniel Biggins' thin face was wary and full of hatred. Oh yes, Rowle had many enemies: by the nature of his position this had to be so.

And I knew how important in so many ways was Silas to
Rowle.

33

You think you know yourself, don't you? You think you have experienced all there can possibly be to experience and you sit back, contented, with that. Ah . . . that's not how it goes Brother Niall, and I know all about that.

'Oh, Amos was good to me,' I used to tell Rowle. 'I was a most special child!' And Rowle never questioned me, Rowle believed me, Rowle never asked me what Amos did and why we were so afraid of him. There were nights when my mother's sisters were turned black and blue with having to protect me.

I feared that wherever I went the taint-mark told the truth – the truth of my birth and the truth of my continuing existence. Amos – I choke on my tears but I did not cry then. You don't cry – you let your dreams come in when you are seven years old. But I was old enough then to have stopped the dreaming . . .

'Yes,' I told Rowle. 'Amos was good to me and I was a special child.' And I didn't want contradicting. I had always loved Amos, under the fear and under the hate. If I hadn't loved Amos he would not have been able to hurt me. And Dooley was Rowle's monster just as Amos was mine.

And Rowle and I would hold each other so tightly. So safe with our lies wrapped around us.

Lucy used to say, 'You have built Silas into a monster. Why? In reality he is nothing like that!' I was frightened of Silas. And no, not just because he was powerful and quite without scruples, not just because he threatened my relationship with Rowle – but because I was drawn to something in Silas, and it was mainly for this reason that I feared him. Strangely, I knew that I could not manipulate Silas in quite the same way that I could manipulate Rowle.

That winter of death that we were now leaving behind us had left Silas more morose than before. Over the winter he had grown thinner so that the bones in his face stood out sharply and hollowed his cheeks, and these days, his wholesome smell was often soured with drink. Even Lucy, who had a great admiration for Silas, expressed her concern because we would be lost in the Combe without his skills. There was no one else except the old women, and they were never so successful with their brews and their cures, as he. It was Lucy who flirted with Silas, not I: she grew quite coquettish in his presence, given to giggles and girlish screams, while I watched and remained silent.

Into the house on the warm spring breeze came the gentle smell of violets and lilies, and daffodils grew in Lucy's garden. I had still to tell her about Rowle and me . . . but there never seemed a good time. And sometimes I wondered over the rights and wrongs of it, and wouldn't it be better to let things carry on as they were? I came to this conclusion as we walked together in the warm spring sunshine . . . daily I swung quite violently between my two options. There were even times when I plucked up my courage and started to say . . . but every time something seemed to happen or, in some absurd way – for this couldn't be correct – it appeared that Lucy managed to prevent me.

'Will you go with Silas to the May dance?'

'He has not asked me.'

'But he will.'

Lucy was a good deal more certain than I. She was also a good deal more certain that Silas was the right man to choose. 'Give him a chance! Relax a bit more in his company, Bethany. See him for the man he really is. And if you decide to go I have found such a brilliant crimson gown for you. It came but a week ago . . . from a carriage bound for London with a caseful of furs. I have shaken it and sniffed it. It is quite clean, and the latest in fashion, almost new.'

I laughed. 'Do you think that I need a crimson gown? Are you so intent on getting me paired off that you think I need to flaunt myself in colours like that?'

'You are so beautiful,' she said to me, without any sense of flattery. 'You don't need colours . . . you could go round in dun-coloured robes with dust in your hair and still attract every eye.'

I fingered the taint-mark – a habit I could not stop whenever I felt uneasy. I had always thought this of Lucy, and now she was saying the same thing of me.

We walked out of the garden and along the sides of the Combe, towards the flattest part, an outcrop of bright green grass where the children played. They had erected a fine maypole and strewn it with ribbons of every hue. They had dragged it into the Combe – a huge thing – using a train of ten horses. It had lain on the ground for a week while the children swirled it with paints of gaudy colours and a great fuss had been made over hauling it up. Ribbons and handkerchiefs streamed from the top. Women and girls had gone out to gather the May blossom, which they bound in wreaths and now these bundles decorated the doors of the caves and the shacks.

As many as could were going to wear green, and put primroses in their hair – so much sweetness and innocence. I was intending to wear green, too, until Lucy mentioned the scarlet. It appealed to me more, for wasn't scarlet a summer colour, too?

Oh, but scarlet was not fresh and innocent like green. And wasn't it the colour of blood?

The straw targets were going up in their usual positions in readiness for the archers. Men lolled in the fresh new sunshine, their backs to the boulders, perfecting their arrows, choosing the most brightly-coloured duck or peacock feathers for flights. Their bows were their most important weapons and so they were cherished and cared for with something like love. Lethal, efficient, the bows were fashioned from witch hazel and the very best quality hemp. And while the men sat making little scraping movements, sharpening their arrow heads and whistling, little Daisy joined the older children, toddling round on her new hobby horse.

Mary and the other women had spent days cooking venison pasties and mince pies. You could tell what they had been doing, for they were all sweaty and wispy. Now they were laying the trestle table with lobsters and chickens, pigeons and sturgeon, round, strong cheeses and piles of sweet, fresh oranges. But the May celebrations meant more than just feasting and dancing to us all. They meant we could walk free in the outside air again, meet together and live together and laugh together, intoxicated with all the wild sweetness of the Dartmoor spring. And summer was still to come. We did not think further than that – and we did recall the winter that lay so heavy behind us.

Silas strode towards us now with his bow over his shoulder and he spoke to me stiffly. 'Are you planning to join us tonight?'

'I was, Silas. I was planning to come with Lucy and Rowle.'

'Is there room for me in that cosy little company?'

'Of course there is, Silas,' said Lucy quickly, embarrassed to think that he had to ask. And I saw she looked flushed – I saw how high were her cheekbones – how luxurious her hair – how deep blue her eyes this afternoon, framed by such neat, narrow eyebrows, such pale gold lashes. 'But it's not Rowle and I you want to join, surely? You are asking Beth.'

'Bethany?' asked Silas, coldly.

And it was quite impossible for me to say no to the proud man with the stormy brows and the cool, officious manners of a noble lord. Whenever I looked into Silas' eyes I saw some secret knowledge there.

'I will wait for you by the house gate,' he said. 'Do not let me down. Do not be late.'

And Rowle? What would he say if he knew I was going with Silas?

We went to sit where the women were washing, dipping the dull, winter-weathered garments into a deep pool of stream-water ringed with stones before it ran on to enter the river below. Everyone greeted Lucy, but I thought the women uneasy with me although they nodded and smiled. This reaction made me haughty. I laughed too loudly, I batted my lashes and I tossed my hair. They thought me a slut and so what? I sat on the grass with my head high and my face to the sun. Even the young ones like Sally – who, when we talked about freedom those months ago agreed with me – even she looked at me sideways through shaded, accusing eyes. So I knew they were nothing but jealous. I pitied them and their drab, empty lives, bending and scrubbing and rubbing until their hands were sore and red and their knees wrinkled and tough.

They did not seem to consider themselves pitiable, however, for they joked and shrieked with laughter while they worked, knowing the night of roistering and feasting was coming. Many of them, I was aware, would be bedding a new man tonight and yet they excluded me, treated me warily . . . because of Lucy!

No wonder these women were evil-tongued, no wonder their thoughts slithered and bit like vipers. Look at their lives compared to my own! Their talk was all of men and children so I stared past them, ignoring the gabble, and thought my own thoughts.

But Bell just sat in her chair and wouldn't stop staring at me. I tried to stare back at the old fool without lowering my eyes, and I told myself that the poor, decrepit old woman had never known love like mine. And I thought of the gold curtains I would have one day, and of the silver thread running through the tapestries that would surround my great bed.

A red sun caressed the horizon and a thin white moon started up in the sky when, having taken great care with my appearance, I came from my room to join Lucy in her chamber. The children were all to the tournament, and the maids and lads were preparing for the dance. There was nobody moving in and out – sometimes total strangers – like there so often was in this house. Perhaps I should tell Lucy now? But no – not with the dance tonight. I must not spoil the evening for everyone. Through the wide open window we could hear music, bagpipes and fiddles, and I could smell roasting meat. The last of the archery tournament was still going on – with two champions left, Rowle and Silas.

The scarlet dress felt coldly lovely round me. It rustled as I walked. I had let my hair loose tonight, I had brushed it a hundred times and it was almost to my waist. Lucy turned as I entered, raised her fine eyebrows high and exclaimed, 'Oh yes, I was right!'

But seeing her made me unsure, for she was in palest blue and neater than I. She was dressed for purity while I was the wildest whore. Did it matter? Should I have dressed in white for purity, also? But it would not have done any good. I looked at myself in Lucy's mirror and, no, it was not the dress that gave me the look that I feared. The dress merely framed the fires that burned underneath. If I had dressed in white, then the white would have looked like the hottest of flames, and even the subtlest blue would have suggested burning on me.

'I never like it, I am never easy when the two of them pit themselves against each other like this. I know that Rowle would like me to be there but I can't watch.'

'For fear he might lose?' I was astonished. The possibility that Rowle might not win the tournament had never entered my head.

Lucy saw my reaction and laughed. 'You have more confidence in Rowle than I do. He is not God, you know. He is fallible.'

'He has to accept all the challenges – he has no alternative but to do so. He must know, before he sets off, that only he can win!'

'He suffers for his reputation,' said Lucy soberly. 'You should listen to what he tells you.' And I didn't know what she could possibly mean.

Lucy paced the room, stepping daintily in her little blue slippers, biting her lips with her teeth and listening for Rowle's return. It crossed my mind how little of our lives we had for ourselves, Lucy and I, because of our love for Rowle. We were almost as weak as reflections . . . turning this way and that according to the way he held his head, his eyes, his chin . . . if he crooked his finger either one of us would gratefully do his bidding. If he went away, would we both disappear? And once again, Brother Niall, in that brief instant, I saw my obsession for what it was. I saw underneath it and round it and understood it – I grieved for my loss of pride, for the loss of my own life with a sadness that was almost unendurable. If only I could have hung on to that moment . . . but then, as quickly and unaccountably as it had come, that moment was gone.

The men came in surrounded by a raucous, back-slapping rabble, and there was best ale provided for all. I saw that Lucy looked anxious and caught Rowle's eye, but he was all cocksure and in no need of comfort. He was quite clearly the victor – and even Silas looked comfortable with the outcome, as though some burning desire in himself had been quenched. He seemed more relaxed than he had been just lately and I was relieved. Perhaps, after all, tonight would go without tension. Perhaps I could find some peace, some happiness, and allow it at last to come in.

34

It was not at all as Rowle saw it.

I did not give Silas tender looks. I did not allow him to touch me indiscreetly. I did not dance alone with him, eyeing him only, all night. Nor did I drink too much wine and flaunt my charms like a harlot.

There might have been some slight truth in Rowle's accusations, but I did not behave as badly as that. It was his fault for returning to the dance after Lucy had been taken home – and that was well after midnight.

I was startled to see him reappear, and it was not usual for Rowle to drink as deeply as that. For a while he stayed back in the shadows with his loyal companions around him. Women approached him, as they always did when Lucy was absent, giggling and flirting, and I even saw the ones who were most reproachful of me standing before him, fiddling foolishly with their girdles and crossing their legs shyly. But I knew that his eyes were on me, and when Silas' hand caressed my breast, when his breathing became deeper and his gestures more intimate and insistent, I did not push that hand away. And then Rowle came forward, his eyes burning black, and said to Silas, 'Forgive me for being intrusive, but I think, my friend, it is my turn.'

I saw that people were listening and watching. The music appeared to have ceased, but I must have been mistaken, for around us couples danced on. Silas hesitated, and that was enough. Before he could protest I was in Rowle's arms and whirling to the music of the mad fiddler, for Jamie Bovey went dotty like that when he played for too long, and he had been playing for five hours now. With his bowed legs and his eyes hardly blinking, he fiddled like the Devil himself, they said, and his eyes looked like a demon's eyes but he weaved magic with his fingers.

Among those who did not dance, some lolled at the tables, picking at the meat with satisfied fingers, singing bawdy ballads and telling stories, while the greedy Amy Trotter scooped up the maggots that crawled from the Stilton with a long silver spoon. Children had dropped from exhaustion and lay like puppy dogs, long-lashed, loose-limbed, sprawled on the ground. Some had taken too much wine and would be ill in the morning. Jugglers entertained in the background, while Dory Kean the fire-eater drew burning faggots over his glistening limbs, the keen whites of his eyes leaping more wildly than the flames that licked the rest of his body. Rufus Siddons ran round the charred white embers of the main fire with bare feet, like a madman, while drunken friends irresponsibly cheered him on. So drunk was he, he felt no pain. A group of drunken bawdy maids had stripped for the men and now danced with painted nipples, caressing themselves erotically with ribbons they had tugged from the maypole. The men who watched their antics called out coarsely, clapping their hands to a rhythm, lurching forward for a fumble now and again and evoking hysterical screams. Couples were openly making love, past concern for privacy. And Happy Blackmore was having to be stopped from cutting himself with a knife in order to prove, it would seem, that he had risen above all earthly matters and was no longer a man but a saint. 'Call me Saint Stephen,' he roared, while blood dripped from the slits in his arm. 'For I am a man of more than seven sorrows.' Most people ignored him.

And all the while the watchman's lantern burned steadily from the hill, and we knew there were men who waited soberly, always at the ready. But most of us danced to the fiddler's tunes while the stars burned frosty above us and little wisps of white ribbon cloud floated around the moon.

Rowle held me stiffly. We circled, and his eyes looked stolidly out and over my head when he asked me, 'What game do you think you are playing, flirting so brazenly with Silas like that?'

'I wasn't aware that I was. But if your accusations are true, what wrong would there be in that? For I do not belong to any man.'

His eyes were still gazing over me, looking out and into some terrible distance. 'Oh? And what makes you say that?'

And I answered sweetly, 'It was you who told me that ownership was unacceptable. It was you who told me how no one could ever own anyone else.'

His black eyes met mine when he said, 'Don't make a fool out of me.'

'I was not making a fool of you, Rowle. You are making a fool of yourself.'

I felt my face flush – was it the wine or the dance or the nearness of Rowle? I had never spoken to him in this way before. I had always been the meek obedient one, the one who was willing to suffer – not silently – but to sacrifice all the same. And, in all honesty, before tonight I think that he would have laughed off my attitude, knowing full well it was merely a front, merely a taunt with no force behind it, no meaning. So how was I to know he would suddenly take me so seriously?

'Yer drunken dog!' A pair of sweaty, brawling men tumbled into the thick of us.

'Yer mangy swine, come 'ere an' let me get at yer.'

Rowle broke away from me, caught them roughly by their collars and threw them out of his path. His temper was quick tonight. At any other time he would have stood back and laughed easily at the rude interruption. When he took me into his arms again I could feel the tenseness of his anger.

Perhaps I should not have drunk all that wine. 'Maybe I should go with Silas. Maybe it's time a decision was made.'

'You must do what you think fit,' said Rowle coldly, 'and not let me be the one to stop you.'

'Silas is a fine man,' I went on. 'Lucy says that you would be quite lost without him. She thinks that we suit each other – Lucy is keen to see me paired.'

The fiddler was playing a slow song now and we swayed to the sadness in it. Rowle was fine in purple and white, and he moved in a sensual way, like a cat. The whiteness at his neck and his wrists was dazzling. I wanted to bury my head in all of it, I wanted to sob out the depths of my need. I couldn't. I held my body stiff and erect and I would not bend to his guiding hand. The scarlet gown flowed round me, catching beads of firelight as we passed it so that I felt that I swirled in pure flame.

I had been unaware of Silas' presence – only dominated by Rowle – so that when I heard his voice coming over my shoulder, slow and polite, I released Rowle and stepped back in surprise. 'I think that, particularly in these circumstances, it is time I demanded the return of my partner.' He gave Rowle a sly little bow. 'If you, sir, would be so kind.'

'To what circumstances, Silas, do you refer?'

'To the circumstances of your own firm commitments, which you seem, so readily, to have forgotten.'

'I don't think I heard you correctly. I would be grateful if you would repeat the words you just spoke.'

'Your commitments, Rowle: your commitments to Lucy and to your children. And may I also refer to the fact that whilst you are taken, I am a free man. And this lady came to the dance with me.'

Now it was no trick of my imagination – the dancing *had* stopped. The sideshows had stopped. Even the whores with their warpaint and nakedness, drooped in the shadows and fell silent. The two men dominated the centre of the stage – that sweet stage of grass where there had been only dancing and gaiety such a short moment ago. Now it was an arena . . . like the cock-pit . . . an arena around which men were clustering, row upon row, and they might have been placing their bets so keen, so avid was their interest. No one stepped forward. Not one man attempted to stop the fight. And I saw Rowle's men together at one end, while a group of others watched Silas sombrely from the other. And it seemed that all the men from the Combe, not drunk now, but wide awake and aware, formed the large circle in between. And I – I was the only woman in the ring. Immediately I felt the flare of an impotent rage towards Lucy for setting me up – for causing me to be here, arranged all in scarlet like this. I stared round, bemused and alarmed, and someone stepped forward to lead me away.

I fought like a wild cat, screaming to be allowed back to the front of the fray. I kicked and beat my way through the boots, crawled on the ground, my face in the dust. But all I could catch before a leg pushed me back or an arm knocked me down once again, were glimpses. I knew they were stripped to the waist, and there were knives in the ring. I heard the clash of steel and I caught the inrush of men's breath. No one was shouting tonight. The silence from the crowd was eerie. It brought me to silence, too, but mine was a raging silence. I needed to call out . . . I needed to stop this. I hadn't meant, oh no, dear God, I had not meant for this . . .

All I could hear were the grunts and struggles of the men in the ring. They were fighting to the death – for hadn't Rowle instructed them at the time of the cock-fight never to leave their enemy unless they were sure he was good and dead! I had heard them then – and had applauded his good sense!

I saw teeth drawn back, an arm bent . . . the glimpse of a leg, kicking . . . the flexing muscles of a man's back . . . the sharp gleam of a knife as it caught the firelight before plunging down. Fire on sweat. And then blood. Sticky . . . on black hair . . . *whose hair* . . . for both men were dark and black. Oh, let me forward! Stand back, you brutes, and let me see! The futile helplessness of my position drove me demented. I tore at my hair like a woman insane and in my madness I considered running for Lucy. But I thought of my wild flight to warn my aunts at Amicombe, and feared that if I did this I might be too late.

What help could I be in this situation, one that I had deliberately caused. And what good could Lucy do? *And oh, dear God, what would Lucy say to me?*

I heard the cold clap of flesh on flesh, the impact of two bodies meeting. The rage in the air was tangible. I turned and saw Jamie Bovey, head down, slumped with the fiddle between his knees – as if something was, for ever, all over. Dear God and I thought of the children and I lay on the ground and tore at the grass. Rowle could lose! There was the possibility that Rowle could lose! Wasn't there? Wasn't there?

No, there was not.

It was Mary who found me. I must have passed out from the horror of it, or caught my head on one of the sharp stones on the ground, for when I woke up there was silence. The people had gone. Mary was kneeling beside me, cooling my head with a rag. When I opened my eyes I looked straight into hers.

'Rowle?' I asked.

Mary nodded gently. ''E be all right, my lover.'

'And Silas?'

Mary gave a wry smile. 'Silas will live ter fight another day, thank the lord.'

'Rowle let him live?'

''Twas a choice 'e offered the crowd.' Mary dipped the rag back into the bucket of water and wringing it out, cleaned my face as if I was just a child. With such gentleness did Mary stroke my face that night. ''E brought Silas to 'is knees. 'E felled 'e again an' again, but Silas came back fer more an' fer more. They said they thought Rowle 'ad killed 'e, such vicious wounds 'e inflicted. But still Silas got up, until 'e could do so no longer, until 'e were right passed out, just as you was when I found 'e. So Rowle stood wi' 'is knife at 'is throat an' everyone thought 'e would finish 'e. 'Twould have bin quite fair an' just – not one man expected no different. But then Ned told me 'e sat back – hung over Silas wi' 'is body all wet wi' the sweat an' the blood, an' out o' the blue like that 'e smiled! Fancy! Rowle just opened 'is mouth wide an' smiled. An' 'twere as if 'e did not have ter kill Silas in order ter beat 'e. 'Twere as if 'e 'ad some secret from the rest o' uz – but 'e weren't goin' to tell it. 'E asked the crowd just the same an' they doan want Silas dead. 'E is too handy around the place. 'Twere sorry ter see the two at each other like that.'

'Where are they now?'

'Rowle has gone back to 'is house an' Silas is to Skinny Joe's. I's thinks 'e carn go back ter Rowle's – not now – not in the circumstances. Well . . .'

I made myself sit up, startled, for I thought there was somebody there. But it was just the ribbons from the maypole fluttering in the night breeze. I leaned over, retching, and held my head in my hands.

'What can I do, Mary?' I whispered. 'Oh, tell me, what can I do?'

'No one can tell 'e, maid. No one can tell 'e what you already knows.'

'I can't pull away – I can't live without him.' And I thought I would see all that angry misunderstanding in Mary's familiar face, but it was strangely sweet, no moralising now. Maybe she knew it was too late. For she said, 'Youm just a child – an' a strange, wild one at that. How can yer know what ter do when yer wracked wi' such passions as these?' And I wished that Mary had spoken to me like this before and not been so staunchly against me. 'You come home ter sleep wi' uz tonight. I still has yer bed in the corner all ready. I never knows, yer sees, when yer might need ter come back.'

I wept, Brother Niall. I wept because I loved her and yet that love didn't touch me, not really. I wept over the harm that I knew I had done and yet I did not feel it. I wept because I knew what I was and I wondered where it would end, and because I wanted to be just a child again, able to hold Mary's hand and go with her, with some purity inside me. Not all black like this.

And I wept because Mary knew, and yet she couldn't help me. I wept because no one could help me, and because I was so alone.

35

You are close to me now, Rowle, very close. You are standing behind me with your arms round me. In a moment I will turn, look up and find . . .

She was everything to you, Rowle, wasn't she – child, wife, mother, lover – while I? What was I to you? Somebody to boost your ego, to play with for a little while until you grew bored. I was somebody who demanded too much in return, wasn't I? I asked for something you could not give. Lucy knew. Lucy understood.

After a little while she got up, stood with her back to me staring out across the moor, wiped her eyes and turned round. Her look was angry, her mouth firm. Her face was white.

'What monsters men are.'

'It wasn't just Rowle, Lucy, it was me, too.'

'How could it be you?' she snapped, running fingers through disordered hair. 'You're only a child!'

'I'm eighteen. Hardly a child!'

'Age doesn't count. You are not mature. He is the one who should have known better. He should not have encouraged you!'

'It was not his fault. It was mine. All mine.' I wanted, desperately, to convince her of this but I felt she was not listening to me. It was Rowle she wanted to blame. She was all suspicious and angry. I had never seen Lucy like this and it frightened me. I was finding no relief in this. This was nothing like anything I had expected. *What on earth had I expected*?

'I would have thought he should have been the one to tell me – not you.'

'Does it matter who you hear it from? He wasn't going to tell you. He said it was better that you didn't know.'

'Ah yes,' and I didn't like that smile she gave me. 'Always the last to know. And why, Bethany, have you decided, at last, to tell me? You have been trying for long enough.'

'Because I thought you already knew. Because I couldn't bear to cheat you any longer.'

No one would tell Lucy the reasons for the terrible fight. Rowle had come home limping, torn and covered with blood and Silas had not returned. So I, half-hysterical with guilt and fear that she might eventually find out from other, less friendly sources, decided the time was right at last. I hadn't expected this cool reaction. I hadn't considered Lucy's reaction very much at all.

'I did know, but not how far . . . How long have you been – cheating me – as you put it?' Her voice sharpened.

'Ever since I came.'

Lucy turned back to the window again, her head high and her shoulders drooped as if she felt the weight too heavy to carry.

'He doesn't know you're telling me?' Her voice was small.

'No. He doesn't know.'

'I see.'

'Do you, Lucy? Do you really see?' I had to keep angry with her. I had to make her argue, to rant and rave. Silence, unhappiness, I could not deal with.

'I won't say I trusted you.'

'You have just said it.' My voice was more bitter than hers.

'What do you want, Bethany?' And I was struck by the fact that Rowle was always asking me that.

'I love him. I want him.'

She turned round again and if the situation wasn't as it was I would have said she was about to take me in her arms for there was so much pity in her eyes and such sadness in her face. And she did begin to hold out her arms before she pulled them back and wrapped them around herself instead. 'Oh, my poor child.' She stared, I stared, but her gaze was so direct that I had to drop my eyes. I shook my head in desperation, not knowing where to put my anger. For I couldn't hate Lucy – I just couldn't hate her!

'Oh, I knew . . .' and she shook her head violently. 'I knew . . . this is just what I feared. It is my fault. I should have taken some action earlier but I knew you both needed each other in so many ways. You are both so childish . . . you both live on dreams. You are fatal to one another. You were from the start.'

'You don't know him as I do,' I said. 'You don't understand

him. You think him fair and just and kind. He is none of those. Some of the things I've heard . . . some of the things I've seen . . .' Perhaps this would be easier if I painted him black.

'Be quiet, Bethany!' Why didn't she call me Bethy any longer? Where was the note of fondness that was always in her voice? Why had the telling of something she'd always suspected changed her so abruptly like this? I wished I could go back out of the room, take time back, I wished I had never started.

'But you have to know the truth!'

'Why must I? And not you?'

'But I do – that's the point – I do.'

'No, Bethany. No. You have made him up. Just as he has invented you, for his own purposes. Some people do that – dangerous people. I know you don't think of yourself like that. You make everything up, Bethany, you invent people at whim, you turn them into who you want them to be to suit yourself.'

'I have never made anyone up in my life.' And the lie flooded me, melted me, so enormous was it. She saw. And smiled. While I scuttled down the passageways of memory and remembered all the times I had done it . . . all the times . . . turned other people into who I wanted them to be. Turned myself into what I wanted to be. Destroying reality as I went along quite indiscriminately. Making myself God of a make-believe universe.

I was horrified to have the truth so calmly laid before me – and in this situation, too, a situation I thought I could control. 'But if I do that,' I began, stuttering, 'if just some of us do that, how can we ever say anything that is true?'

'You very rarely do,' said Lucy matter-of-factly. 'But once you know what's going on it sometimes makes it a little bit easier.'

And I felt very close to Lucy then, beginning to feel that she and I understood one another. So when she said, 'The children will miss you, Bethany,' my heart nearly missed a beat. She saw my shock and said, 'What did you expect, child? Did you think, after this, that life could go on as it was, nothing changed, except you a bit easier with some of your guilt lessened? Did you think I would accept you as you were before, as my friend, my helper, my confidante?' She looked at my face and sighed before turning away. 'Yes, yes – you did, didn't you? Oh, Bethany, you are such a child!'

'I don't want things to change.' Sadness made me heavy, made me sag inside. Losing Lucy was something I had thought wouldn't matter. I wanted to take back what I'd said because nothing had been made any better, only worse.

She wouldn't leave me to nurse my agony. She went relentlessly on, in a voice so cold I was drenched in it, frozen by it. 'Bethany, nothing I could say or do would make Rowle alter his behaviour. We need each other. We have experiences we have shared together that no one could ever come between. I know Rowle as he really is, not as how he would like to be seen . . . as you do . . . No wonder he's playing his games with you.' As she talked I wanted to scream at her to stop – stop – because I didn't want to hear these things. Her words were torturing me. But she didn't stop. She went on talking in that quiet, determined way. There were things she had to say and she was going to go on and say them, no matter what I did or said. 'You think it's me that's keeping him from you, don't you? You are so wrong. I could tell him to go to you, tomorrow. I could say, I don't need you, Rowle, Bethany does. Go to her, build her a house, take her away, have children with her if that's what you need to do. Don't you see, Bethany, it isn't me who holds him. Nobody could hold him if he wanted to go. I couldn't. You couldn't. He won't allow himself to be hurt, to be vulnerable. He can never love you, Bethany. And I doubt if love is what he feels for me, either. Not real love . . . and when he realises he is going to have to let you down, when he realises he is unable to give . . . then he will hurt you, turn on you in anger . . . ah yes, I see from your face that you already know what I mean. He is out of the reach of other people. He has been hurt too much. Don't you see beyond anything he says?'

'But I . . .' my eyes were startled. 'I can't live here any more – why? Why, if I am no threat?'

Her voice was cold, cold as the wind on the moor in winter. 'No, you can't live here any more. And I don't want you near my children. Because you would have destroyed me, Bethany, if you could, as surely and determinedly as any enemy from outside, without a thought. I know you couldn't help it – that you were driven by passions too big to control. I know all this, don't think I don't understand, I do. Perfectly well. Too well. And I also understand the reasons. You wanted to be taken by somebody you thought was very strong, you made him into a god because that was easier for you, wasn't it . . . no decisions of your own to take. Oh, I know, I know. But once we talked about trust, you and I, and I tried to explain about Jessie and why the women feared her. Trust, Bethany, is something we can never have again. And it's for that reason that you have to go.'

This was Lucy speaking – Lucy, whom I had always imagined was soft and weak and malleable. She wasn't – I was the soft one – while she was as hard as iron and her expression showed me so. She wasn't going to back down or change her mind. She was as immovable as Rowle.

'Will you tell him?' and now I sounded like the whinging Bessie. 'Will you tell him I told you?'

'I don't know, Bethany. I haven't thought that far ahead. I am hurting too much inside.'

'Please don't tell him. If you tell him he will hate me.'

Lucy's smile was not one I had ever seen on her face before. 'So you have given me a weapon against you, Bethany. What a strange situation this is turning out to be.'

I wanted to get on my knees, to crawl and to beg. More than anything else in the world I wanted Lucy to keep my secret. Disgusted with myself now, I was appalled at the enormity of my betrayal.

'How will you ever trust me, Bethany? If I say I will not tell, how will you know I am keeping my promise?'

I shook my head. 'I won't know. I suppose you are going to say that I must not meet Rowle again.'

And then Lucy laughed. And it was a real laugh, full of some of the old joy. I even ventured a smile in reply, timid, yes, but still a smile. 'You haven't heard a word of what I've been saying,' she said. She looked young again, as if much of the pain I had brought had left her. And seeing my confusion she bent down and whispered in my ear, 'Rowle doesn't want you . . . don't you understand what I'm telling you! Ah, yes, you are both children, both dreamers, but Rowle has only one dream . . . and that is to go back and take up his life again. It could have happened once. But now it is impossible . . . since the fire, his dream is unrealisable.' And then Lucy shook her head and stared at me sadly. She drew herself up to her full height as if to sum up all she had been trying to tell me. 'But you're not interested in that, are you Bethany? There is only one thing that interests you at the moment . . . so listen, and listen to me carefully. I could no more stop Rowle seeing you than stand on this windowsill, let myself go, and fly right out to the far Tor,' she said. 'And I'll give you that as a parting gift.'

'I don't want a parting gift.' I wanted to stay.

But Lucy looked at me directly and said, 'I want you gone from this house tonight.'

36

'Well?' said Rowle, dragging out the word. When he looked at me I thought I saw hatred there. 'And is this what you wanted?' he asked in a vicious, very quiet voice.

I felt that he was a man who took destiny into his own hands and created it, while I was like a piece of cork drifting in turmoil down the stream. Furious, – for it was he who had made me thus – I got up from my bed and stood before him, pulling my shawl tight around me. 'What else could I do? You wouldn't tell her. Everyone knew! Everyone knew but her!' I raised my fists and held them up helplessly before me. 'We were making a fool of her, Rowle! And you say you care!' I made myself laugh, but it sounded false, hysterical like I was inside.

He kept his voice low when he said, 'So you told Lucy for her own good. Is that what you're telling me now?'

'Something had to happen,' I said. 'Something had to change.'

'And by God you've tried your damnedest to make it change, haven't you?'

After confessing to Lucy I had come to my room to collect my things. I had to get out but where would I go? Who would have me now . . . now that I'd told her? Would she tell anyone else? Did that matter? With each passing minute I felt heavier and heavier, deader and deader, until I stopped my packing and lay on my bed with my face in my pillow, groaning inside. No matter how hard I blinked I could not get rid of Lucy's face and the pain I had put there, but the tears would not come. I could not cry, I seemed to be in a very dry, arid place, my mouth full of sand like a desert, where not even the salty flow of warm water would come to relieve my misery. It bulged inside me, screaming for some way out. I wanted to go back down again and find her. I wanted the awful conversation to go on, thinking, I suppose, that by prolonging it I could turn it and make the ending better. I wanted to talk until everything was all right again, until I felt safe again. Being alone was unbearable, so I might have done that, gone back down the stairs again and pleaded with Lucy to listen to me, depending on her compassionate nature, had not Rowle come in only ten minutes later. I had not even heard his footsteps on the stair, so quiet was he, so silently did he close the door behind him. And he was being quiet now. I did not like him like this.

Hostility filled the room and a blankness roared in the air. Whenever I thought of something to say despair blocked the words before I could speak because I knew that whatever I said would make no difference. I wanted to wipe that look off his face . . . how could I make things right when he was staring that way?

I fought back tears as I said to Rowle, 'I thought she would understand.' When he didn't answer I mumbled, 'Anyway, she knew, Rowle. She knew. I didn't tell her anything she didn't already realise. And if she had kept us apart then none of this would have happened.'

'My God, if this were not so serious your vindictiveness would be absolutely laughable.' And still that expression of distaste did not move off his face and I couldn't remember anything ever hurting so much.

I feigned a laugh again. 'I feel mean and guilty. I feel unloved, and an outcast. I am empty inside except for despair. If you have come here to make this worse, then leave, now! Standing there like that, staring at me like that is helping no one. Since when have you had the right to act so self-righteous and innocent? You are part of all this, just as I am. If you have nothing to say to me now, you might as well go.' Oh, perhaps this was a dream, perhaps I would wake up in a minute and find it was morning and that I could dress as usual, go to Lucy's room, wake the children, go down, laughing, to breakfast as usual . . .

He lifted his right hand and struck me hard across the face. I fell back on the bed, sick and stunned, for it was a heavy blow for which I had been unprepared. Oh, Rowle had hit me before, but never in anger. I stayed there, unmoving, afraid if I did that he might hit me again. I didn't turn round. I kept my face to the blanket. It smelt damp, and of myself, it smelt of despair.

The shock was worse than the pain, and so were his

following words: 'She knows you were merely a dalliance, something I could pick up and put down at whim. She knows you mean nothing to me. She's sorry for you, Bethany. She is nice enough . . . she is decent enough to feel sorry for you. She blames me.'

I dribbled into the blanket. My words were muffled when I asked, 'What else did she say?' I really wanted to know the answer. I really cared.

'She said she was sorry.' And there was so much bitterness in his voice then that I turned over.

'You lied to her. It doesn't matter what you say, I know I was always more to you than that. You care about me, Rowle. If it wasn't for Lucy . . . Rowle, please believe that I didn't think it would be like this.'

He moved towards me and stood over me. I flinched away from him. Once again he spoke softly, menacingly. 'Tell me, my angel, exactly how you thought it would be?' His words hung over the quiet room like pockets of mist on the moor, leaving only his heavy breathing behind them.

But I didn't know what to say then because, to be truthful, I hadn't given a great deal of thought to Lucy's reaction. The telling of Lucy had been to relieve my own guilt, and I'd had the hope – all right it was fleeting and not very realistic – but there had been this vaguest of hopes that she might turn round and say I could have him.

'I hate her,' I said, screwing up my fists which were sweating, and my trapped arms ached under the weight of my body. I looked up at this white-lipped man and I screamed in a mad rage against him. 'The bitch! She has everything. She has everything that I cannot have. She is sly and cunning . . . she holds you in the palm of her hand, but she does it so sweetly you cannot see . . .'

Rowle's whole body was stiff with rage, his face distorted by it, made savage by it. And his hand came down again, harder this time, and I felt one side of my mouth drag down. I touched it with my tongue – warm, bitter, I knew it was bleeding. I sat up on the bed and hid my face in my hands, all screwed up like a knot in case he hit me again. I made sure that even my eyes did not move.

The silence after the violence was awful, cloying. Even the few basic pieces of furniture in the room seemed paralysed, as if they had once been moving. I had no weapons left. And then Rowle said, in a voice tight with bitter control, 'You told Lucy because you don't have a thought in your head for anyone other than yourself. You told her because you hoped she would take the children and leave me, which would, conveniently, enable you to take her place. You told her because you are so spiteful, so needy for love that you can share nobody, and because you couldn't bear your jealousy any longer. You say what you feel for me is love! *Love*! If that is love then I wouldn't like to see what your hatred can do! So help me God, I can never forgive you for this.' And my teeth chattered with fear and anger.

'I cannot be other than I am.' My head throbbed with a steady pulse like a heartbeat, I inhaled and exhaled deep breaths until my choked-up throat was eased. I had to speak, I had to try to say something that might make things right. My terror, now, was not of what he might say or do, but that he might turn round, take three paces to the door, go through it and close it behind him on me forever. I felt as if that possibility was very near. It was unendurable. I could not conceive of the meagre existence of myself without Rowle. It hit me and hurt me as blows never could. I humbled myself before him. I begged. 'I didn't mean to. I didn't mean to. I didn't want to hurt Lucy. I love you. I love you so much I didn't think. I thought that by telling Lucy it would make things better.' I started to cry. My shoulders shook. I was freezing cold and I wanted to pee. 'I even believed she might be able to take this awful need for you away. I wanted Lucy to know for I don't know anyone wiser. I don't know what to do with it, it's destroying me, Rowle. I can't be happy any more, not if I'm not with you. It makes me do dreadful things. Sometimes . . . it feels as if I'm sick. I can't bear it . . . and I don't care what you do. I don't care where you go. I'd follow you. I'd watch you and I'd wait for you. I'd die for you if you wanted that. Yes, I'd even be happy to die.'

I expected another blow but he said, 'What is it you want?' He sounded grim.

'I want to be the most important person in your life.' And that admission slid out between my lips so simply, so easily, so pathetically, that I knew it was the truth.

'And what about Silas?' said Rowle, and his question was threatening.

'Silas means nothing to me.' And then I felt anger again, and bitterness at the pitiful meanness of my small position, here in this room in front of my master. So I raised my voice and shouted, not caring what he did to me, that he should go if he wanted, I'd follow him. I'd stay near him even if he threatened to kill me. I wanted to pray to him, to fall down on my knees in front of him, and it was frightening to be there in that room before my own stone priest, faced with the burden of having to convince him. 'Don't you understand, Rowle? *I can't see, I can't feel anybody else but you!* It is as if nobody else in the world exists! That's what has happened to me.' And I wept, choking, sobbing, not caring what I looked like or what I sounded like, or that he must think me mad, silly . . . I knew he could not understand.

'Do you realise what you have done? Do you realise what will happen now?'

I sniffed and looked up at him, blinking through my tears. 'I won't really have to leave, will I? You can make Lucy understand?'

So then he said, 'You are mad, aren't you? You are quite, quite mad. Either that or a total imbecile. I would have thought that over this length of time, this madness, this passion of yours, would have died away.'

But I was only interested in one thing. I made my voice very small when I asked him, 'Are you going to tell me that we can't meet any more? Rowle, don't leave me.'

He shook his head. I gasped as his fingers twisted in my hair. 'Untie your bodice,' he said, 'I want to feel your breasts against me when I fuck you.' He did not say any more, but just watched while with trembling fingers I drew myself up and obeyed. I was glad to obey, willing to do anything to placate him. With one sweep of his hand he pushed me down on the bed and I know that he bruised my naked shoulders. With another he raised my skirts without looking at me. He pushed them up over my thighs. His mouth came down on mine as he lowered himself on top of me; his hands were in my hair but his thumbs were under my chin so that my face was clamped, so that I could not escape or twist my head from side to side. I tried to speak, to plead. I started to say, 'Rowle, please don't,' but he struck me again across the mouth, and through his own clenched teeth he said, 'Just keep your mouth closed. I don't want to hear your voice.'

I wasn't frightened any more. I felt broken, helpless, and grateful. And then, Brother Niall, I knew I'd really lost something. But it wasn't Rowle, or Lucy, it wasn't a home. It was another, irrevocable little part of me. Soon there would be nothing left, and he, he seemed happy to keep on taking, and I quite happy to give. Because when he hurt me, bruised me, cursed me and devoured me, I knew that everything was all right. I knew that in spite of what I had done, he loved me.

37

Banished!

Back in the days when Mary spoke to me she had said it would burn itself out. 'Obsessions as strong as this, midear, an' they doan last.'

And, oh God, I had hoped she was right because I really couldn't go on living like this. So I waited and waited and hoped and hoped but of course it didn't go away.

How can I tell you, monk – there was nothing else in my life but Rowle. Every second of every minute of every hour I thought about him or dreamed about him or held imaginary conversations with him. And every meeting nudged the whole thing along a little bit more, and every time I heard his voice my feelings became intensified. That's what it was like. That was the nature of the beast.

Banished from the house, banished from the light, I moved to the darker side of the Combe. I made my home in Jessie's cave which was empty since Caleb, his grieving shortlived, had moved in with another woman further up the hill. Oh, and I saw them – men watched me cautiously. Women turned their backs on me. I was a pariah, and when Rowle came to visit me they nodded to him pleasantly as he passed, but tossed their heads self-righteously when they saw me waiting at the door.

'It's not fair!' That seemed to be my favourite expression that year.

'They'll get over it,' was Rowle's response. So simple! 'Never care what people say, Bethy. Never take notice of that.'

'That's easy for you to say,' I replied, angry with him again for his lack of sensitivity. 'Can you imagine what it's like for me, damned and an outcast? Sometimes the look of hatred in their eyes feels like an arrow passing through me. I have no one to talk to, nobody I can call my friend.'

'You should not have told Lucy.'

Why had I bothered to make my surroundings look welcoming? Why had I bothered to find colourful spreads for

264

the bed, fresh rushes for the floor, and why did I keep such a cosy fire burning? Not for me. I didn't notice such things, but for this man, this man who could dismiss my misery with such little concern. This man, who could say of his friend, 'Silas will recover. Things will never be as they were, but they were not perfect even then. Violent change can often improve situations and that's why we should never be afraid of change.' This man, whose own life was so full and satisfying while my own was as dull as it was ever going to get. Except for his visits. Except for our outings. They shone like stars in my long night-times. I was more eager for him now, not less.

We didn't talk much about my confession to Lucy, but in spite of that it was always there with us, sometimes between us. I know they must have talked about it, but Rowle never told me what was said although I fought, bit and screamed to find out. Apart from that, nothing seemed to have changed. He was loyal to her in his old way, just the same. And our meetings continued, just the same. But Lucy was right. I did miss the children. I missed her, too, bitterly.

I was welcome at Mary's but I rarely went there any more because she was cautious with me now and I knew her feelings on my behaviour. It seemed it was the telling of Lucy, now, that was so unforgivable. There was always something that Mary was not forgiving me for. I could never do right for her. Ned was the only one who treated me as he always had – truly glad to see me, joking, hugging, making me laugh and giving me some of the best bits of offal he brought home. Like a father, but unlike Amos. Although Amos, it's true, would never have been affected by the opinions of others, would never have even been aware of such a thing. And Ned was like that, too. Mary, I noticed, would never let me be on my own with him. She bustled round with one keen eye on me and her face all folded up and flat, and once I said to her, 'Mary, what do you take me for? Ned and you – you are like my own! Do you really think I want him to bed me?'

She didn't reply, but turned away with a sniff.

And my days? The lonely times without Rowle? Well, I cut peats, I hitched a sledge to a pony and carted firewood. I fished in the stream and spun wool into blankets. Alone. I, who was used to being alone, was more alone here than I ever had been at Amicombe.

Now that I had a home of my own I saw Rowle alone more often. He used to come and we'd lie in bed after we had made love, and often he'd hurt me these days – proof of his ownership, proof of his love – but afterwards he'd wrap his arms round me and I'd cuddle up to him like a child. Feeling so safe. Feeling that, while I lay like this, I cared not a jot for the opinions of others, nor did I believe what Lucy had told me. In fact, I told myself, I would rather be alone.

At other times I felt restless and would reproach him, 'I am a prisoner here. You have turned me into a prisoner, Rowle. I have seen nothing of the world, and what future is there here for me now? I am holed up here in this cave, only waiting for your visits, dependent on you, sometimes, I feel, for life itself. For I wonder what they would do to me if you cast me off.'

'It is none of my doing. You are closing yourself off. There is no need for you to retreat from everyone – where has your boldness gone? You ought to be out there, facing them.'

'The Combe is not what I mean when I speak of the world,' I tried to explain to him.

But Rowle said, 'There is nothing in the world that doesn't exist here in this small place. The world consists of the same kind of people, wherever you go, and the same petty quarrels and big desires. You don't need to stray further from here to know about the world and its ways. You are safer, here, Bethany, and I will never betray you.'

'It is easy for you to tell me that, for you have seen and experienced the outside world. Why should I take notice of your opinions? I have my own. I might not have felt the same as you did. When life changed for you it was for the better. That is not necessarily always the way.'

'It is what you make it,' said Rowle impatiently. 'You can turn life to suit your own purpose if you are strong, if you are sufficiently determined.'

Yes, life did change for Rowle, and he made the most of it. It could have been a disaster and yet he triumphed over it.

He told me as we sat huddled under a blanket, holding hands and staring in the blank way you do when you gaze into a leaping fire. The wind blew outside the humble hut but we were so safe together inside it. If there had ever been monsters for us then surely, now, they were very far away.

Unexpectedly, Catherine Rowle had shown some feelings when Rowle was due to be sent away to school. She did not want him to go, but her wishes were ignored.

'She wanted to send me to my uncle's house in London,' Rowle told me. 'There had been letters backwards and forwards, letters of which Gideon did not approve. Pressure was being brought to bear: something would have to be done with Anthony Rowle's son. Not all my father's brothers were like Gideon. William Rowle, who wrote offering me a chance to learn to be his secretary, had my welfare at heart. I heard my mother arguing about it with Gideon. I hid at the bottom of the stairs behind the marble lady and listened. "What use has the boy for learning?" she ranted, and I heard her skirts rustling urgently across the floor. "What good did learning ever do Charles? Learning is for serfs, not noblemen! Roger should go to London where he will meet the right sort of useful people and learn good manners!"

'Perhaps she saw a chance for me, a tiny gem of a chance lying down there on the floor and thought she'd try to pick it up. Perhaps she thought that with the power of Gideon's brothers behind me I might be worth fighting for. Or perhaps it was just the mood she was in – who knows? Still it was extraordinary for me to hear her try and gainsay him. Of course, Gideon's arguments demolished her.'

I crept closer to keep warm. He looked down and stroked my cheek. ' "The Mountford School will make a man of him," shouted my stepfather. "It only caters for the sons of the gentry. He will board there just as Charles did and will return here for the holidays. I have made my decision, and The Mountford School is where he is going." '

I understood. It was not in Gideon's interests to send Rowle to London where he would remain out of his clutches forever. So just when his life was beginning to get better, when he had The Turk and he had his reading – it was to change again.

Remembering that conversation with Rowle I can feel a little of the old despair because Rowle smiled when he told me, 'If they hadn't sent me to The Mountford School, if my mother had got her way and I'd gone to London as she wanted, I would never have met you, Beth.' I wasn't certain, from his tone, whether he might have preferred the alternative. I searched his eyes for clues but could find none, so I turned away and stared at the fire and listened to it crackling.

Decisions were made, and thus fate began to play its part, feebly at first, to entwine and enmesh itself round our lives and bring us inexorably together. If he had gone to London, how different his life would have been. At eighteen he would have inherited his late father's estate, could have turned Gideon out of Amberry and his mother too, if he had wished it. Rowle could have taken his rightful place in the world, proud and noble, a man to be remembered. For Rowle was not one to sink into the oblivion of ordinariness.

And I would never have known him.

It seemed to me that the gentry had a strange method of carrying on. Unlike the farming families who welcomed the extra labour once their children were grown, these people sent them away at the earliest opportunity and took in the children of others to act as their servants.

It was unusual for Rowle to have remained at home for so long. People were beginning to talk. Where was the heir to Amberry? What were they doing with him?

Catherine's remaining children, apart from the precious Charles, had all been sent at the age of seven or eight into service to suitable houses as was the custom, there to learn about the running of households – the boys to the estates, the girls to help with the sewing, the cooking, or the work in the nursery. Living with the servants in the homes of friends, they learnt to put their hands to everything. They returned home only occasionally. To their family, to each other, they grew up as strangers. Catherine had taken no interest in their welfare whatever.

Rowle admitted to me that his mother was vain. 'As she grew older she became more obsessed with her looks, taking great care to dry up her milk as soon as she could after childbirth, using plasters made up of oil of roses, dregs of wine, dragavant and arabycke – to stop the curdling, she said. And there was always this woman to do the suckling, a buxom wench with one eye they called Mrs Budd. I only remember how dirty she always looked and smelt – her bodice was always wet and crusty. She consistently dressed in yellow, the sour yellow of old milk. I remember, I thought her one eye made her magic. I used to hide from her.'

I listened hard. I needed to learn all the customs. When Rowle and I were married, when we lived grandly like this, I would need to know how to behave. But I didn't think I would be happy to give away all my children, nor to employ such creatures.

'After she had finished, when my brothers and sisters were two or three years old, then the drynurse, Cattie, would take over. Cattie had one thing in common with Dooley and that was that everything she ever did was done in order to "do us good". Charles told me once that Cattie was in the habit of fetching the children, in turn, out of their beds at night and shutting them in a cupboard. He thought this was the reason he had never been able to sleep through the night without waking up at least once in a cold sweat. Still Charles was always weak and nervous – I didn't sympathise with him. To Dooley this sort of behaviour would have been like playing games, but then Dooley never really frightened me, she never really bothered me.'

I considered Rowle to be too hard on Charles, and once more I remembered my secret and wondered why he had hated his stepbrother so. Something had driven him to murder – what was it, and when would he tell me? Rowle got up to put another log on the fire. I shivered until he came back, and he wrapped me in his arms as he sat down and carried on reminiscing.

'Cattie had a face like a bad apple, and you could hear her coming for the rattling of keys she kept at her belt. Sometimes, after I was in bed at night and her own charges were asleep she used to come upstairs and talk to Dooley. They would drink gin together and talk quietly. On these occasions Dooley might light a fire. I remember lying there, listening, while a dead ivy branch blew against the window, sawing like a bow against its horny stem and making the outside world sound a cold, unfriendly place. It should have brought our inside world together. It should have made us feel safe, but not in that nursery,' said Rowle, laughing, 'not with those two in it.

'Cattie never called me by name but referred to me darkly, over her shoulder, as "that brat". I sensed her interest in me but it was an interest that Dooley, possessive of me in her own peculiar way, did not let Cattie indulge. Other than at those times, when she sat with Dooley talking, I rarely saw her or came into contact with her. Cattie was strongly religious, and yet waspish, vicious and unkind. But, Bethy, Cattie was meekness itself compared to Dooley. I can only be grateful that Dooley was never my wetnurse . . . if she had been I would certainly have been poisoned very quickly!'

Rowle could speak of his early childhood without emotion, but I always felt that Dooley's behaviour troubled him somehow, that he would have liked to understand what drove her. 'Sometimes, Bethy, I think that Dooley must have been insane.'

And I understood why Rowle should want to believe that, that Dooley couldn't help her tyrannical behaviour, that it had nothing to do with him and with the child he had been. I pictured her pacing the floor in that dreadful room, coarse-featured, huge, with a glowering forehead, her large brown face on a line with the hump of her back – she was just like that, I had seen her – blocking out, I imagined, any light that might come through the paned windows . . . the cause of so many unfinished dreams.

But for Rowle, then, it was to be school. Gideon Rowle had not given up on his main objective. 'It is fatal to underestimate people,' said Rowle. 'Particularly to underestimate the lengths to which they will go if driven hard enough. We are all driven by different desires, and Gideon Rowle was driven by power. All that stood between him and his heirs obtaining power forever, he thought, was his brother's son. Me.

'When he came to the nursery to give Dooley the news, Gideon ignored me completely. His face was gaunt, his lips thin and tight. He had failed in his task of destroying me. He was having to hand it over to others.

'He stood in a lordly stance before that empty fireplace in the nursery and announced his decision. He obviously believed I'd be miserable, afraid of going to that spartan place about which Charles always told such grim stories. I saw him glancing in my direction as he started giving Dooley instructions so I turned away, fearful in case he sensed my excitement. The idea of school enthralled me! I didn't care what sort of reputation The Mountford had. I wanted away from Amberry – I wanted something different. And however bad it was it couldn't compare with the unerring boredom of my life at home. Going away held no fears for me, but I knew that I had to be cunning and not reveal my feelings.

'How Gideon must have hated me! I was growing tall and strong, animal healthy. I was arrogant in my bearing – I knew because Dooley told me often – and I was fearless and proud. "Though where you get that from, my charmer, it's hard to tell." I had complete confidence in myself and in my abilities to conquer anything that came at me. I was dependent on nobody – never had been. Gideon thought The Mountford might kill me . . . I knew otherwise.'

Was it true that after his quiet, isolated life at home, when he faced removal to a place that he knew to be terrible, could it possibly be true that Rowle did not feel any fear? I looked at his face, which was all sincerity – and why would he bother to lie to me?

Rowle laughed and added, 'I knew that if Dooley couldn't kill me, then no one could.'

With that dark jest he gave himself away, because only I understood that he had loved Dooley, and I realised then that that little boy *had* felt fear – but that most of it was to do with leaving that terrible, monstrous, all powerful mother-figure behind him.

He went with Tremain. They entered Exeter through the west gate, trotted up the High Street and saw the River Exe swirl dark and rapid, seeping its mists through the air, up and between tight clusters of houses to where, high above, the richly carved gables clasped each other from alley to alley and on.

A cool wind was beginning to moan through the narrow passageways, coming in with the night as they travelled on. It was dusk when they reached the centre and the market stalls were closing. Women in bloody aprons wiped their hands and packed their carts, holding out the last of their wares to the late travellers – lanky fish by the tails – a limp-winged fowl from its cage – baskets of cherries – wool for spindles – and there was a seer with scarecrow arms who tapped towards them with a stick, blinking her blind eyes, cursing, pushing her way through baskets and barrels as she came.

'City of witchcraft, Exeter, be known for it,' muttered Tremain under his breath. Quite surprisingly he crossed himself and led the way from the overripe stench of the market to The Dolphin Inn to secure a room for the night. Tremain was eager. He was a man who liked a pot or two after a dusty ride. 'An' we has to fit in The Mermaid an' The Bear afore we retires, laddy.'

They never reached The Mermaid or The Bear. They enjoyed themselves well enough at The Dolphin.

Rowle told me how their talk on the journey had drifted quite naturally to highwaymen and vagabond gangs; according to Tremain, who carried a short sword and a rapier, there was one particular group it was wise to ride shy of. This was the first time that Rowle heard the name of the Gubbins, and he wanted to know more. Tremain was a voluble talker with drink inside him, dour and silent when he had not, so Rowle was patient while the older man ordered a couple of ducks to be roasted, inspected their rooms and insisted on a fire being lit in Rowle's.

I loved to picture how it must have been in that tavern – Rowle described it to me so clearly. Downstairs, beyond the latch, came a good-humoured clamour. Rowle obediently followed Tremain, who knew his way round. No one looked up as they entered. The energy and movement in the rush-lit room was startling. A mangy dog turned a spit before the roasting fire – and the tiny windows ran with steam. The air was fugged with smoke and fumes of beer and wine and within, like shadows in a dream, rough-bearded captains from Topsham and Exmouth sat telling their tales, hanging about Exeter while waiting for their orders; cloth-merchants making deals spoke behind their hands; worn out travellers sat back with their boots up on chairs and their hands shielding their tired eyes while they exchanged the gossip of the road; and common citizens crammed to get a view of the cock-fight in the corner. Even beneath the Inn the stables were shifting with movement and sound, filled to overflowing with weary, munching packmules.

Rowle told me, 'A skivvy in cap and apron brought our ale, a girl the likes of which I had never met. She was unlike even the lowest servants at Amberry, and, to my mind, almost naked. Her plump breasts thrust like half apples from the dainty puckered lace at her low tied bodice –they were displayed fresh and tempting as fruit for the testing. They matched the fiery roundness of her cheeks and as she rushed about her whole body bounced. The nakedness of her arms was fascinating.

Tremain pinched her as she bent to serve, but it was me that she winked at and when I tried to look away Tremain leaned forward and gripped my chin in a vice-like hand to bring my face back. "You am nearly a man now, laddy . . . you am the son of yer faither, nothing ter do wi' that limp lot at Amberry. Now drink yer ale an' eye the titbits that are here on offer, fer tomorrow, sounds like ter me, you'll be shut in a monastery 'til Michaelmas comes. 'Tis your night, milad, now make the most o' it."

'And it wasn't the heat of the room that made me sweat that night,' said Rowle, smiling as he remembered. 'It was the looks that lass kept sending me and the fear of Tremain's scornful tongue.'

To Rowle's alarm Tremain appeared to have started an argument with a shaggy-faced man who went to sit at their table. The two men banged their mugs alternately, frothing the black ale over the top as their opinions roared to and fro between them, attracting the attention of their nearest neighbours who turned on their chairs to listen. The stranger said, 'Ought ter be hanged the lot o' 'em, an' their heads stuck up wi' the other felons on the castle wall . . .'

But Tremain was not having it. 'How can you speak that way?' he asked the man with the quickly-blearing eyes, thrusting his great face aggressively before him. 'How can you? An' what is the Gubbins ter do, then? What is their alternative? Branded an' hanged fer the crime o' vagrancy, that's what, so wouldn't you be hanged for a sheep as a lamb an' try ter better yourself? What would you do, then? Out o' work, mebbe through no fault o' yer own, an' God knows there's little enough work in the countryside, an' what would you do?'

The opposition to Tremain increased. Others joined the debate. A heated discussion took place as to what should be done with the wayward Gubbins, and how to deter these gangs of vagabonds from roaming the countryside as they did. 'I is all fer it,' put in another man. 'First time caught beggin' an they should take off one ear, second time two, whips an' stocks an' send the varmints back to where they came from. Stop them beggars from bandin' up like that.'

'They comes from nowhere, they is goin' nowhere,' said Tremain. 'An' we force 'em to band together fer protection, they do it ter survive. An' I'm sayin' that I'd do the same if I was in that position which God preserve me I'm not.'

'They hangs 'em from where I comes from,' said a traveller. 'Whipped an' burned fer the first offence, hanged for a second if they carn find work, an' hanged without clergy fer a third offence.' And he smacked his lips together in satisfaction.

Tremain's face was set. He sat back in his chair and drummed on the table with obstinate fingers. 'Personally I doan think I'd care, by then, if clergy were fer me or agin me. I'd probably consider that God had given me a raw deal an' have long since given up on 'E.' He spat viciously towards the fireplace and missed.

'We just carn have gangs o' ruffians roamin' 'bout the countryside,' said Tremain's original dissenter, nodding his head to draw the opinion of the audience. 'We carn come an' go as we pleases. We carn even sleep save in uz beds at night.'

And to that they all agreed. But all the time, while this discussion was going on, that little maid was staring at Rowle, pouting her pretty lips and swinging her hips where they were backed against the serving table. Rowle tried to listen to Tremain, tried to pull his eyes away but he couldn't.

Tremain said to him, 'An' what do you think, Rowle, 'bout all this then?'

The question came so suddenly, and Rowle had not been listening. He had only caught the gist of the subject, that's all. He tried to answer the question but stuttered. He was aware that his face was flaming red but didn't know what expression was on it. However, it must have been a foolish one because all of a sudden the argument seemed to cease as Tremain nudged his opponent with a wicked look in his eye. The shaggy man stared at Rowle and leered down into his cups as he said, 'There's reasons why I regrets gettin' old, by God I do!'

And they all laughed, lifted their tankards towards the maid and then at Rowle, and started singing.

Why did Rowle tell me these hurtful things? Did he not consider them a betrayal, did it not occur to me that I would care what he had got up to when he was only a boy? It was, after all, of little importance.

Rowle leaned back and picked up my hair, touched the

taint-mark in it with reverence, and let his fingers follow it. I shivered.

'She was there in my bed when I went up, naked and on display, free for the taking with all the strangeness and excitements of the night and the new city in her. And oh God there was I, turning the stair with difficulty, dizzy with too much ale, the smoke, the heat and the lust that was new to me.

'That journey was an eye-opener for me in more ways than one. I had no qualms, no fear of the new life ahead. I already felt more at home and safer in this new place, among these people, that I'd ever felt at Amberry. I learned about the Gubbins, about why they were there, swarming over the hills causing chaos wherever they went, and I learned what upright, tax-paying citizens thought about them and what men like Tremain were thinking. I learned about the cruelties of the system, the mire of poverty from which it was quite impossible to escape . . . about how little men were prepared to do about it . . .'

'And you learned about sex,' I said to him casually, staring hard at my nails and trying not to let him see how I burned with rage inside. I knew that encounter had meant nothing to him – as he always insisted these casual escapades of his didn't – but even though it was years ago, years before he met me, knew me, had even heard of me . . . I still couldn't bear it.

Yes, I still couldn't bear it. And I wish I hadn't thought about it just now.

38

He used to tell me everything, during those long hours that we spent together, for we had no life now other than that secret, silent one cut off from the rest of the world. It was important for me to hear his voice – to hear *somebody's* voice other than my own – because sometimes, Brother Niall, the silence in my ears was so terrible it felt like violence. And I longed for those times with Rowle. They were more important to me than the sun in the sky or the food I so rarely bothered to eat, unless Rowle came. And I didn't care what he did to me, as long as he was with me.

Up until the time he went to The Mountford, Rowle had no control over his own life. Things were 'done' to him and he suffered them, as we all have to as children. But after he left Amberry it was different. After that I could begin to understand the truly fine man that he was, for the attitude he took could lead to nothing but trouble. He must have known that – even then – and not cared. Oh yes, I admired him. I listened to his words with shining eyes . . .

Bearing in mind Rowle's background and his temperament, I have to think carefully and ask myself if he did, in fact, have an option. No matter, because once Rowle arrived at The Mountford School and started mixing with that wild bunch of boys, he became set on the path he was to follow, so successfully, ever after.

'We had to break loose,' Rowle explained, 'otherwise we would have gone mad in that bedlam.'

And only a man like that could break loose in the way that he did. I'm sure the depressing aura of the school did not touch him, he would not have let it. Even the buildings themselves, which can easily affect some sensitive souls and seep into their hearts oppressive and cold as the weeping stones, I doubt if Rowle even saw them. Mountford consisted of a long, low building of dark stone, surrounded by a high wall; it was harsh and featureless, with a tall bell-tower coming from the roof and two gabled entrances. A spartan place with a mindless regime dealing out the kind of deprivation that he was used to, there was nothing new or frightening for Rowle at The Mountford.

Contrary to Gideon's hopes, then, school came nowhere near to killing Roger Rowle, although it did occasionally kill others. You could say he thrived on it, because there he met contemporaries similar, at least outwardly, to himself. To survive at The Mountford you had to be hard as nails, and Rowle was.

All the new boys had firstly to endure the initiation ceremony – the fire and water test. This entailed being stripped naked in front of the whole school and thrown into the deepest part of Manet's Pond. Rowle couldn't swim. When he reached the bank, gasping, shivering, coughing up cold lungfuls of weedy water, he had learned to do so.

The fire test was worse. Strapped with his arms round a rough wooden form, the whole contraption was lifted to stand before the hall fire where, every now and then his back was basted with water so that the pain could be longer endured. Rowle never flinched. His back blistered in long, broken weals, so badly he could not bend or lie on it at night for over a month, but he survived, clenching his teeth so hard he ground the tips off them. Did Gideon, knowing Rowle as he did, really believe the system would break his stepson? Fool! The floggings, unhealthy environment, monotonous diet of boiled beef and pottage, bread and beer, the hours of sitting on long, thin backless forms chanting Latin . . . learning pages and pages of it by rote – these were mild privations to a boy who had been tutored by Dooley.

Rowle explained how it was to me. 'But it was the companionship – the sense of satisfaction of being one of a group against the adversary – that's what I loved and discovered there. We found ways and means of getting out undetected. We developed cunning, perfected stealth, and we discovered humour. We had some laughs, some good times. We ferreted, we hunted rabbits: one boy even had a pack of hounds. He paid a local farmer to keep them, and we went coursing. We were fit and hardy, Bethy. Pain and discomfort meant little to us. And every morning, whatever the weather, we washed under the pump in the yard. Oh yes, there was a brotherhood among us that I never forgot.

'There were rats in the dormitories and in that first, bitterly cold winter term, snow blew in through the holes in the roof. You couldn't sleep for the coughing and wheezing that went on, and the weeping,' he told me. And for hours they sat, stiff with the cold, repeating the lessons in boring repetition while from the floor came the sickeningly sour stench of mildewed rushes.

'The worst thing about it was the chilblains,' complained Rowle, although to me, chilblains seemed a minor affliction compared to the other horrors. 'They grew thick in clusters, sticking your fingers and toes together. We used to cut them apart with a knife, and wrap our feet and hands in strips of linen protected against the damp with wax. Some boys, to escape the lessons and gain a few days in bed, rubbed arsenic and ratsbane into the sores to exacerbate them. The bedclothes grew damp in the night and by morning they were stiff on us – they crackled. And all that sitting in the rush-lit, stone chapel in the early morning before lessons began and back there again in the evening, afterwards.

'I was one of the lucky ones. I was not trailing a warmer memory of happier times behind me, a longing for a life I had left at home. I had no comparisons to draw from. And those that suffered in this way quickly went under. The system was designed to drive them under. You would be destroyed, totally, or you would survive. The only other alternative was to make yourself sick and be sent home.

'Yes, I was lucky. We were far better off than the charity boys who worked like skivvies in order to receive this doubtful education – an education fit only for would-be clerks or the clergy. I saw their misery, their depression. I saw the way they moved, tiredly and hopelessly to a place beyond tears. And I thought they seemed dead. Chanting Latin – for the privilege of doing this they sublimated themselves. Their fathers and mothers considered, quite obviously, that at the end of the day it would be worth it. How was this going to benefit them, or any of us, in later life? Discipline, that's what they told us it was all about, it taught us obedience and perseverance, and it sharpened our wits. Well, I never understood the reasons they gave, but I was lucky, I found the lessons easy. My brain took everything in and churned it out without strain.'

What sort of people could run a place like that – for children? I would have needed to blame someone, but Rowle accepted, saw it for what it was and then tried to beat it. That was always his way.

'William Crowcher, the headmaster, was a coarse and brutal man, ugly in the extreme with wide, bad-tempered nostrils and to be avoided at all costs. Mostly this wasn't possible – nobody escaped his cruel ministrations. He ranged through the school like a wild beast snorting, waiting outside doors and listening, padding softly through the corridors and pouncing, when least expected, with hands hard as paws and a voice like a growl.

'The masters and ushers were cold, uninteresting, beaten-down men on little pay, with few aims other than to keep us in line. They thrived, for the most part, on the power their position gave them, but they picked on those they could hurt – the weak ones. The others they let well alone. I knew, after my first week at Mountford, why Charles had detested it so, and to give him his due, he had been three years younger than I. And small. And fat. At Mountford it paid to be strong and hearty with an iron constitution like mine.

'You had to fight your way to the top. I was just thirteen, but there were boys there of seventeen and eighteen and I was determined to be accepted by them. I did not go in awe of them. I was not afraid of them – I merely wanted to be one of them. The boys of my own age seemed to be like small children, they depressed me. I used to lie in bed, the pallet crawling with bugs, unable to sleep at night, listening to the wind and shivering in that blood-curdling cold, and work out who to take on next and, more important, where, when and with what. Strategy, that is all-important – a good strategy and any David can slay any Goliath.

'It took time and pain and no end of humiliating beatings, but I learned to fight. I fought them slowly, one by one, like knocking down an opposing army of skittles. It meant being excluded, at the start, from my own peers, looked on as something odd, someone not to be trusted. They expected me to share their own dreary lives, to wait in turn with them for the power that came with dominance. They expected me to be content with that.'

Rowle made it. How could he, when his mind was set, fail at anything so ludicrously simple? By the end of his first term at Mountford he was battered and bloodied with two black eyes, but accepted by the older group of boys. He soon forgot the sufferings this had entailed: the wounds soon healed.

At every opportunity Rowle and his companions climbed over the wall at night and went into town. Innocent mischief, he called it, pranks! They became masters of disguise, hooking down clothing with long poles from windows as they passed so they collected the wardrobes they needed. They went dressed as monks, gypsies, beggars, travelling players, even whip-jacks who wandered about Exeter quay collecting money for the families of drowned companions. They begged for money, painting on to their faces, arms and legs revolting scars – they cheated for it at cards, playing with specially adapted packs. They wandered through the windy, sour-smelling alleys terrorising the inhabitants with their mimicry of Abraham men – roaring and stumbling, shrieking and falling about, faking insanity so that even the poorest soul paid them to leave and move on.

So cocky were they, and so successful in their nefarious operations in and around the tortuous, winding alleys of the city, that once a week they dressed as dandies in fine clothes and took an upstairs room at The Sign of the Boot in St Thomas', where several times they were actually asked to leave when their merrymaking and raucous behaviour, their cursing, wenching and drinking became too much for the other customers to tolerate.

I didn't like to think of this. I didn't question Rowle about it, for I had my own ideas of what went on in that hot, private room with the vivid hangings on the walls.

And it was often only yards ahead of the constables that they hitched themselves back up over the school walls and fell drunkenly into bed just as the first cock crowed.

'I think that even old Crowcher was afraid of us in the end,' said Rowle with satisfaction, 'for he must have known. Our antics must have been reported by some affronted citizen who saw through our disguise, but nothing was ever said or done about it. Crowcher continued to vent his wrath on the miserable miscreants of pale misdemeanours that were quite without significance, while we roamed the area, came to our lessons well tipsy and sometimes slept through the day, reserving our energies for the night ahead – to the wrath and despair of the good citizens of Exeter.'

And I listened to Rowle and I knew why I loved him.

It was so simple, really. I was dragged towards Rowle by the same magnetic force I can feel even when I think about him, here while I wait. And I wasn't the only one. There are people like that . . . they hypnotise others who spend their lives circulating in their aura. I am among the weak, I suppose, the weak and pitiful who come to burn their wings, night after night, who cannot pull away from the killing flame.

When he told me about his school life, I can see that this power seemed to start way back then, because soon he was not just a member of a group, but the leader, uncontested, so natural was this power that emanated from him. Oh God, people were glad to serve him, they were happy to be near him, they clustered about him and were staunchly faithful to him. And what did he give them back? Nothing but occasional praise and, if they were lucky, one of his brief smiles. One of those wise and subtle smiles.

And if he could conquer a company of great, loutish schoolboys, brats – for this is how I pictured them – with such consummate ease, then how could women resist him?

Who is this man who can do this to you, I used to ask myself during the long, lonely times I spent on my own. Black eyes. Bruises. Hah! I considered them a badge of love . . . he cared enough to hurt me. Who is he? No one special! Dear God, I used to tell myself, over and over I used to tell myself, he is only an arrangement of bone and hair and flesh – so how can you let this happen to you?

Was he really like that, monk? Or was that how I imagined him to be? *Did I create him?* Out of my own needs, then, *did I create him?*

How totally different Rowle's life was from mine. No wonder I found it hard to imagine. No wonder we were opposites and could never, really, know each other.

He stayed at The Mountford for five years, thoroughly enjoying himself there. And all the time Gideon watched and waited as Rowle approached his eighteenth birthday.

I don't know what he learned in school, but he learned a great deal out of it. He must have found life boring at home during the holidays. Things there hadn't changed. Gideon ruled, Catherine simpered and Charles, unimproved, more gluttonous, and lazier than ever, was generally offensive to everyone. In the great hall at night the entertainment went on . . . games of charades, musical concerts, dancing and fencing matches. At fencing Rowle soon became proficient, able to win against Gideon. He was taught by a master from France.

The way the Rowle family lived amazed me. There were always guests at Amberry, balls and parties, and friends came from London for the hunting. Rowle was given a bedchamber on the first landing – 'and a tremendously ornate four-poster bed with the family crest embroidered on the canopy, quite ridiculous after the straw pallets we slept on at school.' They could hardly leave him up in the nursery now and Dooley was gone.

Rowle had never said goodbye. Catherine told him, 'Gideon decided to get rid of her immediately after you left. He had no more use for the crone, threw her out without a penny, and she disappeared off into the darkness, foul old thing, muttering witch-like curses upon the House of Amberry over her humped-backed shoulder, swearing that one day vengeance would be hers. And I think, Roger, that she felt badly towards all of us, as if we'd let her down in some obscure way. Horrid old thing. We were glad to see the back of her. Someone like that is bound to come to no good. I always thought of her more as a man than a woman. I was always a little afraid of her.'

Rowle didn't venture an opinion. I knew how hurt he must have felt and so I changed the subject. 'Did Catherine's attitude alter? Was she glad to have you home?'

'She treated me like any other man who visited Amberry,' he answered. 'She fluttered her fan and her eyelashes, she giggled and tapped me on the shoulder when she wanted my attention.'

'She flirted with you – that's what you're saying!'

'She was that way with everybody. That was Catherine. She couldn't help it.'

'And you, Rowle, how did you feel about her?'

'I felt nothing at all,' said Rowle, looking at me oddly. 'Why? How do you expect I felt?'

'Nothing,' I answered him, flushing. 'I was just interested to know, that's all.'

Oh God, Rowle, I hate you and I wish you were dead.

39

Lucy wept when you left again for school, didn't she, Rowle? She soaked your goose-down pillow with her tears and clung to your cloak with aching arms to prevent you from leaving. You don't have to tell me – with a woman's intuition I know how it was. I ought to know – my God, I have pictured that sweet scenario often enough.

Rowle steadfastly continued to refuse to talk to me about his feelings for Lucy. I'd obtained my information on his early life with her from Mary. I'd asked, and Mary had told me, and I kept asking, wanting to know more and more, not caring that every word I heard on the matter stabbed my heart like arrows hitting the target. Mary only knew what everyone knew, the stuff that was general gossip. But I had to know, no matter what pain it caused. Rowle wouldn't tell me. No matter how I chided, scolded, wept, admonished him, he never discussed her with me. Whether they talked about me I will never know. I fear, I suspect that they probably did, and that fact galls me. It used to drive me to tears.

No, he told me about the other side of that time of his life, the easy side, the side he was so disgracefully happy with. And I sat back with my eyelids lowered trying to look scornful and unimpressed by the way he behaved, but I was excited by it. I could picture that dismal, rush-lit world of Mountford, that bleak life of swishing black gowns and canes and spidery pages of Latin script that had to be enlivened in some way. And listening to him, I think I was even jealous of the cameraderie he found with his dubious cronies. I would have liked to have been there. I would have liked to have been part of that time upon which he looked back so fondly.

He bragged. He loved having an audience who could not, who did not want to go away.

'It was so absurdly easy to take the purses of fools, to cheat

284

and win at cards, to put the fear of God up the stupid young bucks who posed and pranced through the city at night. We would enact a fencing scene in which I was the buccaneer, fancily dressed, leaping down off a shadowy balcony into the thick of them. My companions had bladders full of calf's blood tied under their doublets and when I pierced their chests with the end of my blade, shrieking horribly with blood-curdling anger, they fell down on the cobbles feigning death and it was easy, after that, to con the bags of coins from the fine, long-nosed gentlemen with the loud, braying laughs, and send them packing.

'We would go to the fairs with musical acts of our own – good acts, well perfected, you've heard me play the fiddle, Bethy – dressed in bright colours with bells on our ankles. We would create diversions, fall, play the fool, fight, and the rest of us would be going through the pockets of the crowd, flipping their purses from them and hurrying off to join up later.

'And I always wondered about the poor fools who were caught at it. They had no strategy. They walked into trouble with their eyes open and I watched them taken away by the law and wondered why they didn't stop to think, form a plan, choose friends they could trust. Some of them would sell each other for the price of a mug of ale. It never even occurred to me that I would be caught and hauled before the justice.'

I tried to take him down a peg. 'And had you been caught, they would probably have let you off with a warning, called it a prank just as you did, the high spirits of the nobly born – young men sowing your wild oats.' I scoffed at him, 'While those who needed the money in order to live would have had their arms chopped off, been pilloried or hanged! It was fine for you, Rowle, and you must have known that. There was nothing clever about it. Nothing brave, either.' But my reaction belied the truth behind my words for I did think him brave. And clever.

I know that Lucy would never have admired him like that. She accepted everything he was and everything he did with the same calm resignation. She was never impressed, or dismayed, loving him sweetly whatever. If I had been able to do that, would he have loved me as much as he loved her? If I hadn't always ranted and raved, scratched at him, sometimes, with my nails in my jealous furies, bitten him, kicked at him, attacking that part of him that I felt I had to have – that part I knew could never be mine.

Lucy was a good person. Naturally good. I would like to have been like her. And I know that Rowle didn't hurt Lucy.

And here and now, fearing death, if I could speak to somebody, be allowed to send one last message to anyone in the world before I die, I know that because I am bad and selfish I would send a message to Rowle. A meaningless message, probably, full of the old resentments and a final sting in the tail, a plea to come and get me. But it wouldn't be the one I ought to send, it wouldn't be the one I would like to send. That message should go to Lucy. And it would have to be this.

In spite of everything I've said, in spite of everything I've done, he was always yours, Lucy.

Just before his seventeenth birthday Rowle was expelled from The Mountford School for attacking Mr Crowcher. The staff told him he was lucky not to be prosecuted for such savagery.

However, he did not consider his action of much importance. 'He deserved it. Someone should have turned on him, given him a dose of his own medicine years ago.'

A prefect by this time, he had been given a room of his own, 'more of a cupboard under the stairs,' was how Rowle described this privilege to me. He was caught by an usher with strong drink in his room and a wench in his bed. Two of the strictest rules had been flouted, and Rowle's misbehaviour could not be overlooked. If Crowcher himself had caught the boy out, he might have turned a blind eye, but because it was this particular usher, a disagreeable little man called Biggs, finicky and stubborn, who would never let anything go, something had to be done. At The Mountford this meant only one thing: the traditional severe flogging before the whole assembled school.

Had he been a few years younger, Rowle might have been able to tolerate this treatment, for it wasn't the pain that worried him, it was the loss of pride – and the whole suspect ceremonial approach to the punishment.

The appointed day came, and the School assembled in the dining hall – 'a wooden room full of long, trestle tables. It smelled of milk slops, old meat and damp. Everyone but

Crowcher and a few out of touch masters knew there would be trouble,' Rowle said grimly. 'Everyone was waiting, holding their breath. The atmosphere was tense, and I was the star performer. Even if I'd wanted to, I couldn't have gone in there and just accepted the treatment meekly. There was too much expectancy about for that.

'The eyes of my friends were veiled with laughter. They sat on forms at the front with their legs stretched out and smiles on their lips. The smaller boys stood on tiptoe, jostling for places on the tops of the tables, whispering, nudging each other and struggling to see. Crowcher came in like a black-winged crow, his gown flying behind him, scuttling across to the high table with his cane under his arm. He was a sallow pockmarked man with a streak of hair that crossed his forehead and melted into the general scowl of his face. He always looked grubby, and his eyebrows were like the wheel-arches of heavy wagons, thick with mud.

'My actions weren't spontaneous: I had weighed up the situation carefully. I was seventeen, I had gleaned as much education from The Mountford as I was likely to get, and I was tiring of the games we played – there was nothing left, really, for us to do. The excitement had gone, or was going, and that's when it's expedient to quit. It was time for a change in my life. I knew that expulsion would be the only option left open to Crowcher after I had finished with him. There was no question of prosecution . . . the School depended on names like ours . . . the sons of those who were, or had been, favourites at court. And my father's name was not one easily forgotten. So, yes, I weighed it all up. I was ready to leave, to return to Amberry. In a strange way I had been given the ideal opportunity to pay Crowcher back and to effect the change I wanted in my life.'

Listening to this, I chilled. He was so calculated over everything. Did he then, I wondered, calculate in this way before he made love to me, or rode with me on one of our 'spontaneous' night-time expeditions? Did he sit back and think before he ordered me home, or teased me, kissed me, caressed me? How insignificant did the event have to be before he allowed himself to follow his heart?

Did he have one?

Crowcher called him up. Rowle went, supercilious and grim. I could just imagine that look, for he wears it very often. The headmaster ordered him to bend over the flogging stool. Rowle did so, while with laughing eyes he played to the crowd. Crowcher raised his arm, the cane swished its way up into the air, ready for the downward swoop, and Rowle kicked out with one foot and unbalanced Crowcher, who fell as he stood, with one arm up over his head and that look of determination on his face.

'That look soon changed when he saw me standing over him,' Rowle recalled. 'His unpleasant expression changed into one of disbelief, then of surprise and then horror as I took the cane from his hand, pulled him up by the scruff of the neck and forced him down into my place. Other masters stepped forward, their arms out protesting, but the strongest boys in the room – and most of them were nearly men, now, who could overpower this authority – were behind me. I could hear old Biggs' voice whining above the others . . . "Master Rowle, this is intolerable! Stop this behaviour immediately or I cannot vouch for the consequences . . ."

'An empty threat, for there were no consequences, there hardly ever are!' said Rowle.

He told me, 'Crowcher was lucky, for when I looked down on him from that height, kneeling there, I saw an old and beaten man. He was helpless, and I felt pity for this man with a monotonous life that I know would have killed me had I been forced to live it. No wonder he had turned bitter and vindictive, after years of taking in boys, only to teach them what they did not want to learn, and to exist on wages that would hardly cover what Gideon spent on his best hunter . . . to see the tides of youth come and go like that, all with opportunities he never had, and all despising him.

'He looked up at me, where I stood brandishing that wicked cane. "How dare you, sir! How dare you!" And his voice was strained and a little wild. I thought it funny. The whole, ridiculous situation was funny. Any anger I had started with left me. I shook my head. I let him go. But there was an immediate howl from the crowd. They wanted more. They gave me the thumbs down and so when I beat him I did it for them, not for me, for all those that owed him a beating but didn't have the courage to carry it out. I was not merciful. And in a way I'm sorry now. He was a pathetic man – most bullies are.'

And I thought about Rowle's fight with Silas, and knew why Rowle had let him go.

Rowle rarely criticised others – he laid himself open to attack if he did. I was never slow to grasp such a chance. 'So you don't consider yourself to be a bully?' I asked him innocently.

'Only when I deem it necessary, my sweetness,' he said, leaning towards me and taking my chin in his hand. And I flinched.

Lucy must have been pleased to see him home.

40

Oh, he made it so simple for me to worship him – and I badly wanted someone to worship.

The child was to be an offering, something special and of myself. Something individual, created by me, something good. For Rowle. To make him care for me.

Rowan. I do not want to think about her. I don't think I can bear to think about her. It hurts too much and there is already so much hurting inside me. She is too small and fragile to be brought to this place, even in memory. Too close, too lost to me. Yet I have to look at her, Brother Niall, and I have to face the reason for her coming. It took her four years to be born but all that time she was there, waiting, in my head, and I knew that she would come one day.

Until I made the decision to bear Rowle a child I had used herbs to prevent conception – the juice of savin which we called cover sham – as Jessie had shown me. And Dancy made beads out of ground bitter almonds and swore that one of these in the right place was the safest answer. If these methods failed to work there was always the final alternative: Silas knew how to get rid of a baby but many women, too modest to go to him, preferred to take their chances and go to Dancy, Maud and Bell. This was reputed to be a painful and unpleasant business. Their cure involved a pig's bladder and a tube, gold filing's filched from some church ornament. There was much bleeding and suffering, and dark suggestions that some of the women would never bear children again. It was even rumoured that some hadn't lived. But I would have gone to Dancy rather than risk myself with Silas.

I never saw Silas. I did not want to see or think about him. All I gathered was that he had recovered, body and soul, was much the same man as he had been before, and that Rowle depended on him as usual.

I ceased to drink the cover sham and willed a baby every time Rowle and I were together. It didn't happen, but I had convinced myself that to bear Rowle a child was the answer. And I think, in those in-between years, that Rowle believed me to be happier, more contented. Unwilling to disturb this newfound peace, he accepted my serenity with relief, never questioning it.

Once I grew used to the rejection of the other women I accepted it, considered my independence as something strong, to be proud of. It allowed me to go my own way. But unlike Rowle I found it hard to adjust to the change which had taken place in my life.

Some people didn't ignore me. They spoke to me and didn't go off when they saw me approach, their noses high in the air. There are always some who will speak to you no matter what you have done. The world on my new side of the Combe was a very different place from the one I was used to. Although there were only yards to divide us, the gap between the two sections seemed much larger than that. To reach the other side you had either to climb down and cross the river by slippery stepping stones, and then go up the steep, grassy shale, pulling on tufts and boulders to help you along. Or you had to walk right to the end . . . the east end where the lost ones lived, or along the winding track to the west, towards Lucy's house. The divide was not large, but it seemed so. And I had a clearer idea, now, of what Jessie's life had been like when she lived here with Caleb . . . an outcast . . . bad . . . not fit to mix with the righteous ones on the other side.

It is strange how groups of similar people stick together; even in the small world of the Combe there was a right and a wrong side, a right and a wrong way to behave.

Some nights Sam Gaunt would come, book in one hand, candle in the other, limping and tall in black along the side of the Combe. The preacher considered us all as one flock, the Godless ones, the damned. He stood and shouted in his huge, sombre voice, 'Truly saith the prophet – The wicked is like the troubled sea, which cannot rest, whose waters cast up mire and dirt.'

'We'm tryin' ter rest, yer mazed bugger. Fuck off out o' 'ere an' do yer bleedin' wailin' an' gnashin' o' teeth somewhere else, not 'ere, not where we'm trying to get some bliddy sleep.' This was Rose, the whore – another whore, like me. She disturbed The Countess who lived below me, down a narrow grass run to the right. The Countess always wore a tall red wig and they said she had no natural hair anywhere on her body. They said she took too much opium and that it had reached her brain and turned it. Her house smelt queer, but she was very good to me and showed me how to stuff herbs and meat into a bladder to make a tasty sausage. Nobody knew who she was or why she had come to the Combe, but they could remember her arrival: she had come in a cart pulled by a pure white mule and laden with treasure, jewels and gold. Proud, upright, with a swagger to her unsteady gait, she said she was a woman of high rank. Nobody argued, and she clearly knew about good breeding.

· The Countess shouted back at Rose now in a most unlady-like manner, but the thin-lipped Parson Gaunt continued, fired by the interruption, 'Oh ye barren, wandering fields of foam, going moaning round the world, evil souls, unreconciled to God, tossed by your own boiling passions.'

'If that be it passen', I'm willin' an' waitin' 'ere wi' me legs open an' me fanny all ready fer 'e any time yers pleases. Not fer free, though, yer'll 'ave ter pay fer me entrance ter paradise,' screamed Rose.

'Clear off!' A man's voice this time. 'Yer crazy freak. Go boil yer fuckin' 'ead.'

'I am come to bring light to the darkness,' said the parson, waving his candle.

'There's one sure way o' snuffin' that light at the end o' yer pissin' candle, passen, an' I'll demonstrate in a minute if'n yer doan sod off.'

However, we were too tired that night, and grumbling with sleeplessness, to come out and bait him as we sometimes did. But the Teague brothers, who were not really brothers, who wore broadbrimmed hats and cultivated long ringlets and lived on the mossy platform to the left of me, they went out with their hats on and nothing else, crept up behind him and the parson fled, outraged. The Teague brothers' cave was stuffed with sharp-toothed wolfheads and stags with antlers . . . they had a boar's head over their door outside and the same boar's behind on the inner, and in the mornings, when the sun shone, they would sit outside and polish its gleaming white tusks. They tried to make a garden but the ground was too hard, there was too little sun and nothing would grow. Davy and Garth rarely spoke to anyone else. They conversed in a language they said was French but Rowle told me it was not. Rowle told me it was no language he had ever heard and so everyone knew it was one they had made up.

Sometimes, when I went to the river to fetch water, usually early in the morning when nobody else was about, I filled a pail for them, too. So after I had been there a while, Davy and Garth started speaking to me, beginning with a shy 'Good morning', and on we went from there. They knitted the softest hose and once they left me a pair outside my door. I needed people to talk to although I was rarely bored by my own company because when Rowle wasn't with me I lived in my head. But I needed people to look at me without that mistrust in their eyes. Still, I never asked anyone in. In case Rowle came.

Cherry and Rose were not allowed to ply their old trade in the towns, as it was considered too dangerous to let them out for that purpose. So they practised it on our side of the Combe and beery men would pass late at night, calling out for comfort, belching, staggering and farting.

Sometimes, when they weren't too busy, we'd all go and have supper with The Countess, and we would sit round the table and talk together like proper women with homes and children. The Countess would sit at the head of the table, fine and staunch and made of oak, with Rose and Cherry each side of her and me at the other end. Cherry spread her legs as far as they would go and I wondered if that was because she was fat or something to do with her trade. The Countess would ask how we liked the biscuits – were they too brown or too dry? Did we think that perhaps she should have given them a bit longer? She poured tea out of a silver pot and we drank from special thin bowls. We knew she was after compliments so no matter how weird the biscuits we praised her, for she had a terrible temper and it was said that she'd murdered her husband for gold.

'Do take a jar of my apple pickle,' she'd say as we left, adjusting her wig which was often askew on her head. It was too tall and heavy to sit on that small head properly. Rose and Cherry would giggle, but take the pickle just the same while I never liked to eat mine, because of the queer smell that was always around The Countess and around everything she did.

Rose and Cherry said she was mad.

Rose and Cherry, they fought each other, and sometimes they fought for money. And men would come, just as dusk fell and the women on the right side of the Combe were indoors and getting the children to bed and readying the supper. The men seemed to know when a fight was on although I never did. No one told me: I was drawn outside by the shouts.

They kept on their bodices which hid very little and they kept on their short petticoats. Rose, who was little and quick, with shaggy black hair and a badly pocked face, wore pink ribbons in her hair while Cherry, who was monstrously fat and with tattoed arms, wore yellow. Their arms and legs they covered in goose-grease. They used no weapons, only their hands and their feet, and the men placed heavy wagers. At each end of the ring was a large mug of gin, and Cherry and Rose returned to their corners often – too often for the likes of the audience, who called and jeered when they did so. Money was thrown into the ring and it mixed with the sweat and the grease on the floor. I never saw Rose or Cherry hurt each other; it was more of a tangled, bawdy dance, with clutching, scratching and slapping and tearing at hair. But I saw the money accumulate, and I realised that all the crowd wanted was to see Rose and Cherry pull each other's clothes off. And this they did, but eventually, careful to keep the men waiting.

'We likes to give 'e their money's worth,' was how Rose explained it to me. 'They come fer more than the beer an' the cheese.'

I saw the queue form outside their cave at the end of the bout, and I wondered at the ease of it.

'You should join us,' said Cherry one day, her body bouncing as she struggled down on to the grass. 'We'm overworked, eh Rosey?' She picked her teeth with a sharp chicken bone and considered me between narrow, slit eyes. 'You'd be popular. You'd do well at it yer knows, midear.'

I thought of Rowle and of his reaction and I asked, 'What do I want for money? What do you want for money? What do you do with it and where do you keep it?'

'We don't do it fer the bliddy money,' said Rose, who I thought ugly with her pocked face and her half hair-lip. 'The money, it just mounts up in there. We do it 'cos we likes it.'

There were nights, though, when they didn't like it. Nights

when I was alone, lying sleepless, and heard. Sometimes the customers lost their tempers and beat them, and the girls were black-eyed in the morning. There was one man in particular, Blackjack the ratter, whose hair was red and bristly as a sow's, his beard bright red and tangled, and whose nose was as wide as a tinner's shovel. His eyelids were swollen as if by gnat bites, and all of him together must have weighed twenty stone. No woman would have him, they said. No woman could take him, they whispered. He walked like a giant, swinging from side to side as if it was easier to move his great body that way. When they saw him coming, Rose and Cherry hid, but sometimes they opened their door and he was there and there was no getting away from him. And I was afraid of the pack on his back for I knew it was full of rats. Seeing him, I imagined them live inside it. Along the Combe side he came, and the children who saw him ran to their homes and peered at him through half-closed doors. At times like these I went inside and started humming loudly. For I couldn't bear it.

Once, feeling lonely, I tried to talk to Mary, cried against the black stuff of her dress, but she felt distant, too far away. Something had happened to her silence, and there was no comfort in it now. Only a year had gone by and yet she looked older, heavier. Her hair was greyer, her skin somehow coarser, and yet she was the same woman who had taken me in, with the same monkey features and kind eyes – the same and yet not at all the same. Not to me.

Once I met Lucy out walking. The children had taken to coming to my home and although I knew she didn't like them to play this side of the Combe she didn't prevent them. This day it was getting dark and Lucy, concerned, was on her way to fetch them. Then, seeing me, she didn't come any further but stayed at a distance as I brought them along the path to say goodbye and watch them safely on their way. Bessie was walking well now and Daisy, who adored her, took great care of her and used her like a doll. I had been laughing with the children before I caught sight of Lucy. My laughter ceased abruptly. It was difficult to meet her eyes without lying, or gloating, or apologising – none of which I wanted to do. So we looked, for a time, at each other's hems and spoke politely.

'Well,' she said, pretending she had been taken by surprise.

I saw that her fawn hair reached her waist, that she had it loose and flowing, and it looked fine and soft in the dusk light. I had been imagining her bigger – now I saw that her figure, in white muslin, looked small, fragile and delicate; her legs and feet were bare. She wore on her face an expression of sweetness and simplicity – quite different from the scheming bitch I had turned her into. She was lovely. Enchanted in a special way. And I felt a pang. For a moment I thought I might fail in my plan for a child, and was sick with the weakness this feeling gave me. 'Well,' she said again. 'Hello, Bethany.'

I bent down to stroke a grey cat which had made its home with me and as I knelt I looked up at Lucy. She watched me for a moment, disapproving, for the cat was a disreputable, mangy-looking creature that I had rescued from some lads who were about to throw it on to the fire for sport. And then she said sharply, 'That is bad luck. You know that is bad luck.'

The cat curled and purred, enjoying the attention, its head held high. And I kept on stroking and staring up at Lucy until it felt as though I was working a spell – but I wasn't. I wouldn't know how to. Yet I felt that I was, and I think she felt that, too. She was suddenly afraid. She didn't try to hide that – she just gathered the children, turned and went.

I know that both of us wanted to say more and dared not, or could not, I don't know which. And then the moment was gone. Too many moments went like that. I should have grasped each one and used it, knowing how rarely they come and how precious they can be if you choose to make them.

I was aware of the smallness of my world, and that I felt especially lonely. The sky was going an inky black with a thin veil of stars; there would be a frost later. And would Rowle come?

Seeing me subdued and miserable, The Countess came clutching her wig to my door. She was a person to be avoided, for once she caught you it was hard to get away. She held herself stiffly, her back like a rod as if she was always afraid she might fall over. I did not ask her in. She was always dressed in finery and often carried a bag and a fan as if about to go to a ball. She was the one who chose frivolous, useless ballgowns out of any new consignments of clothes. We used to laugh at her from afar, Lucy and I, but I was used to her now. She was a neighbour of mine, and I didn't laugh any more.

'She's upset you,' said The Countess, staring at me out of her faded, bloodshot eyes and pulling a thick woollen shawl around her preposterous garb.

I wanted her to leave. I did not want to bother to talk. I ached to go and get warm by my fire and hug the incident to me.

'No, Lucy hasn't upset me,' I said wearily. 'I have upset myself.'

'She must have said something to you, to make you go pale like that.'

'Am I pale? It's probably because I am cold.' And again I wished the woman would go and leave me alone.

'All this misery over a man,' said The Countess, opening her fan and fluttering it against a last cloud of evening midges. 'I don't hold with it.' And I thought of the husband she had killed and wondered if she was mad.

The Countess took a clay pipe from somewhere under her skirts, filled it and lit it, so I knew she did not intend to leave but I still wouldn't ask her in. Yet I had to talk to somebody. I felt so very alone. 'Rowle is not just any man,' I told her, aware of the weakness behind my words. I spoke emphatically, as if to convince myself.

'All men are the same underneath and they only want one thing.'

I was not prepared to enter into another conversation over the rights and wrongs of it all. 'Rowle is much more to me than that. And I am more than that to him.' And my mind rolled over all the parts I played for him . . . mother, friend, whore, slave, queen . . . oh yes, we played many games, Rowle and I. And all at his whim. Some of them were sexual, but not all, I told myself, no, not all.

'I was like you once,' she said, eyeing me steadily as she could through her watering eyes and thin puffs of smoke. 'Possessed!'

'Possessed?' I did not like that word. It smacked of magic and curses and spells.

'I had ten years of it,' she continued, 'and that was enough for me.'

I didn't want her to go on. I didn't want to hear about her

husband, or any of the dreadful things she had done. I wished people would realise that my love could not be compared to anyone else's. I wished they wouldn't try. My love was unique . . . and deeper than anything they could have known. And Rowle would love me back, just as deeply, in just the same way, once I presented him with my perfect gift.

'I worshipped the blighter,' said The Countess, coming even closer so she was impossible to avoid. I could not imagine this strange creature worshipping anything, save for the strong black powders that gave her the kind of oblivion she craved. 'Have a biscuit.' And she pulled one of the round, tasteless objects she made from out of the beaded purse round her arm.

I took it and bit it. I asked uninterestedly, 'What did you do?'

'I killed him,' said The Countess with a sudden spark of wild aggression which threw her wig sideways so that she had to raise both arms to clutch it on.

'That's what I had heard.'

'Gossip . . . that is the worst thing about this place.' And I did not like the strange look she put on her face as she whispered, tapping her head with a long, bony finger, 'I killed him in there – where it counts – inside. As far as I know he's still alive in the flesh,' she glared out up to the top of the Combe, as if her husband could be crouching there, listening, still able to get her if he knew where she was. 'Still at it,' she said. 'Still breaking hearts wherever he goes. It didn't matter that it was me,' she said. 'I was there. I was willing, but it could have been anyone for all he cared. Anyone who was prepared and willing to suffer. Are you willing to suffer? Does he hurt you? And do you like to be hurt by him? I think that you do.'

I frowned. I was not going to talk about that. 'So you didn't actually kill him?'

She gave a snort of wild laughter. 'No, no, that's what they take it to mean . . . stupid . . . the lot of them. Missing up here.' She tapped her head again and the burning bowl of her pipe disappeared into the depths of the terrible wig. 'You can do it, too,' she said. 'You can stop this yourself before it goes any further. Well, look at yourself! Look at your life! Think of your future! Where is this getting you? Child, you are going nowhere. He doesn't care whether you are here waiting for him or not. I know his type. As I say, I have met one before.'

Oh, Brother Niall, and I thought how easy it was for jealous, inadequate people to hate Rowle. How they would love to gang up against him with me if I'd let them! I was infuriated – that this silly woman who looked like a horse could stand before me now and say such things – she compared her pathetic, humiliating passion to my own! How dared she? How dared she compare herself in any way at all with me.

'I really don't think . . .' I turned my back and I started walking towards my door.

'Go and talk to Lucy,' she said. And, startled, I turned round.

I shouted, 'How can I do that? She hates me! Don't you know anything?'

'You want to go and talk to her, don't you?' And I was amazed at this woman's perception. For yes, that was the sadness in me tonight. That's what the pain was all about. For once it wasn't for Rowle and I. It was for me and Lucy, the loss of my friend and the wanting her back, oh not as we had it before, but with me being honest and as Lucy had believed me to be. I wanted Lucy to trust me again. I wanted her as my friend! I wanted to feel good about myself again.

'I've gone too far to turn back.'

'It's never too late.'

'Lucy would never agree to see me.'

'I think that she would.'

'Lucy could not help me.'

'I think that she could. Remember, midear, there will be a time when it's too late. That time, it always comes.'

And now this woman, this strange, painted creature, was irritating me almost beyond endurance. Why was I of such interest to her? She didn't know me, did she? And I certainly did not know her. I was not at all interested in knowing her! Or in listening to her unwelcome advice.

'To stop this you have to be prepared to see things as they really are. You have to stop pretending. It's all going on in your head, midear, that's where it's all happening.'

Oh, she promised such freedom, monk! I saw it, oh yes, it was there. In her manic face and her drugged-up eyes . . . she had killed her love . . . and where had it left her? Dear God, what was she now? A wreck. Empty. Finished. Mad as a hatter and crazed by the poppy seeds. If love had brought her down so low then what would it do to me? All right, yes, we were both of us crazy, but which one of us was more free? We both knew the answers. Neither of us could face them.

I thought, oh Rowle, please, please come tonight, and I said to her, 'Leave me alone.'

She said, 'You're not willing to leave it. You refuse to take the first step. You are quite as dependent as I.'

'You are killing yourself,' I said with disgust, for the woman was clearly out of her mind. 'Go home.' Leave me alone! Leave me alone! Leave me alone!

And I heard her answer, bitter in my ears, as I closed my door in her face. 'Dear child, you do not exist. You are without hope. You are already dead.'

I hated that woman. I never spoke to her again. She was bad as the rest of them.

And oh, Rowle did not come to me that night.

41

Rowle visited me less frequently and I stopped my questions about Lucy.

I thought I knew all I needed to know about her, although she hadn't told me herself – she rarely talked about the past. I had found out from Mary years ago. Mary was always the one to go to for information of any kind. She was a gossip, picking up bits and pieces as she went through her day quite gleefully, as Davy next door picked up chunks of horse manure for his garden with his long-handled shovel. Lucy had come to Amberry at the age of fourteen. She was sixteen when Rowle came home from The Mountford in disgrace – just one year younger than he. Lucy was a singer, a juggler, a bear tamer and an acrobat, the daughter of a travelling band which gave their performances in the courtyards of inns and hostelries along an annually beaten track. One winter they left her to take temporary work when times were hard and went on without her, promising to call again in the spring. They never reappeared; she tried to find out what had become of them but failed. Rowle discovered much later that they had been arrested by a local sheriff for putting on a lewd play, and had all died of the plague – her mother, father, brothers and her sisters – while serving their time in gaol. So that spring never came . . . but by then, one season later, Lucy had her own reasons for wanting to stay.

In those days Amberry employed a large and ever-increasing number of servants; already there were twenty at the hall – a chaplain, housemaids, nursemaids, a housekeeper, clerk of the kitchens, a male cook, a butler, a brewer and outside in the farms and gardens there was three times that number, most of them wall-eyed Tremains. Lucy came as a housemaid, though knowing nothing about the duties. She wasn't used to living in a house – this was her first winter under a roof that was anything other than a stable.

No wonder he was drawn to her. As a woman I could

understand why men were attracted to Lucy. She was my opposite, the summer to the winter, the sun to the moon, the light to my darkness . . . Oh, monk, if only I had time to find that light in me! She was all those light, bright things . . . breezy, innocent and happy, that I would love to have been. Her pale pink skin glowed next to her silky hair the colour of sun-bleached corn, and her blue eyes were wide and clear, innocent as a moorland sky; the searching way she looked at you seemed to go on and on just as eternally.

I missed her, for she was good to be near. She laughed a great deal, made people feel important. She made people like themselves.

From the very beginning Lucy shared Rowle's bed during the school holidays, Mary informed me, and fell instantly in love with him. Ah! Apparently it broke her heart every time he had to return to The Mountford. And yet she must have known the hopelessness of her position, surely, for Rowle, being who he was, the heir to Amberry and Anthony's son could never have married her. A circus girl. A housemaid. Never!

And yet her love for him never wavered, although she was courted by very many men who came from the village to invite her to the local hops and fairs, begging for the attentions of the maiden who outshone all the others. Yes, Lucy stayed loyal. And she was always waiting for him when he returned, always obliging, never failing him.

I would really like to know how he felt about her at that time, he, who for most of the year was sowing his wild oats all around town as if there was no tomorrow.

Rowle would say nothing about it.

'When I returned to Amberry Gideon was cold and forbidding as always, but this time I noticed how carefully he watched me. Uneasily I came to realise that he knew my habits – where I'd be at certain times of the day, with whom and where I'd be going. I avoided him whenever I could. I was now six months away from my eighteenth birthday. We never discussed it, but as each day passed his eyes seemed to glint a little more coldly, his mouth to pull tighter.

'I wished that Catherine would talk to me, tell me what was expected of me and how it would happen, but she was afraid of

Gideon and could not. On my birthday would I be handed a great set of keys on a silver dish . . . would the secretaries and lawyers arrive from London . . . would the servants suddenly turn their eyes from Gideon and look for their orders in my direction . . . how would it happen? And what would I do with the power? Dare I expel Gideon, my mother's husband, with a frigid, "Get thee hence!" And if I did, what effect would that have on the nervous, skittish Catherine? Would Gideon force her to go with him? Dare I kick Charles in the backside and chase him all the way down the drive and out of the gates without a penny? And, I asked myself time and time again, is that what I really wanted to do? Is there really any pleasure in vengeance?

'Nobody told me anything, and so we continued to drift towards my birthday, knowing it was coming but unprepared for what might happen. And because I was so unsure I avoided thinking of it and threw myself instead into frenzied activity, loving the excitement of the chase – riding, hawking, hunting, coursing the days away . . . happy, in a way, to accept things as they were. Lazy, happy to enjoy my freedom and the new leisurely comfort of my life. Afraid of the enormity of the change.'

Rowle told me this but all I could think of was Lucy and I wanted to add, 'And loving the nights, I suppose.' I wanted to ask if they discussed the impending situation, he and Lucy, whispering together as I knew that he and I would have done. I wanted to ask if they talked at all, or whether it was just youthful passion that united them at that early stage in their relationship. I wanted to ask if they held hands and watched the dawn come over Dartmoor, making promises in the half-light, tracing pathways on each other's bodies as the first ribbons of sun lit up the hills soft like the fingers of a lover. But I didn't. I thought about it instead, and I seethed with it.

Gideon was not just watching. He was plotting and planning, and while Rowle tried to avoid the issue I am certain that Gideon had little else on his mind but his stepson's inheritance and how, at this late stage, it could yet be avoided.

Everything depended on it – his future, the future of his wife and his heirs. Something would have to be done, and soon.

Gideon was not a stupid man. Caution remained his watchword, but he had left it dangerously late. Any accident now would look suspicious. He had missed his chance during Rowle's childhood, since the boy was too resilient – and the fact that Rowle had actually enjoyed The Mountford was a great disappointment to him. There were many times when Gideon had come dangerously near to achieving his evil ends in the past, but Rowle remained blithely unaware of them.

Rowle said to me, 'You won't understand this, I don't understand it myself, but I missed Dooley.'

I did not answer that, I let it go. Once, I knew, he had tried to find her. I knew because I was there when the messenger came. Rowle had forgotten to close the window and I heard the man say, 'The woman you call Dooley 'as left the district, sir. They say 'er be reduced ter beggin' in London. Tryin' ter find 'er there 'twould be wuss than searchin' a haystack.'

And for days afterwards Rowle was distracted and edgy. Oh yes, I knew he cared more than anyone else would ever understand. Except me. And only because I had had a similar experience myself.

Dooley had let Gideon down. Dooley, on whom Gideon had depended, had made promises she hadn't kept. Women! He was a fool ever to have trusted her. When he employed her he looked at her and listened to her and believed she had the heart of a man, that it would be impossible for such a creature to feel anything for her small charge. However, in the end, after all those years, she had succumbed to some womanish weakness – for how else had the child survived? Gideon was disgusted with Dooley. As Catherine so glibly said, he had thrown her out without a reference, without a penny to her name, she had left casting black looks behind her, and with curses streaming from that ugly face as her misshapen hump disappeared into the winter darkness.

And even Catherine, whom he could control, was becoming more voluble about Rowle and Rowle's future. There was something about him now, Rowle said, that gave Catherine hope. Perhaps it was merely because he had survived, had thwarted Gideon, a feat Catherine had considered impossible.

How frustrated Gideon must have been by then, how full of detestation for his brother's son. Cunning trickled cold into his veins as he sat up late into the nights watching the dying fire, his eyes hooded, intense as a hawk sizing up its prey. There he sat in the high-backed chair, gripping its eagle-head arms and rubbing the sculptured wood with his cold, cold hands. No wonder he watched so carefully, and by all that weary watching he discovered where Rowle was most vulnerable. Slowly he constructed his plan with meticulous care, using all his wiles, all his knowledge of Rowle – the boy's fearless, impetuous temperament, his quick anger, hatred of Charles, of humiliation, his ridiculous pride. And of course, over and above all this, his relationship with the serving wench, Lucy Bishop. All these things were part of Gideon's calculations.

And then he must have had his idea. How he must have smiled at the very simplicity of it.

Treachery, to Rowle, on this despicable level seemed unthinkable. He was seventeen years old, it is true, but he was still just a boy.

I remembered Amicombe and the morning the men from Lydford came for us. Isn't it strange that there is never any sign when you wake up on one of those days which are destined to change your life forever? If anything, they are daunting in their ordinariness, in the way you drift so innocently and inexorably towards your destiny. And then afterwards, being human, you look back for signs. It's safer to believe that you could have known if you'd kept your eyes open, if you'd been alert, because then you allow yourself to think that you are protected against the next time.

So Rowle's morning began the same as any other. He rose, dressed, breakfasted, he ordered his horse to be saddled and strapped his hunting jess to his wrist. He was going with Tremain. Charles and Gideon were otherwise employed, and Rowle was not concerned enough to make further enquiries.

Perhaps there was an omen in the weather. Snow had frozen on the moor and lay there smoothly glittering like ice. It shone like glass in the footprints in the court and in the wagon tracks that zigzagged in and out of the gates. From the stables the heat from the horses clouded into frost above the half-doors and in order to keep warm he and Tremain moved fast. The rivers they jumped were sluggish and slow, filled with old, yellowing snow. They rode with the hunt all day and came home early, a little snow-blind and eager for hot food inside them.

That last day he spent at Amberry was a good one – one to remember. The bitter cold had made his day even more exhilarating than usual, and I suppose he was tired when he joined the family for supper at six o'clock, more glad than usual to ease off his soaking boots, stand by the roaring fire and warm himself with the fiery rum that Gideon offered so freely.

There were no guests that day, nothing in the way of entertainment to keep him up late. As night fell and he played a last, listless hand of cards, listening to Catherine who sat at the virginal and joined in a part-song with Margaret, her visiting eldest daughter, his thoughts must have turned to Lucy.

Sweet Lucy, who promised so much, who waited for him in her upstairs room – so obliging, so undemanding of him that she visited only when she was summoned to do so. And did he wonder where Charles was? Had he not found it odd that his stepbrother, yawning, had merely fiddled with his supper and left a great deal of it on his plate. The gluttonous Charles – not hungry tonight? Didn't Rowle notice the glances exchanged between father and son on that last evening?

'Excuse me, madam.' Eventually Rowle stood up and addressed his mother 'I am tired. Will you give me permission to retire?'

'This early, Roger?' Catherine paused from her playing and half-turned to give him a disappointed smile. She teased him. 'I was boring you?'

'Never, madam. You might affect me much, but never in that way.'

Catherine nodded. She resumed her playing – 'always such sad, wistful tunes', was how Rowle remembered them – and the taperlight caught the diamond clasp at her neck and sparked it.

And Rowle lit a candle from the taper in the hall and made his way to his bedchamber.

He told me how he closed his own door softly behind him and, with his silver cloak swinging from his shoulder, climbed the servants' stairs, jumped them two at a time.

He must have felt so happy! All that sweet love waiting for him – he, who had known so little of it. He knocked softly, paused at the door and listened. There was no reply. He frowned, called, 'Lucy – not asleep then?'

Nothing.

I might have been there, so clear is my picture of this. Rowle lifted the latch and went inside. The room was spartan, containing only a bed and a chest that served both for a seat and a table. A candle flickered and provided the only sense of warmth in the room against a tormented wind that came from the moor and hit the north side of the house with merciless ferocity.

Quickly his eyes adjusted to the darkness. He whispered again, 'Lucy. It's me.'

He heard her whimper. He tensed, stepped forward. Was she ill? Damn this dim light. He lifted his own candle high and approached the bed.

A male voice then, impatient, high-toned: 'God damn you, coming in here and disturbing a man's pleasure without a by your leave . . .'

'Charles?'

Rowle could see now. He could see how Charles lay over her, how Lucy squirmed beneath the great bulk of him, twisting and turning. Once Charles moved his hand and she called, 'Rowle! Oh, Rowle . . .'

No shame? No leaping up and stuttering in confusion? No, nothing of that! 'Get out!' Charles huffed. 'Get out and find a wench of your own – coming in here like this disturbing me!'

Incredulous, fired by the devils of a thousand childhood slights, Rowle was fully resolved, at that moment, to kill Charles. With a howl of rage he was on him, moving like a panther across the room, grabbing him by the hair and pulling him off the narrow bed, banging his head down against the bedstead, again and again. He roared, 'Pig, swine . . . you bastard! Coming in here and taking a wench by force . . .'

Lucy leapt from the bed and cowered against the wall near the window, wrapping her shift around her. 'Leave him, Rowle! Be careful . . . he did not touch me I swear, Rowle . . . please leave him now . . .'

But Rowle didn't, couldn't hear her pleas. Overpowered by his hatred, he must have justice! The candles spluttered out, all was total darkness, but Rowle did not release his hold. Amazed at his own strength, amazed at how weak, how puppet-like Charles was in his hands – a limp, wilting thing without resistance. Rowle's thoughts were murderous. He had

Charles now and he shook him like a dog. 'Only be glad I have come here without a weapon else you, sirrah, would be dead by now . . .'

Weapon or not, the wounds he inflicted were vicious. He punched him, pushed him to the ground and kicked him with his hard leather boots, not caring what happened to this fat fool who had taken such low advantage of so helpless a prey.

Lucy screamed, her hands to her hair, frenzied with horror. 'Leave him, Rowle! Let him go! You'll kill him!'

Rowle stepped back. One moment filled with such fury, the next weakened by a dragging immobility. Lucy! Was she all right? He couldn't see her. She cringed away, part of the shadows on the wall. She was sobbing. Charles was lying motionless on the floor. With shaking hands, from both shock and the cold, Lucy lit a candle and held it high. Charles was white-faced, and from his mouth seeped blood, black blood, which spilled out down his chin and on to his chest, resting thickly on the silk there, staining the blue to purple.

Rowle spat. He watched the spittle mix with the blood. He moved across the room and took Lucy firmly in his arms.

He could only assume that Gideon had been disturbed by the noise, although afterwards he could see that no sound would penetrate the hall below, where Rowle had left him. Afterwards he saw many things, but by then it was far too late. However, an instant later Gideon was at the door holding a lantern, inspecting the scene with a grim frown on his face.

'What has happened here?'

Lucy held her hand to her mouth, shivering, speechless. The sound of the wind was all that could be heard now, and that whined like a banshee to get in, flung itself against the casements, screamed at the shutters. The cold was brittle, but Rowle sweated. The sweat cooled on him as Gideon stepped inside.

Gideon stared hard at Rowle. Slowly and deliberately he knelt on the floor beside his son. He peered in his eyes. He rested a hand on his chest. He bent lower to listen for sounds of breathing.

Then he got up and stood straight, blinding Rowle with the lantern light which he shone directly on him. And all the shadows of the room seemed to move to Gideon's face, giving it hollows and holes, making it shiny cold, smooth as a skull.

Gideon said, 'You have killed your brother.'

'He is no brother of mine.'

'But you have killed him.' So simple – that statement. So full of death. Lifeless. It had a purity about it like Rowle's hatred, but the hatred was all gone now. All gone in. The hatred he directed at himself. What monster was he, that out of his anger could come such harm?

He was seventeen years old but he was still just a boy. A boy caught out in some wickedness – but what punishment was there to fit this crime?

They stood across the body of Charles as they had stood, years ago, across the broken stag. Facing each other, alert, hard-breathing, a question in each man's eye. Who was the conqueror, who the fool? It was Rowle, this time, who lowered his eyes, who let them move across the floor and took them to Lucy's face. And Gideon had no need to wipe his hands of anything. His son's blood was on them and he wanted to keep it there.

'No reasons for me then? No excuses? You will just stand there, next to what you have done, sullen like a dog?'

No silence in this room, the moaning wind would not allow it.

'There are no excuses.' Rowle's voice sounded hollow.

Gideon allowed a small smile of satisfaction to rest on his lips. It looked like a sneer, or the stare of a cat who stiffens to watch something moving in the water.

Lucy rushed forward. 'It was for me that he did it, sir. Oh, he did not mean . . .'

Gideon pushed her back so hard that she fell at Rowle's feet. Her moans merely mixed with the wind and it was as if she had not spoken. And then he said, as if to remove all doubt, 'My son is dead.' And he raised a weary hand to his eyes and stroked them with the back of it.

What to do? What to say in the face of this? The fear and the horror gripped Rowle then, trickling down his back cold as the blood in his veins. His hands fell to his sides, taken there by the weight of their own sudden weakness. He could not bear to look at them, not after what they had done. He never sensed a trap. All cunning left him. He had just the animal instincts he thought that the killing had given him.

'Get out!' The words were spoken as if to an animal. And

because he spoke them in a harsh whisper, Gideon, Anthony's brother repeated them in a stronger voice. He lifted his head higher when he said again, 'Get out! You have one hour, and one hour only in which to leave this house.'

With those instructions given Gideon turned and left, leaving a blackness behind him where he had stood in the dark. But the words he left there filled that space with menace.

Charles remained silent and still on the floor. Rowle did not, could not look at him.

Rowle trembled at the sound of Lucy's wailing for there was great fear in it. He tried to comfort her – they were suddenly children together and the nursery with all its monsters loomed dark and huge around them. They needed the warmth of each other. The shutter banged loose and claimed their attention. They looked outside at the night as they clung there together and saw that the stars had begun to show, and they were frozen stars, shining with frost.

42

So simple, the plan. So devious, the man. And Rowle,
believing, did not look back. Horrified by what he thought he
had done he did not even stop to consider or ask himself why
Charles had offered no resistance, why the blood that streamed
from his mouth was so thick, and so black. After all the pranks
he had played on others, Rowle should have realised. But not
knowing the truth, tormented by the deed he believed he had
done, how could he question the fact that Gideon did not
attempt to get help or try to save the boy.

It had been a daring plan, but the schemers were driven to it
by sheer desperation. Rowle could have killed Charles . . . but
Gideon, listening outside the door, would have stepped in and
prevented that if necessary – wouldn't he?

Charles was a stupid boy, easily led and terrified of his
father, who convinced him there was little risk.

At last I knew why Rowle had killed Charles. And, with a
sinking heart, I also realised that he and Lucy shared a past full
of experiences that were deeper and truer than anything he and
I might have, and something I could never come between. I
knew it, Brother Niall, but I refused to accept it. How could I?

When I think of the night journey that followed, I feel Rowle
drawing closer to me. As he was in reality, shortening the
time-distance between us with every step he took. He wasn't
riding to nowhere that night. He was coming to me. Nearer.
Nearer. And if I stretch out my arms I might be able to touch
him.

As a final gesture of defiance, revenge for The Turk perhaps,
Rowle took Gideon's horse. He collected two bags of gold from
the coffers they kept in the hole in the wall behind the antlers.
He had his sword, he had the suit of clothes he stood up in, he
had Lucy and that was all.

'After the bustle of day, the stables were eerily silent at

night. The house dogs ceased barking as we drew further away and everything that was familiar faded. As we rode out from Amberry I made no calculations. There was nothing in my head – it was strange to be completely empty, like that. It was a feeling I had never known before and rarely since. I didn't know where I was going . . . there would be no sanctuary for me now in London, in the homes of my father's friends and relations. Nowhere for us to go after what I had done. And what's more, I suspected that Gideon would not rest, that it would not be long before he sent the law after me.

'As we rode away that night I felt as if I had no past, no future, there was only the present . . . the moment we were in . . . and that was not unpleasant. The horse moved powerfully under us. We could see the shape of the moor in the moonlight, stretching out in silver like waves lapping a dark sky-shore. We did not know where or for how long we would be travelling.'

Rowle never told me if he was pleased to have Lucy with him or not, and I couldn't gauge his reaction from the way he related the tale. If I had come straight out and asked him he would either have laughed and made a joke of it, or turned away from me, disappointed that my thoughts always went that way, exhausted by my constant hounding. So I didn't ask, but he must have wanted her with him, or he wouldn't have taken her.

And I can't bear the simple truths in that. It hurt me when I first heard it and it hurts me now.

Quite insensitive to my feelings, Rowle carried on. 'We rode south from Okehampton over the Black Down. At first I thought that the men, waiting there so black and silent on Langstone Moor, were standing stones. We were strolling along, half-asleep, heads down, lulled by the womb-like embrace of the night and both of us too tired to give a thought to tomorrow. But then I saw a movement. It might have only been the shift of an eye but in that sharp light it showed and I reined in the horse and drew my sword. I cursed, knowing I should have been alert, in this particular place, for robbers who never slept . . . not even on a night such as this one. And the responsibility that I suddenly felt, for Lucy who dozed behind me, flooded me with a powerful energy. At best I could flee, and probably outstrip them – I thanked God I had Gideon's stallion – at worst I would have to fight. Either way, if I failed we lost.

'But were they men standing there in the darkness? Could they stand so still? Could they wait so long without shivering in this intense cold? Well I could wait, too. I would not move first. The sudden lack of motion woke Lucy up.

'I whispered to her, "Hush. Don't speak. Don't move!" And I felt her grip around my waist tighten almost imperceptively as she saw what I saw and her alarm grew. I cursed the shadows that played with the shapes, subtly altering them moment by moment. I lowered my head to take in more precisely what I saw and I realised that we were completely surrounded. We were at the centre of the ring, and behind every stone there stood a man, just as grim, just as immobile as the granite that sheltered him. As we stood there this band of savages – for surely that was what they were – started moving forward as if at a given order but I had heard nothing.

'Lucy gripped me tightly now and I was torn between spurring on the stallion and taking the chance of pushing past them, in which case Lucy, behind me, would be at risk from the sudden surge or from grasping hands; or holding my ground and attempting to scare them off with threats. I was no mean swordsman. And surely they would have preferred a lost, late traveller on a pack mule, a merchant and his lad, a drunken merrymaker weaving his way home late from the inn. There were far easier takings than I intended myself to be. But could I convince them of that? Tortured by anxiety, I realised that whatever actions I took I would be hampered by Lucy who clung so tight from behind.

'They were more basically armed than I, with picks and staffs, and I saw the gleam of a hunting knife. Their teeth and the whites of their eyes shone bone-white in the moonlight. I glanced behind me and they were moving in from that direction, too. The nervous whinny of a horse from a cluster of blackthorn further out told me there were others, mounted, prepared for a chase.

'They were close now and I could almost smell them. Lucy was trembling violently. The stallion stamped impatience, sensing the tension in the air and wanting rid of it. I pulled one rein sharply and circled, my sword outstretched, tracing a circle of silver flame in the night as the blade flashed behind it.

'The men were like wolves, circling and slyly savage, creeping across the ground. The two bags of coins burned my knees under my saddle and I felt that these figures with their white eyes could sniff the gold. I didn't need to shout, they were close enough to hear my calm warning. "I have nothing to give you. I warn you not to come any nearer. I promise you, you will be sorry. Move off. Back off to where you started and keep stock still." Was my threat convincing? They knew how empty it was as well as I did, but my voice sounded firm, much older than it was. It was the only thing, at that perilous moment, that I could be glad of.

'I could wait no longer. The tension inside me forced me to take the initiative. With all the power I had I pressed the stallion forward at the nearest ruffian and struck with my sword. He fell, and I thought of the bladders of blood we had used at school and I had the time to consider, in the middle of all that mayhem, how different fresh human blood looked from that, thinner, more crimson. I swished the weapon wildly through the air and wounded a second man, and the stallion plunged out of my control, his nostrils snorting and his tail swishing, his ears laid nastily back. I struck out again, my arm held awkwardly above my head because of Lucy behind me, aware only vaguely of the blows that rained down on my arms, legs and my shoulders. I was only distantly aware that they cursed and shouted and sprawled over the stallion's head to hold it steady, and tore the reins from my hands, and hung to the saddle as they tried to slide it down and unseat me.

'I kept them off, Lucy told me later, for a good five minutes which was no easy feat considering how I was outnumbered. Eventually, when I fell, I was still striking out frenziedly, into the thick of them. My fencing master, the man I used to try so hard to please, would have been furious at my lack of strategy, would have wrinkled up his delicate French nose at the crude tactics I was forced to employ. Hand to hand. Heart to heart, that's how the fighting went. I know I shouted "Lucy – run," because I heard my own voice and almost laughed at it, knowing how useless those words were now.

'I should have tried to outride them, but it was too late now, my chance was gone. I was sure they would murder us, rob us first and then murder us. And when my eyes closed, somewhere very deep inside me I thought that this was the last glimpse I would ever have of the sky, of the rogue moon that had played such tricks on me, and of the stars that winked at me. And I felt bereft: a great, billowing sadness filled me as I realised that I was just seventeen years old and would have liked – so much – to live.'

Rowle and I were alike in this, Brother Niall. We loved life so much we had to plunder it, rip from it every ounce it could give us, take from it while we had time, while it was hot and we were hot with it. We had both come near to death. We had seen the things the world could do to people who were weak, to people who were willing to let it run over them and carry them along like bits of straw in a stream to be lost somewhere in the sea. Neither of us wanted that.

So why did we let it happen? I was beginning to understand. And then he turned to me and said, 'And if things had not turned out this way I would have been able to return to that world one day. It is my dream, Bethy, but I fear it is like most dreams. They never really come true.'

'You could return,' I replied slowly. 'You have only to tell them you did not cause that fire. You have only to tell them who did.'

'Such a betrayal,' said Rowle, but it was not to me that he spoke as he contemplated his hands and then raised his eyes to stare at the sky, unseeing. And then he stared at me and I flinched when I saw the despair in his face. His reply was simple. 'If I told them that, Dooley would hang.'

43

Brother Niall, have you ever been defeated by reality?

Whenever Rowle came to me now it felt as if he was coming out of some dark place where I kept him stored away. And if I was beginning to disbelieve in his love – and mine – I could do nothing. I was trapped in my head, possessed. So if I stared at him as I lay in his arms, and asked myself that question, 'Do I love you?' and if I lied in my answer well . . . lying is a way of living, too.

And when Rowle used to come to my cave I'd say, 'Take some soup.' I'd talk to him tenderly, using that, using everything as a trap. 'I made it specially.' And I used to sit and watch him eat it, gently, with that absorbed expression on my face, and ask if he liked it and was it hot enough and did it need more herbs.

When I moved to touch him with my bare arms, accidentally, I positioned myself so the light would catch the angle of my breasts under the thin shift I had chosen. I caught his eye. I knew what these things did to him. I was delicate, dainty, feminine.

Destructive yet helpless, sometimes he hurt me but I didn't care. I was willing to be destroyed in order to add to his power for I needed that power. I worshipped that. I posed for him. I performed for him. I pretended for him. I adored and I worshipped him. And he liked me to do that. It was warm and cosy in there like the den of a she-wolf. I had used curtains for effect, and coloured beads, and every day in summer I picked fresh flowers and arranged them in bowls. I burned sweet-smelling candles. It was primitive, more primitive than his house, more sexual than his house . . . with my cushions and my skin rugs. And I would watch him come in and see the pleasure cross his face as he sank down beside me and relaxed into nothing but the pleasure that I was going to give him . . . sweet . . . simple . . . cunning like an animal.

I rarely ranted and raved any more because he told me, 'You

316

are devouring me with your demands, Bethy. You ask too much from me, you ask for what I cannot give.' No, I became more silent. He demanded submission and I gloried in that, for there were depths that I craved to reach where only Rowle could take me, overpowering me until I screamed out from some primitive core of myself, needing him to take me, hurt me, own me . . . *and therefore to love me.*

I curled up when he climaxed inside me, nurturing the sticky white fluid that would be my child, upset when I had to wipe it from my legs, wanting to hold it tight inside. I was a bee and this was my nectar, precious to me, and honey-sweet.

Sometimes he would stay the night. We still went together to the shepherd's hut and to the gorge, for those were our special places where all our feelings were heightened. Sometimes we went riding out across the forest. Once we came to Amicombe, followed the brook to the lower slopes like two shadows in the dark, stopped and stood looking down at the farm from the peat pass on the black ridge.

The heavy rain had almost stopped and now it was just a fine mist, falling against my face in patters of cold. The grass was swampy; puddles had formed in the hollows and the dark night clouds flew low over us like birds' wings, monstrous, majestic and black, as we stood there. I was dizzy with it. I could put up my arms and be in the sky it moved so close to us. 'Let's go down,' I urged him suddenly.

'There is no light. They are all in bed.'

'No matter. I want to go down. I want to feel how it is there with you by my side.'

For a moment he met my eyes questioningly, but we left the horses with boulders on their reins and moved down softly towards the court. The nearer I came the more I wanted to burst in and surprise Mallin in his nightshirt, drag him from his bed and exact my revenge. Tormented, I said so. But Rowle warned me, 'It's not wise to take action on a sudden whim like that. You have to think about it calmly in the cool light of day.'

'You didn't.' My voice was indignant and I was trembling. Suddenly I was certain of what I wanted to do. My teeth were frozen together with hate, my face wet, tight like a mask with the freezing rain on it.

'What do you mean?'

'When you found Charles on the Tavistock Road you acted on whim, Rowle. You took him prisoner, him and his wife. I saw it all. And you killed them.'

Rowle was very big beside me, lean and slow-stepping down the hill. The wild sky moved behind him, putting a giant cloak on his shoulders. He stopped. 'I did not know you had always known about that.'

'Oh, I know a great many things that you have not told me.' I spoke with uncertainty. This was something I should not have said and I could not cope with his anger.

He thought before he answered, looking straight into my eyes. 'The things I have done on impulse are the things I have regretted most in my life.'

'I might be different from you.'

'Yes, you might well be different in that way.'

'So come with me now! Come with me into that house and help me to punish that man! You know what he did to me! I've told you what he did to me! Just you and me,' my voice was an urgent whisper. 'We don't need men or arms for that wretched creature and his whore.' And oh, I would love to see Rowle deal with Mallin! I would so enjoy seeing all that fear in Mallin's eyes, hearing his screams, watching him cower!

The farm was deathly quiet, much quieter than it had any right to be. There were none of the old night noises that I remembered of old. Rowle had stopped to pick up a stone that had rolled loose from the middle of a wall. 'Look around you, Bethy,' he said quietly.

A little wet wind scattered some listless straw. I pulled my heavy cloak round me, shivering with melancholy to be back once again in this place. I could feel the ghosts. I could see myself as a child, abandoned, lost and frightened. I clung on to Rowle. He felt like the only real thing. I couldn't see what he meant until he showed me. All around was decay.

'Look hard at this farm,' he said. 'It's gone to the dogs. The weeds are reclaiming the land, the hay stinks and is rotten. The thatch has not been renewed – there are holes as big as clouds in the roof of the shippen. The vessels are all in need of repair. The man does not need punishing: the farm is doing it for you, Beth. Mallin is no farmer. The whole place is in rack and ruin and will be vacant within a year. He must be losing money hand over fist. Let's take a look at the beasts.'

I went with him, wanting to find some gratification, to be compensated in some way for the loss of my aunts, and for me – for the long, lost years. We crossed the court silent as deer and peered in the shippen at the motley collection of beasts, ill-fed and sparsely bedded on foul-smelling straw. Amos would turn over in his grave – so would my aunts. And so would I, had it been mine.

Everywhere was a rank, musty smell; nothing was as I remembered. 'There are better ways than killing,' said Rowle. 'Slower. And there's nothing worse than failure. If you fail, there's no one to blame but yourself. We should go away, leave Mallin alone. Let him finish destroying himself in his own time.'

I felt empty and dejected. Outwitted, and I didn't like Rowle's answer. 'I should get no pleasure from that.'

'Do you always demand pleasure from everything?'

I glared at him reproachfully. 'From this, yes. Something is owed me.'

Rowle nodded, understanding that. 'When he's gone we will reclaim this farm, make it worth the work. Then you can come back.'

His words hit me like a blow. I was breathless from them, doubled over. 'What do you mean, come back?' But I didn't want to hear his answer. We whispered there, huddled close to the house, and it was worse because of the whispering. It was so quiet and yet my ears roared with noise. He held my arms to steady me as I stared up into his face and he said, so quietly I could hardly hear and had to watch his lips, 'Go home while you can. Break away from us. Go off alone, stand in the wind and listen to yourself. You don't want all this.'

He let me go to gesture towards the gorge and the Combe. 'All this.' All this, Brother Niall, was the moor and the wild places in it, the gorge and the downs and the valleys he rode. The hunt, the lonely wild span of it all, the laughing wildpower of his life and my love for him. If I was a she-wolf then he was my mate and meant for me: a wolf-man, dark and sinister in this grey night-light. With a look of such seriousness on his face now, serious and sad and full of yearning.

'But I do! I do! I want you!'

He was quiet for a moment before he said, 'Perhaps in another life.' And he kissed me, trying to console me but I turned away, hiding my tears because Rowle didn't believe in anything like that and I knew it.

And I wasn't going to have it like this! No! No! I marched to the centre of the court, shaking with fear and anger, and I stared up at the house and I shouted, '*Mallin! Mallin! Come out. I am waiting for you!*'

A dim light appeared in the upstairs room and wavered before a window creaked open.

'Who is it?' And I curled up inside at the sound of his voice. '*Come Out!*'

Rowle came up behind me but I pushed him away. I felt him release his sword, fall back in the shadows. I was strong, I was powerful, wasn't I? I might have looked small standing there, aggressive, chin up, fists clenched . . . but I wasn't small. Was I?

The familiar door opened softly. Mallin's head came out, with a nightcap on over his wizened grey hair and his tufted, crucified eyebrows. 'Who is there?'

I saw his woman behind him, cowering by the wall, and I thought of Maggie, Lizzie and Birdie. I remembered how they had crouched like that, just like that, by the wall. Women in twilight. I saw all that meekness, the meekness that belongs to the helpless, I recognised it and hated it. I glimpsed the stairs that Amos went up. I stood tall, reaching every inch of the height I needed to shriek out: 'I swore I'd come back one day, you viper, you snake in the grass . . . scorpion . . . evil man, ugh . . . ugh! Do you know what you did? *Do you know?*' I screeched, I spat, I tore at my hair, I flung out my words with all the passion I had in me. And at one time I mixed up the words that I screamed and called out the name of Amos.

Where was Rowle? He ought to stride forward and pull Mallin out. He should march up to Mallin and drag him forward. He should put out his eyes, he should cut off his ears, his nose and his hands and force them into his weak, weak mouth. He should not leave me here like this, alone with it all.

With my face all screwed up I stared at the light. They were not tears in my eyes – they could not be tears that blinded me so, it must be the rain. And I shook, not from fear that night, but I'm certain from cold. And the memories I had were all good memories . . . they were . . . of my aunts, of the rowan pony, of happiness that had been taken away. *By Mallin.*

And suddenly Mallin seemed unimportant, standing there like that so ugly and ridiculous in his white nightgown, squeezing his rheumy eyes up against the dark. I knelt on the ground, hugging myself, and my cloak flew out around me. I sobbed to Rowle, to Mallin, to anyone, I screamed out into the darkness, 'I was a most special child . . .'

'I know, Bethy, I know.' Unconcerned about Mallin, Rowle moved into the centre of the court. He was with me against the monsters –wasn't he? I felt him strong and unafraid beside me – my father, my protector. He would go and get Mallin now . . . he would punish Mallin for what he had done . . . Rowle put his arms round me and pulled me up. My dress was wet. There was dung on my knees.

He seized my shoulders and turned me round. With a cry of anger I tried to pull away but he held me against him and stroked me, and very carefully he stroked my hair, my back, my arms, my face, soothing and healing away the words he had said. The pleasure he gave me was great, voluptuous, and I wanted to stay there forever, enclosed in the private, safe world of his arms, aware of nothing but the touch of his hands and the strength of his body.

Why did he want me to go away? Why had he said that? Why, oh why?

44

I would not go to them for help – those women who were all against me. I told no one I was pregnant, not even Rowle until I was six months gone. And nothing showed. I was just a little plumper, a little more tired. When I bled, and I knew that I shouldn't have bled, I went round just a little angrier against them all, carrying this talisman inside me as if it was an evil eye that would, eventually, protect me from their unkindness.

When I felt ill and sick, when I lay and sweated, grey-faced, hands soaking, I stayed in my cave so that no one could see. Cherry shouted through the door, 'Come out, come out, the sun is shining – we're taking some bread and cheese down to the river. You'll never believe what happened to Rose last night. We have wine to share, red wine from France.' And I yelled, 'Go away!' because you could talk to Cherry and Rose like that and they never minded.

Davy brought me water on the worst days. In his sensitive, quiet way he always knew when they were. He left it outside, and I heard him and Garth muttering on in their strange language together, wondering whether to come in or not. But they never did – they were too involved in something deep in their own lives. They didn't really want anyone else.

I watched the women working on the other side of the Combe. I watched them from my darker side. This was my triumph – not my disaster. I would let nobody see my need. They wouldn't weaken me like that.

I knew enough about sheep and cattle to realise that something was wrong in my condition, but I denied it. I flew to my fantasy again, clung to it hard like I clutched at the sides of my bed when the pains came shooting through me, not even allowing myself to believe that I needed help. That my child needed help. If I was to be safe, to achieve my ambitions, then I had to carry the world alone no matter how heavy that burden might be. And every day that passed I thought, shall I tell him today, or shall I wait until tomorrow, savour it a little bit more, lick my lips around my secret, delighted with it and the visions it gave me. A makebelieve mother with a makebelieve baby. My baby, when it came, would give me Rowle. There would be no talk of my going away then.

And I wasn't going to allow it to take away my pleasures, even if, after Rowle had gone, the bleeding grew worse, the pains sharper. I clenched my teeth and I carried on. He thought my moans were of ecstasy – why should he think otherwise?

And I rode with him, too, to the gorge and to the hut. Many times we raced that summer, as we always did, he on the stallion and me on Hugh's grey mare. She seemed sharp underneath me, sharp like a knife sometimes, and I whispered to her, 'Hey Juno, be gentle, what's amiss with you tonight?' as her muscles moved like a woodsaw and ground underneath me. 'It's the wind in my eyes,' I said when Rowle found me crying. 'You ride too fast.'

'You've never complained before,' he said.

But oh, Brother Niall, I was but a makebelieve mother, a child carrying my dreadful secret with me like a little doll or a stuffed horse . . . a child, just like Jinks Joe, but wounded in a different way. A child pretending to be a woman, pretending to be a lover and a mother.

There was often a trail of children running behind Jinks Joe. When they had nothing better to do, they would seek him out and taunt him and he, too stupid to know any better, always took off so that they could chase him, aiming their peelings and mud pies at him, throwing their taunts and their insults after his lumbering form. They had some justification . . . for at other times Jinks Joe would hide behind boulders and leap out at them in the dark. And their mothers used him as a threat: 'Get ter sleep now or Jinks Joe'll come in the night an' get 'e.'

He was round and pink and fat like a grown up baby, with baby hair smooth and thin on his head. He would cry like a baby, too, squatting on the ground with his legs out before him and his feet straight up in the air, a bundle of sacking, like a nappy, wrapped round him. He didn't appear to feel the cold . . . summer and winter, unless it was very cold, he went about like that.

The children had the measure of him. They had only to

shout, 'We'll go an' tell yer maither on 'e . . .' and Jinks Joe would cower, would sit on the ground with his head in his hands . . . oh, they loved it when Jinks Joe did that. He had been brought to the Combe by a group of women out working. They had found him abandoned and crying in the street and, soft-hearted, had picked him up and brought him home. He'd kicked and screamed all the way. It took time for him to stop wincing whenever a woman went near him. Eventually they let him be, expecting him to disappear and maybe join the lost ones, but I don't think the lost ones would have him – who would? Jinks Joe, like me, like Rowle, had never grown up.

I should not have interfered on the day he came past my door as if a hundred horsemen were after him, but he was such a ludicrous sight, naked and covered with dung and straw. And there was such great fear in his vacant eyes. It was the boy that followed who annoyed me. He was always in trouble, always singling out the frightened ones, bullying the little ones . . . stealing from the inadequate . . . fighting with the weak. His name was Cory Blake, monk, and I think I carry his death on my hands.

I had better confess it.

Jinks Joe, exhausted and reeling, sank down beside the woodpile and started to cry. The boys, led by Cory, surrounded him. I had nothing better to do, so I watched for a while, in the way you do when you are not really interested, drowsy with summer heat and your mind on something else. And then I stood up, fetched a pole with a spike on the end that I sometimes used for the fishing, and wandered over to the small group of boys. I said, quite quietly, 'Why don't you leave him alone?'

'Whore!' whined Cory Blake, out of his thin curled lips.

'I told you to leave him alone.'

'Oh, an' what if'n we decides ter ignore yer? What if'n we decides to chase you!'

I laughed then. I was certainly not afraid of this little rough band. 'Get on and find something better to do. Somebody worth tormenting.'

'How 'bout yousself?' cheeked Cory Blake. He was a thickly freckled, red-faced boy with carrot-coloured hair that looked dirty. The Blakes were a bad bunch even going by Combe standards. The piece of ground outside their cave was a muddled clutter of leavings. They did not throw out their rubbish, but left a pile of bones growing outside until their filth attracted the rats. They were the first to descend on a new load of scavenging, taking what they did not need and then letting the rest go to ruin outside their door. They bred like flies, were forever fighting amongst themselves and hung around all day doing little, barely contributing to community life but taking all there was from it. You could say, I suppose, that I was like that.

I suppose you could say that poor Cory Blake could not help but be as he was.

But this was far from my mind as I walked forward with my fishing pole, holding it threateningly out before me as I went to stand behind Jinks Joe. I wished he would get up and fight for once in his life. He was bigger and stronger than all of them, but he meekly accepted his lot, too silly to respond in any sensible way, too silly to know that his childish behaviour encouraged them.

The lads had been sitting round on the ground but now, led by the antics of Cory, they stood and formed a circle around us. I was caught there in the centre of it, thrusting feebly now and then with my pole, wishing I hadn't interfered and knowing it would do no good in the long run.

I stared into Cory's mean little eyes, and I challenged him to come nearer.

Hands on hips, head on one side, he taunted me, 'Yous thinks you is protected from the fact that yer goes wi' Rowle.'

'Don't be silly, Cory. Rowle would not be bothered with anything so pathetic as this.'

'Youm callin' me pathetic?'

'Yes, Cory, I'm afraid that I am. What else should I be calling you?'

'I'll teach 'e that I is not so pathetic as I carn handle a wench who is naught but a slag. We'll teach her, won't we?' And the rest of the lads nodded.

'Why don't you get up now, Jinks, and walk away? Go to the river and wash off all that filth and straw. Don't worry, they are not going to touch you.'

But the stupid Jinks took no notice. He sat there blubbing at my feet so I had to remain, holding my pole, feeling silly and wondering how long this situation was going to last.

They had made him roll in the dung-pile again, and the stench that came off Jinks Joe was deathly. But I could feel Cory's breath on my face and that was not pleasant, either. The gang were all near us now and taller, not quite the harmless young lads I had imagined. I sensed a menace that came from Cory and spread like a burning hot rash through the rest, dotting their faces and making them sweat with the fever of anger. I wished, more than anything else, that I had not interfered.

Exalted, it would seem, and sensing forbidden territory for once in his life, Cory Blake stepped forward and yanked my hair. 'Witch! Witch!' he said, low and under his breath as he tugged at it. 'Rowle goes wi' a witch. Her should be tied ter the stake an' burned.'

'Witch! Witch!' the lads started chanting, enjoying the novelty from their worn-out old taunts to Jinks.

Suddenly I was powerless, full of guilt and fear, and the suspicion that the taint-mark was giving me away. Was it exposing my shame, telling the world what I was? I was Amos' toy, to be taken and fondled at nights at his will. And all those nights of hiding . . . 'Get out, child! Get ter the moor . . . get out o' this house fer I carn be responsible fer the savin' o' 'e, not any longer. Stay out until mornin'.'

And all that crying and talking by Birdie's baby's grave, as if she would ever understand . . . But did I cause Amos' desire? By the way I moved, breathed, cowered, ate, slept, breathed . . . Did I cause the bruises that I saw on my mother's sisters . . . and had I also, somehow, because of my wickedness, been the cause of their death?

'Witch! Witch!'

I felt myself shrinking inside. I wanted to cover my face with my hands, I wanted to hide. I held my belly where the child grew inside . . . protecting her from this, the worst thing . . .

'Yer bleedin' bastards, away wi' 'e! Fuckin' lunatics wi' yer mazed behaviour, get off away from 'ere and take yer bad selves elsewhere.' With her sleeves rolled well up and her tattooed arms waving wildly, Cherry flung herself into the crowd who became lads again . . . just lads . . . wanting some fun, passing an hour on a long summer's day. They scattered, leaving nothing but the fear inside me behind them. And Jinks Joe sitting on the ground looking up at me out of tearful, wondering eyes. All covered with stinking straw.

'Take yer silly self off,' went on Cherry impatiently. 'Doan yer know yer brings it all on yourself! Yer should stop yer wild jumpin' out, I've seen yerm hidin' behind the bushes an' boulders like yer does. Doan yer see it makes 'em afeared o' you? Keep yourself ter yourself an' yer'll be all right!'

But she was talking to someone who couldn't quite understand her. Jinks Joe stood up unsteadily and ambled off. 'Hopeless,' said Cherry, her arms across her ample chest, her great, blue-veined breasts bursting almost completely from her scanty bodice. 'What can yer do?'

But I know that she was staring at me and feeling puzzled: why had I been unable to deal with a harmless rabble like that? She had seen me cowering there, about to sink to the ground. She frowned on me . . . disapproving of weakness. 'Yer should not have got yourself involved,' she said at last, 'in somethin' yer obviously couldn't cope wi'.'

And I didn't want Cherry to think badly of me but I couldn't think of anything right to say.

After that episode, I used to find little gifts left outside my door – river oysters, pears, a couple of quails, a bright, shiny stone with silver seams glittering in it. I knew they were from Jinks Joe but I never caught him leaving them. And I thought little of it until Rose told me once, ''E's often out there, hidin' behind the woodpile, watchin' 'e. Yer'll have ter be careful,' she cackled, ''e'll force 'is way in an' have his batty way wi' 'e one dark night.'

But I did not feel uneasy because that was not the way of the childish Jinks Joe.

And then, alone one night, I heard a heaving and a sobbing and I knew it was him but I could not imagine what gift he could bring that would cause such terrible exertion. I slipped my cloak round me and opened the door, glad that Rowle was not there for he could be nasty when interrupted. Rowle would not take much care in dismissing poor Jinks Joe.

He was sitting by my door in his baby way and lying on the ground, over his legs, was Cory. Without a face. His head all smashed in. Tears were flowing down Jinks Joe's face, wild tears rushing like an overflowing river.

'I's gone an' killed 'e,' he said. And Jinks Joe had never spoken to me before.

'Why?' I dragged him inside, and the body came with him. Jinks Joe seemed reluctant to let it go. There was blood on my floor, and blood on Jinks Joe's arms, and his hands, they were crimson, they shone with it.

'Why?' I stared wildly around like a madwoman, checking to see if anyone was looking before I shut the door.

''E were comin' fer 'e,' sobbed Jinks Joe. 'I've bin guardin' the place an' I watched 'e. An' night after night that lad 'as bin watchin' this cave. Tonight 'e startin' comin' . . . I watched 'e draw nearer. I didn't mean ter kill 'e, but 'is head broke in when I got it in my hands . . .' And he rocked, sat there on the floor, with the body over him, rocking and crying like a baby.

'Here.' I gave him the special strong ale that I kept for Rowle. The pains had been nagging me again that night. I had been glad I was alone, relieved that Rowle wasn't calling.

I tried to keep my thoughts on practical things – for this could be bad for nobody else but Jinks Joe. There was only one possible outcome: the fool would be hauled up before the council of men and he would be banished from the Combe – sent back to the streets from which he had come – no wiser, no more grown up, just as childish, the same fool. Nobody would miss Cory Blake, least of all his family who had too many children anyway and took no notice of the ones that they had. But they would make a great song and dance out of their son's murder, would milk the situation for all it was worth.

No one would stand up for Jinks Joe. Why would they? He was just an imbecile. No one would miss him, or be sorry to see him go.

And Rowle – could I enlist his help? Could I trust him to be on our side? Would he, for the sake of a fool, listen to my entreaties, be influenced by my sympathies? I didn't dwell on that thought for long. To ask Rowle's help would be pointless. He would say, as he always did, 'You can't let it go. People are led by example. If they see one get away with crimes lightly they are quick to follow suit. The discipline here is so tenuous, it can so easily break down. We hold control, not by luck or chance, but by conducting matters out in the open, fairly, where everyone can have their say and see that justice is done.' And he would add, 'No one would support an appeal for leniency for the likes of Jinks Joe.'

I knew where I'd stand with Rowle.

And Cherry – Rose? It would be unfair to pull them in. As for Davy and Garth, I did not really know them.

I floundered around, searching my brain for ideas. It boiled down to the fact that I was alone with this. I could take the easy way out and take Jinks Joe – right now – to Silas, or I could deal with this thing myself . . . with the help of the blubbering Jinks Joe. The awful fact of his crime somehow did not concern me, no, not in the slightest. For he was always a most gentle soul . . . until now. And was this my fault?

'Wash yourself down in the bucket.'

While he was doing this I wrapped Cory's head in a sack. All sticky and sodden, it didn't feel like a person, and I tried not to look. I did it all with my eyes half-closed and my head half-turned away.

'Now,' I said to Jinks Joe, whose face was all mild and obedient. 'Go and make a deep hole, right in the middle of the dung heap.'

I opened the door and watched him go. The dung heap was out of sight and sound, as far from the caves as it was possible to make it. In spite of this fact, on hot summer days it reeked, and people had to go round with hands over their noses. The stuff wasn't used until it was quite rank and rotted. It was high, and thick, and wide. It seeped black juice at its edges. If Cory was stuffed in the middle of that it would be more than a year before they'd find him. And by then no one would suspect Jinks Joe, no one would know who had done it . . . if there was anything of him left not rotted. And Jinks Joe, the one most likely to give himself away, by then I knew that he would have forgotten.

It was some time before Jinks Joe returned and then I smelled him before I heard him. And all the while I paced my floor with the body of Cory on the ground, trying to pretend he wasn't there, avoiding him with my eyes. It was horrible having him in there like that . . . horrible.

Jinks Joe carted him over his shoulder, limp like a doll, but stiffening. I followed after, creeping through the night, terrified of being found out. You would think it was I had killed Cory. You would think it was I who had blood on my hands.

Jinks Joe was strong – the body seemed just an empty sack on his back. And he was only too familiar with the dungpile; he

329

seemed to know his way around it. Nor caring for the sticky mess or the vile odour he shoved Cory Blake deep inside, pulling him this way, pushing him that, until he was deep inside and steaming. Steaming away, boiling away there until, we hoped, he would be all gone. All done with and finished.

'Now just leave it be,' I whispered to Jinks Joe who was puffing and panting with his baby hair all sweated down and his sack nappy all covered with filth. I wiped my own hands as if they had muck on them, but my muck was only the sweat of fear and I wiped that off on my skirt. 'Now we can just forget all about it. Completely forget. And what will you say when they ask you?'

'I'll say he's in the dungpit,' said Jinks Joe, trying so hard to please me.

'You will not say that.' I tried to keep the exasperation out of my voice. 'You will say, "I don't know. I have not seen him since yesterday." Do you understand?'

Jinks Joe repeated my words again and again; over and over them he went until they were sharp in his mind.

And several days later I heard them ask him. 'I have not seen Cory,' said Jinks Joe. 'I have not seen him since yesterday.'

I cringed, for Cory had been gone for five days then.

But his questioner just looked at Jinks Joe sorrowfully and moved on. And I knew we had done it! It didn't matter what Jinks Joe said now because nobody was ever going to take any notice.

But ever after that I had to put up with Jinks Joe crouching out there beside the woodpile.

45

I walked in the dim, misty light of an autumn morning, stepping through bracken, detouring boulders. It was early. Rabbits scattered as I went, the few stunted trees that I passed dripped rain from their branches; they grew angled and some quite grotesquely in their efforts to survive against the prevailing winds. Why did they fight such a battle, I wondered, and I thought how much luckier were those who had put down their roots in the soft, deep earth of the valleys, where they could grow straight and tall, washed by a gentler rain and warmed by a more trustworthy sun.

I carried a broken iron pot and blew on my hands to warm them. They were red and sore and in danger of chapping, for I had been helping Garth and Davy with their hopeless patch of garden.

'How long do you think you're going to be able to keep your little secret?'

I had not noticed Silas. He made me jump and I thought he referred to Cory Blake who was on my mind at that moment. I wished he had not approached me for I was passing the house and did not want to be seen by Lucy.

'I don't know what you mean.' I was aloof and distant, although merely to see this man made my heart flutter wildly and I feared my face must be scarlet.

'You're going to have to tell him one day, you know, and it would be sensible to start making plans for the lying-in.'

Now I knew I was scarlet. My wet hands were clenched by my sides and the pot grew heavy. How could Silas know? Was he merely taunting me, as he used to so often in the old days?

He abandoned his saddled horse and came through the small gate. The geese in the court hissed angrily as he shooed them aside. We stood beside the court wall and I leaned my back against it for I was rarely well these days and standing did not help me. And I thought how little Silas had changed. He still wore his wolfish grin . . . his face was sharp, his eyes insolent, and his mouth was forever teetering on the edge of a sneer. I had not seen Silas to speak to for nearly five years. When we passed we raised a hand, or, more often than that, whenever I saw him I reversed my tracks and took a safer route to my destination. But this time there was no retreat and he seemed determined to waylay me.

'When is your baby due to be born?'

'What business is that of yours?'

He shook his head wearily. 'Stop fighting, Bethany. It is precisely my business. If it were not I should not be enquiring.'

'You are assuming the role of my physician, are you, Silas?' And the cutting scorn in my voice reminded us both of the last time he tended me . . . after Jessie had left . . . in my room at Lucy's house. I could hardly hold his gaze but his eyes were bold, remembering.

He said slowly, 'That was a very long time ago.' And I did not know how to answer. 'Have you told Rowle?'

'I have not.' I was maddened by his attitude. This was my business, not his, and yet he was forcing me to discuss it.

'When do you intend to tell him?'

'I have not yet made up my mind.'

I did not like Silas' smile. I remembered that smile: it knew too much. 'I am surprised at you.'

'Because I am to be a mother?'

'Oh, Bethany! Why should I be surprised that you are about to bear a child?'

I held up my head and stared at him hard. 'You think me unable to do that? To bear a child – to love it properly?'

His smile disappeared into the icy silence, and his eyes were bemused now, wide with questions. But he asked me nothing. He told me, instead, 'You have a strangely low regard for yourself, and there is much in that that I find hard to understand. You consider yourself different from other women. I see it, in the way you walk and talk and carry yourself . . . but you do not see yourself as higher than them. For some absurd reason I think you are ashamed of yourself.'

I hated the way this conversation was going. I loathed talking about myself – I was always afraid of being found out. I was always afraid of Silas. 'I am ashamed of nothing!'

Silas shrugged. From behind the wall I could hear Rowle's voice directing the man who was putting a newly-broken horse through its paces. I was desperate not to be seen with Silas, talking like this, for Rowle would ask me why. He knew my opinion of Silas, knew I would not willingly stop to converse with him. And I was also afraid that Silas might tell of the baby . . . depriving me of that pleasure.

'There is nothing wrong with your feelings, Bethy, nothing wrong with love, about making love, about allowing yourself to enjoy your natural desires.'

I was stiff with defence, feeling vulnerable and hurt, and I disliked the sound of my own voice when I said, 'If I remember correctly, Silas, on both the occasions to which you refer I had little choice in the matter.' I sounded like a liar.

Silas was silent for a moment while he stared at me with serious eyes as if summing me up for the first time. We had been apart for five years, and yet we had not been. 'Ah yes, the Lord of Misrule. The wild man who wore the wolfskin – that was a wonderful image, wasn't it? Everything about me bad and evil . . . taking advantage of what? Tell me, what were you then? An innocent child with no idea of what was to happen? Helpless – you? There, with the whole Combe sat at the table. Couldn't you have called out for help? And Rowle just a whisper away? Don't deny it, Bethany. For your own sake, please don't deny it. You wanted me then . . . even if the reasons were wrong, even if it was merely to attract the attention of Rowle, you wanted me Beth, and I knew it! Did you think I would bother with someone who was afraid and unwilling? Did you think I did not have the pick of the girls in the Combe . . .'

'Stop it, Silas! You are speaking too loudly! They will hear . . .'

'Who, Bethy? Who are these people of whom you are so afraid? Are you sure they are not all there inside your head?'

'You turn events round to suit yourself, to suit your own guilty conscience!'

He contradicted. 'No, you are the one who does that. And in your room, yes, I came as your physician. Do you think I play games like that with every maid I tend? Do you think I wasn't responding to some need that I sensed in you? And a very great need in myself. I wanted you then, Bethy. Just as you wanted me.'

'But I called Lucy in! I prevented you!'

'Yes. And I have always wondered why.'

'For a reason you will never accept, Silas, because you are so proud and hate to be rejected. I denied you because I loved Rowle. I have always loved Rowle and I will always love Rowle. You could never mean anything to me. Never!'

Silas caught my arm to prevent me from pushing by and leaving. 'There is safety for you in loving Rowle. He made the decision for you, didn't he, that first night he took you when you came to the Combe. And you were safe with that. It was nothing to do with you, was it? His lovemaking was inflicted on you, you could see it as something to be endured . . . not shared. I would guess you enjoyed that night . . .'

I raised my arm to strike him. 'How dare you, Silas! How dare you suggest . . .'

He caught my wrist and held it. 'And ever since then, oh, how easy it has been for you, hasn't it? You could go round the Combe aloofly rejecting all the others, keeping yourself for the one man with whom you were perfectly safe because you had created, in Rowle, a makebelieve figure, a god, an idol . . . and idols do not have the feelings of mere men, do they, Bethy? Idols do not have raw desires, rampant passions, idols do not make excessive demands, and you could feel, quite safely, that you had no real choice in the matter. You do not have to respond to a god . . . you can go, blazing in white, as a sacrifice!'

Nausea rose in my throat and I had to swallow. I sank back against the wall, folding my arms across myself. I gazed away over Silas' head, pretending I was not listening. A curtain of rain tormented the bracken, and next to us the rowan leaves on the little tree turned their pale backs to the wind, and the red berries shone with wet pixie caps.

A woman went by and loitered, tempted to pause and listen. She peered through the slit her cloak made, and to me she seemed all eyes. Silas frowned at her and she went on, throwing me a hard look. I saw the satisfaction on her face and I knew she would take away the fact she had seen me here with Silas, take it away with her and spend hours chewing over it with the others. We waited until she was out of hearing. Then Silas said, 'All men are not like Amos. Your body is lovely. Your feelings are lovely. You do not have to hide behind a god to make pure your feelings.'

'You know nothing about me!'

334

'I know that you are afraid, lonely, and expecting a child in less than three months from now. I know that Rowle has become your life. You have made him into your life to protect yourself from your passions. I know that no one, not even Rowle, is big enough to fill that need in you. Rowle will destroy you, Bethy, as he destroys all that he fears he might love. Does he beat you? Has he scarred you? To conquer a woman is Rowle's way of conquering himself and his own fear of weakness. You seek cruelty as if you cannot enjoy love without pain. I know that you are sweet, and good, and gentle, and kind, and that you ought to find someone nearer your age, make a home and have children.'

I flirted. I softened my voice and my eyes. 'You left out the fact that I am beautiful.'

'I left it out deliberately. Yes, you are very beautiful, but that comes way down the line of importance in my mind when I look at you.'

'You cannot see into my head. You assume, you come to conclusions, but you do not know!' I grew angry. Angry and frightened. I had come out to get a pot with a missing handle mended, not to cope with Silas in one of his most difficult moods. He was a most manipulative man with absolutely no scruples: he would say anything, do anything, to get his own way. And I couldn't imagine why Lucy was ever staunch in her support of him. She was almost wanting to throw me into this man's arms! Hah – they were probably in collusion together, both keen to get me away from Rowle. I bent down and pretended to scrape the mud off my boot.

'You are right, I cannot see into your head. Your head is your own. Your body is your own, Bethany. You own it: you can decide exactly what to do with it. But sadly, I don't think that is something you will ever understand. You do not have to give it away as an offering. Your god is merely a man, Bethy, and men are contemptuous of offerings. Worship is hard to swallow.'

'And who are you to say these things to me? Oh, you are wasting my time. I have better things to do than stand talking to you and I need to get on.'

He took no notice but went on talking as if I had not interrupted. 'I only know that I am not the evil, makebelieve man that you want me to be. The stag's antlers and the wolf fur

335

are costumes, Bethy, fit only for pantomime. I am a man who loves and admires you for what you are, as Lucy loves Rowle for what he is. That that is not enough for you both, that you have to create and live with illusion is something I find very distressing. It is also, unfortunately for you, full of danger.'

I was withering with my scorn. 'Don't pity me, Silas!'

He stared at my stomach. Silas could be so sly with words. 'I pity the child. I pity the pawn. Sacrificed for the sake of the King.'

This time I did hit him, hard, a slap across his supercilious face. He did not reel or fall back. He merely smiled, and followed up with, 'You know where I am. And I will always be here for you.'

And I stalked away, swinging my pot behind me.

46

I told him beside the waterfall. Well, you know me now, Brother Niall, so of course I did.

I decided to tell Rowle when I began to feel a little better. Six months had gone by and I was beginning to show, but I stayed small. I was never huge and rolling like some of the women, never had to walk like a duck and sit back in my chair with my belly like a table.

My God – it was only months ago. We were down by the waterfall in all the gold of last autumn. It rained on us. It played on his face. Gold, russets, bronzes, and the water was pewter cold. And I remembered the first time we had come to the waterfall, I could remember everything about it, every sensation, everything we did. How we had sat by the falls, down by the lichened falls with our feet in the water, and he'd touched my hair and the white tress in it, 'a stream of white water,' he had said to me. Even the sky had been green there then, and the vegetation was soft, lush, bursting with sap and juice, exhaling an earthy sort of scent, the scent of sex.

Today it was colder. Under the vaulted sky the silence down here was thick as a blanket, save for the constant splashing of the fall. But rarely, when I was with Rowle, did I feel cold or discomfort. At those times I lived with an aura of happiness tight round me, an absurd sort of happiness, impenetrable like armour. Many times I had rehearsed the moment. All life, everything we had ever said or done seemed to come together for me, at this moment, in some great truth. It was such a precious moment for me in my dreams. I could have told it a hundred different ways, every one of them as beautiful, but all I said was, 'I am going to have your baby after Christmas – there's three months to go, that makes it January. Perhaps it will be snowing. Perhaps we can bring her here in the snow.'

Oh monk, I had pictured that scene so many times.

I sat with my back to him while I told it. I had no need to look at his face – I had seen the joy my words would give him many times in my dreams, so I turned round slowly, eyes wide with love, expecting to see that look there, for me.

His face was terrible. His eyes were closed and he put his hands to his head, stroking the sides of his forehead. He reeled in a kind of blind, hopeless wretchedness.

'You're ill! You're ghostly pale!' I moved near to him, hugging him, keeping him warm until he was himself again. This was not what I had imagined – no, nothing like what I had imagined. 'What is it? Tell me! What's the matter?'

Rowle shook his head as if to put the bad pictures out of it. Every muscle and every nerve in his body was taut like an animal sensing great danger. It seemed as though he was paralysed. At last he opened his eyes and they looked as though they had been bruised from within. He stared at me. He opened his arms and he held me close and I could hear the wild beating of his heart as if he'd just returned from the chase with all the Queen's men riding close behind him.

'Tell me!' I demanded, for I knew he'd seen something. He shook his head again and his face was still grey. 'Tell me – you saw something –one of your pictures – you saw something, I know you did!'

I was hysterical, desperate. Something bad – about our baby – that's what he'd seen. And it was something so bad that he hadn't been able to hide it from me. Something terrible. Many times we had laughed at his visions – he'd had them before. It was a gift he was not proud of and I used to tease him and tell him I believed him a wizard and that he ought to be tried for a witch! He'd agreed. He'd confessed to me that he had them often and when they came he tried to dismiss them although they'd proved useful in the past. He'd had warnings: on the strength of them he had avoided certain places and certain times and stayed safe because of them.

'Tell me!' I was not prepared to leave this.

'I was ill, Bethy,' he said, forcing a weak smile. 'It was nothing, I promise you. I merely felt a sudden pain.'

'No! It was not that! Don't pander to me!'

'I wouldn't lie to you.'

But I knew that for the first time in his life he was lying to me. He was bothering to lie! What, dear God, could that mean?

'You haven't said anything – about the baby – you haven't answered me.'

'The baby.' That hard pain again, behind his eyes. It was there and piercing.

'My baby. Our baby!' It was as if I had to remind him! 'It is coming after Christmas.'

He nodded. 'It will be a girl child.'

'That's not so clever!' I tried to lighten the ominous atmosphere. 'I know that, too. That is not so clever and there's no bad luck in knowing it.'

'I didn't know you wanted a child. You didn't tell me. I thought you were protecting yourself.'

'I have been wanting a child for a long time now. I didn't tell you for fear you would not agree.'

'That's not very fair.'

I couldn't bear this! This wasn't the way our conversation should be going at all. 'You are the one who keeps telling me nothing is fair! Rowle, you haven't answered! Are you glad? Are you happy for the new life we have created between us? They won't be able to ignore me now! They'll have to include me – and we'll be a family – you and I and the baby.' And they came again, those visions of settling down, finding a home, going to church with a line of little ones trailing behind us. Me with him – and his – for always. Lucy didn't enter into my picture, nor did his children. No, not at all.

His reaction was far from the one I had hoped for. It was all sadness and consolation and I wanted to shout, 'No! No! Don't deprive me of this moment! This is unfair! This is cruel!' I was threatened, then, by a kind of numb apathy. Weakened by it, as if nothing mattered, and why should I fight any more. Where would I get the strength? And I saw, then, that nothing was going to be as I wanted it, and if I could, I would have put the child back and thought of some other way. Because I was afraid of the birth, feeling so weak and ill as I was, and I was afraid for the health of the child after the bad start we'd had.

No wonder he staggered, Brother Niall. No wonder he sighed and paled. No wonder he found it difficult to look at me then.

He had seen it . . . all of it . . . all this mess. All this sorrow. I wonder that he didn't weep, then and there by the waterfall when I told him my news with such evident glee.

We had gone too far, both of us, and there was nothing we could have done to prevent it. There was a terrible inevitability about all of it, life flowing on as irreversibly and as surely as a rushing river taking its rusty tin ore down to the sea; light and dark together, good and not good, rushing like a river or like Rowle's black-eyed stallion, galloping unchecked and wild-eyed for God knows where.

And I? I started on him again then and there, obsessed like a madwoman. And perhaps I was not quite sane. 'Leave the Combe, Rowle. Take me and the baby with you. Let's start another life somewhere far away from here. Let's have a family of our own, lots of children. A proper life, not like this one. A free life, so we can go where we like without fear, so that we can be around ordinary people, get away from savages and criminals. Surely, deep in your heart you feel the same way? You do, Rowle, don't you?'

The close-growing trees shut off the sound of the wind and left it to come as a low, quiet moan. 'And Lucy? And my children? My friends? Everything I have built up here? Oh, Bethany, Bethany . . .' He held his face in his hands and I have never seen him more despairing. 'I have told you again and again that I will never leave here. I cannot leave! Why do you refuse to hear me? When will you believe me?'

'But you love me! You love me, Rowle, not Lucy! And I am having your child.' I crawled like a beggar crawls, hat out for titbits, leering with scabs on my face like want.

'It is not like that.' And his words came slowly as though he recoiled from trying to untangle something so fateful and hopeless.

I stood up then, my back very straight, staring at the waterfall and hating it because it could fall so coolly, so simply, with one way to go, over the lip of the fall and down into happiness. My hair flowed wet behind me, I let the water spray on my face. Why wouldn't my life go like that? Why was nothing so simple for me? 'How is it then, Rowle, if it isn't like that?' I don't know where the question came from. I only knew I didn't really want to ask it. And that I shouldn't have asked it.

'What we have isn't love.'

There! It was said. And for the very first time I actually heard it.

The walls of the gorge loomed vast above me, gleaming with silvers and golds. The sky was far away, suspended in such a great space, and I was very small and far away from it all. I felt the ridge of the scar on my hand; I fingered the taint-mark. Was I really here any more and was all this actually happening? I said, 'I love you!'

'This madness – this craziness of yours – of ours – it is not love.'

'Oh?' I stood even straighter, trying to move away. But he followed me. Carefully. We did not touch each other. And I flung at him over my shoulder, 'And you know, do you? You, who are so wise, you know what love is, do you?' Oh, and my voice was cold, the words frozen stiff as an icicle dripping its cold down by the banks of the water.

I turned round to face him. He stood, head bowed, like a penitent before me. 'No, I don't. I don't pretend to know.'

'So how can you possibly say that what I feel isn't love?' What words can you find to convey utter desperation? Why do words always let you down just when you need them so badly? Why do the most important questions always sound absurd?

'All right, Bethy, have it your way. I can argue with you no longer.' His face was all strain and his body sagged, exhausted.

'So! You're not going to leave the Combe and take me away? Ever? Is that what you're saying?'

'That's what I'm saying.' And his eyes were hard. Why was he doing this to me? What made him so hard, so cruel? Why did he use me as he did if he didn't love me, had never loved me, didn't want me? Those questions were all in my eyes, they brimmed in my tears and fell over. Stinging.

'So you're sorry about the child?'

When he sighed he sounded as if the weight of the world dragged on him, and his silence was horrible. I repeated my awful question. I wanted to stuff the words I needed to hear into his mouth so I could hear him regurgitate them back out at me. Oh, turn this moment around – give me something to hold. Make this a dream and let me wake up, sobbing, on to my pillow. Rowle tried to hold me but I pulled away, hatred and accusation in my voice as I shouted, 'It is a curse! She is cursed by her father before she is born! You, with your silence, with your evil eyes have cursed my daughter, Rowle, and I will never forgive you!'

'Bethany . . . no!'

'What else then? What else can I think? Oh, Rowle, if Lucy knew, if she knew the real you she would not love you for one

341

more minute!' I waded into combat, using my most powerful weapon, thinking in my despair that I was a match for my antagonist, throwing away all commonsense that might weigh me down.

'Lucy does know, Bethy, and Lucy accepts. I cannot be other than I am. I am not the man you imagine me to be . . .'

I did not want to hear this! This was pathetic! 'Lucy accepts, oh Lucy accepts . . . well, how nice, how convenient for you! I do not know how you can bear to live with yourself. How can you? How?'

He was vulnerable. He was defensive. He was just a man. And I could not bear to see him like this. I watched his hands, his strong, capable hands, nervously rubbing together, as if they were trying to comfort each other, as if he could find comfort, now, nowhere else. I couldn't bear to look, so I lifted my own, put them together as if in a prayer, but there was no answer to it and they told me nothing.

'Sometimes I don't know. I only know that I don't want to hurt you . . . I don't want this. It is all my fault. I let this happen, but can't you see what I've done to you? Why, oh why, do you let me? I allowed you to see me as I wanted to be . . . but I am not like that, really . . .'

So I laughed in his face since he hated being mocked, wanting some bold response from him, wanting to turn him back into my god. But this time there was to be no relief. I twisted and turned and struck out in my turmoil. Let him attack me, then! Let him strike me . . . let him claim me like that. But he would not. He submitted, like a dog, to my attack. I scratched and I clawed and my hands slid down his face and his body, wet and weak and watery as the rain. There was nothing to cling to, nothing to hold on to. Rowle was a vapour . . . just rime on the grass . . . just sky, just image and I could not grip him. There was no relief from the pain – not anywhere, and I felt so brittle just then that I waited to fall apart.

But monk, I still believed that love, passion as deep as ours could not be destroyed by anything I said or did. I also believed that if I could get Rowle away from the Combe, that if I could only get him out of the clutches of Lucy, away from his friends, then he would be mine. I clung tight to this belief, this dream of mine, hanging on to the last threads of it with lacerated hands.

Until it broke.

47

Brother Niall, I stole gold.

I went to the cave of Rose and Cherry and I stole gold. They didn't want it, they had told me that and I'm sure they meant it. They worked for the pleasure, not for this solid bag which hung so provocatively from the timbers at the back of the room where the added wooded section met the wall. I crept silently into the room when I knew they were both gone out, the candlelight hidden inside the curve of my hand. Hardly breathing.

I reached up, felt the weight of the bag. I had it . . . all I must do now was unhook it and bring it down. For I had been to see Dancy and I had pleaded with the old woman: 'Take this away from me. Put me back to how I was. If you don't do it then I'll do it myself.'

And Dancy, half-hidden in shadows as she sat and rocked before the small fire in her shack, had lifted her shrivelled head and looked down on me as I stood, nervously, only just inside the door, afraid to go any nearer.

'Can you do it?' I was ready to beg if she asked me.

'Aye. Fer a price. Anything can be done fer the right price.'

'Money?' For the first time in my life I realised how precious money was.

'What else?' And her voice crackled like the wood on the fire, and her skin was the colour of ashes. She plucked at a goose she had on her knee, and she didn't cease with the plucking, no not all the time I was in there. So I watched her gnarled hands as they flew, making a great pile on the floor on a rug she laid there for the purpose. The words we exchanged were soft as the feathers that flew that night. She did not stop plucking and she did not stop rocking and she did not move her eyes off me. Not once.

'I am all of six months gone.'

'I know.'

'Will there be danger?'

'Oh aye, certainly.' All in the same tone of voice.

'But will you rid me of the child?' Dancy nodded.

'How? How will it be done?'

''Tis better you not know.'

'Will it take long?'

'Depends.' And she took her eyes from my face for a second and let them travel all over my body.

'Are there others who have . . . at this late stage . . . are there others?'

'Not so many.'

'How much money?'

'Fifty sovereigns.'

I knew that Rowle would not give me the gold . . . not because he would be averse to the loss of my baby but because he would fear for the danger to me. I did consider swallowing my pride and going to my old enemy, The Countess, for we had not spoken since the night she taunted me and compared my obsession with her own . . . with the drug opium. And we sniffed and tossed our heads when we passed each other. But I was worried about any hold she might have over me after that. I did not trust her. It was not possible to trust anyone so totally dependent on her particular poison.

I would have asked Rose and Cherry, but I was sure they would want to know why I needed it, and I could not be certain of their reaction. I did not know Garth and Davy well enough to ask for such a vast amount and anyway, I was fairly certain they would not possess such a sum. They were not interested in money, only in each other.

Jinks Joe would have stolen it for me. I had only to ask him. He still lurked by the woodpile some nights, thinking I didn't know he was there. However, I felt it was too much like asking the innocent to collude in something evil, and I did not want Jinks Joe to have the death of myself on his conscience, however muddled and impoverished that conscience of his might be.

So I was in there, taking the gold. I had my hand under the leather bag, about to reach higher when Rose's voice came questioning from the pile of bedding in the corner. 'What are you doing?'

I sagged. I shook with shock. All the breath in my body came out of me in one burst. I gazed about me but there was

344

nowhere to look and no excuse came to mind. There was I, reaching up, with the unshielded light of the candle upon me. What could I say? I said nothing.

Rose was small and pocked and ugly. She was naked under her blanket. Now she threw it over her shoulders and held it loosely round her before she got up and came towards me. 'What are you doing?' she asked again.

I bit my lip. I couldn't stand there, silent, forever, I had to give an answer. So I said, 'I have come after the gold.'

She looked at the bag, still strung up there safely, and then she looked at me out of curious eyes. Her hair was wild and untidy – she must have been deeply asleep. I had thought her out. I had heard someone go out earlier, and had assumed it was both of them.

I could see she found the situation hard to understand, perhaps because she had just been asleep. 'You wanted *gold*? You wanted our gold?'

I cleared my throat before answering miserably, 'I wanted any gold. I need fifty sovereigns, and I thought you might have . . . You told me once you had . . .'

'What for?'

I took my eyes to the floor, fatigued and defeated. 'For my own reasons.'

She set off round the room then, quite restlessly, her hand to her lips and her forehead wrinkled. She paced. She stopped and I scented the musky smell of her. She looked at me and she paced again. 'You is a little late wi' your decision, I thinks.'

'It is my life,' I said.

'An' 'tis my gold,' she replied, stopping for a moment and staring once more at me.

'You don't have a need for it.'

'An' you do? An' that 'tis good enough reason fer yous ter be comin' in 'ere an' takin' it?'

'I suppose I thought that, yes.'

Suddenly she seemed to be struck by an important idea. 'You never though o' askin'?'

'I thought you might not give it.'

'Ah.' And she set off with her pacing again.

Time went by and every second thudded its way through my head. I could hardly see out of my eyes with the shame of it and I boiled inside with the mixture of shame and fear. Stealing in

345

the Combe was a serious matter. People had been thrown out for less. Everyone went round saying, 'If'n we's carn trust each other then who can uz trust?' It was easy to see this was true. And here was I, breaking that trust, and choosing the only people I had left to call friends.

Finally, after what seemed hours of silence, she said, 'Take it. Go on, take it.'

'No, I said. 'I can't.'

And then she smiled, and said in a different manner, 'Go on, maid, take it. We'm women together an' if we carn help each other then where are we at?'

'I feel I can't take it now.'

'Very well then, I'll hook it down fer you myself.' And she did so. She handed it over, too, and when I refused to put out my hand for it, she leaned forward and brought it up so there was no alternative but for me to take it.

'What about Cherry?' I asked.

'Doan worry 'bout Cherry. I'll tell Cherry. Cherry woan mind.'

I hovered at the door, uncertain about how to take my leave in this embarrassing situation.

Seeing this, Rose said, 'There's just one thing I want yous ter do in return fer the gift.'

I turned round, surprised. I hadn't expected her to want anything back. I didn't know I had anything she could possibly have wanted.

'I wanted yer ter listen ter me. I want yer ter have the gold but I doan want yer ter spend it. 'Tis your decision an' I would never dream o' takin' that from yer. 'Tis just the stage you are at, maiden, 'tis that which worries me. An' understand that wi' the money you have in yer hand you do not need to get rid o' it. Yer can leave the Combe and make a steady livin' fer yerself wi' that bag yer have now. A livin' fer youself an' protection fer the brat.'

'And what if I decide . . .'

Rose shook her head. 'What yer choose ter do wi' yer own body, child, 'tis nothin' I has a right ter speak on.'

So I left her, and went to my bed and shook for what must have been over an hour.

There were more than fifty sovereigns in the bag. Many more.

I slunk across the Combe towards Dancy's house at the appointed hour, creeping past the shacks and caves, afraid their occupants might hear my loud breathing. I was afraid, oh yes, but I felt that the time was good; it was the early hours of morning and there ought to be no one about. And then, suddenly, a door opened, light flooded out, there were loud sounds of goodnights being said and then I was face to face with Silas. I was breathless and startled, he cool and brusque as ever, taking every situation quite in his stride.

'Goodnight, and I'm glad all is well with her now,' he said to the closing door.

'I must be going.' I tried to hurry past.

'Just wait for me one moment . . .' I rushed on, walking straight by Dancy's house, imagining that she would be waiting. I had not given myself time for unexpected incidents.

Silas followed me. I hurried. He hurried.

'Are we going to wander the Combe all night like this? We have to stop somewhere, some time – surely?'

And in my fear I started to laugh. The situation was so ludicrous . . . I sank down on the ground and put my chin on my knees, looking down at him as he climbed towards me, a despairing smile on his face.

'I will not bother to ask you,' he said, 'so you don't need to bother to tell. Nor to lie, either.'

Suddenly, yes, it seemed like a waste of time to do either. 'I saw no other way out. Unless you. . . ?' I clutched at the last chance.

'Earlier, yes of course. But now . . .'

'But now it's too late.'

'For such drastic action as that, yes, it's too late. Dancy's cures would have either had no effect at all, or they would have killed you. The woman's a menace. Either way you would have suffered great pain,' and he put out his hand to take the bag that I held behind my back, 'and a great and unnecessary loss of money.'

He came up beside me and sat down. We looked down over the Combe together. It spread out before us, dropping below to the river and then up on the other side. The sprinkling of lights could be fireflies, but the brightest light came from the house to the left of us. Our eyes were drawn towards it. I said to Silas: 'Thank you for not telling him.'

'It is not to do with me.'

'You could have told him. You could have spoilt it for me.'

'I let you do that for yourself,' said Silas wryly.

'Does Lucy know? Has Rowle told her?'

Silas picked grass and chewed a stalk between his teeth. He turned to me directly when he said, 'No. I don't believe Rowle has told her.'

'So she does not know.'

'Lucy does not know. Why? Were you hoping for something from her? Like forgiveness – sympathy, perhaps?'

'Sometimes, Silas, you can be very cruel.'

'Or very honest,' he said. 'Would you like me to tell Lucy?'

I thought. I gazed into the deep blue darkness and I shivered. 'No, Silas, there is no point.'

We left it then, and went on to speak of other things. I was surprised how relaxed we were together. All the tension seemed to have gone, and once he said, 'We could have been good together, you and me, Bethy. It could have worked between us.'

And once, when I shivered, for it was cold sitting there under the new white moon, he put his arm around me and I did not feel the need to pull away. I liked it.

It seemed we had much to say for it was dawn before we left each other. He didn't kiss me goodbye. He looked at me and said, 'I want to be there, Bethy. I don't want you to bear this alone. I want you to promise to call me, any time, day or night. I want to be with you.'

So I promised him that, knowing I would break that promise, for I wanted to be alone when I gave birth to Rowle's child. Hating it one moment, and yet setting such store by it the next. It was all confusion inside me. I wanted to make it mine, created by me, without any help, no muddling midwife or doctor coming along before I was ready with knives and scissors and salves to get it out before it was ready. Keep away from me – with your good intentions and blood-spattered aprons. For in this way, and only in this way, could I make it real, could I create the sacred offering that I had to give to Rowle.

He might still, when he saw it, change his mind and let me stay near him.

48

Rowan. I'll let you come then, but not for long. You mustn't stay long in this place which is so cold and evil. You are safer, much safer, where you are.

She slid into the world one night, Brother Niall, when I was alone. She came smoothly, early and without fear. What had she to be afraid of? She was dead.

Exhausted, I slept with her beside me, warming her out of her frozen blue death. There might be something I had failed to understand —perhaps human children take time to catch their breaths. They are not on their feet immediately, pulsing with life like animals are, so perhaps they do not breathe immediately, either.

I dripped milk into her mouth – bad milk with yellow in it. Her lips were white and wouldn't move although I pushed them with my finger. The milk slid out down her chin and it looked as if she had spat it there.

Cross about this, I cleaned her. I went for water and warmed it, laid her on my knee as I had seen the other women do. Shouldn't her eyes be blue? Why were they black? Was black a bad sign? There she was, stretched out like a skinned rabbit, blue and bloody and mine. Who else's was she but mine? I cooed to her as I washed her, coming to the black hair that stood all tufted on her head, startled hair, with a white streak in it like mine. Tainted.

The child Marnie came to the cave mouth, a wraith in the misty dawn. She had taken to coming here lately and I hadn't minded. Neither of us had spoken before – the lost ones never spoke. Now I fumbled around, picking the wet baby up in my arms and I screamed at Marnie, 'Get out of here! Leave me be! Don't you think I've got other people to care about 'stead of waitin for you! Get out of here and don't come near me again. Skulking about. Take your mad, staring eyes away from me.'

But Marnie, defiant, took no notice. Just stood and watched

me and the child with her head on one side, wonderingly, blinking slow as an owl out of strange, grey eyes. And then she said, in a voice that was clear as a bell, ''Er's dead.'

I pressed my lips together. I gripped the baby tightly as I whispered defiantly, 'She is sleeping.'

'I's seen 'em dead. 'Er's dead. You must let 'er go. 'Tis wrong ter keep 'er.'

'How can I let her go? Where would I put her?'

'Doan know. Doan matter. 'Er woan care.'

My hair covered my eyes. I threw it back from my face, tossing my head like a wild mare when I said, 'You're mad, Marnie, and you don't know anything. You're mad and you're stupid and I don't want you here, staring, dirtying everywhere up.'

'I'll go fer Rowle if'n you wants me to.'

I gave her a black look under my hair but she took no notice. She just came nearer, quiet and light as a fairy, quite unafraid of me and my ravings, staring all the time at the dead thing in my arms. So I thought she was after it.

'Gi' 'er a name.'

I sat down, but gave up the washing, and wrapped the child in a blanket. Her lips were blue and her eyes were wide, surprised to be born and find nothing. Blackly surprised.

'You'll have to clean yerself up, youm all mucky.'

I hadn't felt real since the baby was born – it was as if I no longer existed. Now I looked at the mess and thought it was somebody else's. Who had been in here – what had they been doing to make the place so bloody. It smelled of blood in here and I smelled hotly of blood. The only thing that didn't smell of blood was the baby and she smelled of turves which had gone stale and wanted burning.

'I'll do it.'

She came nearer, all four foot of her witchy, scrawny self, and looked at the water I had used. 'That'll do.' She built up the fire, blowing on the embers. She hung the pot over the fire, and held out her dirty hands for the baby. 'Gi' 'er ter me.'

'No, I'll not give her to anybody.'

'Gi' 'er a name, then. We carn allus call 'er it.'

I thought of the thing I had truly loved best in my life. I thought of the rowan pony. 'Rowan.'

'Gi' Rowan ter me then.'

'No.'

'Yer carn keep 'er. Yer carn keep hangin' on ter a dead thing.'

'Somebody cursed her,' I muttered.

'Aye. It do look that way.'

'Nobody wanted her to be born.'

''Tis often the way. There's worse handicaps than that. That woan have killed 'er.'

Marnie was quick and efficient. And all the while she worked she watched the door, fearful that someone might come and that she might find herself trapped. But her scrawny hands were gentle – not the hands of a child. Nor were her eyes, or the things she said to me that night. How old could she be – twelve, thirteen? She was ageless.

She stayed all day and she stayed with me that night, lying in the rushes on the threshold, pretending to be asleep. But she didn't sleep, because every time I woke and raised my head she was there, awake and watching. And in my fevered dreams I imagined she was a dead child, too, that they all were – those little spirits who waited, whispering out there. Had she come for Rowan, then – could I bear to think of the little one in my arms leading a life like theirs, scavenging in the dark, huddling together for warmth, the blind leading the blind in that nursery of hell?

I held my baby tighter. I kept watch. I wanted Marnie to go. I said so and she refused. A pocket of stone dripped cold dawn water. The splashing sound it made was sad. I heard men's voices, and women calling. The world went on, but inside the cave it was warm and dreamy and unreal with me and Marnie in her grey gauzy dress. Marnie watching. Me waiting for my baby to breathe. Quiet, warm, peaceful desolation.

I didn't notice time passing, but then Rowle was there. I woke to find him beside me, his lean dark face on the mattress beside mine, shut against me.

I sat up and shouted, 'Where's Marnie?'

'Marnie has gone. Marnie was worried about you. I would have come at once – you should have sent someone to fetch me! You should have had a woman with you all this time.'

'Where's Rowan?'

Rowle shuttered his eyes and looked away from me. I leapt

from my bed, weak from not eating, dizzy, scrabbling around in the room to find the well-fingered bundle, grubby in grey blankets.

'Come back to bed,' he said softly. 'You're too weak to be up and about. Mary is coming. She will stay with you tonight.'

'I don't want Mary to stay with me. I want you!'

'I will stay with you if that is what you want. I will stay with you for as long as you need me.'

But I knew now, Brother Niall, that this was just his way of speaking.

'Where have you put Rowan? She might need feeding. I have the food for her – more than enough – look!'

He shook his head sadly. My body seeped, sticky in a mess. 'Later, Bethy. Feed her later. It's you who needs feeding now. Mary is bringing you broth.'

Mary Mary Mary . . . what did I want with Mary? I wouldn't listen. I heard his horse munching on the scrub outside. I pushed open the door and saw the bundle, wrapped in the same dirty blanket hanging on the saddle hook, pathetic, lonely, there for anyone to get at – rats, buzzards, owls. I screamed. I lurched towards the stallion which backed away, white-eyed, sensing madness. 'Give me that! Give me that!' I screamed. 'Give me what is mine!'

Rowle watched as I took Rowan gently back into my arms and shuffled back to bed with her. 'You haven't said if you like her yet.' I pulled down the blanket and stroked her face. 'Have you looked at her? Do you know I've given her a name. She has my hair.' Proudly I held her up. Coughed. Gurgled. And was sick. I held her to Rowle. I looked at Rowle with pleading eyes.

She was my gift but I could tell he didn't want her.

'She's lovely,' he said softly. 'But perhaps she is too lovely to live.'

'Yes,' I said slowly. 'Yes, I see that.'

'You can't keep her here.'

'I don't want anyone else to have her.'

'Do you want me to take her up to the ridge?'

'Can I come with you?'

'You're too weak to come anywhere.'

'You'll not go without me.'

We went to the black ridge. We buried the box.

Afterwards he left me alone and I talked there, on my knees, as I had talked to Birdie's baby about all those secret things when I was a child. It was just like meeting an old friend again. I whistled softly, remembering how I had practised there once. I looked down on the newtakes, expecting to see those three familiar figures there. But there was nothing, no movement. Just great, open sweeps of earth. The grass tickled my knees as it had done then, making crisscross patterns on them. And the wind stirred my hair, carrying all the flavour of the sea with it. The moor was rusty red against a darkening sky – a glow seemed to come from the earth itself – all life was in it. And all around me rose the crags and tors of home, familiar arms cradling me, shapes to turn your face into, shapes so firm, so loyal they would last for ever and ever and not go away, never pretend.

And all I wanted to do was to sleep. To lie down, in this place, and sleep.

And I knew why Birdie had chosen this place for her baby – why she had staggered so staunchly up the hill with that cross. And if this place was good enough for Birdie's baby then it was good enough for mine. So I made my offering, finally, strangely, a little secretly and shamefacedly, to the Forest itself, for I felt it to be stronger than Rowle and I wanted Rowan protected by something strong. And it was not a betrayal. It was just a small change of mind.

'Do you like me?' I whispered into the wind. 'Am I pretty? Am I your friend? My name is Bethany Horsham, Bethany Horsham, and I am quick and sly, Maggie says, and good at catching salmon. And that's all I know and all I want to know. And I'll find you again one day when the cuckoo comes.'

And that was my prayer.

49

Rowan. The wind helps me to moan the lullaby. I will not remember you again. While I thought of you I felt you in my arms, light as a feather and cold as ice. You left a small dent on my pillow, that's all. And I don't know if I loved you. I don't know what I felt about you – you are just a scar on my heart and if I touch it it bleeds like a wound never healed. I will not demean you by pretending that is love. I had you too short a time, I never knew you. You spat out my milk and you closed your eyes at me.

Perhaps you were the only person I didn't make up. You didn't stay long enough to let me.

There was a kind of small wisdom in your eyes. I wish I hadn't noticed that. Did you not want to live? Did you decide to die . . . knowing who your mother was?

And now I have to have something strong to take the pain away. Here it is, monk . . . here it is . . .

'E 'as other women. Mary woan tell yer that, nor will Lucy, they're not the kind. But I'm tellin' yer that fer yer own good. You is not the only one. I've seen 'e.' She told me this thing and could feel unashamed!

I couldn't believe Marnie. I shook my head and I closed my eyes to get the sight and the sound of her out of it. She was a crazy girl, all mixed up. She might think she had seen Rowle with other women but she had obviously been mistaken. He would have told me – wouldn't he? He wasn't the sort of man to slink about telling lies and afraid. He prided himself in his honesty, telling me lies would be too small for him.

So I told Marnie that.

'Have you ever asked 'e?'

'Why would I?' I wished she would leave me alone and go away. She was always coming in . . . and without knocking. Even when I went out, sometimes I came back and she was waiting.

'Well, 'e wouldn't lie, would 'e, if'n 'e never had to.' And I thought her eyes glittered with malice, but when I looked again they were calm, the simple eyes of a child wanting some company.

'I would have known,' I said flatly, turning away, not wanting to look at the tension on her face or the well-meaning there. And I thought that I would have known – if such things were happening surely I would have sensed it. I felt her small hand on my arm and I shook it off.

'Others know,' she said. She would not stop! I wished she would be quiet. 'Yer friend, that Jessie knew . . . her who left wi' all that trouble. Everyone knew, 'twere goin' on even back then. 'Tis allus gone on. 'Er knew, but 'er were too kind ter tell 'e.'

I snarled, 'But you're not too kind, Marnie, are you?' Yet my eyes dug into her like clutching fingers, wanting to, having to know.

'You should know this,' was all she said before she slipped away, and I noticed a pile of flat cakes were gone from the recess next to the fire. I never knew when she was coming or going, she moved so silently and so quickly.

Agony. Much more powerful than jealousy – burning much deeper than jealousy. The fear of loss, and he was my sole preoccupation. I had nothing else, I hadn't had anything else for seven years. My skin prickled with unease. My hands were wet and my heart was a leaden weight, so heavy was I that I could hardly move around the small space that was my home, couldn't get a proper breath in it. Temptation – of course – here in the Combe . . . too much for Rowle to take. Of course! Of course! All these women so freely available, flaunting themselves, wanting him. Happy to oblige him and then let go, not obsessed like me. They offered him so much more than I could – pleasure, fun, enjoyment, things I seemed to have forgotten about. Was it true? Was it?

Of course it was true. And yes, it had always been true, but I had refused to see it. Oh God oh God oh God . . . the knowledge was unendurable. That something so ugly could rise from the deep and poke its head over the pleasant, shimmering image of my own fantasy! Out of my reach and out of my brain's control! If Rowan had lived then perhaps . . . oh, what was the use of fooling myself any longer? Rowan was dead, and Rowle was going elsewhere for his pleasure as he always had. And there was nothing, absolutely nothing I could do about it.

Had I known all the time and not felt strong enough to face up to it? Could it be . . . and if that was so, then why didn't I continue to bury it, push it down under the water and continue to sail smoothly over the top. Pretending. All day I paced, a thin, haggard creature, trying to gauge the situation correctly. All day, up and down, up and down, carrying the dead weight of my misery on my shoulders. I wouldn't watch him . . . nothing so demeaning . . . no, I would ask him outright the next time he came. And watch his face when he answered. Listen to his tone of voice. Watch for the lie and jump on it.

Oh, Brother Niall, why didn't I leave it alone?

Eventually he came. I knew it was him when he opened the door – he had a special, firm way of doing it. Not like Marnie's – she kicked and pushed and came, but all soft and fluttering.

There he was, I studied him – this idol of mine – this creature that I worshipped. Tall, the sharp curves of his chin settling on his collar, the wet patches across his shoulders, his simmering black eyes, his curling hair twisted by damp to a line on his forehead. The way he also smiled so ruefully when he saw me. And I tried to picture Rowle getting old, the black hair turning grey, the face thinning, the back bending, and I tried to see him as a child, frightened and lonely and crying, screaming for help . . . as I had sometimes. None of my pictures made sense. I had to see him as he was . . . or as I had created him, with scraps of my world thrown together like somebody else might create a pot out of good clay. Scraps . . . like fear, and joy, and beauty, and lightning; sensations . . . most of them frightening . . . they had all formed Rowle and built him strong like that. He had to be strong. There was so much of me inside him that he had to carry.

He frowned at my blotched and swollen face. I had been crying all day. Knowing what I must look like I turned away and buried my head in my pillow. He came and sat beside me and grasped my shoulder, hurting me. 'Is it Rowan?'

Through my sobs I said, 'No. It's you. You don't love me any more.'

His voice was cold and even, and a little relieved, I thought.

Only that . . . could he have been thinking, or muttering under his breath . . . only that. I can deal with that. But he said aloud, running his hand through his damp hair, 'What has brought this on?'

All I could do was cry louder. 'Stop it,' he said, 'Turn around and sit up.'

Slowly, wearily I obeyed, weak with misery, wanting so much to hear him deny what I was going to ask next. There was no other way to put it, so I said, 'I know you have been with other women. Everyone knows it. Everyone has always known it but me.'

He paused before he answered, and in that pause was my answer. There was really no need for words after that. And I thought that outside in the Combe the cooking pots would be burning and children would be running in before it got dark. The sky would be rosy with the last of the sun. People, men and women, would be holding each other, softly. Then, very slowly with measured consideration he said, 'I always told you how it would be. I never pretended it could be otherwise. It doesn't mean to say that I care for you any the less. My feelings are just the same.'

Was that your second lie, Rowle?

I wished I had something to do with my hands. But the thought of getting up, spooning some dough on the hot stone, perhaps, making a few little scones, the thought of even doing a simple, ordinary thing like that seemed immense, impossible, like climbing a mountain. The soup I had made for him laughed at me. It simmered there, in the pot, the smell of it giggled a tasty vapour into the air. How many times had he come and eaten here, straight from the bed of somebody else? How many times had he loved me with other women fresh on his hands? A log fell from the fire with a crunch, the ashes shifted and sparked. Somewhere in the distance I heard a baby cry.

My voice was dry and burned from an ashen throat as I said, 'Was it my fault? Was it something I did or didn't do?'

I watched him get up and feared he was leaving me, leaving me here with this freezing cold space beside me. He had energy, then. I noticed that he could still move . . . do little things, for he poured himself ale and stood at the far wall, caressing the dented tin pitcher. He turned and he said, 'It's not a question of blame. If anyone is to blame then it's me, but I am not going to blame myself for being who I am because there's no good can come from that. I cannot be different, Bethany. And I thought that by now you had come to realise that.'

Some people say that life is a dream. And I felt then, that my life had literally been lived like that. A kind of troubled, tangled sleep, full of nightmares and troubles, yes, but balanced by golden moments of pure delight that left me soaring and singing, feeling as if I was flying, no destination impossible. Well, if my life had been a dream then now I was, for the first time, wide awake, exploding into wakefulness and desperate with the need to return to my sleep again . . . forever . . . never to awaken.

And my wakeful voice seemed like some other voice, not mine, when I said, 'Who? Who are they? These women!' And my voice thickened and broke. I could not control the sobs and I didn't want to any more. To talk like that was a kind of defence. I had to attack him and hard. I could not discuss this reasonably although, somewhere deep down I knew that I should. I did not believe that he loved me the same – if he loved me at all he would not hurt me. If he cared even slightly he would not hurt me. And yet . . . and yet I realised that I had never believed it . . . somewhere in love there is always pain . . . the truth was awful to comprehend, for I never honestly felt that Rowle loved me unless he was hurting me.

And Lucy – poor Lucy! I had the nerve, then, to feel sorry for Lucy! Sorry for myself. Sorry for everyone but Rowle.

He said, 'It doesn't matter who they are.'

'I want to know! I must know!' More pain? Was it more of the pain I was after, grovelling for it like this?

His voice was hard and low. 'I don't intend to go into this any further with you. I want to stop this – now, and realise that there is no threat to you.'

'How can I believe you? How can I possibly believe anything you tell me any more?'

'Because I have never lied to you.'

'No! No, you haven't! You've never lied because you have never cared enough to lie! If we had gone from the Combe this wouldn't have happened. It is only because we are here, prisoners here, leading this peculiar life hidden away from the real world, that all this has happened! If you had done what I asked you to do, what I begged you to do years ago, and taken me away, we could have been happy, Rowle. We could have been together, and happy, not arguing and crying like this.'

But it was only me who was arguing and crying. It was only me who was unhappy. He just looked slightly troubled, uneasy, that's all.

I held my breath, looking up at him. Something in his face gave me a glimmer of hope – some love I saw there, or pretended I saw there. It must have been pity I saw. I mistook it for love. I plaited my blanket between my fingers, carefully. Oh, monk, every movement, every word was careful. He came back beside me, took my hand and stroked it. It was tense and cold under his own, all hard and wet with tears. 'You've always believed that, haven't you, Bethy? You've always blamed the Combe and my life here, believed that was what stopped me from loving you as you needed to be loved.'

'Yes,' I sobbed. 'And I know that to be true.'

Rowle shook his head. 'Perhaps it would be better if you thought about going . . . no, wait . . . let me finish. The time and the place is wrong for us. Life, for you, is different here. You are caged and you shouldn't be caged. You have only me, now the child is dead. You do nothing all day but conjure up things for yourself in there,' and he tapped my head and he smiled – he actually smiled as if I amused him!

He went on. He had more to say. How dare he! 'Life in the Combe – I neither like it or dislike it, I accept it. There is no place for me out there any more. At first it was Charles, I believed I had killed my brother. For years that held me here, I could never return or take up my life outside again. But after I realised Charles was alive, after I took my revenge on him and his wife, well after that Amberry burned and my future was decided forever. But even if things had been different, even if I was pardoned tomorrow and free to walk out of here and my dream came true, it would be Lucy who would come with me, not you. I can never give you what you want from me, never, do you understand that? God! I've tried hard enough to explain. You have never understood. You will not accept me for what I am, and I am half to blame for that. I know. I accept that. Lucy has told me.'

Did some look on my face cause him to go on? Did he always

see, and respond, to this need of mine for punishment? Harshly, savagely, sparing me nothing Rowle went on, 'I never wanted a child by you. I do not want a life with you. I am not what you see, Bethy, nothing like what you want. And I will never be. It would make no difference if we were in the Combe or out of it. I would be the same person – and so would you.'

I felt him inside my head, but I could not touch him or reach him. 'I wish I had never loved you.'

'So do I, Bethany, so do I.' And he didn't look at me when he said that . . . the biggest betrayal I have ever heard, harder than any blow, making everything worthless, turning all the gold into cobwebs. He stared over my head at a place very far away and his voice was queer and distant. The voice of the vanquisher, hard and cold.

It was over. And the hopelessness of that was too hard for me to contemplate.

For more than at any other moment – the pain that he gave me was so intense – it was then that I recognised with total despair that this was my love as it had to be, and oh, monk, I loved him. I saw how it was. Yet I loved him.

50

Now the hard shard of moonlight has moved to the furthest end of the cell. It rests on the wall between us, preparing to leave. For dawn is nearly here and the moon-clock has run its course.

Rowle must come soon. He must come soon. For I cannot believe that my life is almost over.

At the start of this night I was screaming inside, hysterical with the pain and the fear of it. Now? Now I am calmer, beginning to turn into somebody else. I have to. I can't stay here, as me, any longer. I almost want to die, Brother Niall. I cannot live with the shame. It isn't for that they are killing me. No matter. The reasons don't matter. I only know that I am not fit to live, probably never have been fit. And that it would be right if I died now. I cannot carry any more horror inside. The memories are all I have left but the memories are too painful. I could not use them again if I lived, and without memories what are we? Something other than human.

Am I other than human? That at such times I can turn myself off – feel nothing? What am I then, Brother, what am I?

Not only did I refuse to listen to what Rowle said, but I forced him to say otherwise.

'Perhaps,' I wheedled, 'perhaps, if we were not in the Combe, then perhaps . . .'

And Rowle turned away from me and, in order to stop me weeping he agreed, 'Perhaps.'

'Perhaps if your name was cleared and you could go free? Perhaps, if that happened, things might be different?'

'Perhaps.' His voice was uneasy.

So I clung to my plan as I had clung to Rowle because I didn't have anything else. Rowle had said, 'In another time, another place.' That was all I had left of him and I attached to that my own meaning.

My plan became my life and dominated it as Rowle once had. Once again I lived in a dream as I plotted and planned, deciding which way to tackle it, which move would be best to make, and when. Out of misplaced loyalty Rowle could not tell them of Dooley, but I was the only one who knew the truth and I was under no such constraint.

Would they believe me? Would they act on the word of a scoundrel's moll, a woman of ill-repute, of no standing? Would they call me a woman possessed and turn me away, mocking? But one person would believe me . . . John Furze would believe me. And I had the words of John Furze to hold on to, 'If you ever need help, midear, if you are ever in need of a friend, there's few with so much influence as I in this fair part of the country. I, John Furze, am at your disposal. Remember that, my child.'

Oh yes, I was not without an important friend out there. John Furze, that little fat man who had once come to supper, he would listen to me.

And there was no other way out for me. Did I really believe, after all Rowle had said, that if he was free he would choose me? Leave his Lucy and choose me?

Dear God, I had to believe it. For I could not bear to remain in the Combe knowing that everyone thought me a fool, knowing I had been duped for so long – like poor Biddie Canter. And one day Rowle would stop coming to me. When that happened the women would mouth their consolation but I knew exactly what they would be thinking. I knew that they would be glad to see a wicked woman put in her place and suffering. They would cluck their sweet words, tell me I'd get over it but add, ''Tis best, 'tis best,' in that awful soft way people have of speaking when they think they know best and it isn't at all what you want to hear. Like spooning food into the mouth of a baby who doesn't want it. Cunningly. Falsely, with encouraging eyes. And I knew what they would be thinking and saying behind my back.

And Silas? I did not think about Silas. Thinking of Silas confused me. It always had.

There were a million stars in the sky the last night Rowle and I made love. And he was not brutal. And I was not afraid.

'What is it, Bethy? You have gone cold.'

'Not cold, Rowle, just distracted, thinking of other things.'

'Good things?'

I turned and looked at him. 'Different things. Things that you would never understand.' I got up. I made myself busy. I stacked the dishes neatly and wiped the spoons dry. And then I started to wipe the table; every stain and every crumb was most important to find.

'Why don't you try me?' He turned over on the bed, naked, watching me.

Sometimes I feared I was losing my mind, or giving my soul to the powers of darkness. Would Rowle hate me for telling his secret, for declaring his confused, childish love to the world? No one would understand his need to protect the terrible Dooley – not even after recognising the fact which I only suspected – that her revenge had been taken on Rowle's behalf. After meeting Rowle on the moor that day she must have gone to Amberry and discovered what they had done to him . . . to her baby. She had wreaked her own, terribly flawed revenge. And how much of burning that house down had been to do with a twisted desire to destroy her own miserable part in Rowle's life? I had seen her face when they met. I had watched her. And after the deed was done she had fled to London; Rowle had been unable to find her and save her, but what if others were to find Dooley and hang her for her crime? What would Rowle think of me then? Miserably I pushed these concerns aside. I had to make something happen, I had to change things. I only knew that if I was successful Rowle would be free, and then, perhaps, he would choose me. My need for him drove me mad. My jealousy drove me to the wildest of fantasies. 'Do you believe in good and bad?' I asked him now. 'In God, and in the Devil?'

'We have them both inside us. They do not exist without us.'

'Do you believe in an afterlife?' And then I dragged the peat indoors, leaving a line of mud behind me, and having to kneel and clean it up for I did not like mud in the house.

'I have seen nothing to tell me of it, in this one.'

'But they say . . .' I stacked the peats beside the fire. My face was damp and hot and my hands being busy, I had to blow the hair away from my face.

'People who are afraid say many things.'

'Am I bad, Rowle?'

'This is a strange line of questioning. You are in a strange mood tonight. Do you think that you are bad?' He was smiling. He thought that I joked.

'You prefer me as I was before?'

'I prefer you to be who you really are.'

'Ah yes, but who am I, Rowle?' Now that I know you don't love me – who am I? I stopped what I was doing. I went to sit beside him. It was smokey in the room tonight, and the candles cast shadows in the corners. When I moved my shadow was tall, and I saw there was a kind of violence in the way the black shape of myself crossed the ceiling. He pulled back my robe and ran his finger between my breasts. Then he cupped them, terribly gently, and I let my head fall so my hair covered his chest. I did not want him to make love to me now. I wanted to hear him speak.

He lifted my hair. He kissed my face. And I felt my need for him growing inside me, burning there. I wanted him to tug my hair and pull me down, take me in the most brutal way he ever had taken me, so that I cried out with pain and fear. But I pulled back away from him and let him speak. We played our favourite game. 'You are probably a princess, fathered by a lord, brought up in a magic world of glittering rivers and jewelled pools. You rode through your childhood, wild and free, hair flowing out behind you, you and your enchanted pony. You have wings on your feet. You are a special child . . . special to me . . . You are beautiful. You know how to love a man. You are loyal in your worship. I know that you will never let me down.'

'And you,' I stroked his face. It was important to know the shape and the feel of it . . . in case something went wrong. 'You are a king . . . you overcome . . . you kill all the monsters. You are strong and able and passionate and gentle . . . when you want to be gentle. You are like granite . . . you are the moor . . . and I will always love you.'

Rowle said, 'You are more beautiful, now, than you have ever been.'

And I knew that it was my distance that intrigued him, and my strange, unpredictable behaviour.

Oh yes, we still talked and went to the gorge together, but it was gripped, silent and eerily cold now, wintry, and the water hung in icicles that felt sharp as my heart and as dead. All the greens, so vivid in spring and summer, were pearled with frost. When we joined our mouths together our breath came as one, white on the frosty air, and I wished we could be joined inside as easily and as truthfully as that. I stopped asking him about his 'other women'. It was pointless. My questioning only made him angry and got me nowhere. I was past all that. Everything seemed pointless except for my plan. It was the only, really positive thing that I had.

51

The day before yesterday I saw lighted tapers, women's fires, glowing faces. I saw the men's fur coats and the women's layers of sacking, pile upon pile to keep them from the cold. I saw wooden trenchers and tin pitchers on the long trestle table and the sunset reflected by the distant clump of trees. A cold sunset, and clouds steaming gold, rising up behind it.

Rowle was there, very large, very real, although now he has no substance. His four children slept under blankets, watched by Lucy who was pressing to be taken home. A man with a rushlight moved across the valley like a small glow-worm inching closer to the group for warmth, and a winter moon was waiting, pale and thin as Bible paper, an afternoon moon waiting to take its place up in the real sky.

Rowle's house was there, dominating the far end of the Combe, and lights came from the caves and shacks, grunts and moans from satisfied pigs, and goats clanked their chains – everything was fat and contented like the men who drank wine and shared jokes across the table. They looked like normal, jolly, healthy people, families together, surviving together, and who can ask for more? Certainly not Rowle. This is what he loves to observe. You couldn't see the sad children from there – the lost ones. They were hiding somewhere in the dark. The watchman stood still on the bracken-strewn hillside, just another dark shape among the boulders and tortured trees. All was well. All were content.

Except for the figure of Bethany Horsham as she crept across the darker side of the Combe, alone and dark but for the jewel of the little dream which she clutched in her hand. Only I could hear her breathing in my ears. And see the disordered shapes of the hilly contours, spiky grasses and marshy places that framed tracks for me in her eyes.

And that was the sight I took with me from the Combe.

Oh, I was very frightened, Brother Niall. Still unsure. I had no knowledge of how to behave in front of other people. I had lived like a hermit for seven years, in a cave, in a hole in the ground among savages. And before then my social learning was little better, buried away at Amicombe with my three weird aunts and Amos. Hardly a suitable background from which to demand to see one of the most important and powerful men in Devon. Hardly a firm basis from which to put Rowle's case.

But put it I must, no matter how long I had to wait there in the cold, cold night outside the doors of Lydford gaol, going over and over my story. What should I say and how should I say it? And would my plan work?

I had chosen my clothing with extreme care . . . cunning, I thought to myself. I had used the key I still kept to get into the stores to find the special coat that I knew to be there, the coat I must wear over this simple white dress. I found it – a grand one – lined with fur and with a hood. I liked to finger the fur, finding it comforting, for there was little comfort outside this grim place. I found the special boots, too, boots that did not fit me properly and made my walking tottery. I was not used to going with anything on my feet – even in winter I preferred to keep them bare, but I wanted to make myself look important – these people had to listen to me! I tried to pass the time by sleeping, and I think I did sleep, for a moment, in spite of the cold. I curled up on that wide, granite step before the door, pulling the cloak tightly round me, and in my confused, half-waking moments I tried to dispel the evil vibrations that seemed to ooze from this sinister place.

There was no other way out for me. I had to do it.

Maggie, Lizzie and Birdie – I saw the spot and went round it, averting my eyes, trying not to remember, but the worst memories are always the strongest, the ones that won't go away. Why is that, monk? I passed by the gravestones where I had waited that day, and watched them die. So long ago. Did it really happen – could it have? Tired and anxious, I began to wonder why I had come here. I longed to be back in my safe place, covered in blankets which smelt of my hair and were mine, by my own fire which was mine, with the door which was mine closed tight against the rest of the world. For the first time Rowle was not in that picture. For the first time I saw a place where I could be self-sufficient and have some pride. Be my own person. But I had left that behind and I came to this place flushed with purpose. I wore boots and a coat. I was a stranger in a strange place and I had my part to play.

I thought of John Furze's friendly face and that memory encouraged me. It seemed that some part that was written for me by an alien, unfriendly hand was urging me on, and I was too involved to draw back. But it was too late to dress up as somebody else, to learn a new role. I was steeped in this one. It was far too late for me then.

The first of the morning fires smoked out of a village chimney and hung, with curled indecision, blue on the morning air. Early-morning voices came shrilly into the dawn. The graves in the churchyard made hollow shapes and the spire loomed grey, like the leaden sky. The Gaol took on a firmer form . . . the walls precluded all sound. They gave off a tearful, stone sound of their own. In a while the village people would wake, warm in their beds, feeling safe and secure. And back in the Combe they would not yet know I had gone.

Then came the moment for which I had been waiting: the sound of keys, of determined footsteps. The door opened suddenly; the business of the day had begun.

They were not giving me time!

'I have come to see John Furze.' The name of the man gave me comfort, a firm handle to hang on to.

The burly man's frown deepened as he grunted, 'John Furze? A friend o' youm then, is 'e? 'E's away till the morrow, but what has such as you ter say ter 'e? Not much I'll wager . . . not likely.'

My heart sank to my stiff new boots. The courage drained out of me. 'Then I'll go and come back when he's at home.'

But no, he would not have that. I had no alternative than to follow this man with the brutal, stupid face to a bare room which smelled of stale beer. Was he the man with the sheep's head who had done those things to Lizzie? I shuddered but could not tell. The bones in his forehead shone white like a bird-pecked skull, and his ears were sheep's ears, shaggy and torn. There was no humanity in his eyes. I was very small following in his footsteps – if I hesitated he gripped my arm roughly – I heard the sound of my own boots and they were unfamiliar to me. And I knew I should not be here.

I waited. I waited all morning for the constable, but he, uninterested in my tale, was suddenly intrigued when I mentioned the name of Roger Rowle and Amberry. Time after time, he kept interrogating me about my coat.

'I borrowed it from the stores, and my boots.' I opened the coat and showed them my rags. I felt ashamed when I said, 'These are mine. But my clothes are nothing to do with the reasons I stand here before you. I have come to tell you about the fire and about Roger Rowle. The authorities assumed it was him and he didn't deny it . . . he took the blame because he was afraid of what would happen to Dooley. He has been outlawed ever since, but please listen to what I say: Rowle is an innocent man! If John Furze were here he would listen to me. He would understand. He would know that what I tell you is true.'

'That doan make no sense, wench. An' I's doan likes ter hear the names o' the gentry, fine people such as they, on the lips as such as you. They are fancy boots fer a maid of your kind. You stole that coat, too, didn't you? Where was you workin'? Did the work displease you? Did you think you would help yourself ter what wasn't yours in order ter get your own back on your mistress? Oh yes, maid, I know the likes of you.'

'Then why am I here? If I stole this coat and these boots, then why would I come to Lydford? Why would I waste my time standing here telling such a tale?'

They didn't bother to answer. They whispered together in the corner of the room with their hands before their mouths and their beady eyes still upon me as if they saw something succulent; they could almost have licked their lips. I could not hear what they said but when they came back to confront me they asked me again about Rowle. 'You say you were 'is woman? You say you bore 'e a child?'

'Yes.'

'So you must be important ter the man?'

'I am important to him, yes. And he is important to me, else I would not be here.' I tried, once again, to tell them about Dooley, to explain why Rowle had kept silent, to convince them of the reasons why he had taken the blame. Both men, the constable and the gaoler, threw back their heads and laughed at each telling. I saw old food in their beards, and the constable's remaining teeth were black. The gust of their breaths was foul in the air and I held my hand to my face.

'Ah! Wait till the steward hears this story . . . this 'un should amuse 'e.'

'Aye, if'n 'is gout is not playin' 'e up too bad today.' And the constable with the bad teeth scratched his stomach, his soiled, broken nails making a tearing sound.

I said again, 'Dooley started that fire. She found out what they had done to Rowle, probably spoke to Tremain. By then she was a poor travelling woman, selling pots with a vagabond band. She probably spent a great deal of her time begging for her living. She had been thrown from the house when Rowle went to school without sixpence in her pocket, without a word of gratitude. She must have blamed her miserable circumstances on the Rowles. The night they dismissed her they probably laughed at her protests – knowing Gideon, he probably cursed her. But no matter what she had done to Rowle, following Gideon's orders, over the years she had come to love him. In her way. In her own dark, complicated way. And in spite of her cruelties he had loved her. It is possible!' I protested, seeing the looks on their faces. 'Believe me, I know it is possible to love those that hurt you, especially when you are a child and there is nobody else!' I let my imagination take me, I pictured how it must have been. And I told them, 'She crept to the house late at night when she knew them all to be sleeping. She took a taper from the fire and put it to the tapestries. She started the blaze and fled away into the darkness. It was a terrible deed, committed by a madwoman with a black, tormented mind. Everyone in the house was killed – Catherine Rowle, Gideon Rowle, even the children who were staying in the house at that time.'

'Put that aside,' said the man with torn ears. 'Put that aside a minute and tell us again that you have been livin' – as you puts it – wi' Roger Rowle the outlaw?'

I nodded. Perhaps, now, they were understanding me. Perhaps they could hear me. 'Yes. I went there from Amicombe when my grandfather died and my three aunts were killed.' But they had stopped listening to me. The constable was cleaning out his ear.

Both men smiled and I feared the greedy beams on their faces. The constable turned his back to me when he asked again, 'Where did you get your coat an' boots?' And the turned back was more threatening to me than the front of him, for I knew he would whirl round again and bring his great face back to mine when he turned.

They made me remove the boots and I was quite happy to do so for they were pinching my toes. I was more reluctant to give up my coat, for underneath I had little, and there was no warmth in that room. My feet were cold on the stone floor. It was colder in there than in the Combe. Cold, damp and musty – and misery seeped from the walls. They had to have a rushlight burning in order to see even in the daylight.

The constable squinted up his eyes. He read the words slowly, following them with a grubby finger. '*Abigail Varney*. The writing here says these boots belong ter a person called Abigail Varney. Where did you get them?'

I shouted in my desperation: 'I have not stolen these boots! I have come here to tell you of Roger Rowle and of the Amberry fire. Why won't you listen? How loud do I have to speak to make you hear me?'

'Silence! That is enough from you. Take 'er downstairs, Tom, until they call fer 'er.'

The courthouse chamber is high up the steps on the second floor, and if I stretched I could see the distant moor. Rooks swooped past the tiny window. The chamber was used as a stannery court, they said, and on a box before me was the stannery weight – a hundredweight heavy. The Queen's arms were on one side and there was a coronet between two ostrich feathers on the other. It was all meaningless to me.

But yesterday there was no stannery court. Yesterday was for the hearing of small offences, poachers and thieves and those who had fallen behind with the paying of their taxes. Bewildered, I did not know what I was doing there among them.

There was a brighter light in that grand room – but the same smell of rotting dampness. I stood across the room from the three robed men with my legs trembling and my heart hammering. It was all going wrong: how could I make them listen to me?

'An unlikely tale of forgeries and lies from out of the mouth of one who has no understanding of the oath.'

'A woman destitute of grace and goodness as well as a home. A vagabond, a beggar, homeless save for the house she took in the valley of the Lyd. She tempts the anger of the Lord by her sheer audacity.'

'Aye! Aye!'

'And it is we who must make an example of these perjured wretches who think they can come here with their bizarre stories and lies, who think they can use the law of the land for their own ends . . .'

'Aye! Aye!'

Speaking was Master John Nosworthy, steward of the court. Behind him stood Tom Wekes and Jed Whiddon, his clerks of law.

'This is a most unlikely tale and therefore must be omitted, and we must ask ourselves instead why this graceless varmint who comes in rags should be wearing on her shoulders a coat of velvet and silk and sable fur, and boots of the finest calf leather with the name Abigail Varney imprinted in the cuffs of one . . .'

This seemed to have nothing to do with me.

The man in the red cloak leaned forward over his bench, narrowed his little pig eyes and stared at me as I stood in that cold timber room, shivering. He rested his chin on his pudgy hand and age-marks mottled his fingers. His hair was white as unsullied snow, and his lips were big and red. Blood . . . the berry of the rowan . . . and I pulled myself back to concentrate on all that was happening. I was exhausted with trying to tell them. I wished I had not come here. I did not understand these people, what their methods were or what they were trying to prove. I had met nobody like them in my life. They were strangers to me and their ways were strange. Even their manner of speaking was strange. I would have given anything to have been able to walk out of there as easily as I had come – to take back the events of the last twelve hours and pretend that they had not happened.

What was I doing? Oh, what was I doing there, making myself the martyr . . . flinging myself into the fray for my own selfish ends. Did I half hope, even then, that they would not believe me? Had I secretly wanted to be taken, so that Rowle would come to prove his love? Oh, dear God . . . was that true, monk, was that the real, the terrible truth? Driven by fantasies. Oh, but it was real . . . it was real . . . in my head it was real! Something drove me on – some terrible need that was lodged there. If they would only listen to me then Rowle could be pardoned, Rowle could go free, take up his birthright once again . . . and perhaps . . . perhaps, hearing of what I had done he might love me?

Which of these did I want? Which would I have preferred, or was the pathetic truth that I would have been happy with either result so long as I got him? Oh yes, monk, it's too late to lie.

There were others, poor wretches like me, waiting behind me, and they were restless and anxious. A stench came up through the floor, a stench I could only compare with a midden gone rare, and the herbs that were strewn among the rushes did nothing to curb it.

'Where did you get that coat?'

'It is my coat. I borrowed it from the stores.'

Master Nosworthy glanced round at his clerks and frowned. 'The wench talks nonsense. She speaks of the Rowle family with a familiarity which disgusts me – as if such a person, even an outlaw, would dally with such a person as she. She has made up every word of this extraordinary fabrication. 'Tis impossible to comprehend the wildness of such an imagination.' But I did not trust his cold smile.

'There would be a fine bounty paid for the capture of Roger Rowle. The family of Anthony Rowle is a fine one, sir, and monied, with influence in high places. There are brothers at court with the ear of the Queen. 'Twas a terrible thing that happened at Amberry, if you remember, sir.'

'Roger Rowle did not cause the fire! That was Dooley!'

'Be quiet!' they shouted at me.

The steward leaned back in his carved chair and winked at the lean young man beside him. 'If it were true . . . if this extraordinary story were true, tell me then, my good sir, do you think you would have the gall to communicate with these people, the Rowle family, on the strength of the false testimony of a wench such as this we have here before us today?'

'No sir, I would not,' replied Wekes, his pinched face flushing slightly. 'Nothing she says can be relied upon. All I say is that if this maid is who she says she is, if the relationship she had with this savage be true, if, as she says she did, she bore his child, then there is a good possibility that Roger Rowle should attempt to collect her from this place before too long. And we would have the notorious Roger Rowle in the net and the bounty in our hands. The ruffianly gang have been known to rescue others of their number, many times, from the gibbet rope, and we seem to have here before us today a perfect opportunity. And we would reap any rewards there might be – by accident – so to speak.'

'And in the meanwhile . . .'

'In the meanwhile justice must take its natural course. She must be held below, and, having no defence worthy of hearing, she must suffer the proper penalty for theft laid down by the law of the parish of Lydford. She must hang for the theft of the coat and the boots.'

I tried for the last time. 'But sir, it was Dooley who started the fire . . . it was not Roger Rowle . . . you must communicate with his uncles and tell them that so that he can be cleared of a crime he did not commit!'

'Silence!'

'With no defence?'

'There is no defence worthy of presentation, sir. That is patently not her coat. Neither are these her boots. No, she must hang with the others tomorrow.'

They had my outer clothing displayed on the table in the centre of the room. It looked as pathetic, as inconseqential as myself. What had I done? I was cold and frightened . . . didn't know what to say. Didn't understand what they were saying, for half the time they whispered together, and only occasionally did they speak out loud for all the court to hear.

But I did hear them speak of the bridge coming down. I did hear them say, "Twould be such a simple trap. We could mount a guard of men by the bridge and trap the savages should there be an attempt at rescue.' The man called Wekes picked his teeth and wiped his fingers on his braided sleeve. His voice was low, but not so low that I could not hear him. He wore an earring in his right ear. It caught the light and sparked when he said, 'That's if there would be anyone left, for they would not notice the lack of the bridge in the dark. We would be well commended should such a simple trick work. And we would have nothing to lose by it.'

Nosworthy's chin got lost in his ruff. He chortled, 'We would lose nothing by doing that – that's what you're saying, eh, Tom? And you think that such a bizarre attempt at rescue would be likely? After all, here we are saying the wench's story is rubbish and with no substance to it.'

'I think it is rubbish,' Tom Wekes assured the fat man, 'but if we catch Roger Rowle tomorrow we can dispose of him quickly and cover ourselves against the possibility of any smattering of truth. Let me remind you of the size of the bounty.'

'Cover ourselves, yes, cover ourselves.' He took the other man's words and moved them between his teeth like gristle. He looked over the bench again and seemed surprised to see me still there. 'Take her down,' he said to the constable, staring at me out of cold little eyes, and his fat lips smacked together as he moved his glance towards the next felon, a tiny boy not six years old who was accused of stealing a hare which he found in a trap. ''Twas dead already, sir, I swears 'e were dead when I took 'e.' I heard the lad's voice, shrill with honesty, as they pushed me down the stairs and took the last of the daylight from me.

52

Brother Niall, this is a truly terrible place. It is dark in here, and cold, and the floor is wet so I am better standing. I wonder who was last in here, waiting: I wonder what happened to them, how they spent their last night if they were lucky enough to be given one. Were you here, monk? Did you listen, as you're listening to me now? Are you immune to pain, to fear, to all the horror that is Lydford Gaol?

I fear that I might sleep, yes, even with death looming over me, for the terror makes me drowsy. My brain calls for release from the torment of dread. It is trying to protect me, to cheat me. Like Maggie, my brain thinks it knows better than I do – but do I really want protection? Wouldn't I be better to stand in the open and accept, now it's the end? To sleep my last hours away would be somehow neglectful and cowardly.

There is no time left! *Where is Rowle? Where is Rowle?* Is it possible that he has abandoned me? Oh, what is it like to hang, Brother Niall? How long will it take me to die?

So it is not for my brave endeavours that I die. There might have been something noble in that, for there is always something noble in love, no matter how twisted it might have become. I die for the theft of a coat – that is my crime – and boots. Fine boots made of calfskin and belonging to one Abigail Varney. The boots gave me blisters – they didn't even fit me properly!

This is what Rowle is fighting against – this injustice, this cruelty. Protected as I had been, how could I have known? Blind and hungry as I was, how could I have known the extent of the brutality of the world outside? I had thought that the death of my aunts was a crime committed against justice by Mallin, but I ought to have known – the Combe was living proof; I lived with the consequences of British justice, it limped and hobbled each day all around me.

But I had been blind – unthinking of anything save for my love. Unwilling to think, unwilling to see . . . was it self-defence, or just this terrible gift for pretence with which I have been born, with which I surrounded my life.

I might not have known of the world, but I thought I did know Rowle. I believed he would come for me, even if it meant putting his life, and the lives of his men, at risk. I thought he would come for me. He is bigger than all of the men here – if he had come he would have seen through their sorry little trap. Their plan could not have worked. They could not hurt him.

Don't look at me like that, monk. Why, do you think it is possible that they might catch him and kill him? What are you trying to tell me . . . *that he is only human?*

I am thinking of Mary and Ned, now, and the time she grouped her children to her, waiting for Ned to come back and protect her. I have time to think as I pace. I think about Judd . . . Marnie and the skylark she mended with such gentle fingers. I think about Garth and Davy and their hopes for their futile garden. I think about Bell and her memories. I think about Lucy and of all the times she tried to warn me. And I think of the silent watchman, always there with his lantern, guarding a family. And I am one of that family . . . I am not alone.

A rattle at the door above our heads! Dear God, there has been a mistake! They are coming to set me free! Or is it . . . could it be . . . at dear last?

I stand flat against the far wall, trembling and unable to breathe with the hope of it. Is it merely the wind? The voice is small, as if it can hardly penetrate the thickness of the wood. Is it the voice of a child . . . a man . . . a woman . . . it is so muffled that I cannot tell.

'Your name?'

My name? What is a name. 'Who is asking? Why are you there? What do you want?'

'Your name. Just your name.'

'For why?' What are they going to do to me now?

'For Roger Rowle. Do they hold Bethany Horsham? Are they to hang Bethany Horsham in the morning or do they set a trap? Answer me quickly! I haven't much time and he will have it from no other source but this.' And now I hear a scrabbling, like a rat, and straw falls down the stepladder and lands, yellow, in a puddle of watery floor.

What is a name? It is everything. My voice is clear and honest and I can hardly believe it is mine when I answer, 'My name is Abigail Varney, and I hang for the theft of a coat and boots. I do not know of anyone called Bethany Horsham. I have never heard that name.'

No answer. No sound either. The messenger has gone and I – I have caused my own death! I have no breath left to call but I want to cry after the messenger. I want to scream, 'Wait! Wait . . . take a message to Rowle. I have so much to say . . . don't leave me alone here like this. Tell him to come for me, ask him to save me. I do not care about the trap or the threat to the Gubbins clan. There must be a safe way round it! For the love of God don't go! Don't let me die!'

But I am silent. And all the different people I play – they stay silent.

I am empty. There is nothing left now, nothing inside me. I slump down on to the floor, cowering and covering my face with my hands. I remember how I always thought that Birdie's soul had flown from her, like a sparrow, while I believed I had been born without one. But something has left me now and I feel bereft without it – bemused, bewildered. I have saved Rowle from danger, but what is there left? What has happened to me?

I am free.

I am free and disenchanted.

I did not need to be rescued. I have freed myself and yet I feel overwhelmed as if a great tragedy has just happened to me. I cannot stop shaking. Rowle is merely a man, just a man, just a frightened, confused, human being as I am, not a king. Not a god. I saved him, he was not able to save me. The world has suddenly gone so small, and if I lived now, with my love gone, what sort of silver would the stars be?

And there is the whole world out there and I have spent twenty-three years upon it and missed it. I could have loved – I could have laughed. I could have danced with the rest of them. Others see rainbows, others bathe in moonlight, so these things must be real. I did not need Rowle in order to see them. The colours might not have been quite so vivid, but soft colours have a gentler, more beautiful dimension. I have my own colours, I did not need to take Rowle's.

And I would have liked to have known peace. And gentleness. I would like to have stopped being breathless, and spent some time with soft, silent flowers that fade quickly.

Don't touch me don't touch me don't touch me. Come no nearer, Brother Niall, I can't stand you near me, and take that pitiful look off your face! No monk . . . back off . . . don't hold my hand and I do not want your crucifix! It is right that I die for my wickedness. For I am evil and justly judged. And I wish that the morning would hurry and come. I am ready, now, for death.

53

I am an old, old woman, cramped and hardly moving, cringing from the light which is white. After so much inaction – now all is crazy around me – shouts, the scraping sound of the stone from the wooden hatch that covers the stairs. And legs are coming down, legs bound with hide strips with dark boots on. I hear the leather creaking of the boots and I see the cracked lines across the toes.

No, not now – not already. Where is the moon? I didn't see it go. Why did it seep away like that with no goodbye. Where is it? I thought there was more time . . . not now. *Not now.* I thought I was ready, but who is really ready to die?

There is no time to try for madness, no time to assume some other personality. No time to conjure up from my vast store something protective, thick enough to shield me from this.

'Is it time?' Why does the silence roar? Why doesn't he answer or look at me, this man with the brutal hands and the staff he holds defensively before him as if he fears I might break loose and attack him. Why would I? And how could I?

I'm not going to resist. If I cringe against the wall and refuse to leave my dungeon the struggle from that would make the terror worse. No, no. I have to go willingly, pretending that every step is not a step towards annihilation, towards no more sunshine, no more pain . . . I'm not ready. I'm not ready at all.

He just looks at me, meekly almost. As if we have an understanding –as if I have agreed to something and now we both know I must honour my pact. But I agreed to nothing! This was decided for me – a long, long time ago – before my birth, even? Lizzie would say that, call it destiny. So could nothing I might have done prevented it? Could it God, could it?'

Oh yes, I call upon You now – doesn't everyone at the end. Being so alone is impossible to comprehend. There has to be someone else there, even to a woman without a soul, who doesn't know right from wrong. They didn't tell me at

Amicombe: shall I tell the gaoler that? Would it make a difference?

No. Nothing can make any difference now.

With my body protesting I go up the dungeon steps, feeling every notch and bend in the rough wooden stairs as if I am part of them, have lost my identity and am already dead, rolled out and become part of it all. Yes, there's the sky and I feel part of that, too, and my feet take to the bare earth as if that's where they'll always be, not hanging there in space . . .

There it is – the instrument of my death – high on the little knoll before the Gaol. Brown. Simple. Effective: up, across and a rope hanging down. Steps that I must climb and a bare platform. How can such a simple thing, disguised as a gibbet, really be the great door that it is, the doorway to Hell itself. Such a simple thing.

Rowle, hold my hand.

Maggie, tell me a story in mellow lamplight.

Lizzie, make a wish.

Birdie, sing a song.

Jessie, be there for me.

Lethargic, I can hardly move. I am so terribly tired. My legs weigh me down and my heart hammers hard against my chest. Why is everywhere white, I begin to ask. What a stupid question, and what does it matter to me anyway. Who would bother to answer someone who is about to die. What a waste of time. It has snowed in the night and all the edges of the world have been softened. A grey snow-sky goes over the wintry moor and into the distance, like a series of waves, wild and sombre.

I climb the slope and look down and only now I see the people, snow on their backs like floury pie-crusts, huddled there, pale and drawn and blown-out by all of it. But they won't miss the last bit of fun, the dying. Lots of dying. Lots of themselves to be hanged today at Lydford. Me and the boy with the poached hare and how many others, I wonder? I see the high-towered church, the bare fields, and far away the landscape that is as familiar to me as my own hands. And everywhere a curious winter stillness as if the whole world waits and holds its breath to see the sinner go.

My gaoler turns up his collar and grunts against the cold. His nose is red and dripping. The snow falls fast now, great soft flakes on to the already thickly-white grass, falling softly between the limbs of the churchyard trees. My eyes are dazzled with the frenzy of their falling. My feet move soundlessly. All around is silent, all around is telling me that it can never, ever end.

How – and in what way is this going to hurt? And what will I do with the last pain? There are even rabbit tracks in the snow.

I feel a rush of sickness and terror as they guide me up and I sense the earth under my feet for the last time. The steps are slippery with ice – they haven't put sawdust down then. I must be careful – that's funny. I laugh. The gaoler looks at me quizzically.

I want to do this properly. I don't want to make him cross with me – I don't want him to hurt me.

I look down at the scraps of me. Oh, Maggie with your reassuring stories – 'all will be well when the cuckoo comes'. Tell me, tell me where I'll be when the cuckoo comes. The rope has ice entwined in it. It is alien, the one thing, this morning, that I don't feel part of. It bites like a chain, as cold and as hard as a chain. It doesn't give.

So this is death.

I let my hands hang straight beside me. I am no longer conscious of the snow, just the gaoler's face, watching for the moment. No, no. I can't have that vision as my last. The pull will have to come without my knowing, because I am going to turn my eyes to look at the Forest, and listen for that cuckoo. There are words being spoken, not for me to hear. They are lost to me, smothered by the snow and taken away by the wind.

White and smooth and restful – the outlines of the hills. Granite and eternal. Dartmoor, which we called the Forest. My land is a gaunt land where the wind sweeps over the raw-boned frame of the earth, the giant breakers in the distance threatening to roar towards the lapping land-waves that are ours. Life – sweet with campions, honeysuckle, celandine and violet, and foxgloves grow between the blackthorn. And always, there in the distance, beside us or behind us, the mast of our ship – the cone of Brent Tor with the dark church on top, a pennant against the sky.

*

Only a few steps from here to the waterfall. The skies will take me there.

The world is dark and I am cold and I remember when we made love by the waterfall. That was like this, like waiting, helpless, between two worlds, with sheer cliffs before and behind to shield us. I remember . . . I remember . . .

54

No pain no darkness just a moment of rest.

And a deep booming voice shouted, 'Hold! What the blazes is going on here and who gave orders for the bridge to come down? Hell, blast and damnation.' The padded, well-muffled figure of John Furze struggled clumsily from his horse and dragged it after him down the hillock, half-striding, half-slipping, towards the base of the grisly platform. 'Hell's teeth, what is this business? I have only to be away for three nights and all Hell is let loose behind my back. Martin Richards – slip that noose! The girl has fainted. Don't stand there and stare as if you're being faced by some ghoulish apparition, you great gormless dolt! Pick her up, man! Rub some warmth into her arms and legs . . . get away . . . move back you vultures and let me pass!'

For a moment there was no movement, not from the watchers who stood back dizzily as if woken from deep dreams, nor from the burly man who stood, arms akimbo, beside the girl, staring down at John Furze with a look of stupidity on his face. Only the snow drifted silently down, forming a soft backdrop which made the people unreal as if everyone there was merely an actor miming on a stage. John Furze strode to the edge of the wooden platform and gazed up out of rime-rimmed eyes. His face was a purplish red from his early morning exertion and from the biting wind; he could feel the sweat running under his doublet. He turned his fiery eyes from the sight above him and flicked them around the crowd to search for his clerk.

'Master Wekes!' he called in a quieter voice. 'A word.' And then, returning his sharp glance to the executioner. 'Get her down for God's sake, before I have to get up there and do it myself.'

Tom Wekes, at the edge of the little crowd, quailed beneath his heavy coat of royal blue velvet. He rasped his clerical hands together as he stepped forward through the silence. John Furze, who was a good deal smaller than his learned clerk, was forced to look up, but this did not detract from his power, for he was a square, squat man, planted into the ground and immovable as a small bull. His chin came up aggressively and he steamed from his nostrils. He narrowed his eyes. His voice was hoarse when he spoke and hardly above a whisper. 'So . . .' he hissed, and it was his clerk who yearned for diminishing size. 'Once again, Tom, I go and you and John Nosworthy take the law into your own greedy hands. You well know my feelings on this. Trials you may hold . . . but the sentencing must wait until my return so that I can scrutinise carefully the matters in hand. Our reputation is bad enough, Tom. It has even reached London – they are maligning us there. They say there is no justice to be got at Lydford and I will not have it, Thomas! I will not have it. What is the meaning of this business? You have some explaining to do.'

'We could not wait, sir. We had the chance to snare Roger Rowle, you were away and we took it. We ordered the bridge to come down because we felt there was a good possibility he might attempt a rescue this morning. There has been a guard down by the gorge all night.'

John Furze was having trouble removing his gloves. The heavy leather was stuck to his hands and he wrestled with first one, then the other. 'Oh . . . and what led you to this fanciful conclusion?'

'The thief, sir. The vagabond you see by the gibbet. She freely admits that she was his mistress, bore him a child. She came here yesterday talking such nonsense we had to dismiss it and follow our instincts. She is nothing but a whore and a thief. Even now, sir, 'twould be better to order the execution to go on. It would be better to mete out justice to a liar and a thief such as she.' Wekes stumbled and stuttered over his words in his eagerness to convince his master.

Done with his gloves, John Furze stepped back for a better view. Away for three days in Exeter, he would have been back last night, but the snow had forced him to take bed and board in Mary Tavy. He had not slept a wink there. The tavern was a poor, mean little place and he had had to share a bed. The condemned girl must be frozen stiff. All she had on was a thin dress of white . . . her face was white . . . her hands and her feet almost translucent, and against all that white that black hair tumbled. John Furze frowned and pushed his clerk aside, for he thought he caught sight of a streak of pure silver. 'I'll be damned! I know that poor creature!'

'I doubt . . .' But Wekes fell guiltily silent, cursing his ill-fortune, as his hard-breathing master took the gibbet steps two at a time and climbed to the top. He pushed the ungainly Richards aside and kneeled down beside the limp girl.

When Bethany Horsham opened her eyes she saw snow falling on a pure white head. She saw small, twinkling eyes of periwinkle blue and a strawberry nose. She smelled horse and sweat and essence of roses for it was dried rose leaves John Furze used to hang in his clothes. She brought her hands slowly to her neck. She tried to swallow but found she could not. Her mouth was dry. Her eyes were dry and, panicked, she could not feel the beat of her heart. She felt shrivelled up, hardly able to remember where she was or what was happening.

'Your name, girl,' said the fat man crouching beside her. 'I ought to know it . . . I have known it once . . . give me your name.'

It took Bethany a while to speak, a while to make her mouth obey her and form the words. Her jaw was tense and her teeth had started to chatter so hard she feared she was losing control. But she told him. She watched the snow fall silently round her, and she told him. Dimly, like a faraway thought, she recognised this man as her saviour . . . he had come to save her from something that had been happening. She must be nice to him. She must do what he asked. They might not hurt her if she did what he asked.

'Bethany Horsham! I know now!' he shouted down to Wekes who stood like a miscreant child in the snow below him. 'This woman lived with the Gubbins in the Combe . . .'

'I have been trying to tell you that,' the thin clerk replied. 'She is the mistress of Roger Rowle. We might have caught him.'

John Furze turned back to the girl. Some colour was returning to her cheeks. Her eyelashes swept them with shadows of black and her face looked bruised and pinched. 'Can you hear me, child? Can you understand what I'm saying? Do you remember me? I dined with you once.'

Bethany thought – do I want to remember? Is it safe to let myself remember. Will I go mad if I do? She felt terribly weak, vulnerable and afraid, but the loud man's face was reassuring. He spoke with excitement but sincerely. 'I think I do remember . . .'

'Enough of this,' said John Furze, rising with difficulty. 'Wrap her up in a blanket and get her to my house. Someone go ahead and alert my wife. There is something about this that I do not like, something that smells like bad fish. And I will get to the bottom of it, Master Wekes, if it's the last thing I do.'

'There is a long list of others . . .'

'Hold everything. Pack up and go. There will be no more executions carried out at Lydford today. And you . . .' he turned on the crowd who stamped their feet against the cold and muttered together, deprived of their entertainment, '. . . get to your homes. Have none of you anything better to do with your time, by Christ?'

Safe and in the home of John Furze, whose wife was as gentle as he was blustery, Bethany Horsham told her tale. 'The memories hurt me. I don't want to go back too far. All I want to remember now is that I came to tell the truth and was disbelieved. I came to appeal for a pardon and found myself with a rope round my neck. I had one night waiting outside in the cold, but the night in the dungeon seemed colder.' And she shuddered and wept again, unable to go on, until Hettie Furze shoved her belligerent husband from the room and said, 'That's enough for tonight, John. The child is in terrible shock. Let her explain things to you slowly . . . You always want to be doing everything at the same time.'

Hettie Furze sat up with Bethany, beside her bed, next to the roaring fire. 'Rowle could not explain to anyone why he would protect his nurse . . . for no one would understand. No one but me.' Hettie leaned forward and poked the fire. Her presence was calming. She was a big, comforting, unflustered woman who gave the impression she had all the time in the world to listen and nothing else more important to do. Every now and then Bethany wept and Hettie held her.

'I was so afraid. I did not want to die. I was not ready to die.'

'You have the whole of your life in front of you now.'

Bethany shook her head and her sobs wracked her body. 'But nowhere to go. There is no one who cares.'

'Hush, child. Eventually the terror will leave you. You will not feel so alone and desolate when you have come to yourself.'

But Bethany feared she would. 'Maybe they should have let me die.'

'Quiet now. Quiet.'

'Rowle did not come,' she sobbed.

'Rowle did not come because you told him not to. You risked your life in order to save him. You came to Lydford in order to free him. You must think good of yourself, child, and get rid of some of this blackness inside.'

'You don't understand . . . I did it for my own purposes! I am evil!'

'Everything anyone does, even the kindest action, is done for selfish purposes. No one chooses to do anything unless they want to. We are human, Bethany, we are human and, aspire as we might, we cannot join the angels. We would look silly if we tried. And I don't think we'd be very nice to know.'

In the morning John Furze came in, a good deal fresher and more rested after his good night's sleep. Some of the raw redness had gone from his face. He raised his shaggy white eyebrows. 'Is she ready to see me now?'

Hettie Furze shook her head. She walked to the door and whispered, 'She's sleeping. Let her rest. I think you'll have to get to grips with the fact that she might never be ready, John. You are asking too much to force her to relive that whole nightmare again.'

'No matter,' her husband replied, trying to whisper, but even his whisper was loud. 'I have found the Jesuit. I have him downstairs in my study. I am giving the wretched man breakfast and I'll see what he has to say.'

'You are concerned in this, John, aren't you? What is your involvement?'

'I swore to William Rowle many years ago, after the unfortunate business with Charles and his wife, that I would do all in my power to help the family. The young man's revenge was terrible but, powerless as he felt at the time, and cut off from justice, understandable. Unfortunate, yes, but understandable.' John Furze peered over his wife's broad shoulder towards the sleeping girl. He went on, 'Many aspects of this bad business have been unfortunate. He took the law into his own hands. He should not have done. With time, with money and influence, eventually that business was smoothed over – and he knew that, Hettie. I told him! But setting fire to the house, to the guilty and innocent alike, was an entirely different matter. With that second crime on top of the first, young Rowle had gone too far. And yet his uncles never believed that Roger Rowle, no matter how hardened he might have become, could deliberately have burnt his immediate family to death. And neither did I believe it. How could he be so foolish, just when matters were turning out right? The handsome blaggard never denied it, but he never admitted it, either. The family have spent a fortune endeavouring to discover the truth. They are desperate to avoid having Gideon Rowle's second son inherit. Gideon's sons are a feckless, unworthy lot. The brothers of Anthony Rowle are eager to learn anything that might help them to arrange a pardon. And I think we have it, Hettie,' he banged his fist in his hand and Hettie turned a concerned face towards the bed, frowning. She laid her finger on her lips. 'At last I think we have it, woman!' and in his loud way he crept out. Hettie Furze made sure it was she who closed the door.

While Bethany rested, spoiled and cosseted by the motherly Hettie Furze, sometimes remembering, sometimes choosing to forget, and not forced by her protector to do either, John Furze, pleased with himself and feeling important, penned an urgent letter to his friend William Rowle. In it he described the picture which Bethany had painted for the monk.

'*It was the old nurse,*' he wrote, squeezing his little eyes to see in the candlelight as he paused before scratching on, '*who was undoubtedly employed to do away with the lad. A relationship developed between them, those two who spent so many unhappy hours alone in that cold room upstairs. She might have been a hard and cruel woman, but she had a heart. She appeared to grow quite proud of the boy in her own strange way, after he triumphed over all the trials and tribulations, after he survived. He grew into the kind of boy any real mother would have been proud of . . . and who is to say, William my friend . . . maybe she thought it was her skill that had turned him into such a fine young man.*'

John Furze paused again and reached for the port. He felt the bottle's outline with his fingers, brought it towards him, and automatically felt for his glass and poured. There was nothing in it. It was empty! He lifted the bottle upside down and pulled a wry face. Drat the woman. His wife played dead in bed these days, so the least she could do was to make sure his other comforts were provided. He dipped his nib into the ink and carried on. *'When Roger went to school they threw Dooley out. Can you imagine what her feelings must have been then?'* John Furze was asking somebody else to imagine . . . but could he? He stopped to think for a moment. There she was . . . thirteen years in employment . . . and then thrown out like an old boot. Not only that, but in her heart she must have wished things could have been different. Bah! He smiled to himself. He was nothing but a sentimental old fool. He was putting thoughts into the old rogue's head which she probably did not have, warm feelings into her cold old heart. Well, if not that, then she must have felt anger towards the family who could cast her off so simply, without giving a thought to her future welfare.

'They met, once, quite by accident, out on the moor by Belstone. I won't go into the details of the circumstances here. They are best forgotten. But, up until that time, Dooley had probably imagined that her charge had grown up and claimed his birthright. She could rest assured that matters had turned out well for him, even if she herself had come to a sorry state of affairs. But when she saw him . . . realised with shock what had come to pass . . . she decided to find out the truth. Then it was she discovered the foul trick that Gideon and Charles had played on Rowle, the trick that had forced him to abandon his home and live as he could, as an outlaw.'

John Furze tried to wipe the ink off his cuff. He could not. He tried to make sure he did not spoil the paper for this was a long letter and he certainly did not want to do it again. His wife called him a messy man . . . she was upstairs with the girl now, she seemed to thoroughly enjoy her company. And Bethany was certainly very much better. Ah, thought John Furze to himself, stretching out his legs towards the fire, manipulating the cramp from his fingers so that the bones clicked like the small white logs, if only I was a younger man . . .

He heard the firm knock on the front door. Who could be out and about on such a dreadful evening? He threw down his pen and half got up . . . would somebody else go or was he expected to do everything in this house? He inclined his head to one side and listened.

Little Jennie answered the door and John Furze heard her say, 'Yes, who is it?'

'We have come to see Bethany Horsham whom we have heard is temporarily lodging with you.'

'Just a moment, I'll ask the master. Who shall I say has come?'

'No names. Just friends.'

John Furze sat up, all alert. The maid came in and he nodded. 'Take them up,' he told her. 'Don't keep them dithering out there on the step.' But after he heard the front door close and the tread of the visitors on the stairs he got up and shuffled over to the door. He was in time to see a man . . . very dark . . . very dignified . . . and a woman, fair and beautiful. He could not say if he had seen them before, for he only caught a quick view from behind. He hurried away before Jennie, coming down again, could see him, and he groaned when he looked down and saw he was only halfway through his important letter. I am the man of this house, he told himself angrily. I ought to have gone to the door myself to find out who the visitors were. But his wife was always telling him he was far too inquisitive, getting worse as he grew older, and it was that which had prevented him.

'I'll leave,' said Hettie Furze politely.

Bethany raised her head, saw Lucy and lowered it again. Timid, ashamed, she could not face her, but there was no such reticence on Lucy's part. She rushed forward and folded Bethany tightly in her arms. Silas stood smiling beside the bed. Before Bethany could ask it Lucy said, 'Rowle could not come. It would not be safe for Rowle to come.'

'Is he angry?'

Lucy held Bethany's hand. There were tears in her eyes, which made them look very bright when she said, 'He is angry because you were so foolish, because you took such a very great risk. He would have come for you, Bethany. He was determined to save you. And then they told him you were not there, it was another . . . Abigail Varney . . .'

'But you have come, Lucy.' Bethany pulled back her hand, uncertain of Lucy, unsure how to respond. She could not hold Lucy's eyes, they were too bright, they saw too much, they always had.

391

'Of course I have come. How could I stay away after I'd heard what nearly happened to you.' She looked around the room, her appraising eyes taking in the comfortable furniture, the glowing fire, the colourful covers and curtains. 'When death comes so close it makes all else seem unimportant. I care about you, Bethany. I had to come to make sure you were all right.'

Bethany glanced up at Silas. He stayed silent, but his eyes never left her face.

'After everything that's happened, you still came? How do you know I am not pining again for Rowle, planning to get him away from the Combe, plotting to take him away from you?'

Lucy smiled and it was one of her old smiles. 'Well, if you still haven't learned, if you still have not woken up to the human face of Roger Rowle then all I can do is pity you. Bethany, I do not fear you . . .'

'You turned me out of your house.' Bethany bit her lip hard. Talking of those times still hurt. The shame was the worst part. 'And he still came to me. He came to me often. We made love, Lucy.' She had to make sure Lucy knew. Perhaps she hadn't properly understood . . .

'And do you think that I do not know?'

'You allow him to do these things. You ask nothing of him. You love him and yet in return he cheats you.'

'I am a fool,' said Lucy simply. 'In a different way from you, and yet I am a fool and I always will be. I love him, Bethy, and I live in hope that one day he will change his ways . . .'

'But if he does not?'

Lucy laid down her cloak – there was snow on the hood. 'Ah, if he does not, do you think that I can stop loving him? Do you think I have not wanted to . . . many times? We cannot change our feelings just because we are wounded by those we love.'

'You are too gentle. Too noble. You make me feel small and mean against you. You always have made me feel that way. I would like to be like you.'

Lucy laughed. She reached up and held Silas' hand, bringing him into the ring of warmth she could feel surrounding them. 'Then let me tell you a secret. How would you feel if I told you that I had always yearned to be more like you? Strong . . . wild . . . determined to get your way . . . you make me think of the heart of the moor. Beautiful, too, and warm, so full of love if you could only have found the right person.'

Bethany gazed at Lucy, her dark eyes wide. Was Lucy telling the truth? Or was she mocking her? 'I don't believe you.'

'Well, I can only assure you that what I say is true. And something else, something you might just laugh at. Bethany, I would have so loved to have been your friend and I was always so sorry . . .'

Now Bethany felt that her own answering words were inadequate. 'But it was I who always longed for that . . . it was me who wanted, yet felt I was never good enough . . . too dark . . . too black . . . as if I might flaw you, touch you with it.'

Lucy leaned forward and put her arms round Bethany once again. Together they cried. When she released her she reached for a tress of Bethany's hair. 'Ah yes, the taint mark,' she said. 'It is always with you, isn't it, Bethy. It grows with you. You can never leave it behind.'

Bethany turned away from that and said, 'Silas, I'm glad you came.'

Silas answered, 'I had to see you, I had to know you were all right. And if you want to return with us now I will take you.'

Hettie Furze returned with a silver tray on which was balanced a jug of mulled ale and some hot ginger biscuits. She stayed in the room while they talked and Bethany tried to explain, tried to tell about Dooley, without mentioning Amos. But the honesty that they had that night, and all the love and the caring made secrets seem shameful between them.

'So that's how I understood,' she told Lucy. She felt released, as though she were flying, after talking of the hurt and the shame she had kept to herself for so long. 'That's how I knew Rowle would feel that way . . . I knew he was protecting someone, for he could not have started the fire. And gradually I realised who that person had to be.'

'If we could only go back to that life,' said Lucy, and hope made her gentle face more beautiful. 'If we could only go back . . . Judd, Matt, Daisy and Bessy would grow up in such a different world.'

'My husband is doing what he can,' said Hettie, thrilled to be part of this happy reunion, excited and warmed by it all. 'He is a stubborn man and if there is a way of proving your story to be right, believe me when I say he is the man to do it!'

They talked about hopes and dreams. They talked about difficult, frightening things that had only stood between them before. And it was late at night before Silas and Lucy got up to leave.

'It is too soon for me yet,' said Bethany, strangely shy of Silas. 'I want to come back, I want to see Rowle again, but give me more time.'

And downstairs, John Furze put down his pen, satisfied with himself after scratching a forthright ending to his letter.

55

It was the third week of the search, and it was proving to be difficult. Finding one beggar in a city where it was thought there might be twelve thousand, had never promised to be an easy task.

Sir William Rowle, Lord Chief Baron of the Exchequer, sat back in his carriage and waited. He never failed to be saddened by the changes he saw in London, and the worst of it was that they were happening so quickly. His journey today had taken him far from his own splendid house between Whitehall Palace and the mouth of the Fleet River. He disliked the new, sprawling suburbs which even now joined the villages of Whitechapel and Stepney, Shadwell and Limehouse and extended right along the river at Wapping. And all this in spite of the law which forbade anyone to build within three miles of any London gate. But pressure from the desperate poor, the swarming immigrants, proved the enforcement of this law to be impossible. Row after row of squalid tenements were going up everywhere .. hidden behind screens if necessary. William Rowle considered that the sad, straggling suburbs were somehow draining the heart from the city.

He smiled sadly. Oh, much was still the same. As Sir William passed over London Bridge, the heads of traitors stared down at him. There they would stay, impaled until they rotted, or were blown down into the river on a gusty night.

Two wagons were stuck in the narrow alley between The Ship Inn and Williams' apothecary shop. Pedestrians attempted to squeeze by and avoid being pulled into the loud fray between the two draymen. Fury steamed into the mists of the chill March morning, and the affair was threatening to become a bloody one – understandably so, for both waggoners were likely to be wheel-locked and imprisoned here for half the day. Beyond this bottleneck was a hotch-potch of stalls, and there it was even more difficult to avoid becoming embroiled with the pushy vendors who approached every man, woman and child, flapping their wares at the passing faces and calling, 'What do you lack, sir, what do you lack? Soft boots, see, made with the best hides, and cheap, the cheapest you'll find in London this day.' 'Musk boxes, beard-brushes, toothpicks . . . buy, buy, buy' and so, all around the man in the carriage, the song of London went on.

He closed his eyes to the rush of noise and bustle. An old man now, white-haired and slightly stooping, he preferred to stay within the high-walled confines of his house where his younger brother Alfred eagerly waited for news. Younger than him by five years, Alfred was nevertheless ill and feeble, crippled by the gout. Neither brother had married, and so they had been particularly pleased when Anthony, the brightest, most energetic and promising of all four of the Rowle sons, had become betrothed to Catherine.

And then – the tragedy.

William did not like to think of Gideon. His death had been no great loss to the family, nor the world, either. William held his handkerchief to his nose. John Furze's letter he kept to his chest in his right hand, as if he was afraid some passing pieman might stretch his arm through the opened door and whisk it away. The letter, to William, was a precious thing. He felt vulnerable in so public and degenerate a place so at all times he kept his silver-topped cane at his knee, defensively at the ready.

Dogs barked, a crier rang his bell and called out in the distance, and from the workshops came the constant ringing of hammers, the sting of iron on an anvil, as horses were shod, barrels were hooped, coffins were sawn, and over all this was the general clamour which came from the tangle of opened windows.

'We are too late,' said James, his servant, hurrying back, quick to close the carriage door and take refuge in the velvet upholstery. His short hair was grey and lavishly powdered and he always trod carefully in the streets, taking care to keep the dust off his silver buckled shoes. A fastidious man, he was obviously distressed by his task. 'She has just lately been turned from the tavern, unable to pay, and putting the customers off with her constant whining. Now they say she is stricken with the pox and has gone to Bankside.'

Sir William leaned forward and instructed the driver, but

without much hope in his heart. Their search kept taking this familiar turn, leading to another blank wall. The filthy creatures amongst which the old woman lived would say anything to earn the fourpence which would buy them a mug of ale. Such wretched poverty, such desperation. John Furze's letter suggested an understanding of why the notorious Gubbins clan had ganged together as they had. '*I would oust them,*' he wrote, '*if I had men brave enough, or sufficiently well armed, or if I thought it would do any good. But there is more hope of containment where they are than if they dispersed and roamed about singly or in pairs and I do believe they would cause more crime. I know where they are. And although they be pests of the worst kind, apart from the nuisance they cause roundabout here, at least they are all in one place.*'

The carriage travelled on, stopping and starting through the busy streets. Again he dispatched his servant to the new address, and again William Rowle, tired now, sat back and waited. This time his servant returned more quickly and William leaned forward to hear his news. 'I gave your description to the lad at the door who says she arrived here last night.'

They found Dooley in a wooden brothel at Bankside, where a broken tavern sign dripped and beckoned listlessly to barges in the rain. Ramshackle steps led down to the Thames that ran below it. The windows were grey and cobwebbed, and a dubious woman of the lowest type halted them on the stair. Clearly syphilitic, for she was almost blind and supported on two rough crutches, she called to them through broken teeth, 'You pay me afore yer climb these stairs.'

But William was already on his way up.

The woman wore woollen mittens up to her elbows; they were moth-eaten, crispy and a dirty brown. Grey ringlets hung from under her bonnet like spirals of horsehair stuffing and her skin was yellow but daubed with false colours that gave her the look of a broken, badly-painted doll.

'We do not wish to take advantage of your wares,' said James, affronted, waylaid in the dirty hall and considering his encounter with such a person unspeakable. 'We are looking for an old beggarwoman whom we heard has taken a room.'

'Oh, 'er,' said the madam sourly, her indigo-painted mouth turning down as she realised there was no great fortune to be

397

made in this matter. She waved one crutch in the right direction and the smell that wafted from her was more rank that that which oozed from the dark flowing river outside. 'Now then, an' what would the likes of 'e be wanting with such as' er?'

'Surely that is our business,' said James, while in front of him William Rowle was mounting the dark staircase painfully and with difficulty.

'Yer might be in time, yer might not. 'Er up there be on 'er last legs. I doubt she will last the night.' The proprietor of one of the cheapest houses in London – and that was saying something – remained at the bottom of the stairs, large and menacing, blocking James' way, so he was only too willing to give her a shilling to get her to move to one side. The old man creaked up the stairs a few steps ahead, having to stop now and then to find his breath.

When they found Dooley they saw a large cat asleep on the white ashes where the fire ought to have been. William Rowle supposed there must be some warmth left in the fireplace, and if there was, then certainly it was the only warmth in the room. And the cat had it all.

He was prepared for a dreadful sight, so he was probably not as shocked as he otherwise might have been. Not so poor James, who stepped back and moved quickly to the closed window, attempting to force it open to let air into the squalid room. Dooley lay on her side on the bed, propped up on yellowing pillows, chattering to herself. She was thin to the point of emaciation. Her head disappeared almost completely between her hunched-up shoulders and her hair – she wore no cap – was a frazzled, matted grey. He small black eyes had lost their lustre and now looked ashen like two dead coals peering out of a waxen face. Her large nose must have been broken many times and now stuck out starkly between the skin of her sunken cheekbones, skin that was covered with a crust of suppurating scabs. She had two teeth left and because of the black gap between them they looked long and pointed like an old dog's fangs. The lines on her face crisscrossed like a map and sunk into folds of immeasurable sorrow, and yet William found it hard to feel pity.

And this . . . this grotesque, rotting, stinking carcass of a woman was the object of his nephew's fierce and unrelenting loyalty. And love? William shook his head, unable to believe it. Time and circumstances had undoubtedly ravaged her, but even in her best days the woman he saw on the bed must have been a daunting sight. The thought of this uncultured hag administering her attentions to any one of the Rowle family, let alone a child, a fearful, lonely boy, was almost too much for William to bear. Ancient as he was he felt hot young rage boil up inside him.

Unwilling as his senses were, he forced himself to move nearer. And then he spoke her name. 'Dooley?' And she ceased her chattering, went quite stiff on the bed, and brought one listless eye to rest upon her visitor. And in a voice just as awful as the rest of her, the dying old woman cackled out, 'Well, fine sir, and what do you want with me? Can't you see that this old body's dying?' And for a second her face moved into a smile . . . as if she was glad, wanting her life to end!

'My name is William Rowle and I have come to see if you will have the goodness to talk to me about something so important it is the closest thing to my heart.' He beckoned to James to leave the window alone – the smell of the river air would be almost as bad as the smell in here – and William wanted the paper James carried, the paper he had gone to such lengths to have drawn up.

The old crone watched him. Hopeful, but not certain if she understood him, William carried on. 'I had not expected to find you in such dire circumstances. I had expected to have to pay you a great deal of money to comply with my wishes. I had even made plans to carry you to a safe place.'

She shifted slightly on the bed before raising a claw-like hand and putting it on his arm, prior to interrupting him. It was all he could do to refrain from pulling back in disgust.

'William Rowle, you say? That black bastard's brother! That evil demon!' And she sucked and rolled her mouth around until she mustered enough saliva to spit. William Rowle looked away and breathed deeply before he summoned up the strength to carry on.

'I know, Dooley. I know all about that.' He made sure he pronounced his words very clearly. 'And it is for that reason that I have come.'

'He would have had me kill the boy.' She muttered in between her moments of coherence so that William had to lean over her to hear. 'Oh, 'twas a melancholy place, 'twas a melancholy life the both of us led. But I didn't kill him . . . oh no . . . I didn't do that. I could see he was better than all of them put together . . . and he needed me . . . do you know that?' She struggled to lift her head off the pillow but started coughing and fell back weakly.

'And you found out what had happened, didn't you, Dooley? One night when you were travelling the moor with your friends, you met young Roger with his outlaw band . . . and he saved your life. Do you remember?'

Dooley did not reply but started grovelling under her rags, trying to straighten the ties and folds, cursing as her movements pained her and she found it hard to manoeuvre.

William Rowle carried on. James had moved nearer and now he stood behind his master, his nose wrinkled up, his eyes trying to find something more pleasant in the room to rest on.

'And then, when you'd been to Exeter and sold your pots, you went back to Amberry, didn't you? You couldn't believe what had happened. You expected that Roger would have taken his position as master of the house by then. And you were furious with Gideon for sending Roger to school, away from you, without so much as asking your opinion, let alone for his actions three days later. For he dismissed you from his employment, did he not? He threw you out into the night.'

William hoped that what he was saying was something approaching the truth. If the story the Horsham girl told the monk was untrue, then all this searching, all this hoping, would be a complete waste of time and effort. And, worse than that, he and Alfred would die knowing that Roger, the rightful heir, was doomed to spend the rest of his life holed up in some primitive ravine, cavorting with a bunch of marauding savages. For on their deaths the passing of the estates could not be held back any longer. Gideon's second son, George, a weak and embittered young man, was already well over age, and champing at the bit to get his grasping hands on the family fortune.

Dooley's eyes closed. William leaned forward, fearing, all the time, as she breathed her painful, rasping breaths, that each one would be the last, that he would have come so close and that it might yet be too late.

'Dooley, can you hear me? Do you remember?'

In a voice that sounded like a rusty wheel, between bouts of hideous coughing, Dooley spoke through her scabbed lips. Mucous wept from the corners. 'Oh yes, I went back to that place. They threw me out without a thank you. Penniless, I was, and homeless. Not a soul on earth and nowhere to go. And my charmer had gone off and left me . . . my little man . . . my charmer . . .'

William leaned forward and touched her. Had she gone to sleep? Her breathing seemed a little easier.

'After I met my charmer on the moor I went to the big house first, in order to beg for food and a night in one of the stables.' Dooley's eyes started from her head and she gasped wildly before spluttering on. 'I was turned away. Gideon saw me hanging about by the gates as he rode by. He leaned forward and touched my shoulder with his whip. He asked me what I was doing. I told him, I stood there and raised myself up and I told him.' Her hands clawed at her clothes as she struggled to continue. 'I said I had met my young man on the moor . . . I asked him what had happened in that house to force my charmer out into the cold like that . . .' And she subsided into a terrible bout of coughing.

'And what did Gideon tell you?' William paused before asking gently.

Dooley's face, terribly thin, appeared to go thinner as she composed her muscles to speak. 'He said that Charles had been away for some years, abroad, visiting, and that when he came back he was murdered by Roger. For no reason at all, he told me. Out of sheer, black-hearted malice.' Dooley's mouth gaped open, her tongue came from between her teeth, black and dreadful with plague. William thought she had stopped, that she could not go on. But she moistened her lips as if, now she had started, she was determined to continue at any cost. 'He said that he didn't know where Roger was and why should he care? He told me I had always been a meddling old fool and that I should take my ugly old body away from the house. I spoilt it, he told me. I should take my ugliness off and get it as far away from him as I could if I knew what was good for me.'

'Ah yes. They did send Charles abroad for a while, after Roger left Amberry, as soon as they considered it safe. They thought that Roger was probably dead . . . and then Charles returned with his new bride. But fortune frowned on their wicked plot, for he met Roger on the road,' William mused, half-talking to himself.

'How did you find out the truth, Dooley?'

'I had only to ask Tremain.' She spoke remarkably clearly.

'And why, if Tremain knew the truth, did he not contact us?'

'He was threatened, quite terribly, to keep his mouth shut. Gideon told him that if anyone ever found out the truth he would know it was Tremain's doing.'

'And yet Tremain talked to you?'

'What harm could I be?'

'And after the fire? After Gideon was dead?'

'Tremain died in the fire,' said Dooley, her dull eyes lighting up for a moment. 'Tremain died. They all died. Roger and his men were there trying to save them, attempting to do what they could, aha, but by then it was way too late.' Dooley chuckled and the sight and the sound of that was awful. 'Tremain saw me leaving. He died in Rowle's arms. Tremain should have left the fire to burn. He should not have tried to help them. He might have had time to tell Rowle it was I. And after that, well, I came to London.'

'Tell me about the fire, Dooley.'

The old woman snapped closed her face like a trap. She continued to delve inside her clothing, pulling and scratching, as if something was itching her there. William stifled the need to scratch himself: she must be seething with lice. 'Why should I tell you? Why should I tell you any more?'

William spoke to her very directly, trying to conceal the great need in his voice. The truth of it was he could hardly bring himself to continue. 'Because it is the fire, which has been blamed on Roger, that is now preventing him from taking his place in the outside world once again. And now, now that you have not got much longer to live, if the fire was anything to do with you, your confession would absolve him, Dooley. We could get him a Royal Pardon, and he would be a free man. He took the blame, woman, he took the blame in order to protect you!'

Dooley hesitated only for a moment. In that time she brought her wasted face round on the pillow to stare at the grandly clad nobleman who sat on her bed. She was summing him up, he knew. She was assessing him, wondering if, even at

402

this late stage in her life, she could trust him . . . trust anyone
. . .

She closed her eyes again before she spoke, as if it was easier to see the past that way. 'I crept back to the house after nightfall, after I saw the lights go out.' Her voice turned from a snarl into a hiss. The words she spoke were pushed through her lips with venom. 'I hated them . . . God help me I hated them . . . all of them . . . every single one of those who dwelt in that monstrous place. We could have had it so different, my charmer and I, if it hadn't been as it was . . . if I hadn't been coerced into doing what I did. I had no option,' and her voice turned pleading, like a beggar whining for bread. 'But over the years, over the years oh yes, it was different. He grew, you see, into such a fine lad. And he was mine! Really, truthfully, he was mine. I raised him. I nursed him.'

William Rowle could not imagine a worse fate for anyone than to have this creature as a nurse.

But Dooley talked on. 'Oh yes, I went back and I crept into the kitchen and took a torch to the fire. And then I went, all silently and quickly, into the hall where the tapestries hung. I lifted the torch and I watched them burn. I smelt the flames and the smoke and the hot material burning.' Once more Dooley attempted to lick the scum from his lips. 'They were all to their beds, the house was of wood, I crept out after and watched from the park. It lit the whole night with its roaring and crackling and great flames flew and swept in the wind, they seemed to be licking the moon itself so high did they rise in the black night sky . . .'

She stopped suddenly. She pulled her hand from her tattered garments and held up a roughly carved wooden horse. She handed it to Sir William Rowle, who went to take it, but Dooley would not give it up. She managed to raise herself up an inch or two to stare at it proudly when she said, 'He made me that . . . 'twas a model of The Turk . . . the first horse he had, when he was just a small lad.'

William Rowle gestured to James to bring out the paper. He spoke very carefully, as though to a village idiot. 'This is a confession, Dooley,' he said. 'It tells, very simply, what happened on the night of the Amberry fire. It gives your name, and it tells everyone who might ever need to know that you did it. It is a short, straightforward document, and that is all that it says.' He edged himself closer to the woman in the bed. He took the quill that James handed to him. 'And if you were to hold out your hand so that I could guide it, your signature on this would make sure that Roger Rowle could return to his rightful position, take up his place in the world where he properly belongs.'

What had William been expecting? A tussle, arguments, hours sitting there in that miserable room trying to convince the dying old crone?

Dooley stretched out her hand. And, taking it into his own, he formed the letters for her and she signed the paper.

56

It was a joyous time. For this, Rowle's last night in the Combe, a great feast had been prepared. It was a sultry June evening after one of the first real, fizzy days of summer, and every member of the Gubbins clan was there, greatly excited by the changes, avid to know what was happening and to bid their final farewells before they were too steeped in drink to do so.

There was no trepidation, no feeling of abandonment, for they were in the hands of a new leader who was greatly respected – Silas had always been at Rowle's right hand. Everyone understood that freed from the confines of this place, with his new influential connections, Rowle could achieve far more in his aims to convert the world outside to a greater sympathy for those who suffered hardship and poverty.

Rowle and Lucy might be gone, but they were safe; life would go on much the same and the new order did not worry them.

Women spread cloaks on the short grass and fed their babies. Children chased butterflies, or tumbled and fought together. A group of boys were heaving stones about in the river and trying to build a bridge. The preacher was already flat on his back under a clump of blackthorn, dead to the world until morning. Garth and Davy held hands and nobody took any notice. Everyone kept their eyes on their pockets for Daniel the Nip's eyes were beady sharp tonight and he had no compunction, no idea that there might be a right or a wrong time . . .

A month before, Bethany Horsham had returned from Lydford and was taken in at Mary's house. There she stayed, protected at first from would-be clacking tongues quite firmly by Mary, quite rudely by Ned. And she was happy to be there. 'I am not ready to be on my own yet, my dreams are still too terrible, and although Lucy asked me to stay at the house, I don't think that would be right. I would not feel easy there.'

But even though Lucy encouraged her to talk to Rowle, 'For

you must see him soon, you cannot forever hide from him. There are things between you that must be resolved,' Bethany would not. She could find no reason to give to Lucy, save to say that she was embarrassed and still full of shame at the way she had humiliated herself. But it was to Mary she could confide, 'I dare not. Not yet. Oh Mary, I am so afraid that if I see him again I will find myself back where I was and that I could not bear. Not after all I've been through. Not now I have found myself again.'

'Nonsense. You must trust yerself,' said Mary. And they talked and talked, sometimes most of the night, with Mary saying, 'You has yer whole life before you now. Cherry an' Rose insist that you keep the gold . . . so you has the opportunity ter go from here if'n you wish. Silas badly wants you ter stay fer you know that 'e has always loved you, right from the start 'e loved you. But you didn't want ter see that, did 'e? You were too afraid o' yer feelin's. An' the thing you desired most in the world has happened – Lucy wants ter be yer friend. There isn't a day when 'er doan ask after you, or come ter visit you bringin' you gifts.'

Bethany was thoughtful. 'I don't want to touch that gold. I buried it, for shame, when I left the Combe . . . for even then, sick as I was, it felt bad on my fingers. One day I might feel differently, and there will be better ways to spend the money. And I have no wish to leave the Combe,' she said, seeing that when Mary looked at her now her eyes were soft and full of forgiveness. Everything had changed. Everyone had changed. She was the reason for Rowle's freedom, and, not only that, she had risked her life to save his. Her obsessive, selfish behaviour had been quickly forgotten; she was no longer a wicked woman to be shunned and ignored, she was a heroine and yet she appeared to be repentant, meek, willing to smile and converse with the others, interested in their children and their lives. And everyone suspected that eventually, when she recovered, she would be Silas's woman. 'This is the place where I feel at home. There are people here that I love. And now that I'm better,' she smiled at Mary, 'not sick any more, I can run Lucy's school. I can learn about cures from Silas and Bell. I can even ride with the men, sometimes, Silas told me. My future is here, Mary. This is where I want to be.'

Mary's little monkey face broke into a wide smile and she put her arms around her.

Lucy insisted that Bethany sit beside her for the feast . . . Lucy was on one side, Silas on the other. And Bethany knew that Lucy, above all others, was glad of the outcome of the whole affair. She was longing to make the new start. 'For the sake of the children as much as for myself.' She shelled an egg as she spoke, her fingers deft and certain; she turned around and fed it to Bessie who came up behind her, dark curls bouncing. All Lucy's children resembled Rowle.

The night grew dark. The blackness became soft, scented and secret. The lanterns were lit. The fiddler began to play with magic fingers and couples got up to dance casting revolving shadows. Silas, looking very fine in white and gold, stood up and invited Lucy to join him. Bethany felt Rowle very near; the distance between them pounded, full of her own heartbeat, and when she felt herself flushing she was grateful for the night. How long was he going to stay where he was, staring at her like that? She could feel his eyes. But they had to speak . . . they had to . . .

He got up from his chair and came to sit beside her. 'Bethy?'

She did not answer but held out her empty goblet and he filled it. Together they watched the red wine glow with lights that the lantern cast on it. It seemed to Bethany that everything she had ever said, or would say, had been said before. It was done with. Perhaps Rowle would speak first for she could think of nothing to say.

'I have to thank you,' said Rowle.

'For what?' She had not expected this. Why was he so stiff? So formal?

'For understanding. For being someone who knew. I thought no one else would know what it felt like – to love a monster!'

Neither of them smiled and their conversation was careful. Their eyes did not meet. Each spoke as if to a third listener out there somewhere in the darkness.

'We were never honest with each other,' said Bethany. 'We made each other up. We told each other stories. You were right when you said what I felt was not love.'

Rowle fell silent. And they both turned away from the conversation to watch the dancers who twirled in their sparkling finery; a sudden thin wind sighed at the candles on the table so they wisped their ribbons of soft black smoke. She felt her eyes stinging. With his head turned away and his voice low so she had to strain to hear him, Rowle said, 'I will miss you, Bethy.'

She said, 'You have Lucy. Lucy's love is real. Lucy will never ask too much of you, see too deeply into you, challenge you, anger you . . . Lucy is so good . . .'

'We could meet,' said Rowle, taking his hand to the base of his goblet and turning it so that a little wine overflowed and stained the table like blood-red tears.

Close to tears herself and knowing why she had loved him, Bethany raised her head and faced him. His overpowering vitality showed in his eyes which were hard as the granite of his native land. She held his eyes with her own, black held black, and there was fire in both. 'I am not the person I was. You speak to me as if I was still the same poor, besotted, possessed wretch that you knew. I have changed, Rowle: circumstances have changed me. My feelings have changed . . . it happened over one night while I spoke to the monk in the Gaol. I believed that my life was ended and I looked back and saw myself as a hopeless addict who had never been able to choose her own destiny, nor to see people as they really were. I needed a god, someone to take me, possess me, someone to whom I could give myself completely . . .' She had rehearsed this. She stopped, seeing that her hand was trembling. She lowered her eyes. How had she meant to go on? 'And I do not want to go back to that creature I had become. She had no pride, Rowle, do you understand that . . . no pride or self-will. All she did and all that she thought was directed towards one being – and that was you. The only aim I had was to please you. I was not happy. It was not pleasant being me.'

He asked his next question softly, and his hand moved gently to touch her own where it came from the simple pale blue silk of her sleeve. She saw. She felt. She decided to let her hand remain. 'And are you happy now?'

'Don't ask me about happiness, you who so glibly deny its existence. I am free. For the first time in my life I am free, and that's all I ask.'

'Free to love again?'

'In time, if I can, yes Rowle.'

'And so we are left with the memories.' He clenched his fist on the table. 'And so we will never meet again. Never ride out, wild, as we used to. Never bathe in the water together, never curl up by the fire in the shepherd's hut.' There was cold desolation, like anger, in his voice.

'I could never betray Lucy's trust again. Not for you, not for anything in the world.'

'You sound so certain.'

'I have made up my mind. There is no going back. Going back, for you, would be merely a game. You hurt me, Rowle. You treated me badly. For me, going back would be blackness, misery and despair. I do not despise myself that much.'

They were not finished. They could have talked together all night had not Silas interrupted. He held out both hands to Bethany. He was tall and fine, his jewels sparked against dark skin.

Bethany smiled and stood up, giving Rowle not a backwards glance. She looked very lovely in such simple blue silk, demure and innocent with her black hair piled up high on her head. The silver streak looked brighter tonight and matched the gown she wore. She was watched and admired by many men as she moved, that night, in the arms of Silas. They looked well together, he so tall, so powerful, so dark . . . she such a beauty beside him. The wine and the music flowed like the dancers. Silas whispered, 'I am so happy to see you relaxed, enjoying yourself, liking yourself again. It seems as though a terrible spell has been lifted from you, and the most important thing is that you lifted the spell by yourself.'

'I am myself, for the first time in my life I am myself,' she said. And Silas believed her. Well, why wouldn't he? She almost believed it herself.

Silas closed his eyes in happiness as he felt the woman he had loved for so long, so close to his heart. If I give her time, he thought to himself, if I don't rush her and make her afraid, all that I ever wanted will be mine. He was satisfied that Bethany was not indifferent to his charms, and since her return to the Combe they had spent time together – when Mary would allow it. They enjoyed the same pastimes, they shared the same humour, they had the same hopes for the people of the clan. I have never felt so close to her as I do tonight, he thought, more happy than he had ever been in his whole life.

He opened his eyes and saw Rowle and Lucy, and Lucy looked calm and lovely tonight and she smiled as the two couples passed one another. The fiddler played the haunting music of love. A warm wind moved through the Combe lifting the women's hair, weaving between the dancers and scattering their soft whispers and the fireflies.

A predatory owl flew from one side of the Combe to the other, screeching and rustling its wings . . . he met his mate, and the eerie cries they exchanged were like nothing from this earth. Familiar sounds, the singing of the skies and the breathing of the Forest. As she listened, Bethany's closed eyes opened – and met Rowle's! They should not have, oh God, they should not have. For an instant they held . . . for the shortest of seconds . . . for the most minute of moments . . . and all the words she had practised during her long hours of lonely walking, all the promises she had made to the skies, they laughed at her then as they turned into notes and plucked at her heart like the music before fluttering, lost, into the night.

Her heart ached with the awful, familiar pain . . . she had not felt alive without that sorrow. Her eyes filled with bitter tears as she fingered the silver streak in her hair. *She was his. Totally, utterly his.* As the moor was his. As the skies and the valleys and downs were his. She was incapable of life without him. For pity's sake, why hadn't they let her die . . . she could have been free. She looked away. She closed her eyes and let her head rest on Silas' shoulder. Ah, but this time it would be different, there would be cunning. Oh yes, she might pretend to love Silas, looking up into his eyes as she was doing now. She might even move into his house, bear his children, sit by his side as he grew old, in the evenings, like a good wife would. No one would know . . . she would keep her dark secret from all the people who would rather not know . . . they would not call her names any more, laugh at her, scorn her and despise her.

All the colours of the waterfall beckoned. She writhed as she felt herself bathe in the spray.

Oh, but what of all the hopes? All the good, new feelings? The freedom she thought she had found . . . *born out of terror and killed by one smile?* For obsessions as powerful as this do not die. Freedom is an illusion. Bethany thought she had found it but she should not have listened to others who always think they know better. Knowing herself, she should have known.

She whispered his name, loving the sound of it, over the music and into the wind.

For there is, after all, no light to this darkness . . . not even in the morning, no, not even at the end of the longest, blackest of nights.

Author's note

Little was ever known or written about the Gubbins because local men were so disgusted by them that they did not want the world to know they existed. The Gubbins grew into a pagan colony of several hundred, started by two 'strumpets' who were with child and fled there to hide themselves in Tudor times. Their 'occupation' of the Lyd valley and its combes lasted for at least 250 years.

These 'abominable moormen' were horse thieves, sheep stealers, deer stalkers and cattle marauders and they lived in cots, hovels, caves and shacks. They were given the name of 'Gubbins' which meant dregs of humanity . . . rubbish . . . trash. Hardy, tough and athletic they could outrun horses over short distances and it was said that many of them lived to a great age. By the 17th century they seemed to have held such domination of the area that people walked in terror of their lives. It was unsafe to journey from Plymouth to North Devon over the western fringe of Dartmoor. Those brave enough to get near could tell if it was black Dartmoor mutton or red deer venison the Gubbins were having for dinner because they cooked in the open air. Their dialect was unintelligible to the people beyond the boundaries of Devon. So barbarous was their speech that even men from other parts of the moor found it difficult to follow.

By 1660 there were signs that the tribe was breaking up. They started bringing their children for baptism, and getting married. The influence of Jesuit priests who hid from Cromwell amongst them was said to have done them good.

By the early 18th century the tribe was absorbed by local society, their cots started crumbling and their shacks tumbled down. The cave-mouths became overgrown with weeds and nettles. Some Devon people still bear the name of Gubbins to this day, and there is a pool at Lydford Gorge next to the Devil's cauldron – now owned by the National Trust – called Rowle's pool.

Nothing at all is known about the king of the Gubbins, Roger Rowle. Charles Kingsley used him as a fictional character in Westward Ho, and killed him off.

> *'And near here's to the Gubbins Cave*
> *A people that no knowledge have*
> *Of law of God or men.*
> *Whom Caesar never yet subdued*
> *Who've lawless lived of manners rude*
> *All savage in their den.*
> *By whom if any pass that way*
> *He dares not the least time to stay.*
> *But presently they howl.*
> *Upon which signal they do muster*
> *Their naked forces in a cluster*
> *Led forth by Roger Rowle.'*